PRAISE FOR ALLYSON BRAITHWAITE CONDIE

First Day

"Condie raised the creative bar for LDS fiction in her debut novel, *Yearbook*. Now in her follow up, *First Day,* she's cleared it by a mile! Condie's characters jump off the page and will linger at your side long after you close the book."—Jason F. Wright, author of the national bestseller *Christmas Jars*

"Ms. Condie has the unique ability to easily steer readers through each main character's viewpoint, making this book a brilliant, insightful, and very enjoyable read!"—Holly E. Newton, M.A., *Meridian Magazine*

Yearbook

"An engaging, unique portrayal of high school life by a talented new author."—Kay Lynn Mangum, bestselling author of *The Secret Journal of Brett Colton* and *A Lov*

"I appreciated the important moral lessons learned. I highly recommend it for today's teenagers!"—John Bytheway, bestselling author of *What I Wish I'd Known in High School*

"This book will captivate you from the beginning and hold you to the very end. . . . Well suited for teens through adults!"—Holly E. Newton, M.A., *Meridian Magazine*

"*Yearbook* is right up there with *High School Musical*. I love it!" —Meagan Cherry, 14, Marquette, Michigan

"If I only read one Mormon young adult novel this year, I don't regret it being *Yearbook*. I enjoyed the jaunt back into simpler high school days, back when the world was wide open, when there was so much to learn, and when I was having regular encounters with so many interesting people around me . . . all pleasantly accompanied by that background buzz of hormones at work. I recommend this book not only to Mormon teens, but to anyone interested in them."—Holly Jones, *Association for Mormon Letters*

FIRST DAY

OTHER BOOKS BY
ALLYSON BRAITHWAITE CONDIE

Yearbook

FIRST DAY

A NOVEL BY

Allyson Braithwaite Condie

DESERET
BOOK
SALT LAKE CITY, UTAH

Visit us at DeseretBook.com

Library of Congress Cataloging-in-Publication Data
Condie, Allyson Braithwaite.
  First day / Allyson Braithwaite Condie.
    p. cm.
  Sequel to: Yearbook.
  Summary: Alternating chapters follow four Mormons—Andrea, Ethan, Joel, and Cate—as they struggle to make the right choices and decisions regarding jobs, college, missions, and love.
  ISBN-13: 978-1-59038-775-7 (pbk.)
  1. Mormons—Fiction. [1. Mormons—Fiction. 2. Universities and colleges—Fiction. 3. Church of Jesus Christ of Latter-day Saints—Missions, 4. Missions—Fiction. 5. Dating (Social customs)—Fiction.] I. Title.
  PZ7.C7586Fi   2007
  [Fic]—dc22   2007008315

Printed in the United States of America
Publishers Printing, Salt Lake City, Utah

10 9 8 7 6 5 4 3 2 1

For my parents, Robert and Arlene,

who were there on my first day

and who have been there for me

ever since

CONTENTS

CONTENTS

ACKNOWLEDGMENTS

My deepest thanks to my husband, Scott, and to our two boys for the love, encouragement, and occasional early bedtimes that made this book possible. I am head over heels in love with the three of you.

I am grateful to Bob, Arlene, Elaine, Nic, and Hope for their feedback, baby-sitting, phone calls, and encouragement. What a family.

I am indebted to Chris Schoebinger and Lisa Mangum at Deseret Book for their patience, good humor, and talent, all of which they have exercised on my behalf many times. They both deserve an all-expenses-paid visit to Ithaca. Maybe someday . . .

I owe more than I can say to the amazing women of the Cornell Branch/Ithaca Ward. Thank you for the playdates, the morning jogs around Beebe Lake, the baby-sitting swaps, the meals you brought when I had my sons, the testimonies you bore, the girls' nights out, the trips to the park, the long talks, the shared toys at church, and the examples and love you showed me during my five years in New York. I will remember you and love you, always.

And, last of all, my gratitude to another woman of the Cornell Branch/Ithaca Ward: my grandmother, Alice Todd Braithwaite, who was also a young mother in Ithaca, and in whose footsteps it has been a privilege to walk.

CHAPTER 1

DECEMBER, SEATTLE

Andrea Beckett

The airplane was getting ready to land. I looked out my window, down at the furry pine trees and gray, satiny water, and I felt glad to be home, even if there was uncertainty waiting for me there. As the plane descended lower and lower, I looked at all the houses lined up along the roads like buttons on a coat, and thought about how clear everything looks from above. The cars look busy and purposeful, and the cities seem so neat and tidy, bisected by their little streets and intersections. Buildings are so crisp and square, and they don't give you any idea of the mess and chaos that might be inside.

We touched down, the wheels hitting the ground solidly. I looked away from the window and up to the front of the cabin, waiting for the door to open.

• • •

As I made my way through the rest of the holiday travelers, I felt very streamlined, with nothing to carry but my single light bag, slung messenger-style over my shoulder. Other people had lots of luggage and coats and children and holiday shopping bags. Someone even carried a wreath through the throng, making me wonder what it was about that particular wreath that made it worthy of a plane ride.

I wove through the crowd, past wheelchairs and strollers, a single fish in a very crowded ocean, swimming against the current, darting in and out whenever I saw an opening. Every now and then, as I headed away from the gates, I caught myself unintentionally following the metal fish embedded in the walkways there at the Sea-Tac Airport. Even when I was little, I didn't like to step on the fish when we came to the airport. We used to come there a lot to pick up my dad when he would return from business trips. Things have changed, both within my family and at the airport. My parents got divorced. And you can't meet people right at the airport gate any longer. It's too bad in a way. It takes some of the excitement out of the landing.

I wondered who would pick me up. My mom would be there, I knew, but I wasn't sure if Chloe would get out of school to come too. I was sad as I thought about the people who wouldn't be there. I would see my dad later, but not at the airport. Ethan, my brother, was on his mission to Brazil. And Grandma wouldn't be there. Although it had been several years since she'd died, it still seemed strange that she was gone.

I knew my family, all of them, loved me. I was sure of them. But there was someone else I *wasn't* so sure about. Someone I hadn't seen in two full years. And it was that person, not my family, who was causing the jumble of feelings I felt inside as I neared the escalator. Uncertainty, excitement, nervousness . . . all those feelings could be traced back to a certain Dave Sherman, who was fresh off his mission to Australia, and whom I would be seeing for the first time in two years during my visit home.

I didn't know if Dave would be coming to the airport. We'd left it vague; he'd come if his family didn't have something else planned for him. Talking to him on the phone had been both awkward and exhilarating. We'd both tripped over our words and laughed a lot. I knew we were both still interested in the versions of each other we'd been when he left, the ones we'd written and sent pictures to for the past two years, but I didn't know how either of us would feel about the people we'd become and all the changes that had taken place while we were apart.

I edged onto the escalator heading down to the baggage claim and craned my neck to see if I could see my family. I'd worn my bright red Cornell sweatshirt so I would be easy for them to spot. I looked for my mom's reddish hair or Chloe's signature dressing style—a riot of pink and blue and purple and green that didn't always match. I didn't dare look for Dave. Part of me wanted him to be there, wanted to see him as soon as possible. Part of me wanted a little more preparation before we came face to face.

What I saw, as the escalator moved down toward the ground floor of the airport, was an enormous sign with my name—Andrea Beckett—printed in huge letters with different colors of marker. It was the only sign there. I felt like turning around and running back up the escalator to hide out of sight, but I didn't. It was like watching a group of clapping, singing waiters bringing a piece of birthday cake toward your table. You don't want the attention, but there's no way out of it. What was my mom thinking? Then I realized that it wasn't my mom holding the sign—she was standing to the left of it. It wasn't Chloe either—she was bouncing to the right.

The sign moved down a little and I saw Dave's brown hair and his huge smile. My heart didn't miss a beat, but it definitely started pounding faster. He looked older, a little different, but it was Dave. Of course it was Dave. That explained the sign. I was suddenly very fond of the sign.

"I smell like airplane," I warned him as he approached me at the bottom of the escalator. He laughed, that absolutely contagious laugh of his, and that made me start smiling too. He gave me a bear hug, smushing part of the sign, and I hugged him back. Then I hugged

Mom and Chloe too, but I couldn't stop looking at Dave. "How are you?"

"Great," he said. "I conned your family into letting me come along. I couldn't wait any longer to see you."

"I imagine this was your idea as well," I said, gesturing at my name in print.

"Of course." Still holding the sign, he looked around. "But now I don't quite know what to do with it."

"I'll hold it," Chloe offered, reaching for it shyly. She thought Dave was the coolest person on the planet, almost as cool as Ethan, whom she's always adored.

Dave handed it over and reached for my hand. I was a little surprised that he would do that right in front of my mom, not to mention the first time he saw me, but it was fine. Holding hands with him felt nice and comfortable. I smiled at him and he raised his eyebrows and grinned at me. We were both back on the same patch of earth at the same time for the first time in two years. I decided that it felt pretty terrific.

• • •

After wrestling my giant bag into the trunk of our car ("This is the part where you're supposed to declare 'My hero,'" he told me, and I rolled my eyes), we were off. Chloe sat in the front seat with the sign, which was getting a little worse for the wear. Dave sat in the back with me. He still held my hand in his.

He tried not to monopolize the conversation between my family and me, but I couldn't help asking him lots of questions too. How had his homecoming talk in church been? I wished I had been there to hear it. How was his family? How was his sister Addie? It felt good to be talking to him and to hear his voice and remember the way he said things. He had picked up a slight accent and a few little phrases from being in Australia, and he asked his questions with a lilt at the end. I thought it was cute, but tried not to let on that I did.

When my mom stopped to drop him off at his house, he leaned over to me and said, "Would it be asking too much of you if I invited you to my family Christmas party tomorrow night?"

I should have known he'd jump back into things with both feet. He's never been a hesitant guy. I looked at my mom and she smiled. "Go ahead. We get to have you all to ourselves tonight."

"That sounds like fun," I said to Dave. "I'd be happy to come with you." I'd been to a Sherman Family Christmas party once before, right before he left on his mission, and it certainly hadn't been boring.

"Great! I'll come get you around six. Thanks for letting me come to the airport, Sister Beckett! See you, Chloe!" Dave squeezed my hand briefly, before he left the car. I waved to him from the window as he went up the path. We all watched him go in the door and close it behind him, and then my mom waited for a second before she shifted into reverse. She glanced at me as we backed out of the driveway.

"Well," she said, finally. "David doesn't waste any time."

"Nope," I agreed. There was another pause. "And since I'm only going to be home for five weeks, that's probably a good thing. No time like the present I guess."

"I wonder if you guys are going to get married," said Chloe, turning around in her seat. I opened my mouth and was about to say something sarcastic, but the look on her face stopped me. I could just see that she was picturing the kind of flower girl dress she would get to wear. My mom and I exchanged smiles. It was good to be home.

• • •

I'm not usually big on sleeping in, but I woke up very late, almost noon. The semester must have taken its toll on me. The coursework for biology majors is no joke, and I had been working hard at school. Even though I don't know if I still want to go to medical school, I know that grades will matter in whatever I decide to do. I put a lot of myself into keeping up my academic record—maybe too much. I'd had almost no social life that semester because of all the studying and labs and papers to write; finals week had about done me in.

I could smell my mom's celebrated orange-cranberry bread baking downstairs and hear Chloe playing Christmas songs on the piano. A few years ago I would have groaned and ducked under the covers to hide, both from the prospect of having to help bake and from the sound of the piano. Absence, or college, really does make the heart grow fonder.

I showered and went downstairs with my hair still wet. You can get away with that in the winter here, barely, but if I tried that in Ithaca, it would freeze on the way to school, no joke. Seattle felt positively balmy.

"It's cranberry bread time," I remarked, while I looked in the cupboards for something to eat. There were several different kinds of cereal in there, all the boxes were full, and none of them involved marshmallows. It seemed like the land of milk and honey. I sighed happily; I wasn't at school anymore.

My mom nodded, and continued grating orange peel into the bowl. "We're going to bake today and deliver tomorrow," she said. She'd recently gotten a master's degree in library science and now she worked as a librarian at the middle school. In addition to it being a job she loved, it also meant that she had the same holiday and summer breaks that Chloe did. Mom was wearing her hair in a ponytail and she was still wearing her pajamas. It was nice to see her so relaxed. I think that seeing Ethan and me safely off into adulthood has taken away a lot of the stress. It wasn't like this a few years ago, when she was trying to figure out what path she wanted to take with her career and we were all trying to decide how our new family situation was going to work.

"What do you want me to do?" I asked, pouring a bowl of cereal. "I'll help as soon as I'm finished with breakfast."

"Actually, if you'd sit there and keep me company, that's all the help I need for now," she said.

"I can do that."

"Soooo . . ." Mom said, drawing the word out meaningfully, "you and David seemed to be getting along fine. Are you excited to go out with him tonight?"

"Yeah," I said. "It's nice that I have such a long winter break so that we can kind of get reacquainted again. I don't know what's going to happen. He's still the same Dave, and he also *isn't* the same Dave."

"I bet he's thinking the same thing about you," Mom said. "I'm interested to see how things go between the two of you."

"Me too."

She tactfully changed the subject and we talked about Ethan's latest letter and the phone call he would be allowed to make on Christmas Day. I finished my bowl of cereal and carried it to the sink to rinse. While I was there, I started doing the dishes from the baking Mom had started. Now that I've been cooking for myself, I can appreciate my parents a lot more—they are both amazing cooks. *So what happened to me?* I thought as I pictured the fridge in my apartment, which was almost always bare. Maybe learning to cook would be one of my New Year's resolutions. I made a face to myself. Maybe not.

I called my dad at work to tell him that I wouldn't be able to see him that night since I had to go to Dave's, but I had the afternoon free. Dad said he'd take a late lunch and asked me to meet him at a restaurant near his office if I had time. I had time. For the first time in several months, I could relax. My finals were over, the grades would be in soon, and I knew I'd done well. Dave was home and our first meeting was out of the way. I could catch my breath, for a minute or two anyway.

• • •

Dave picked me up that night in the same car he drove in high school. It was a monument to durability, or else extreme denial.

"Wow," I said, as we walked to the car hand in hand after he gave me another enormous hug. "I would have thought she'd be long gone."

"You'd think so, wouldn't you?" He patted the car affectionately on the hood. "I hope she lasts long enough for me to save some money for a new one. I'll be riding the bus to the University of Washington for school, so she can rest during the week."

"Are you excited to start school again?" I asked him as we clattered out of the driveway and clunked onto the road. It was surreal to be doing this again. Driving in the same car, heading over to his family's house . . . it was just like old times. Except for the two years of different experiences behind each of us, that is.

"Yes and no," he said. "Yes, because it's a means to an end. No, because it's . . . well, it's school."

"What are you going to be when you grow up?" I teased. "In one of your letters you mentioned teaching or coaching. Are you still thinking along those lines?"

"I don't know." He shook his head. I almost caught a hint of grumpiness or annoyance in his voice. "I'm not as good at planning ahead as you are. You've known from Day One that you were going to be a doctor."

"Not necessarily," I interrupted. "Yes, I'm still majoring in biology, but I'm not totally sure that med school is what I want to do. There are a couple of other programs I've been looking into." In fact, there was one program in particular that I wanted to talk about with someone. I hoped that Dave would ask me what other careers I was considering, but he didn't.

"Well, at least you have a few possibilities," he said instead. "You have multiple career ideas before I can even think of one. It's a good thing I still have plenty of general credits left to take."

"You'll figure it out. You'll be fine. You'll do well at whatever you decide to do." I wanted to say more, something less generic, but we were at his house and it was time to go in and see all the Shermans.

I thought I was prepared to see Dave's family again, but I forgot how overwhelming and fun it was to walk into a roomful of people I hadn't seen in a long time. After I'd been exclaimed over and hugged by all the female Shermans and slapped on the back by all the guys, the two of us went into the living room where the annual Sherman Family Gingerbread House Contest had started a few moments before our arrival. People waved to us from their chairs. Some worked alone, others in groups. Almost anything in the contest was fair game, as long as all of the ingredients you used were edible and the walls and roof of the house were made of gingerbread. Oh, and the only adhesive you could use was the same kind of frosting as everyone else, a huge batch that Dave's mom made ahead of time. The Shermans have their standards.

Dave and I were paired up, of course. Our pointed roof kept collapsing, so Dave decided that flat roofs were better anyway. We made a sort of Frank Lloyd Wright-esque gingerbread house (if Frank Lloyd Wright had been marginally talented and had worked only in pastry). We spent most of our time creating an elaborate garden out of candy that was heavy on Santa-shaped garden gnomes.

Dave's dad had his Santa stuck in the chimney. One of the aunts had him falling through the roof. Eric had him being gored by a pretzel-antlered Tootsie Roll reindeer. No one has ever gotten more mileage out of chocolate foil-wrapped Santas than the Shermans.

Dave's family is a lot like him: loud, boisterous, genuinely good-hearted. Dave and I sat right next to each other and our knees kept bumping under the table. It felt so good to be so close to him again and to be laughing so much. I got a serious fit of the giggles, which doesn't happen to me very often. The hilarity was contagious—everyone was having a good time being together.

Except for his little sister Addie, who had turned into kind of a surly teenager. It happens. She didn't put much effort into her gingerbread house and then wandered away partway through the contest to watch TV by herself.

My heart hurt a little for her. I remember being that age and feeling those feelings. You couldn't pay me enough to be fourteen again. I'm glad I won't have to deal with that age again for years, not until Chloe turns fourteen. Unless, of course, I get called to work with the Young Women or something crazy. That can't happen for a while, though, since I'm in a student branch without any youth programs.

"All right," called out Mrs. Sherman, and everyone hushed. "While the panel of judges is deciding which gingerbread house is the winner, the rest of you are going caroling." A couple of people groaned. She held up her hand. "No whining. You know the routine. When you get back from caroling, we'll have hot chocolate and announce the winners."

Dave and I went to a couple of houses with his family, but then doubled back to his house for hot chocolate and Christmas cookies before everyone else returned.

"Oh no, you don't," his mother exclaimed as we tried to sneak in the back door. "You get right back out there and sing. We're not done in here yet." She made shooing motions at us. Dave's favorite Aunt Leslie and another relative whose name I couldn't remember were deep in discussion, judging the houses.

Dave smiled at his mom. "Please, Mom? I just got home, and all I want to do is sit here in my very own home and have some hot chocolate . . ."

Of course he got his way, though we had to wait a few minutes while they finished judging. A mild debate ensued about whether or not they could award the grand prize to Eric, since his entry was a bit macabre. Aunt Leslie argued that he still deserved to win, due to the combination of undeniable creativity and sound architecture. I couldn't wait to see Eric's face when they told him he'd won. He'd never won before, according to Dave, and the grand prize was always the same: you got to keep the giant gingerbread house trophy for a year. The trophy had been created years ago by Grandma Sherman out of clay and actually fired in a kiln, and it was a sight to behold.

You also got bragging rights and dinner out at the restaurant of your choice, but those things were secondary to the trophy itself.

Dave and I sat at his kitchen table with our mugs of hot chocolate and it all felt so warm and familiar. Part of the roof of our gingerbread house had caved in while we were gone, so we ate the evidence of our unsound architecture.

"Do you remember our first date?" I asked him. "This kind of reminds me of that."

He laughed. "The hot chocolate part, yes. But this time we didn't go to the ballet beforehand and we're not sitting up in my tree house freezing while we drink our hot chocolate."

"That's true," I said. "And we're both much more mature and grown up."

"Definitely," he agreed, walking a chocolate Santa over to my cup and dropping him in.

"So, when are you going to break out the mission memorabilia?" I asked. "I'd love to see some pictures."

"Be careful what you wish for. I've got a lot of pictures and even more stories." He looked wistful for a moment. "It's been hard to come back in some ways. It's nice when you have a lot of focus in your life."

"Yeah," I said. "Obviously I haven't been on a mission or anything, but I always feel like I'm at a loss when it's vacation time. You know me. I'm a structure fiend. It's weird after being in school and working all the time to come home and then have nothing to do for a few weeks but hang out."

"You'd love being in the mission field," he told me. "There's all the structure you could ever want there."

"That's what Ethan says, too."

"How is old Eth doing?" Dave asked. "I need to write him a letter. How long has he been out? Six months?"

"He left at the beginning of May, right after the school year ended at BYU, so it's been about eight months now." I missed my brother. I was looking forward to his Christmas call almost as much as my mom, I bet. My dad was coming over to our house Christmas afternoon so that he could talk to Ethan too. That was going to be interesting. "I can't wait to hear his voice at Christmas. We're arranging the entire day around his call. It's weird how lonely I've felt since he's left."

"You guys got pretty close, didn't you? I remember you talking to each other a lot his senior year, that semester before I left on my mission."

"Yeah," I said. "Chloe and I are already counting the days until he gets back. I bet Addie was doing the same for you."

"And what about you?" he asked, and there was that mischievous glint in his eyes. "Were you counting the days until I got back, too?"

"Don't you wish," I said. "Actually, I had no idea when you were coming home. I was totally surprised to see you at the airport. I thought you had at least a couple of months left. I haven't been thinking about you at all."

Dave shook his head at me, smiling knowingly. "You're a terrible liar." He was right. I had thought about him every day for the past two years.

• • •

At the end of the night, Dave drove me home, back through the night to my house. "Thanks for coming tonight," he said. "You were a good sport."

"I still think we were robbed," I joked. "Our house was much better than Eric's."

"No kidding. So you had a good time?"

"Of course I did."

"Do you want to go to dinner or something tomorrow?" he asked. "Just the two of us? Tonight was fun, but there were a lot of people around. We could talk more then."

"That would be nice." I liked the idea of the two of us out on a more formal date, even though this had been fun, too. Basically, I liked the idea of being with Dave, period.

He opened the door for me and helped me out of the car. He closed the door behind me, but he didn't step away from the car, just stood there looking at me. I looked back, hoping that I knew what was coming.

It was our first kiss in two years.

It was just the way I'd imagined it would be.

CHAPTER 2

DECEMBER, BRAZIL

Ethan Beckett

When I woke up on Christmas morning, I tried to forget that it was Christmas. It shouldn't have been hard to do, because everything was different from the way Christmas usually went at home. To start with, I had woken up at 6:30 A.M. to the sound of a beeping alarm. The early hour wasn't new—like every kid, I'd gotten up early on Christmas morning for years—but the method sure was. Usually, instead of an alarm, I had Chloe bouncing on the foot of my bed, feverish in her excitement to get to the presents.

I dragged myself out of bed, remembering to put on my flip-flops before I walked across the bedroom floor to the bathroom. Since all kinds of wildlife and vegetation grow in Brazil that don't back home, going barefoot can mean trouble. No spiders or bugs this morning, I noticed. That was a good sign.

The water in the shower was lukewarm at best, but that didn't bother me too much. It was around ninety degrees and humid in Brazil in December. It hardly ever gets that hot in Seattle in the summertime, let alone at Christmastime—another difference. I showered and put on my clothes and somehow managed to sweat through them by the time I'd finished eating my breakfast—again, nothing like my usual Christmas morning breakfast. It was cereal with fresh ripe mangoes. Okay, so some of the things that were different weren't all bad.

I was trying to pretend that it wasn't Christmas so that the day would fly by until the afternoon when I could call my family. I didn't want to give in to the inevitable homesickness until then.

But my companion, Elder Vickers, wouldn't play along, and my plan was over almost before I could start putting it into practice. After breakfast, Elder Vickers went straight for the cupboard where we'd stashed the Christmas packages from our families.

"Come on, Elder Beckett," he said, plopping the boxes onto the kitchen table in front of me. He reached over to switch on the Mormon Tabernacle Choir Christmas tape on an ancient tape deck, both of which had come with the missionary apartment and both of which appeared to have been there since the mission was opened.

"I was going to wait until later," I protested.

"Why?" Elder Vickers asked, already tearing into his package.

"I'm trying to act like it's not really Christmas, so that I don't lose focus on the work," I said lamely. "I'll open everything later, after we call our families. I don't want to make it any harder than it already is, you know what I mean?"

He didn't. Elder Vickers fixed me with his are-you-serious stare. "That doesn't even make any sense."

I shrugged. "I know, but I still think I'm going to wait." I walked over to the couch, leaving my box on the table.

Elder Vickers held up a cellophane bag with holly printed all over it. "Come on, Elder . . . my mom sent her famous Christmas candy."

"No thanks," I said. "But I appreciate the offer." I sat down and opened up my scriptures, trying to find where I had been in my personal study the day before. A piece of toffee wrapped in waxed paper landed squarely on the pages. I looked up at Elder Vickers.

He pelted me again. "It is time to have fun, Elder. You are Scrooging my Christmas." In a high and squeaky voice, he started singing, "Rudolph the Red-Nosed Reindeer," but he completely botched the names. "You know Dasher and Dancer and Mancer and Nixon, Comet and Cupid and Dapper and Flicken . . ." he sang.

"Elder, that's not even close," I said, laughing.

"Who cares?" he asked. "The only one that matters is Rudolph, right?" He nudged my box of presents. "Come on, open it."

I gave in and walked back to the table. Elder Vickers was already tearing through his package, with some of his mom's candy lodged firmly in his cheek. Two weeks ago, when we first became companions, I didn't know how to take him. He's from a little town somewhere in Vermont, and has a deep bass voice, a take-no-prisoners attitude, and a heart of gold. He's also huge. I'm fairly tall myself at six two, but Elder Vickers has at least two inches on me. He's also amazing at Portuguese and can fix almost anything. Sometimes I feel like the little city boy, following around the man of the people. It's lucky he's a good guy or I might get bugged by everything he does right when there's so much I'm doing wrong.

I'm struggling with the language more than I should be this far into the mission. I'm starting to worry that I'll be the only missionary in the history of the Church to remain a junior companion the whole time because I can't figure out the language. Elder Vickers listens very patiently while I make a mess of everything when we try to teach our investigators, and then he steps in to clear things up. "You'll get it," he always tells me, and I nod and act confident, as if it's only a matter of time before I become outrageously fluent and articulate.

Serving a mission has been one of the most humbling experiences of my life. I'd always thought of myself as a reasonably smart person, well-liked, a good guy, fairly competent. I'd even had a few talents—running, soccer, getting decent grades at school. On my mission, though, it was like all those parts of my identity had been stripped away and I was left with—what? With my testimony, I guess. I wished that I were better at sharing it—both at finding the right words to share it in Portuguese and at sharing it in general.

・　・　・

The first gift that I pulled out of the box was from Chloe and when I saw her handwriting on the tag, a wash of homesickness went through me. It was so easy to picture the way Christmas was at home. I could see Chloe sitting at the kitchen table wrapping the present, using way too much tape and cutting way too much paper for the size of the gift. I could picture the large plate glass window behind her and how the world would look outside that window. The sky would be gray and the grass would be matted and greenish-brown and the hedge in the backyard would be hanging on to its thick green leaves, but they wouldn't look as bright as they would have in the summer.

Christmases in Seattle are not white Christmases with snow and heavy coats and hats and snowmen and all of that. But there's still a Christmas mood about them, even if they're different from the pictures in the magazines. You can *feel* the cold from the lakes and from Puget Sound in the air, something that only happens in a place with a lot of moisture. And there are evergreen trees everywhere. Chloe used to think they were all Christmas trees and that every evergreen tree in the state of Washington existed for her own personal satisfaction at Christmastime.

I sighed. Elder Vickers looked at me. Before he could accuse me of ruining his Christmas again, I tore into the present. Chloe had sent me some peanut butter, which she knew I missed, and also a huge box of Red Vines licorice, my favorite.

"Score," said Elder Vickers when he noticed, and before we continued, we both stuffed some of the synthetic red licorice into our mouths. Artificial flavoring never tasted so good.

Andrea had sent me a box with a bright red water bottle inside.

It was the huge, clear plastic kind that you see people carrying around campus a lot. It said "CORNELL" across it in huge black letters and had a cheesy, cartoon picture of a bear—Cornell's mascot—along the side. Crammed inside it were dozens of bright red pencils also emblazoned with "CORNELL." There was also a red notebook with the Cornell logo on the front. I started laughing. Ever since we ended up at different schools, the two of us had had a rivalry going about which school was the best. Last year for Christmas, I'd given her an "I ❤ BYU" T-shirt and she'd vowed to get me back. It looked like she was making good on her promise.

"That's the ugliest water bottle I've ever seen," Elder Vickers said through his mouthful of toffee.

"It's from Andrea," I said, and his eyes lit up. He's seen her picture and thinks she's beautiful. He's always referring to "when you set me up with Andrea" as if it's a given. He doesn't have any sisters, so he doesn't understand that asking a guy to set you up with his sister is basically never going to happen. Even though he's a good guy, I'd have to sit him down and read him the riot act first, and that would be the end of our friendship.

I tried to open the package from Mikey surreptitiously so Elder Vickers wouldn't give me any grief, but it was impossible. "What did your girlfriend send you?" he asked.

"I don't know yet," I said. "I'm still reading the card."

Dear Ethan,

Merry Christmas! I'm mailing this early so I hope it gets to you in time. I know you probably only get to wear T-shirts on P-Day, but I still thought you'd like to have at least one Mariners shirt around. We'll have to go to a game again when you get back.

When I was trying to think of something extra I could do during the Christmas season (some kind of service project or something), I kept thinking about how you are already doing lots of things, every day, that are all about the spirit of Christmas. I think that's awesome. I hope you

have a great Christmas and I will be thinking about you and praying
for you (and missing you a little too, if that's all right).

Love,

Mikey

I read the card a second time through, making sure I caught every word.

Elder Vickers cleared his throat. "Are you going to keep sitting there grinning like a fool or are you going to tell me what she gave you?"

"A Seattle Mariners T-shirt," I said, holding it up for him to see. "Feast your eyes on the insignia of the finest team in baseball." Elder Vickers—a devoted Yankees fan—rolled his eyes and turned back to his gifts. I folded the shirt up and read the last line of Mikey's card a few more times, not caring if Elder Vickers noticed or not.

• • •

After we finished opening our presents, we headed over to the da Silvas' house for lunch. The big meal in Brazil is lunch, not dinner, and that goes double for Christmas Day. As we started to get ready, we both kept looking at our piles of gifts on the table. Elder Vickers read my mind.

"We should take them something," he said. "We don't need all of this candy and stuff."

I nodded, and we combed through our gifts to see what we could give. We decided to give the da Silvas some of Elder Vickers' candy, some homemade popcorn balls from my mom, and a few candy canes for the kids. I worried we were going to give those kids a sugar overload so severe it would last until next Christmas.

There was a baseball I'd asked my mom to send that I'd already planned to give away. After some thought, I added the Mariners T-shirt that Mikey had sent to the pile. One of the little da Silva boys was intrigued by baseball and kept asking why on earth we'd play that in the States instead of soccer (which they called football). Even though I felt kind of bad about giving the shirt away, I knew they would love it, and I also knew that Mikey would understand. At least, I thought she would. And I'd still have the card she'd sent and the knowledge that she'd remembered me.

Elder Vickers added the tie that his parents had sent him to the pile. Brother da Silva only had one tie and Elder Vickers was convinced that he would love this one. I hoped so. Elder Vickers has his own standards of taste and this tie was deep purple. Only a guy Elder Vickers' size can get away with wearing purple ties. Skinny runner types like me stick to red or blue or black.

Last on the list was Sister da Silva. I grabbed the Cornell notebook and a handful of red Cornell pencils. I mean, what was I really going to do with forty-eight pencils? Besides, I knew Sister da Silva liked to keep a journal and thought she might appreciate the gift.

We put everything back into one of the big brown shipping boxes. I decided that next year I would ask my mom to send tons of stuff that I could give away. I kicked myself for not having thought of anything besides that one baseball for this year. It felt good to be doing something Christmassy. To cover up the addresses and postage, we salvaged the wrapping paper from the different gifts and pieced it together into a big sheet to wrap the box. It didn't look perfect, but we figured they would cut us some slack.

"Your corners are absolutely unacceptable," Elder Vickers commented, as I taped down the last edges of our makeshift wrapping paper.

"This is harder than it looks," I told him, sticking on one final piece of tape for good measure. "We should put something on top to decorate it."

He looked around the apartment until he found a ribbon from one of the gifts we'd opened earlier. We tied it on, but somehow the bow didn't look right. It was uneven and off-center. After a couple of tries, we gave up.

"It's fine," Elder Vickers decided. "Plus I think it's getting worse every time we try." He picked up the box, and I opened the door for him.

"I'm glad we're going to the da Silvas' for Christmas," I said, locking the door behind us and following him down the steps.

"Me too," he agreed. "They're one of my favorite families of all time."

"They're so strong." Brother da Silva was quiet and kind, a gentle man who lived the gospel with his whole heart. His two sons, Mauricio and Reynaldo, were growing up to be exactly like him. Sister da Silva was warm and kindhearted, and she thought my language problems were endearing rather than annoying. She was also the best cook ever. Sister da Silva was awesome.

"And Sister da Silva is an amazing cook," Elder Vickers said, reading my mind again. "I'm going to have to watch myself with that good food so I don't get greedy."

The members in Brazil are so generous to us that it becomes a problem. Sometimes we sit there eating the food and we know that they have put the very best of the best in front of us, even if it means that they are going to have to go without. It's humbling. My first week, I tried to give some of it back right after the sister had dished it to me, telling her that I couldn't eat so much, that she should keep some of it, and I'd hurt her feelings. I hadn't done that again. I still worried, though, about eating all their food.

We knocked on the door and could hear the boys' running feet. The door opened to their smiling faces and I thought of Chloe with a pang. The older boy, Reynaldo, was about her age, and he was the one who opened the door, beating out his younger and noisier brother, Mauricio. Their parents appeared behind them, warmly wishing us a Merry Christmas and guiding us towards the feast they'd prepared.

Brother da Silva offered a blessing on the food that even I, with my problematic Portuguese, could tell was beautiful and heartfelt.

He asked the Lord to bless us and our hard work and I knew that He would with someone like Brother da Silva doing the asking.

"Here you are, Elder," Sister da Silva said in Portuguese, dishing me a helping of meat. I thanked her, and she responded quickly saying, *"Tem que ser forte pra casar com uma moça bonita."* I couldn't tell what she had said. I looked around for help and everyone started laughing at me, even the boys.

"She said she is going to fatten you up so you can go home and marry a beautiful girl," Elder Vickers repeated, slowly, in Portuguese.

"See him blushing," said Sister da Silva, smiling at me. That I could understand. And I *was* blushing, of course. I always do. I bent my head and started eating the mixture of chopped-up onions and tomatoes that Brazilians call salad.

After we had finished eating, we went out to the backyard so the boys could run around. Elder Vickers and I brought out the box of presents and let them tear into it. The boys were excited about the Mariners shirt and baseball, and Sister da Silva loved the notebook and pencils. "You are such a thoughtful boy," she said to me, smiling. Even my worries about the tie turned out to be unfounded. Brother da Silva loved it. He folded it carefully, taking it back to his room to put it away immediately.

With their new T-shirt and ball, the two boys decided that it was time they tried to learn the great American pastime. "Will you teach us baseball?" Mauricio said, hopping up and down. The Mariners T-shirt came almost to his knees.

"What about hockey instead?" Elder Vickers grumbled good-naturedly, since that was his sport of choice. He was always trying to get them interested in hockey, but that was even more foreign to the boys than baseball. He pretended to refuse to play, but the boys knew he was joking, and he finally agreed.

We set up some bases using three old newspapers for first, second, and third, and an old deflated soccer ball for home plate. Elder Vickers placed them carefully in the dust and kicked enough dirt together into a little pile to serve as a makeshift pitcher's mound. The da Silvas' backyard connected to several other families' yards, and I could see some of the other kids looking at us with interest. There were no fences, only a few laundry lines strung up, so they had an unobstructed view.

We found a piece of wood that would work as a bat in a pile of wood Brother da Silva was using for his latest home improvement project. It was long and skinny, about the right size. I showed Mauricio where to stand and how to hold the bat. Reynaldo stood warily to the side, watching his little brother carefully. I lobbed the baseball slowly to Mauricio. He swung wildly, chopping vertically through the air with the bat as though he was chopping wood, and both Elder Vickers and I burst out laughing. He grinned back at us. Reynaldo was laughing too.

"Let me show you how," I said. I'd forgotten that these boys wouldn't have seen baseball on TV. Elder Vickers pitched me the ball and I swung, connecting with it on the first try and sending the ball across the yard. The boys jumped up and down. *Minha vez! Minha vez!* the boys cried. *My turn, my turn!*

They both practiced a few times. Reynaldo was the first to get a hit. When his bat connected with the ball, he stood there in perfect surprise, mouth open, watching it fly.

"Run! Run!" I reminded him, and he tore off around the bases, head down, moving fast. He made it all the way to home. Neither Elder Vickers nor I had the heart to tag him out, though I chased him with the ball, laughing along with him. Brother and Sister da Silva clapped from where they sat watching. Mauricio pumped his fist in the air.

After Reynaldo and Mauricio had had their fill of baseball (Reynaldo got three more home runs and Mauricio connected with the ball at least twice), they wanted us to play football with them. "Please! Please!" they begged. "It's Christmas!"

Elder Vickers checked his watch. "We've got time for a quick game," he decided. The boys cheered, and ran inside to get their ball. Elder Vickers positioned himself at the goal since that was the position he played in hockey. I didn't care where I played. I was excited about having the chance to run around and kick the ball a little. The boys burst back out the door with the ball, laughing together. Brother and Sister da Silva were smiling too.

When some of the neighbors saw that we weren't playing that weird American game anymore, they came over to join us. There were kids all the way down to Mauricio's age (about four years old) and even some adults older than I was. Since it was Mauricio and Reynaldo's ball, they got to choose the teams. Reynaldo went first.

"Elder Beckett on my team!" he called. We divided up sides. I could see the other players looking at me in my dress pants and white shirt and I felt out of place. But, even though they nudged each other, it was Christmas Day and they were too polite to say anything.

We started the game. Mauricio's team got to have the ball first. Since there were so many little kids, it wasn't an all-out game, but I could tell that the others were surprised when I didn't embarrass myself and when Elder Vickers proved to be a decent goalie. I passed the ball a lot, which always helps things. Then, later in the game, Reynaldo passed it to me as I neared the goal. I caught the pass neatly and dribbled it in closer.

"He's *good*," I heard Reynaldo say in surprise, and I laughed out loud as I sent the ball sailing straight into the goal. It didn't occur to me until later that he had chosen me for his team before he knew that I could play. When I realized that, I thought it was one of the nicer Christmas gifts I'd received.

• • •

We finally said our good-byes and left to go caroling at the homes of some investigators and inactive members. After that, it would be time to go home and call our families. Home. Thinking about home didn't make me feel as sad as I had felt that morning.

The warm sun beating down on my head, my full belly, the sound of the da Silvas' laughter ringing in my ears—all of those things made it easier. So did feeling the da Silvas' love for Christ and love for us.

I remembered the one year when we did have snow at Christmas. There was a little skiff of it on the lawn. Chloe wasn't born yet, so it was just Andrea and me. Andrea and I woke up and saw the snow on our lawn and couldn't believe our eyes. We went right outside; we had to touch it to see if it was real. I think we got a snowball each out of what was on the front lawn, and by lunchtime, you'd never have even known that it had been there. But we remembered it and talked about it all the time. Some of the other Christmases were lumped together and when I thought back on them I couldn't pick out specifics. But I knew this Christmas would be one of the stand-outs, like the snowfall in Seattle. One of the special ones.

"Not such a bad Christmas so far, is it, Elder?" Elder Vickers asked, humming "Silent Night" to himself as we went along.

"Not so bad at all. Pretty cool, in fact."

"It won't be as hard next year," he told me. "This Christmas was a lot easier than my first, not that the first was that terrible or anything. But I'll remember both of them forever."

I knew he was right. I would remember the taste of salad and caramel flan and candy canes in my mouth and hear the sound of the da Silvas singing "Silent Night" to us in Portuguese as we left. I would remember Reynaldo hitting the baseball for the first time, and his smile, and the way he forgot to run the bases at first, and stood there instead, beaming.

I started singing "Silent Night" along with Elder Vickers' humming as we walked. A few measures into the song, I realized I was singing in Portuguese, without even thinking about it.

CHAPTER 3

FEBRUARY, ITHACA, NEW YORK

Andrea Beckett

My roommate Emma burst through the door to our apartment. I'd been back home in Ithaca for less than an hour, and it was cold and boring without anyone else around. The minute I heard her key in the lock, I hurried into the front room. Neither of us are really what I would term screamy huggy girls, but we both screamed and hugged when we saw each other. Five weeks of winter break will do that to you.

"So . . ." said Emma meaningfully, shoving her suitcase out of the hallway. "How did everything go with Dave? I need the whole scoop, not the bits and pieces you were giving me over the phone."

"It went fine." I was trying to be nonchalant, but I knew my grin gave me away.

Emma gave me a closer look. "*What* on earth are you wearing?" she exclaimed. Then she looked around, rubbing her arms. "It's freezing in here!"

"You answered your own question," I said, waddling toward the kitchen where I had left some water boiling for hot chocolate. "The heat hasn't been on in here since we left, remember? We left it barely high enough to keep the pipes from freezing. So I'm wearing—"

"Your ski pants and your coat to keep warm," she finished, shaking her head.

"I'm also wearing my flannel pajamas," I told her, pulling out two mugs from the cupboard. "Do you want mint chocolate or regular?"

"Mint, please," Emma said. "Let me put these suitcases in my room and I'll be right back." She started down the hall, but called back to me, "Don't think I've been distracted from the issue at hand. We *are* going to talk about Dave. All night if necessary!"

• • •

"I'm too tired to be coherent," I warned Emma, sliding her hot chocolate toward her. "I didn't get much sleep over the break, and I can never sleep on airplanes."

She brushed aside my words with a wave of her hand and pulled the mug toward her. "Who cares about coherent? I'll forgive you if you're not, but you'd better start talking."

"Well . . ." I couldn't quite think of where to start. "He's still more fun to be around than anyone I know. That hasn't changed. It feels like he has more layers to him, now. Or maybe those layers were already there, but now they're more developed."

"But the sparks were still there?" Emma demanded.

"The sparks were still there," I admitted, and I couldn't help smiling.

"Did you kiss?" Emma asked bluntly.

"Yeah . . ."

"And . . ."

"And that's all I'm going to say," I informed her with an arched eyebrow.

Emma rolled her eyes and sipped at her hot chocolate. "So how did you leave things? It sounds to me like you guys left it that you're still together, like you're going to give it a shot, right?"

"Yeah," I said. "Definitely. We're going to try to talk on the phone every day and I'm going back home to Seattle for spring break. We still haven't really talked about this summer and what will happen. I think that if all goes well, maybe I'll try to get a job there for the summer. We'll have to see what happens. But it went really well. It was so much fun to be with him."

"You're so happy when you talk about him," Emma declared. "It's not something I ever thought I'd see—Andrea Beckett in L-O-V-E."

"I didn't think I'd ever see it, either," I admitted, slouching down in my chair a little. "But something about Dave gets to me."

"I can tell," Emma said. "So what did you two do? Did you hang out the whole break?"

"Almost," I admitted. "We were together nearly every day. My mom complained that she didn't get to see enough of me, but I don't think she was too mad about it. She likes Dave. And we took Chloe with us sometimes, to the movies and stuff, so she was okay too."

"Did you hang out a lot with his family, too? Or just him?"

"I was with him a lot, but I saw his family some too. I went to their family Christmas party, and his sister had a birthday while I was there so we all went snowboarding. And on top of all that, our group of friends had a big welcome-back party for him on New Year's Eve. There was a lot going on."

"Well, I'm glad I got to hear all the details," Emma told me. "But you're going to have to repeat it all when Shannon gets back."

"I know. She already warned me that she expected a full report."

Shannon, our third roommate, was returning the next day. The three of us had been friends since freshman year, when Emma and I were the only two LDS girls in our freshman dorm (the only two LDS female freshman on campus, as it turned out) and Shannon was one of the only girls in our dorm who wasn't interested in partying every weekend. She was a conscientious Catholic and the three of us had sort of gravitated toward each other and had been inseparable ever since, even with the inclusion of Shannon's boyfriend, Rich, halfway through sophomore year.

My phone rang and I grabbed for it, sitting bolt upright. Dave. "Hey," I said. Emma raised her eyebrows at me, and when I mouthed the words, "It's Dave," to her, she smiled and went to her room to give me a little privacy.

"How are you doing?" Dave asked. "How was your trip?"

I told him about the plane ride and the apartment and about Emma getting back, and he laughed at all the right times (like when I told him about what we were wearing to keep warm in our freezing apartment) and sympathetic at all the right times (when I described how my two-hour layover in Chicago had turned into a five-hour layover). I could picture him talking on his parents' cordless phone in the kitchen, hunting through the cupboards for something to eat, which is what he always did when he was on the phone.

"What are you going to do tonight?" he asked, and sure enough, I heard him start unwrapping something. "Anything exciting?"

"I think I'm going to unpack and get some dinner and crash," I told him. "What about you? And don't talk with your mouth full."

Dave paused, mid-crackle. "How did you know I was about to eat?" he asked, laughing. "You know me too well."

• • •

After I'd hung up the phone with Dave, I wished that I were back in Seattle, going to the University of Washington, hanging out with him. I missed my other friends, too. Since I had spent so much time with Dave, the only time I'd seen them, really, had been at his welcome-home party on New Year's Eve.

"Have fun!" my mom had called out as I left the house. She refrained from making any sly comments about how much time I was spending with Dave, for which I was grateful.

"I will," I'd called back over my shoulder.

I'd been looking forward to the party. It's always bittersweet to get back together with people from high school. Everyone is changing and doing different things, so it's impossible to feel quite as close as you once did. Still, there is a bond there, the kind of bond that comes from being friends during such a pivotal time of life. The kind of bond that happens when you remember how the halls looked when they were decorated for Homecoming. Or how lame the theme was for Prom your junior year. Or how you felt the day you found out your principal had cancer.

I decided to go early to help Mikey with the party since it was being held at her house. I called Dave and told him I'd meet him there. That way Mikey and I could talk about Dave and Ethan as much as we wanted. We hadn't had a chance to do that yet. We'd grown closer the summer before I left for Cornell, when she had been dating Ethan a lot, and we'd kept in touch ever since.

"Hey," I said when Mikey answered the door.

"Andrea!" she said, giving me a hug. "It's so good to see you! Where's Dave?" She looked behind me, as if she expected him to pop out from behind a tree or from underneath one of the bushes. It wasn't an entirely irrational expectation.

"He's coming later," I explained. "I thought I'd come help you and hang out a little, since I haven't seen much of you this break."

Mikey led the way to the kitchen. "Yeah, I wonder why that is?" she teased. "It seems like you've been spending a lot of time with someone else, someone who just got back from Australia, someone whose party we're getting ready for right now." She handed me a platter and a bag of vegetables. "Will you make the relish tray? I'm going to mix hummus for the dip and then we should be almost ready. Julie's bringing the desserts and Elizabeth is bringing the soda."

I began slicing the carrots and celery. Mikey started mixing the chickpeas together for the dip. I looked at her, trying to see how and if she'd changed. The last time I'd seen her had been in the summer, a couple of months after Ethan left. She still wore her hair long and she was still skinny, but you could see she was finally starting to fill out a little from being rail-thin, and her haircut was different—she had a few long layers now.

"So tell me about Dave," she said. "I've seen him here and there for a minute, but that's about it. How are things going?"

"We're having a good time," I admitted. "It's so fun to be with him, you know that. There's no one quite like him at Cornell that's for sure."

"There's no one quite like him anywhere," Mikey agreed.

"How is your second year at BYU? Do you miss the dorms?"

Mikey laughed. "Not so much. It's weird there without Ethan, though. He was there for my whole freshman year; we hung out all the time. He was part of the BYU landscape for me, part of my whole freshman year experience. Now that I live off-campus, all the guys are older and have already served missions and it was really weird at first. But I'm getting used to it."

"Do you miss him?" I asked her, and then wanted to kick myself. Of course she missed him. The real question, and one that I knew from experience was hard to answer, was: How much?

"Yeah," Mikey said, not taking offense. "You know how it is. It's kind of a weird combination of missing him but not letting yourself miss him, because who knows what's going to happen when he gets back."

"That's so true," I said. "You kind of have to keep everything in balance, because you don't want to stop thinking about him entirely, but you also don't want to pine away."

"Yup," said Mikey. She cleared her throat. "Does Ethan say anything about me to you?"

"Not much," I admitted, "but what he does say is good. I know he misses you and that he thinks about you. He's never been all that comfortable talking to me about dating stuff, but he has told me that."

Mikey smiled. "Well, at least that's something. He's good about writing, but his letters are so friendly and businesslike that you'd never even know we'd been anything more than friends from reading them."

"Dave was a little like that, too." I paused. "I think it's good that they're so focused on their missions."

"Oh, definitely," Mikey said. "I wouldn't have it any other way." She paused, scooping the dip into a serving bowl. "Well, I might like a *little* more emotion—" She stopped as she looked at my relish tray.

I had arranged everything in pie-shaped sections on the tray, alternating the green vegetables with the brightly colored ones, but I had ended up with a handful of carrots that wouldn't fit. My hand was hovering, as I tried to decide where to put them.

"Just dump them in the middle, or anywhere they'll fit," she told me.

"Then it won't be symmetrical," I said, and she laughed.

"Maybe we could eat them," she suggested, taking a few from me. "We'll take one for the team, in the interest of symmetry."

"It's nice of you to throw this party for Dave," I told her, snapping a carrot in half before eating it. "How did you get conned into doing it, anyway?"

"Oh, I thought we should do something to welcome him back and I wanted to do something for New Year's Eve anyway so I asked him for a list of people he'd want to come. I should have realized it would be a long list. It's turned into quite the endeavor."

"I can imagine," I said, right as the doorbell rang. Mikey's mom answered it. A couple of people stood on the doorstep and coming up the walk behind them was Dave.

"Well, here we go," Mikey said as we walked out into the foyer.

Being on dates with Dave in a group setting is always interesting because he's the life of the party and everyone wants to talk to him, but it was obvious from the start that that dynamic was going to be even more pronounced that night. It was his welcome-home party, after all. When I went out into the foyer with Mikey, my eyes met Dave's immediately, but everyone was in between us and all we could do for a minute was smile and wave.

Finally, he detached himself from some of his well-wishers and started toward me, but Mikey inadvertently stepped between us and stopped him to ask him a question. I kept walking toward him anyway and he hooked his arm through mine when I got close. Mikey was telling him about some of the people she'd invited who hadn't been able to come.

"Avery Matthews couldn't make it," she said, talking about one of Dave's good friends from high school journalism. "I forget why, but it was a good reason. She sent this for you though." She gestured to the end table next to the coat closet. There was a small toy red wagon with a card in it. I didn't get it, but Dave started laughing.

It ended up being quite a party. There were plenty of people from our ward there, the kids who had been our age and a few from the groups that were just older or just younger. Mikey had invited a lot of people from the school paper staff and from track. She'd also invited a lot of Dave's friends from the University of Washington (he'd gone there for a semester before he left on his mission). I'm sure some of them thought it was weird that they were spending at least part of their New Year's Eve at a Mormon party with no alcohol in sight, but they were good sports about it. People *like* Dave. It was a feeling I could understand.

The doorbell rang again and Mikey went to answer it. This time it was a few more of Dave's college friends. I didn't know any of them, and neither did Mikey, so Dave hurried to rescue her.

I was alone again. "Hey," said a voice behind me. I turned around to see a familiar face—Tyler Cruz, basketball star and genuine good guy from high school. He stood there, all six foot five of him, looking a little out of place in his bright red University of Utah sweatshirt. Tyler had taken Lakeview High School by storm and not only because of his undeniable talent on the court. He was also one of the only guys at school to have stood up to our slimeball-in-residence, Everett.

"Tyler!" I said. "I haven't seen you in forever! How are you doing?" Even though I hadn't actually seen him since graduation, I knew from Mikey that he and Julie still kept in touch.

"Great. I'm here with Julie, but she's putting something together in the kitchen," he told me. "I'm hoping you'll talk to me so I don't feel like a fool for crashing Dave's party."

I laughed. "You're not crashing it. We're all glad to see you. It's been a while."

"Yeah," he said. "I had another year at school with Julie and Mikey and Ethan and those guys, but you and Dave headed off to college right after I came to Lakeview. You're still at Cornell, right?"

"Yeah, I am," I said as we sat down on some folding chairs near the Christmas tree. "Where did you end up going to school?" I asked him jokingly.

He looked down at his U of U sweatshirt and grinned. "Basketball scholarship, but I sit on the bench more than I get to play."

"That must be frustrating." I'd never actually seen him play, since I graduated a year before he did, but I'd heard about him from Ethan.

He shrugged. "It's okay. Hopefully it'll get better next year. I redshirted my freshman year so this is my first real year playing and I've still got a lot to learn. There are some good things about being on the team whether or not you get playing time. We're playing University of Washington this weekend, so it worked out nicely to come back so soon after Christmas. Last year we had to practice, so I ended up staying in Utah and hanging out with the team on New Year's Eve. It was a lot different than this."

"This is probably a little less of a party than you're used to," I said, trying to be sympathetic to him in case he felt like a fish out of water. I gestured to the refreshment table, full of root beer and lemonade and cream soda. One of Dave's University of Washington friends was standing there, looking at the beverages in puzzlement.

Tyler looked at me, confused as to what I meant. Then he seemed to figure it out. "Oh, I don't drink," he said with a smile. "I decided there was no way to take my playing to the next level if I was doing stuff like that to my body. So, it's kind of cool when I hang out with you Mormons because I don't have to explain myself the whole night long and drive a bunch of drunk people home afterwards. Although I still have to ask Julie to decode half of what you're saying."

"What do you mean?" I asked.

"I'm getting pretty good at Mormon terminology from living in Utah, but there's a whole new set of terms everyone's using right now that have to do with missionary stuff."

"I bet," I said. "Are you doing okay or do you need a translator while Julie's in the kitchen?"

"I think I'm doing okay," he shrugged. "But I'll let you know if I don't catch something." He held out his cup of root beer and took a drink, slouching down in his chair so he didn't look so tall, and smiled.

"So tell me more about Utah," I said. "Have you been skiing yet? Does your coach let you do stuff like that?"

Tyler and I talked for a few more minutes and then Julie came back. She looked beautiful and gentle, as usual. She had always been cute, but her sense of self-worth had increased over the years, which gave her a quiet self-confidence that was nice to be around. She wore a light blue sweater that brought out her eyes, and Tyler was obviously happy to be with her. I wondered what was going on there— was their friendship about to evolve into something more? Of course, I didn't ask.

Dave caught my eye from across the room and was starting to weave his way toward me, when one of the University of Washington guys called out to him. He gave me a mock-exasperated smile and went over to talk to his friend.

And so it went for the rest of the night. In a way, it was good because I had a great time catching up with Julie and Tyler and Mikey and other people from high school and church. Mikey and Julie and I made plans for them to come visit me in Ithaca during the summer, something we'd talked about for a while. This time, it seemed like it might actually happen and I was excited at the prospect.

But as the night wore on, I got a little tired. Sometimes it's a little hard to keep your game face on. Parties can be fun, but there are also quiet moments, moments when you're in transition between comments and talking to people, when you let down your guard a little. It was a moment like that, right before we were all going to gather while the clock struck midnight, when I was sitting alone on the couch and thinking. Everyone else was gravitating to the kitchen where Mikey was handing out noisemakers and hats but I stayed where I was, looking across the room at the lights on the Christmas tree and not thinking about anything in particular. That's when Dave found me.

"Did you miss me?" Dave asked, sitting down next to me. He handed me a noisemaker and put his arm around me. I rested my head on his shoulder.

"Do you mean tonight or while you were on your mission?"

"Either. Both."

"Oh, I don't know," I teased. "It's good to see you, but I hadn't really noticed you were gone."

He didn't buy it for a minute, of course. And neither did I. I'd been waiting a long time to see him again.

"Happy New Year," he told me, leaning closer. Someone yelled, "It's time," and people started chanting as they counted down to the New Year. "Ten, nine, eight"—I tilted my head up a little more and we both started smiling—"seven, six, five, four . . ."

"Do you think I should kiss you in front of all these people?" he whispered. I didn't say anything, just waited, just looked at him.

"Three, two, one . . ."

I closed my eyes for the kiss.

"Happy New Year," he whispered a few seconds later.

• • •

Now, on opposite sides of the country, our nightly phone calls took the place of our dates. Sometime after dinner at Dave's, which was 7:00 P.M. his time and 10:00 P.M. for me, one of us would call the other and we'd talk for a while before I went to sleep. After that first night, I always went into my room to talk to him. I'd sit at my desk and doodle while we talked, or I'd organize a drawer or my closet while I was on the phone. I had so much nervous energy; I had to burn it somehow. And after we were done talking, it always took a while before I could fall asleep. I would be laughing at something he'd said, or wondering what, exactly, he'd meant by something he'd mentioned.

For the first few weeks after winter break, I walked around campus feeling like I had something extra, some insurance against the cold and the loneliness that can happen during winter. Someone cared about me, and even though he was thousands of miles away, we would talk on the phone or text message or send e-mails. I kept those warming thoughts inside as I walked around the freezing campus. When I walked around a couple holding hands or saw people kissing good-bye before they separated for classes, I reminded myself that someone cared about me, too. And that was a big deal. That was almost enough.

I had almost always been able to get school and running and work to go my way if I worked hard enough. But dating was another story. That always went wrong for me. And for once in my romantic life, things were going just as I had hoped. Dave was home, we were dating, albeit long distance, and the five weeks of Christmas break had been exactly how I'd pictured they would be. Everything had been perfect.

The only little problem was that he was so far away. He wasn't across the globe anymore, but we still had an entire country between us.

On the weekends, when Shannon went out with her boyfriend, Rich, and Emma always had something planned, I usually stayed home and studied or researched different grad school programs. Because of a class I was taking, I found myself intrigued by marriage and family therapy and the possibility of getting a master's degree in that area seemed appealing. During my Friday nights researching online, I found programs all over the country that looked interesting, including one at Syracuse University and one at BYU.

To my disappointment, the programs offered at the University of Washington didn't seem to be as good a fit. I wanted to talk with Dave about all of this but when I tried to bring it up, it never seemed to work. Our conversations tended toward either joking and kidding around with each other or superficial small talk. I tried to bring up serious things, like my growing uncertainty about medical school and my confusion about what I really wanted to do as a career, but it was hard. I hadn't expected it to be that way. We'd always had fun together, sure, but we'd been able to talk about the serious things too. It seemed like I couldn't get past the joking and the façade. It seemed that we did better talking in person. I couldn't wait for spring break.

"I've been thinking about getting a master's degree," I finally told him one night on the phone, when the conversation hit a lull. I had to get it out.

"What about med school?" he asked, sounding surprised.

"I don't know," I sighed. "Remember at Christmas, when I told you that I was thinking about changing programs? If I did a master's degree, that would only take two years. That's a lot shorter than four years of med school, plus the residency. And even more than that, my interests have changed. I had to take a psychology course this fall for my major and I think I'm more interested in that field now."

"You mean you're going to be a shrink?" Dave said.

"No, a social worker, who works with families. The degree I'm thinking about is a master's degree in Marriage and Family Therapy." It was the first time I'd said the name of the program out loud to anyone. I hadn't even told Emma or Shannon or my parents exactly what I was thinking about doing. I liked the way it sounded.

"Well, I'm sure you'll do well at whatever you decide," he told me sincerely. And then we were off to the next topic. I knew that he meant what he said and that he didn't want to push me in one direction or the other, but I still wished he had said something else. Something more.

As February drew to a close and March began to arrive, the distance seemed to matter more and more. I couldn't get a feel for what he was thinking. Some nights I would hang up the phone and feel like we'd connected, like the distance between us was easily bridged with our feelings and our jokes and our camaraderie, and other nights I would hang up and feel like I'd had a chat with a nice acquaintance. It was so hard to tell which feeling was more accurate. I wished fervently that Cornell's spring break wasn't at the end of March. I wanted to go back to see him as soon as possible.

Then came the time when he didn't return my call until late the next day. He apologized, "I'm so sorry, I stayed late studying on campus and when I got on the bus to come home, the battery on my phone died and by the time I got home, it was too late to call you . . ."

I knew he wasn't making things up. It was all true. But I also knew that a few weeks ago, he would have found a pay phone, or checked his watch while he was studying, or sent me a text message while his phone was charging, or something to make sure that he didn't miss talking to me. Were we drifting apart? Or was this a good sign, a healthy sign of being comfortable in a relationship and not feeling like it had to trump all else?

It was so hard to tell.

FEBRUARY, BRAZIL

Ethan Beckett

The water in the font was cold. We had waited and waited. At first, everyone who'd come to the baptism stood close together and talked and laughed, and then, as it became more and more apparent that there might not *be* a baptism, people got a lot quieter and more subdued, and then they started to drift out of the room and away.

After Elder Vickers and I had done everything we could think of to try to locate Eduardo, the bishop had a little discussion with the two of us to say that it didn't look like there was going to be a baptism that day. He said it very gently, and it was obvious that he was right, but it still hurt to hear the words echoing off the tile as we stood near the font.

The three of us stacked the chairs. Elder Vickers emptied the font. I think the sound of draining a font for a baptism that didn't happen is one of the emptiest, most melancholy sounds I've heard. I changed out of my baptismal white pants and tie and shirt and back into my missionary clothes. I clipped my nametag back onto the pocket of my white shirt. Elder Vickers turned out the lights and I locked the building and we started walking home.

For once, we had nothing to say to each other. We both knew how the other was feeling. Elder Vickers was going home in two weeks and we had both been thrilled that Eduardo's baptism was happening before Elder Vickers left. We'd been working with Eduardo the entire time we'd been companions and now something had gone wrong. But what? I couldn't get that question out of my mind as we walked through the streets to our apartment. *What had happened?*

Was it because *I* was going to baptize him that Eduardo hadn't come? Elder Vickers had a better command of the language and was funnier and more dynamic. Maybe if *he* had been the one doing the baptism, Eduardo would have shown up.

Or maybe I shouldn't have challenged him to be baptized after our most recent meeting with him. I had felt good about it at the time, but obviously he hadn't been ready since he hadn't shown up.

Then the darker thoughts started to intrude. Was there something wrong with what we were teaching? Who was I to tell someone like Eduardo, whose life had been a battle and a struggle in so many ways, that everything could be okay? It seemed almost arrogant sometimes. I'd never been drunk, never battled temptations like alcoholism. I'd had a mother in my life, and a father too. The only times I'd gone hungry were times when I'd chosen to fast, but there had always been food available. I cringed in embarrassment as I thought of times when I had been younger and had complained because I didn't like what we were eating or because there was no dessert. I'd always had plenty of clothes to wear and a warm room to sleep in and a bed of my own. When I had decided that I wanted to go to college, there had been money for it. Neither of my parents ever hit me.

It was *really* unfair, when you thought about it. How would Eduardo, struggling with poverty and addiction, feel about someone like me, who could talk so easily of sacrifice and the Savior's power to heal everything, when I'd lived such a charmed life?

No, it wasn't possible to be mad at Eduardo. I gave up on that. But I decided that it *was* possible to be mad at myself and wonder how I'd failed him. It was even possible to be a little bit mad at the Lord for not helping Eduardo have an easier, more comfortable life.

We arrived at our apartment. Out of habit, we slowed and I checked the mailbox. Neither of us had had any letters from home for almost a month. We didn't know how our families were or what they were doing. The mission office was supposed to forward our mail on to us, but it hadn't been happening for some reason. It had bothered us a little before, but now it felt like another fresh slap in the face when we got home and looked into the empty metal mailbox with its long streak of rust on the side like a gash.

"Nothing," I told Elder Vickers, and he shook his head because he already knew. We went up the steps, empty-handed.

• • •

The next morning, the alarm went off and I sat up, still trying to shake the feeling from the day before. We'd both gone to bed feeling pretty down and the weight was still sitting on me when I woke up. It was P-Day. There was laundry to wash, letters to write, grocery shopping to do. But all I did was sit in bed, holding my scriptures and trying to read them, waiting.

I wondered what I was waiting for. I realized, as I watched Elder Vickers read his scriptures, that I was waiting for him to cheer me up. I was waiting for him to come up with one of his signature plans, to figure out something that would make us feel better. I was waiting for him to take the lead, like he usually did. I was waiting for him to fix things. But he kept reading and turning the pages, one by one.

I knew it was unfair that I expected Elder Vickers to fix things every time. But I still wasn't sure what to do. I racked my brain for something that I could do to pull us out of this funk. Nothing. I sighed and stood up.

"What do you want to do first today?" I asked him, listing the things we usually did on P-Day. "Laundry, letters, or grocery shopping?" Then, I realized with a start that this was his second-to-last P-Day. Sometimes we could do a little sightseeing on P-Day. "Is there anywhere you want to go?"

"Não," he said. *No.* He stood up. "Let's get the grocery shopping out of the way first."

• • •

We stood in line at the *supermercado* with our basket full of fruit, dry spaghetti noodles, cereal, laundry soap, and some milk (which came in bags and tasted flat compared to the milk back home). While we waited our turn, Elder Vickers idly read the newspaper headlines out loud to me in Portuguese. Just like the headlines in the supermarket lines at home, the newspapers in Brazil made the world sound even crazier than it is. Or maybe it really *is* that crazy and I'm just naïve.

We started walking home. "Are you *sure* you don't want to go anywhere?" I asked him. "The animal park? The cathedral?"

Elder Vickers shook his head. *"Não,"* he said again. "Maybe after we do our laundry."

I groaned. "Don't remind me. I keep trying not to think about it." One of the promises I've made myself is that when I get home I won't complain about doing the laundry ever again. It's my least favorite task on the mission because we don't have washers and dryers. We wash our clothes ourselves, scrubbing them as hard as we can on the built-in washboard in our washtub. Then we hang them out to dry when we're finished—on a clothesline in the yard if it's sunny, on a clothesline in our apartment if it's raining.

I unwrapped the bars of thick, waxy soap, while Elder Vickers brought the laundry baskets into the yard. We separated our whites and darks into our plastic buckets and put soap in with them to soak. We ate lunch while they soaked, still not talking much. When we walked back out in the yard to start scrubbing our clothes, a dog was by one of the buckets, about to try to drink the soapy water. Elder Vickers pretended to throw his brush at him.

"*Sai fora!*" I yelled. *Get out of here!* The dog ran off.

It took us a good hour and a half to scrub out our clothes and hang them on the clothesline in the yard to dry. The dog kept coming back to visit. When he realized we weren't actually going to throw anything at him, he kept to the edges of the yard and watched us, panting and licking his chops. Elder Vickers gave him a bowl of clean water to drink so he wouldn't keep trying to get into our laundry.

"Don't feed him anything, though," he warned. "Unless you want him to follow us around forever."

We spent the rest of the afternoon cleaning out our apartment, which needed it, and trying to keep the dog away from our clean laundry. Then it was time to write our letters. Letter writing in the late afternoon is always the most perilous time for me for some reason. P-Day is almost over and I'm tired and so my guard is down a little bit. I owed letters to my parents, Andrea, Chloe, and Mikey.

What made writing letters even harder this time was that I had no idea what was going on with them because of the mail situation. For all I knew, Mikey had a new boyfriend and had "Dear John"-ed me, and here I was like a fool, writing stuff like, "We had a good week, except for a baptism that didn't pan out." What if she didn't even care about that, or about me? I hurried and finished her letter and moved on to my parents. At least I knew they would always care about me. They had to. They were my parents, even if I did have to write to each of them separately, instead of writing a single letter addressed "Dear Mom and Dad."

When they got divorced, it was a dark time for me. When I couldn't talk to my sister, and I could see her changing and withdrawing, that was hard. When I was flying on the airplane to Brazil, stiff and hot and uncomfortable in my white shirt and tie and nametag, and all the other passengers were laughing at us and speaking in rapid-fire Portuguese that we couldn't understand, that had been rough. I had thought about turning right back around and going home. I'd tell my parents, "Sorry, I gave it a try, and it wasn't for me."

Nothing to compare with Eduardo and what he'd been through in his life. But still. I'd had some bleak times too. Everyone walked around with the scars of their own trials and did the best they could most of the time. You had to remember that when you talked to people and tried to offer the gospel or you'd forget the whole spirit of compassion the Savior showed in His ministry. Some days you rose above it all and some days you just put one foot in front of the other and tried to keep your chin up and did what you were supposed to do.

Which is what we did the rest of the evening. One foot in front of the other. We mopped up the mess the stray dog made when he ran into the kitchen and tracked mud all over the floor. We put away the laundry tubs and hung up our clothes in the closet. We made dinner. We washed the dishes. We walked down the street and talked to a few people. We did our personal scripture study. Check, check, check.

"You're a great comp, Elder Vickers," I said after I'd said my individual prayer and climbed into bed. Nothing in response. I closed my eyes and tried to go to sleep.

Just when the silence had gone on so long I was sure he was asleep, I heard him say, "You too, Beckett."

MARCH, ITHACA

Joel Hammond

I came to Ithaca, New York, by myself. Snow was falling, so even though it was late March, the town had a wintry feel, a night-before-Christmas mood about it. Later, when I saw some forgotten Christmas wreaths left on some of the houses, it seemed more appropriate than it did out-of-season. It was easy to forget that we were actually closer to Easter with this kind of setting. I even started singing "Have Yourself a Merry Little Christmas," under my breath after I picked up the key to my rental car.

There were peppermints in a basket at the rental car counter. I took one and lodged it in my cheek as I headed to the car. My feet made the sound of walking in deep new snow—halfway between a squish and a crunch. I was glad I'd brought my down coat and wished that I'd brought some boots. Snow was melting in my running shoes.

No one had cleared the snow off the car yet, so I turned the heater on and started brushing off the windshield. As I worked, I wondered what I had gotten myself into, spending three days alone in a little town I didn't know. It had seemed like a good idea to investigate each grad school thoroughly before making a decision about where I wanted to go to get my PhD in economics. Cornell was the last visit of three. I'd gone to Arizona first and it had been fine, but then I'd spent the weekend at UCSD, in San Diego. I was sold on the school, the program, the city, the beach. I was going through the motions with this last visit mainly because I'd already purchased a ticket and because I'd never been to New York.

I turned on the dome light inside the car and tried to read the directions I'd gotten from the bored employee at the rental car counter. Time to find the motel and crash until morning. It had been a long flight from Utah and I was tired and disoriented.

Luckily, the motel proved relatively easy to find. I set my carry-on bag down on the fake wood-veneered table in my motel room and pulled off my wet shoes and socks. I retrieved a mashed granola bar from the bottom of my carry-on and decided to invest some money in vending machine nutrition instead. A bag of microwave popcorn and a Snickers bar later, I felt better, but not by much. I couldn't wait until the morning when I could find something involving a real food group.

Before I crashed, I gave my girlfriend, Lauren, a call. She picked up after only one ring, which made me feel good. "Hey," I said.

"Joel!" she said and the excitement in her voice made me smile. "How are you?"

"I'm good. What about you? Did your presentation go okay in class?"

"Yeah, it was fine, but I want to hear about you! How was your flight?"

"Long. But I made it here safe and sound. It snowed, so they had to deice the runway before we could land, but other than that it was completely uneventful."

"What's it like there?" I could hear loud laughter in the background. "Sorry, let me go outside. There are a lot of people here." I heard her open a door and then close it behind her. "That's better," she said.

I knew she was standing on the little balcony of her student apartment in Provo, where it would still be chilly, but not as cold as it was here. I could picture Lauren sitting down on the white plastic chair she kept on the balcony, maybe sitting cross-legged to keep warm, wearing her oversized BYU sweatshirt or her parka. Man, I missed her.

"Tell me everything," she said.

"Ithaca is freezing. That's all I know right now," I said. "It should be interesting. I'll be meeting with some people in the Econ department tomorrow and then Saturday I think I'll go up to the Sacred Grove before I fly out that night."

"Sounds good," she said. This was all stuff she'd heard before. "So do you think you're going to find anything there that makes you want to give up on the San Diego idea?"

"I don't think so," I said. "San Diego's still looking good. But it will be nice to know that I checked into all the options."

Lauren laughed. "That's you, all right."

"What about you?" I asked. "What have you been up to today?"

"Not much," she said. "Went to class, went to work, came home. The usual."

The usual seemed very far away from that little motel room in Ithaca. I knew what classes she had today, Thursday, and the path she'd take home from her job on the BYU campus, and the way her apartment looked.

"So, any opinions?" I asked. "Where do you think I should go?"

Lauren thought for a minute. "You shouldn't make your decision based on me," she said. "Do what you think you need to do."

That was as close as we ever came to discussing the issue at hand, which was: What were Lauren and I going to do about *us?* She and I were at a crossroads. She had another year of her undergraduate degree, and I needed to start graduate school so that I could one day go on to gainful employment. Would she try to transfer and move to wherever I went? Would I defer admission and stick around in Provo for another year? Were we going to try to do the long-distance thing? And—the biggest question of all—were we going to take the plunge and get married?

• • •

The next day was better than I'd thought it'd be. I found myself liking everything—the department, the faculty, and the students—more than I'd expected. If it weren't for the weather and the location and being so far away from most of my family, I might have to give Cornell a shot. I liked the feeling of walking in the snow, past the old stone buildings on the campus. Some of them had high ceilings and ornate chandeliers that threw light out of the windows and onto the drifts of snow as it grew darker.

There were a few snowflakes drifting down as I walked through the middle of campus toward a red brick building that caught my eye. It looked like a church. The doors were closed, but I read the name: Sage Chapel. There was a small plaza next to the chapel and I sat for a moment on a bench I found there. Bare trees stretched their branches above me, arching across the courtyard. I watched the snowflakes tumble, fat and lazy, around the warm red brick of the chapel. I looked up at the stained glass windows and at the carved stone angels over the doorways, watching them as they disappeared into the darkness while night fell around me. I wondered what it would be like to belong here.

But it was getting darker and colder, and I couldn't stay on the bench forever. I went back to my tiny motel room to kill a few hours before dinner. Being alone on a Friday night seems extra depressing. No one feels bad for themselves if they're alone on a Tuesday night.

I flopped onto the bed and turned on the TV. I watched some of the NCAA tournament without anyone to comment to or trash talk with. It had been a long time since I'd spent so much time alone inside four little walls. I thought about calling Lauren again but figured I'd better wait until I had some actual news if I was going to bother her on a Friday night. She would have things to do, friends to hang out with.

I had to get out of my room. I decided to find someplace to eat and consulted the list of places given to me by the front desk clerk. It was still snowing outside as I made my way to my rental car, which was muffined in a white drift of snow. I scraped off the car and started out. I drove the wrong way on a one-way street and was pulled over by a police officer, who was nice but made me feel even more inept than usual. I tried to order a steak at what turned out to be a vegetarian restaurant. After all of that, I decided I'd finally generated enough news to rate a phone call to Lauren, but she didn't pick up either her apartment phone or her cell phone.

After scripture study and prayers, I fell asleep to the sound of another tournament game starting on TV.

• • •

Thankfully, it thawed enough the next morning that I could still make it to Palmyra. I'd never been to the Sacred Grove before and I had my heart set on visiting. I couldn't be so close and not go, since who knew when I would ever be back in upstate New York again.

The route that the clerk recommended wrapped around Cayuga Lake, which was frozen at the edges. I was tempted to walk out on it and see how far I could get, but I didn't try. The ice was white and the water was a smooth, metallic gray.

Looking at the landscape in front of me, I was surprised at how beautiful it was, even though it was painted mainly in shades of black and white and gray. It's amazing what He can do with even a limited palette. There were lake houses and docks right against the lake, propped up in the icy water or sealed up against the winter. It was hard to imagine a time when people would sit on those docks with lemonade and a suntan and when the water would be blue instead of slate in color.

I made it to Palmyra right before it started to snow again. It wasn't a serious snowstorm, just the kind that reminds you that spring isn't here yet and won't be for a while. There had been enough flurries, though, to scatter a dust of fine white snow across the sidewalks and roads.

I'm not sure how many people visit the Sacred Grove in the middle of a mild snowstorm. I assume the number is lower than it is in the summer when the weather is nice and school is out, but maybe it's when it's cold and bitter outside that you most need to be reminded of what happened in that grove. It was beyond frigid, but I'd driven all that way and couldn't leave without going in. A look through a rental car window wasn't going to cut it—snow or no snow—and once I was there, I was too excited to wait out the flurries. I wanted to have a chance to kneel and say a prayer in the Grove before I left.

At least this trip won't be a total waste, I thought. *I'll go home and send in my acceptance to San Diego and I'll know that I explored all of the options and that San Diego was the one.*

I got out of the car and pulled my hat down over my ears, zipped up my coat, stuck my hands deep into the pockets of my down jacket. I willed my running shoes to show more resistance to the wet than they had done up to that point.

The paths had been cleared with typical Mormon efficiency and I looked up at the trees. In the songs and in the pictures, the leaves are always green and it is always spring, because that was when the First Vision occurred here. The season was off but it was still the same place and that was connection enough. It was beautiful this way, too. The leaves were gone, but each dark branch was precisely outlined in pure white snow. Without the leaves, you could see how high the trees grew and how strong they were.

And it was so quiet. Now and then I could hear a little sigh as a bush or a tree branch released a little of its burden of snow. But that was all, except for me walking and breathing.

I stopped and knelt in the snow. I bent my head to pray. It was one of those prayers where you don't so much form actual words as send feelings up to heaven. If you could put what I was feeling into words, it would be something like, "I'm here, where Joseph was. Thank You for this, for everything. Please help me do the right things in my life too."

There have only been one or two experiences in my life where I have had very clear answers to prayers. Usually I go along, doing the best I can and asking if I'm on the right track and usually I get that warm feeling when I pray about stuff that means "Go ahead." But this was different. I hadn't had such a clear answer hit me with such force since deciding to go on my mission.

As I stood up and brushed the snow off my knees, I knew. I knew the answer to a question I hadn't realized I had asked. I knew I was going to come back to New York for graduate school. I knew that I would be in this place again. In spite of the traffic ticket, the embarrassing social situations, the freezing weather, the fact that the girl I was fairly sure I could happily marry lived a few thousand miles away, I still knew that I would be coming back. This was the place for me.

It was strange how something so complicated could be so simple.

MARCH, ITHACA TO SEATTLE

Andrea Beckett

"She wouldn't let me check it, or put it in a bag," apologized the man sitting in seat 12A. "Her grandma gave it to her during this visit and she loves it." He nodded to his daughter who was holding a gigantic stuffed whale on her lap. She was sitting in the aisle seat—12B—which meant that her dad was squished against the window to make room for the whale. A flipper dangled into the aisle, and I brushed against it as I stepped into the next row.

We were in pretty close quarters for the ride from Ithaca to Philadelphia. It was a tiny plane, the kind that has only one seat on one side of the aisle and two seats on the other. The whale was so big that I couldn't even see the little girl herself, just some socks and red patent leather shoes sticking out, dark sprigs of pigtails, and her round little nose and eyes over the top of the whale's black-and-white head. She looked like she was around three or four years old, and it made me think of Chloe and how she'd been at that age. She wouldn't have relinquished a stuffed whale either.

"There's no way that's regulation size," I said, laughing, sitting in the window seat and fastening the seat belt.

Her dad looked back and shook his head ruefully. "It's not," he said, "but it fit through the X-ray machine and no one's going to take a toy away from a kid. Plus it's soft. I don't think anyone can get injured with it."

A young, dark-haired guy stopped in the aisle, checking his ticket against the printed labels above the seats. He slipped his carry-on into the small overhead bin. "It's a very nice whale," he said to the girl, catching my eye as I looked at him. He smiled and sat down in the empty seat next to me. Rats. I was breaking one of my cardinal rules by engaging in conversation with people before it was 15 minutes until landing. It looked like I was going to be stuck making friendly conversation with *everyone*. Good thing this leg of the plane ride was only about an hour long.

"I wish they'd let *me* bring something that big on the plane," I told the little girl. "I'd never have to check my bag again."

"Wouldn't that be great?" asked the young guy next to me. "I hate standing around in the baggage claim area waiting for my stuff. One time, some guy grabbed my bag and took off with it. I had to chase him down and get it back."

"Was he trying to steal it?" I hypothesized, interested in spite of myself.

"Nah, I don't think so. Our bags looked alike and he was in a hurry, so he took mine by mistake. He was kind of a jerk about it, though, considering he was the one in the wrong."

"That's too bad," I said, my interest already waning. I wondered if I should get out my book now to read and let him know that the conversation was over. I had been a victim of my own nervousness about the trip home and had let down my guard—I hadn't meant to talk to *anyone*—but it wasn't too late to salvage the situation . . . yet.

As the plane took off, I vowed I was not going to share with him any of my own baggage claim stories. I was not going to inquire politely about his destination and whether or not he thought his luggage would make it there in time. I was not going to ask him where he went to school or how many brothers and sisters he had or whether or not he was following the NCAA tournament. I did not want to be making small talk for the duration of the ride. I turned toward the window a little more, but then I dropped my water bottle, and it rolled next to his feet. He reached down and handed it back to me.

"Where are you flying?" he asked. "Are you from Ithaca?" Well, I was in for it. We were having a conversation, in spite of my best efforts at being polite but distant. I threw caution to the wind, for a second anyway. It would help to have something else to think about besides Dave for a little while.

"No," I said. "But I go to school at Cornell."

"Really?" he asked. For a dark-haired guy, his eyes were surprisingly blue. "I might need to ask you for some advice then." He turned as far toward me as his seat belt would allow.

Yup. I was definitely in for a conversation, and it served me right for breaking my own rules. I should have known better. My own rules are for my own protection, after all. "About Cornell?"

He nodded. "And about living in Ithaca. It looks like I'm going to be doing both next year." He had a nice way of speaking, with almost a cadence to it. His voice was the kind that would be perfect for broadcasting or commercials, I noticed without wanting to notice. I decided, without wanting to decide, that he could be considered good looking after all. "I've been out visiting for a few days to see what it's like."

We were interrupted for a moment by the stewardess, who slung some miniscule foil bags of pretzels onto our trays and gave us teeny tiny bottles of water to drink. She asked us what we wanted to drink in addition to the water. The young guy wanted orange juice; I wanted more water. In front of us, the little girl expressed a strong preference for apple juice. I popped my bag open and shook the pretzels out into my napkin.

"You seem kind of old to be graduating from high school,"

I observed, "so I assume you're coming to Cornell for a graduate degree?"

"You're right," he said.

"Cornell's a great school. And Ithaca is a good place. You'll get used to the cold, if you decide to come here. Maybe." I thought for a second. "I guess I can't guarantee that since I still hate the cold."

"I'm Joel Hammond," he said, looking amused and sticking out his hand.

"Andrea Beckett," I answered, shaking his hand once.

There was a commotion in the seat in front of us, and suddenly two heads—one human, one whale—popped up over the back of the seat. "I'm Mia Hales," said the little girl, ignoring her dad's requests to sit back down. She lifted the whale up a little more. "And this is Whaley Whale."

"Pleased to meet you, Whaley," said Joel, reaching out and shaking one of Whaley Whale's flippers seriously. It reminded me of something Dave might do, only the execution was completely different.

"He can't talk," said Mia, fixing him with a solemn stare. "He's not real."

"Right," said Joel. He looked at me as if to say, "What now?" I shrugged.

"Mia, sit down," Mia's dad whispered loudly, glancing back at us apologetically.

"Whaley Whale doesn't talk, but he loves pretzels," said Mia holding out her hand over the back of the seat.

Joel grinned wryly and handed her his bag of pretzels.

"Mia!" her dad hissed, yanking on Whaley's flipper. Both Whaley Whale and the pigtails popped out of sight.

Laughing, Joel lifted his cup of orange juice and took a drink, but someone walking down the aisle jostled his arm and it spilled down his front. He set the cup back down and looked at me with an amused glint in his eye. "You have a very refined fellow passenger," he said seriously. "Not only will I smell like orange juice for the rest of the trip, but I think I've just been shot down by a stuffed whale." His sense of humor was so quiet, so understated, so different from Dave and his effusiveness. I knew Dave would have had that little girl laughing by now. But Airplane Guy Joel was still sort of funny, I guess, if you knew how to take his sense of humor.

I wondered when I was going to stop comparing everyone—even random guys on the airplane—with Dave.

I handed Joel my napkin to help with the orange juice spill. Mia's dad also slipped us a handful between the seats. Joel got himself cleaned up a little, but tiny bits of orange juice pulp still clung to his wool sweater. He tried to pick them off but gave up, looking resigned.

He pulled off the sweater, nearly impaling me with his elbow in the process—"Sorry," he said—and underneath his sweater, he wore a gray T-shirt with "Cornell" printed across the front. He had obviously bought it at the bookstore, because it had little creases down the sleeves where it had been folded and the tag was still stuck to the neck of the shirt, hanging out of his collar. He balled up the sweater and stuck it under his seat. Airplanes are so small and so forcefully intimate, you notice these things even when you're pretending to earnestly peruse the safety card.

"Have you figured out the safest route for us in the event of an emergency?" Joel asked, pulling out his safety card and pretending to read it too.

I joked back a little. He wasn't bad to talk to, even if his humor was a little dry. "I can't decide. Remember, the closest exit *may* be behind us."

Joel craned his neck to look around. "I don't see one."

"It's the row in front of us, silly," said Mia, peeking around the edge of her seat.

Joel laughed. "I'm glad someone around here is on top of these things."

"If we have a water landing, we could all ride Whaley Whale to safety," offered Whaley Whale's . . . dad. Mia let out a shriek and clutched Whaley Whale more tightly.

The captain chose that moment to make a loud and largely unintelligible announcement about what was going on up in the flight deck. Joel leaned back in his seat. I stared out the window, and yes, I was thinking about Dave.

"You know," Joel said after a few minutes. "You never answered my first question."

"What are you talking about?" I turned to look at him. "Which question?"

"Where are you flying?" Joel repeated, stretching out in his seat. He was tall, like me, and had to angle his legs out into the aisle to be comfortable.

"I'm going home to Seattle for spring break," I told him, wondering if he would be on the same flight. Then I would truly be in for it. "What about you?"

"I'm flying into Salt Lake City," he said.

I looked at him sharply, wondering if he was Mormon too. He could be. There was a noticeable absence of swearing in his conversation. He was clean cut. And he'd ordered orange juice, without any alcohol to go with it. I looked for any blatant signs—a CTR ring, a wedding ring, a Book of Mormon in his hand. Nothing obvious. I thought for a second about asking him, but I didn't know if it would offend him if he wasn't. Sometimes I get tired of everyone asking me about coffee and Kurt Cobain the minute they hear I'm from Seattle, especially since I don't know that much about either of those things anyway. I don't drink coffee, and Cobain was before my time.

Joel's blue eyes met mine. "Are you trying to decide whether or not to ask me if I'm Mormon?"

"Yeah," I said. "Are you Mormon?"

"I am."

"Me too," I added, and he smiled.

"I thought so," he said.

"Why?" I was curious.

"I'm not sure." He looked thoughtful. "I think it's because you haven't sworn once this whole plane ride. Or it might be that glow you have about you." He was joking—I hoped. "So, was it mentioning Salt Lake that gave *me* away?" he asked.

"That, and you're kind of clean-cut." I shrugged. "Nothing else. It was a guess."

He looked slightly sheepish. "I guess neither one of us has a Book of Mormon in our bag to give away to people on airplane rides, then."

"Guess not," I said. "I should be better at missionary work than I am. My brother's on a mission and he has to knock on the doors of perfect strangers and talk to them in a language he's still learning, even though he's been out for almost a year. You'd think I could at least get up the courage to ask someone if they're Mormon or not." *What's wrong with me?* I wondered. I couldn't seem to stop talking, which was very unlike me. It must be the nervousness about Dave.

Joel laughed. "I actually do have a Book of Mormon in my carry-on, but as you can see, I didn't really do much about handing it out. I could do better, too, and I've *been* on a mission. Where's your brother serving?"

"Brazil," I said. "Where did you serve?"

"Texas, Spanish-speaking."

"And now you go to school at . . . ?"

"BYU," he said. "Maybe you've heard of it?" He gave me a wry smile.

"Oh yeah," I said. "Mostly I hear about it along the lines of, 'Why didn't you go to BYU?' After the University of Washington, that's where most of the Mormon kids in my area go to school. Plus, my parents went there, and so did my brother before his mission."

"I'm sure Cornell is very different from BYU," he said. "Is there a ward in Ithaca, or a branch, or do you have to go to another town for church?"

"There's a ward for the permanent residents of the town and a student branch as well."

"Just one?" Joel whistled. "I guess I'm used to BYU where there are something like 12 stakes and over 200 wards for the students alone."

"I like being in a small branch," I said. "It has its benefits."

"So tell me some more things you like about church and about Ithaca. I'm going to need all the information you're willing to give if I come back in the fall." He paused for a second. "*When* I come back in the fall."

I surreptitiously checked my watch. Only about twenty more minutes left until we were due to land. I might as well go for broke and talk for the rest of the plane ride. Thank goodness this wasn't the Philly to Seattle leg. That would have been a whole lot of conversation. As it was, Joel was just enough of a distraction that I could divert at least part of my mind from thinking about Dave. But Dave was always there underneath everything, like a rock in your shoe that shifts now and then so you don't notice it as much, but you're always conscious that it's there.

"If you don't have somewhere else to go, that is," Joel said with a touch of friendly sarcasm in his voice.

"Sure. What else do you want to know?"

He wanted to know a lot. At first, I was worried he was just interested in asking me more personal questions, but he was very serious and wanted to find out every little piece of information he could about Cornell and Ithaca. He asked a *lot* of questions. He even laughed at my jokes sometimes. Some of his questions I could answer, like where most of the single grad students preferred to live and where I thought the best place to grocery shop was (Wegman's, hands down). And some of them I couldn't. "I have no idea how far away the Baseball Hall of Fame is," I told him. "I didn't even know it was in New York." He made a face of mock disgust at me.

The plane bumped a little as the wheels touched down on the runway and Whaley Whale popped out of Mia's hands. Joel reached out to catch Whaley, but missed, and Whaley bounced down the aisle toward the back of the plane as it touched down. "My whale!" Mia shouted, and she frantically began to tug at her seat belt.

"What the—?" I could hear from people a few rows ahead of us, as they watched Whaley's wild ride down the aisle.

Another shriek from Mia let them know exactly where he belonged, and someone snagged him and started passing him back up to where Mia was sitting. People handed Whaley Whale over their heads and down the aisle. "Whaley's crowd surfing," I observed to Joel, and he laughed.

When Whaley finally made it back to Mia, her dad took charge of him and sent us a commiserative glance over the seats. "Do you think it's too late to gate check this thing?" he asked us, and we both laughed.

We taxied to the gate and people began to unsnap their seat belts and grab their bags and books and jackets. Joel pulled his sweater out from under his seat. Mia's dad gestured for us to go first, but Joel told them to go ahead. "You'll clear a pathway for us," he said, and it was true: Whaley Whale was a like a battering ram clearing out the aisle for us. We followed them off the plane and out into the airport.

"Maybe I'll see you around in the fall," I said to Joel.

"I hope so. Thanks for all your help." He looked like he was about to add something else, but didn't.

"Look me up when you get back. You remember my name, right?"

"Andrea Beckett," he said, shaking my hand and smiling at me. "I couldn't forget that sense of humor." Then he hurried off to catch his connecting flight.

I stared after him for a minute. *My* sense of humor? Was he kidding? I realized he wasn't. Then I laughed. He had no idea who he had been talking to. The last thing I am is funny. I can laugh at stuff going on around me, but I've never been good at making jokes or kidding around. Except with Dave.

When I found the waiting area for my connecting flight, I shook my head and smiled. It turned out Whaley Whale was going all the way to Seattle with me. But I didn't get to sit by them this time. I watched Mia mash him through the aisle and sit next to someone else a few rows up. I guess gate-checking him hadn't been an option. I pictured Dave and what he would have said. Dave. What was going to happen with Dave? Was I ever going to have a plane ride again where I didn't spend the majority of it wondering about Dave and where we were headed?

• • •

I didn't have to wait long to find out what was going to happen with Dave. We'd planned on seeing each other that night after I got home from the airport, even though it would be late. What I hadn't planned on was that Dave would be waiting for me at my house, standing next to an unfamiliar car in the driveway.

His brown hair was still short like it had been after his mission, not the mess of wild brown curls it had been in high school. His face looked older. He leaned against the car door and half-waved at me as my mom, Chloe, and I pulled up next to him.

"Did you know Dave was going to be here?" my mom asked.

"No," I told her. She looked at me and I tried to smile. I was tired and disoriented from all the traveling, but my heart lifted a little at seeing him in person. I wanted desperately to fix the little nagging worry inside and convince myself that everything was going okay. I was thinking like an optimist, which wasn't my style, and it made me a little nervous. Why was I so anxious for everything to be okay? Did it mean that it probably wasn't?

Mom looked from me to Dave and gave my arm a quick

squeeze. She gathered up Chloe, who had fallen asleep in the car, and went inside, exchanging smiles and hellos with Dave on her way to the door. A few moments later, the lights inside the house flickered on in the deepening twilight.

"Hey," he said, still leaning against the car door, and from that first moment, from the way he said that one word, I had a feeling about the way things were going to go. And it wasn't a good feeling. The distance I'd felt on the phone wasn't something I'd made up. Something was different in the way he looked at me, in the tone of his voice, in absence of one of his trademark bear hugs. I could feel myself starting to break a little inside.

"Hey yourself. It's good to see you." I moved toward the porch steps and sat down. I tried to sound as normal as possible, tried to keep my tone light. Somewhere inside, my mom flipped the porch light on, and I sat in the spotlight waiting for him.

"You too," he said. "We haven't talked in a day or two." He slowly crossed the driveway and I scooted over to make room for him on the steps.

"I know," I said. "I guess we've both been busy."

I looked down at the scuffed toes of Dave's sneakers. Sitting side by side made it hard to look him right in the face. He wasn't looking at me, either, when I glanced up for a second. He was looking somewhere in the distance. As I watched him, he started to say something, then stopped. Then he tried again. "I know. It's been a long winter. It's not so easy to do this long-distance thing, is it?"

"I thought we'd be good at it by now, since we were fine while you were on your mission. But it's been . . . harder. For the last few weeks, anyway." I was still looking at his shoes. There were pine needles and dirt stuck to the bottom of them. Based on the brand and the way the soles were worn, they had been his running shoes at one point before they had become his everyday shoes. I stared at his feet while he talked. I tried to keep my teeth from chattering.

He agreed with me. "Yeah. When I was on my mission, we could keep it casual without feeling like we were losing ground. But now it's time to either go forward, or not, and it's hard to figure it out when we're not even together most of the time." I could tell Dave was getting cold too. But neither one of us scooted closer to the other for warmth.

"I know," I said. "I've thought about trying to get a summer job here, to see if that would help." Finally, I risked a glance at Dave to see what he thought of that. We'd discussed it before, but not recently. He was quiet, looking down, not at me. That almost told me everything I needed to know. Almost. I had to hear the exact words, so that I wouldn't have any leeway later to misinterpret what was happening or keep dreaming that everything was fine. Even though I wanted to, I couldn't make it easier on either of us. I had to have it spelled out, even though I was sure that hearing the words was going to hurt more than anything had hurt in a long, long time.

"But you don't think that would do any good, do you?" I asked. I started pulling at the inside of the cuff of my sweatshirt, trying to find a loose thread to unravel, trying to find something to hold onto.

"I don't want you to change your whole life around for me," he finally said. "What if it didn't work and you'd come back home and left your job and school and friends in Ithaca for nothing? That would be a lot of pressure."

"Yeah, but the alternative isn't really working either, is it?" I looked over at him again and this time he was looking at me. As our eyes met and held for the first time in a long time, I knew how different things had become. I'd gotten used to the luxury of Dave looking at me as if there was no one else he'd rather see. His eyes were still kind. But it was different.

Seeing him look at me that way made me feel a little like I did the one time I had been in a car accident. I had hit a patch of black ice and the car had started sliding, sliding, and I knew instantly, without a doubt, that things were out of control and that what was happening was not good.

"There's something else, Dave," I said suddenly. "What is it? Everything seemed to be going okay for a while, and then all of a sudden it's gotten a lot harder. "You've gotten a little more distant. I feel like there must be something else happening here."

"Do you remember Avery Matthews? From high school?" he asked, still looking straight at me.

"Yeah, of course. She wrote for the school paper," I said, picturing her in my mind. It was a vague picture: someone with long dark hair, a locker near mine—hadn't she written a poem I liked?—but I knew who she was. I knew she was Dave's friend, the one who hadn't been able to make it to the New Year's party. And then I remembered more. "She had a crush on you." I stopped for a moment. "Oh." So *that* was it. I should have figured out that it would be something like this, not just busyness at school and work or a lot on his plate as a member of the Institute council.

"She joined the Church a few months ago, I guess," Dave said. "Which took me by surprise because she wasn't interested in it at all in high school. And I kind of lost touch with her during my mission. I'm not the best letter writer, as you know. I wrote you more than anyone else except my parents."

I waited.

Dave, without realizing it, was getting more and more animated as he talked about Avery. It was hard to watch, so I ducked my head to listen instead.

"Anyway, we'd seen each other a few times after I graduated— just as friends, you know—but it all came to a stop after I gave her a Book of Mormon a couple of weeks before I left on my mission." He paused. "I think I told you about that." I nodded, and he went on. "I figured nothing had worked out, especially after she didn't show up to that New Year's party and everything. I thought I'd probably offended her, and even though I felt bad about it, I sort of wrote it off because I didn't know what else to do. Then I ran into her at Institute one day in February. She goes to U Dub too, and she's taking some institute classes. I was excited to see her there. I asked her what she was doing, and that's when she told me she'd joined the Church."

I waited.

"To make a long story short, she told me that she went through a lot of questioning and took the discussions twice—one time during her senior year in high school and another time last summer—and that's when she finally decided to be baptized." Dave stopped, looking uncomfortable. "I promise that all of this has a point."

"I think I know what the point is," I said. "Let me help you out a little. She's always had a crush on you and now you're reciprocating it." I was ready to move this conversation along, now that I knew the worst. It was cold out here and night was falling hard.

"Well," Dave said slowly. "Yeah. Kind of. I feel like I *could* reciprocate it. We've been hanging out some, always with other people, but it's starting to seem like maybe . . ." He stopped talking and shook his head. "I'm such a loser. We haven't even been on a date yet or anything. It seemed like I should talk to you first. But this might be even worse. I'm sorry." I'd never seen Dave look so miserable—at least not in recent memory.

I stood up. Dave looked at me, not sure what I was going to do next. I wasn't sure, either, so I folded my arms and looked at the driveway.

"That isn't your car," I blurted out. It sounded like an accusation.

Dave was puzzled by the change of topic. "No, it's my mom's. The old car is in the shop. It broke down."

Neither of us knew what to say, so we were quiet.

Dave finally stood up too. "Andrea?" he asked quietly. "Are you mad at me?"

I'd thought that uncertainty was the worst possible feeling and that knowing something, anything, would be better than not knowing. But I'd been wrong. I'd gotten what I'd asked for and all I wanted to do was go back. Knowing for a fact that Dave was interested in someone else was a hundred times worse than not being sure what was going on. There wasn't any room for denial now.

I wanted to be mad at him. But I wasn't. I'd never expected to like Dave so much. He was never supposed to be more than a funny, crazy, wonderful friend, and somewhere along the line it had evolved into so much more. Even when Dave was gone on his mission and I had dated a couple of other guys, nothing had ever come of it. I'd never come close to dating someone else seriously. No one could compare to Dave, and now I was losing him.

I expected to be angry and cause a scene, like I'd always done with breakups in high school—like when I caused a scene and dumped Connor Manwaring right before Homecoming. I'd never left a relationship without the upper hand, without getting the final parting words. But somehow that didn't seem important anymore. I didn't feel angry, just sad. Sick and sad. I would trade this feeling for mad in a second. Now I knew why I'd always gotten angry during my breakups before. It was a perfect defense mechanism.

"I'm not mad," I finally said. "I guess you could say I kind of saw it coming. We have bad timing, Dave. First you had your mission, and then I stayed in Ithaca for school. Long distance relationships aren't easy. Bad timing from the start."

Dave's eyes will always be the eyes of the first guy I fell in love with. They were still kind and friendly, which seemed unfair for some reason. "Actually, I think we have great timing," he said. "You made my senior year in high school the best ever. You were great to me on my mission. We've had a lot of good conversations this year. You've been a huge part of my life at a very important time. I'd like to think that it wasn't all bad for you either."

Stupid Dave. Now I really couldn't look at him because I was tearing up. I shook the tears away and looked up into the sky.

"This might sound kind of weird," Dave continued, "but I still love you." He cleared his throat. "I love you as a person and as a friend and everything. I guess I'm not in love with you the romantic way, even though I do care about you a lot."

"I know," I said. "That makes sense. I think I feel that way too," I admitted, then I laughed in spite of myself. "Although this still hurts a lot and I can't seem to stop crying." I pulled my sweatshirt sleeve over my hand and rubbed my eyes with it. Dave finally reached out and gave me a hug. I wanted to hold on tight and not let go. But of course, I didn't. My arms felt so empty afterwards.

"I'm making a habit of this with you," I said, trying for a joke before I completely fell apart. "Remember the night at Homecoming when I bawled in your car for hours?"

"Yeah," Dave said, smiling a little, and I could see his eyes were a little wet too. Was he crying too? This was so awful. I couldn't stand it.

"Ugh," I said and kicked the porch rail hard. It was a childish thing to do, but it made Dave laugh, which didn't tick me off for some reason.

"I feel the same way," Dave said. "It's always hard when something ends." To prove it, he kicked the porch rail too.

"I'm waiting for you to tell me that we're still going to be friends," I said, trying again to laugh.

"We *are* still going to be friends," Dave said seriously. "I'm good at being friends with people." He looked a little sad. "It's taking it to the next level that gives me trouble."

· · ·

After Dave left, I did feel mad. I kicked the porch rail a few more times. "You seem to do fine taking it to another level with Avery Matthews," I muttered to myself under my breath. "We had invested so much time in this. Would it kill you to give it another couple of months, until I can come home and convince you otherwise?"

Feeling mad made me feel a little better since it was what I expected. Like I said, I've always gotten mad after my other breakups, so this at least seemed normal. But it didn't last long. I realized there was little point in fighting for a relationship with Dave if he had already abandoned the battle. There was nothing left to fight for.

So instead of feeling angry, I ended up feeling exhausted. I wanted to go for a long run despite the midnight hour, but it was too dark. I was starving, hungry for food and for someone to talk to. But the house was dark, and quiet. My mom must have given up and gone to bed. I went into the kitchen and saw that she had left me a plate of dinner labeled with my name. I ate every bite. I was ravenous, completely hollow inside.

· · ·

The next morning, I was standing at the front room window, waiting for . . . I didn't know what. The window in our front room is a huge plate glass pane, with the windowsill only about a foot off the ground. I used to sit on the corner of the sill and watch people and animals and cars go by when I was smaller, and then, when I got older, I would sit on the floor by the window to do my homework, propping my books along the sill and sitting cross-legged on the floor.

Oddly enough, it was the one place I could count on for solitude. In our house, the front room was the least used room. You could always count on someone being in the family room or the kitchen or needing to get into the bathroom. My bedroom was sandwiched between Ethan's and Chloe's and they both made a lot of noise. The front room of the house for some reason was always colder than everywhere else, so we never went in there unless we had some kind of formal company, which didn't happen often. It was an easy place to claim for my own. And once I had carved out that little space as my own, it stayed mine.

I liked it because I could watch people go by and see things happen through the glass. I could hear people talking or dogs barking or the other sounds of life going by, but in muted tones. I was still a part of it, but removed. The hard edges in the conversation usually didn't make it through the glass, and the people were there, walking by and going about their lives, but only when I looked up. Only when I let them into my life. I didn't have to interact with them at all if I didn't want to. I reached up to touch the glass of the window and it felt cold, as it always did.

• • •

"Why is this so hard?" I asked Emma a few days later on the phone, trying to make a joke out of it. "People break up all the time. So we're not dating anymore. So what?"

"You're mourning the loss of your entire relationship and that's rough," Emma told me. "You're not dating anymore, but you've also lost a longtime friend, too. That part doesn't have to be permanent. If you're lucky, the friendship will return, even though it will be different. But it's going to take some time."

It seemed like what I had plenty of was time. Lots of time to think about what had happened. Lots of time to rehash our conversation. Lots of time to replay moments that Dave and I had shared together. Lots of time to get through before I felt good again.

Isn't it funny how the memories you cherish before a breakup can become your worst enemies afterwards? The thoughts you loved to think about, the memories you wanted to hold up to the light and view from every angle—it suddenly seems a lot safer to lock them in a box, far from the light of day and throw away the key. It's not an act of bitterness. It's an act of self-preservation. It's not always a bad idea to stay behind the window and look out at life instead, is it?

CHAPTER 7

APRIL, BRAZIL

Ethan Beckett

I put down Andrea's letter and sat back on the bus. *"Como está a sua irmã?"* asked my companion, Elder de Oliveira, sitting next to me. *How is your sister?*

"Está bem," I told him. *She's well.*

But I had my doubts. This was Andrea's longest letter to date—four pages—and even though most of it wasn't about her breakup with Dave, I could tell that she had written more because of it.

I'd grabbed her letter on the way out the door. The mail came early in our new area, for which I was grateful. I stuffed it into my pocket to read on the two-hour bus ride to zone conference. "Anything for me?" Elder de Oliveira asked, and I had to shake my head no. He nodded good-naturedly and we continued on our way, walking through the pleasantly cool air of an early morning in Brazil.

For the first time, I was the senior companion. My greenie, Elder de Oliveira, was Brazilian and new on the mission. He was a man of almost inhuman patience, since he had to listen to me make mistakes in his language all the time. It had taken a full year for me to be senior comp and I knew that at least part of it had to be because of my struggle with the language.

I was getting better, slowly but surely. I could still see Elder Vickers holding up flashcards, labeling things in our apartment with pieces of paper, sitting on the couch across from me and pretending to be an investigator while I stumbled through the concepts, and making me laugh when I was on the verge of getting mad and giving up. I missed Elder Vickers. Even though I liked Elder de Oliveira, we'd only been companions for a little over a month and were still learning how to interact with each other.

I followed Elder de Oliveira's lead and pulled out my scriptures, but reading while in motion always makes me carsick, and we were definitely not on a smooth ride—plus I was already feeling kind of queasy because I'd read Andrea's letter while we were moving. Our bus was one of the nicer ones, the kind that looks and feels like a chartered bus from the states, but the road had plenty of potholes and bumps to make up for the relative luxury of our ride. When my queasiness turned to flat-out nausea, I gave up reading the scriptures. I found myself looking out the window at the road going by and thinking about Andrea instead.

They don't tell you how often you're going to have to read between the lines when you're on your mission. There should be a class on *that* in the MTC. Take this letter of Andrea's, for example. In it, she had written the lines, "Dave and I broke up. The long-distance thing was too hard and he wanted to start dating someone else—remember Avery Matthews? It's been harder than I expected. I guess I really thought things were going to work out between Dave and me."

It was straightforward, and precise, and honest, all of the things that Andrea is. Reading between the lines, though, I could tell that she was hurting a lot. For her to have admitted that something was hard, let alone harder than she expected, meant that she was probably struggling quite a bit. Maybe she even felt the way I had a few months ago when I was having a particularly hard time on my mission. For a while it was a struggle to even get up in the morning. I'd go through the day and think, *There's something I'm trying not to think about. What is it?* and then I'd remember. Even though it was always near the surface, I'd be hurt all over again by the pain as it broke through. Kind of like thinking about Eduardo and the missed baptism.

I was sad, genuinely sad, to hear that Andrea and Dave had broken up. She had always gotten such a kick out of him. I was surprised, too. He had had a crush on her for years. I had always figured that if their relationship ended, it would be the other way around—Andrea would be the one to call it off. But I was wrong. I tried to think of what I would write to her. As the bus moved along through the streets, I started composing the letter in my mind. Then I could sit down on my next P-Day and put it into words and send it off as soon as possible:

Dear Andrea,

I'm sorry to hear that you and Dave broke up, I really am. You always had such a good time with him and he was always crazy about you. I could tell from what you did and didn't say in your letter that it was tough and I feel bad about that. By now it might all be water under the bridge, but I have a feeling it might not. You and I are alike in that we do a good job of keeping ourselves safe from emotions and going out there on a limb, but when we do decide to go for it, it's no-holds-barred. I know you don't want to hear this but I know how it must have felt and I am sorry.

I could, too. I knew how it felt, from past—and possibly, from present—experience to lose a relationship with someone you cared about deeply. I still worried about that with Mikey.

Mikey. I had to read between the lines of her letters too. We'd decided to keep our letters casual and friendly, which was good for both of us—I could stay focused and she would be free—but sometimes, as I read her letters and her cheerful, happy account of the classes she was taking and what was going on in her ward and which roommate said what, I found myself wondering what she was really trying to say, if anything. When she talked about her ward and what amazing people she'd gotten to know this year was she referring to people in general, or was there someone in particular that she liked? When she talked about how much fun she was having, did that mean she didn't miss me at all?

Sometimes reading between the lines is a good idea, so you can find out the truth, and sometimes all it does is send you down a road of unprofitable thinking. Like now. I turned my attention back to my companion.

Elder de Oliveira had struck up a conversation with the man in front of us, not an easy thing to do considering the noise level on the bus. He spoke with such ease, so fluently, with his hands matching his words with gestures. I watched as he said something that made the other man smile and say something back, and then they both began to laugh. I smiled too, because I had caught the gist of it, if not every word, and *that* was something that wouldn't have happened a few months ago.

I have gotten much better at the language, better than I would ever have thought I could be. When I looked back at how far I had come over the past eleven months, I couldn't believe it. But still, when there were two native Portuguese speakers talking to each other, there was nothing I could do but smile and go along for the ride, nodding now and then but not quick enough to interject a comment of my own. I could understand most of the words, but it was the pace, the quickness, the matching of gestures to words, that eluded me. I was competent, which was something I had never thought I might be, but I wasn't fluent.

Sometimes I wonder if my family is like that—struggling with the language of love. We can speak the basics, but there's a certain fluency that we miss. We try to do all the right things, say the right things at the right time, be dependable and good. But still, we get something wrong, miss a nuance, skip a beat.

"He is my teacher," Elder de Oliveira said to the man.

Who, me? I thought. I listened more closely. Elder de Oliveira was telling the man that I was the one who helped teach him how to teach the gospel, that I knew many things he did not, that I had been on the mission longer and was teaching him how to be a missionary.

I looked out the window again so that they wouldn't know I'd overheard them. I hadn't known that Elder de Oliveira felt that way. I had always felt that *he* was the teacher, in spite of my senior comp status, because he was always helping me with the language and culture and explaining the implications behind certain situations or phrases. If Elder Vickers had helped me become adequate in the language, it was Elder de Oliveira who had helped me become competent. Now that I had the basic vocabulary down, Elder de Oliveira was endlessly patient in explaining the little things I still didn't understand. I had been convinced that no one would help me as much as Elder Vickers had, and now something entirely different was unfolding, part of the Lord's plan. I'd seen that happen time and time again. You'd think I would know by now that what I think and see and want isn't always what the Lord has in mind.

Well, this is the part of the letter where I tell you that you're awesome and any guy would be lucky to be able to date you. You know that. You broke enough hearts in high school. It could be that this had to happen so that you could see what it felt like from the other side. Or maybe it had to happen so that you could meet someone totally perfect for you. Whatever the reason, there must be something in store for you, some plan in the works.

I'm learning on my mission that when I think I have a plan, I mean really have *a plan—something that's going to knock everyone's socks off— that's when the Lord comes up with something better. Of course, sometimes it involves the humiliating downfall of my plan first, but it does work out eventually. I have faith that will happen for you too.*

Okay, okay, I know it's easy for me to say since I'm not in your situation right now. But for what it's worth, I do believe it.

The bus ground to a halt. Elder de Oliveira and his new friend shook hands and exchanged good-byes. "What a way to travel, Elder," he said to me in Portuguese. "I like traveling by bus because you can talk to people without being worried about where you are going, like when you are driving."

We climbed off the bus and the two of us consulted our directions to the zone conference. We had about six more blocks to go, straight ahead of us, before we would be at the chapel. Side by side, we started walking. The clouds lay dark and heavy above us, the air thick with humidity. We were moving at a fairly fast pace, but I still felt itchy and caged. Elder de Oliveira noticed.

"What's wrong?" he asked me.

"I'm sick of walking. I want to run."

"Why not?" he asked. "We could beat the rain. I'm a very fast runner. We can race to that bus shelter, down the road. See?" And without another word, he started running down the street toward the bus shelter.

"Elder, wait!" I yelled after him. Right on cue, the first raindrops smacked the pavement around me. Elder de Oliveira just kept running down the street, head down; he *was* fast. Maybe even as fast as me. I grinned.

I started after him. Dress shoes aren't ideal running shoes and asphalt isn't the greatest running surface. I was glad I didn't go skidding onto my face. Our shoes made slapping sounds on the pavement, the noise drawing attention from other pedestrians to our race down the street.

When I caught up with him, he looked over at me and laughed. I was out of breath, but I was laughing too. "Even faster," he shouted and we sprinted to the end, stride matching stride. We stood in the bus shelter for a minute, hiding from the rain and catching our breath, still laughing.

I reached down and loosened my shoe. "I'm going to have a blister tomorrow," I told him.

"Me too," he said.

A weird thing about the mission is that you can be reminded of something from home, something familiar, by something absolutely foreign and unfamiliar, but the reminder is so complete that it takes your breath away. That happened now, as I stood with Elder de Oliveira, breathing hard after running in the rain. Even though the temperature was different and I was wearing dress shoes instead of running shoes and living in an entirely different country, I thought of Andrea and running in the state meet my senior year.

Andrea had graduated from Lakeview by then, but she was still there to cheer me on. She had left Ithaca after class in the afternoon, flown to the Tri-Cities area in Washington where the state meet was being held, and stayed in a hotel there so she would be in time for the races in the early afternoon. She did it all last-minute, without telling me.

She wanted to surprise me. She did. I stood at the starting line and saw her standing there on the sidelines, waving, and I couldn't believe my eyes. And then she ran to all the hardest parts of the course, the ones where she'd taken pictures of me the year before, the ones that no one knows about unless they've run the race themselves. I came to those places in the course with the rain on my face and my hair in my eyes and the taste of metal in my mouth and there she was, cheering in her own way, which isn't yelling and screaming, but saying in her voice that carries, "You can do it."

I wished I could tell her, right now, without the delay of letters:

You can do it, Andrea. Hang in there and keep doing what's right. Things will get better. When I look back now at how far I've come, from being literally the worst Portuguese speaker in my group at the MTC, to being able to teach discussions and have conversations with people on the street, it blows me away. It happened step by step, though. It's like it was when Chloe changed from a toddler to an actual person. We both looked at each other one day and said, "When did that happen?" But it had been happening all along, a little bit every day. One day you will look back and think, "I made it through and came out stronger than ever."

"What are you thinking about, Elder? You look very serious," Elder de Oliveira said as we headed into the building for our meeting.

"My sister. She is having a hard time right now. I wish I could see her."

"You will do what you can," he told me. "You will pray for her and you will write to her. She will be in your heart and words. That is the best you can do for now, and she will understand."

You can do it. You'll get through it, you will. I will be praying for you. Something good is going to happen. Someone else must be right for you. Hang in there.

Love,
Ethan

JUNE, ITHACA

Caterina Giovanni

I'm seventeen and the jobs I've had so far are baby-sitter, lawn mower, and berry supervisor. That last one is this summer's job and has been the best one yet. When I apply to colleges this fall, they should be dazzled by the variety and impressed with my work ethic. I hope so because my grades aren't anything to knock their socks off. I'm a hard worker and I don't sit around, but there are lots of other things I'd rather be doing than studying. I wish I could be a berry supervisor for the rest of my life but the strawberry season and blueberry season combined are less than three months long.

So here's how I got my awesome job. My friend Kayla's parents own the Dunford Family Farm. At the beginning of the summer, Kayla asked if I wanted to be a berry supervisor. I think the name was what got me. Supervising berries sounded easy. Super easy. How much trouble could berries get into? It turned out I actually supervised the *people* picking the berries and not the berries themselves, but fine. It was still easy.

Kayla's farm is a "U-Pick" farm, which means that anyone who wants to can bring baskets or bowls or buckets and pick their own berries. All we had to do was show them where to pick and teach them how to tell if the berries were ripe. Then we weighed their haul at the end and took their money. Like I said, very easy.

Supervising something other than screaming kids (like I did last summer) sounded good to me. Kayla and I even got to work together some of the time. Plus I could wear shorts and a T-shirt to work every day. And flip-flops or sandals. Any summer job not requiring socks was high on my list! I think you should spend as much of your summer as close to barefoot as you can.

At the beginning of the day, I'd arrive at Kayla's house and we would head out to the strawberry fields, a mile or two away from the main barn. We had a little stand with a cash register, a scale to weigh the berries, and a couple of lawn chairs. Kayla's mom, who worked in the main barn, would send the people who wanted to pick berries over to us, and we would send them out into the fields and weigh their berries when they got back, and that was it. You could do it in your sleep. I think sometimes I did. It was awesome.

Once in a while, my parents wondered aloud if I should be doing something else, something that paid better or had more career potential. I love my parents, but they were totally wrong. School would start up in a few short months, and I would be a senior in high school, trying to pass my classes and figure out what to do about life post-graduation. I needed time to breathe and be outside and think about whatever I wanted to think about. The job was perfect.

It was one of those few times in life when something that you think is going to be great turns out to be . . . great.

• • •

It was turning out to be the summer of daydreaming. As I sent another family into the field to pick strawberries, I thought to myself, *What should I think about today?* I'd forgotten a book. I'd forgotten a journal to write in or even a pad of paper to doodle on. I popped a strawberry into my mouth and chomped down hard. I feel bad for people who only eat strawberries that come in plastic containers from the store, room temperature and not quite ripe. A strawberry should taste like a summer day, so fat and ripe that it will plop into your hand with the littlest tug. Strawberries like that you can eat all day long, without once having to make a sour, puckery face.

A few berries later, the air started to get heavy and the sky turned low and bluish gray. A summer thunderstorm was coming, and it was moving in fast. A deep, grumbly roll of thunder sounded very close. The berry pickers noticed the change in weather, too. I saw them start to gather up their things and run for their cars. Kayla hurried toward the old car we used to drive out to the field each morning. I kicked off my sandals and stretched out in my lawn chair.

"You're crazy, Cate," she called out as she past me. "You're going to get soaked."

A lady ran to her car, holding a huge bowl of berries as she sprinted. Berries bounced out of the tin bowl now and then like kernels escaping from a popcorn popper.

An older man walked slowly though the rain had started to fall. He waved his bucket at me. "No point breaking a leg to keep from getting a little wet," he called out, and I laughed and waved back, agreeing. He got to his car before the worst of the storm hit.

What would I be like in the face of disaster, if this were a real hurricane or something instead of a normal, everyday summer storm? I wondered as I watched the rain and the people. Would I grab everything I could and run like crazy, or would I try to be calm and collected, or would I do something else I couldn't even predict? Hunker down and hope it would all go away? Would I pack anything?

I remembered my mom telling the story about how she always packed her bags in plenty of time when she was expecting a baby. That way, when the time came, she could grab the bag and go without a second thought. She told me that by the time I came along, she thought that she knew exactly what to pack and felt pretty good about how prepared she was. But then I wasn't like any of the other kids and nothing went the same and she had to send my dad home for things she'd never even thought of needing, like teeny tiny T-shirts that buttoned up the front because I hated having anything put over my head and would scream so loudly that people would come in to see what on earth was happening.

She tells this story a lot because she believes that it illustrates my personality perfectly. My personality, according to her, is surprising and unpredictable. "Cate is the most fun to watch," she tells my brothers and sisters. "You don't know what's going to happen, but you know it's going to be entertaining."

I liked the story about my mom packing. When I was little, I used to pack a little bag in case I ever had to leave in a hurry to go outside. I didn't want to get caught somewhere without my crayons and my fruit snacks and maybe a cool rock or two. The problem was I always ended up cheating and using my little bag for a non-emergency. So I was always out of fruit snacks when I really needed them, like when I was in the middle of playing something extra fun and had no time to come inside for a new pack. Now *that* was a real emergency.

It was a fast storm. One minute the raindrops were coming down flat and gray and fast, spattering and slapping the leaves of the berry plants and the stiff plastic awning covering me. The next minute, they were slow and bright and sparkled, because the sun had suddenly returned. Then they were gone altogether, except where they hung from a leaf or slid briskly down a windshield.

Car doors slammed, voices chattered, birds started singing again. "Guess we won't have to wash our strawberries once we get them home," joked the old man on his way back out to the field. The prissy pickers, not wanting more strawberries enough to get wet or muddy, came over and had their berries weighed, paid for them, and went home muttering about the weather forecast. Most pickers didn't care. They went out and got good and wet and muddy and laughed and joked with each other as they picked, as though the rainstorm, that brief shared experience, had created a bond between them. It was like the one time I went to Disney World. We were in the line with the same people for so long that we started to feel connected. When we finally got on the ride, the people behind us clapped and cheered and waved good-bye. "We'll miss you! Don't forget to write!" called out one lady, joking.

After 5:00 P.M., more and more families would come to pick berries once the parents were finished with work for the day. On Mondays, I often saw a few families from our ward who liked to come berry-picking for family home evening. My parents and I would have family home evening when I got home at seven. Sometimes I joked around with them and called it "Cate Home Evening" since I'm the only kid left at home now. We all have to take a turn saying a prayer or doing the lesson every week. You can't slack off when your numbers are low.

But there were a few hours to go before 5:00. Kayla drifted over from her end of the field, holding her lunch. "Mind if I join you?" she asked, plopping onto the lawn chair next to me and kicking off her flip-flops.

"Of course not. This is your farm," I said. She pulled her sandwich out of her bag and we sat there, eating and looking out over the strawberries. The strawberry season was already almost over. In a few weeks, it would be completely finished and we'd move on to blueberries. I could feel the summer slipping through my fingers, so I hung on to the lazy pace as much as possible, trying to make it last.

Kayla's older brother, Matt, sometimes came and joined us for lunch, and I was happy to see him coming across the field. I waved him over to us. He was getting way too tan for his own good, so tan I almost couldn't see his freckles. There were only the two lawn chairs so he sat on the grass. There's a little chivalry left in the world, or at least there is when Matt is around.

"That grass has to be soaking wet," I said, thinking of the rainstorm.

"It's not too bad," Matt said, shifting a little. Kayla lazily took another bite of her sandwich. Matt took out a brownie. He always eats his dessert first. I always eat mine last.

Our conversations had been like this all summer. We say what we want, when we want, and sometimes we sit together and don't say anything for a little while. We're in our summer rhythm.

"What would you guys take from a burning building if you could only grab one thing?" I asked dreamily. "Say your families and your pets are all safe and all of that. But what *one* thing would you take? What would you pack?"

"That's such a Cate question," Matt teased. "Why on earth are you sitting around thinking about stuff like that?"

"No reason," I said, choosing not to bore him with the details. When you actually do trace one of your thoughts back to its origin, which I like to do as a summertime diversion, it can be kind of a long road.

Matt laughed. "I'd probably grab the first thing I saw and get out of there." He shrugged. "If the people and the animals were out, that's all that would really matter to me."

Kayla was more thoughtful. "I guess my photo albums. It would be hard to have to put them all together again."

"I'd take my journal," I said. Kayla nodded, like that didn't need an explanation, which it didn't. "At least, that's what I think I'd take. Maybe if it got crazy I'd be like Matt, grabbing the first thing I saw and ending up with something ridiculous, like a textbook or a tube of toothpaste or something."

Matt rolled his eyes at me. "You know what I mean. If there was an actual fire or something, you might not be thinking clearly."

"That's true," I admitted. "It's just an interesting question to think about."

"Here's an interesting question for you," Kayla said. "Where do you think we'll be this time next year, when you and I have graduated?"

"Who wants to think about that now?" I leaned back in my chair and closed my eyes. "Don't ruin a perfectly good summer day making us think about something like *that*."

CHAPTER 9

JULY, BRAZIL

Ethan Beckett

The paper was snarled and stuck in the mission office's ancient printer for the third time that day. I grabbed the pair of tweezers I kept in the desk drawer for this very purpose and sighed as I scooted over to the printer in my office chair. I had to lean forward because one of the back wheels was missing and if I distributed my weight evenly while I was in motion, the chair would make a nails-across-the-chalkboard sound on the office's tile floor. I made it to the printer without offending the ears of anyone in the office. The assistant to the president, Elder Campos (my senior comp), didn't even look up from his desk. Stealthy. That was me.

I reached into the printer with my pair of tweezers and extracted a twisted slip of paper. Part of the bottom was missing, so I reached in again and surgically removed an even more warped shred of paper. It wasn't a piece of plain old white printer paper that had caused the jam. It was a check. A check that would now have to be voided and printed out again. It was the third one today. I kept suggesting to the mission president that we write the checks out by hand, but he wanted them to look official, plus he pointed out that all of us in the office had horrendous handwriting, which was true. So the printer it was, and I was stuck learning its temperament and idiosyncrasies.

"Think of it as an old car that you have to pamper and treat kindly," Presidente Marques had told me when I showed my frustration, laughing at the expression on my face.

The printer was on its last legs, as was about everything else in our mission office. Luckily, the office was due to receive a serious overhaul. Even our mission president was scheduled to be released in about a month, and he wanted everything to be in order for the new president. So while we waited for new equipment, we had to try out new systems of doing things (like figuring out how to print checks). As a result, the atmosphere was more tense than usual and I, as the blundering new financial secretary, came in for a lot of the chastisement.

Even though I respected Presidente Marques, sometimes I wanted to tell him, "If I'm so bad at this, send me back out into the field." I had to laugh at my "the grass-is-always-greener" attitude. At the beginning of my mission, the office had seemed like it would be a safe place, where almost everyone *could* speak English if they had to, and where you didn't have to proselytize on the street every day.

Now that I was in the office, I caught myself staring out of the window at the streets all of the time, daydreaming about street contacts and tracting. The day before, I'd seen my old comp Elder de Oliveira at a zone conference, and it had made me miss the few months of our companionship, when everything had worked so well. It's strange how some segments of time on my mission felt like small lifetimes, complete in and of themselves.

I heard Sister Marques call to Elder Campos, and he went out in the hall to talk to her. I could hear the urgency in her voice and hoped with all my heart that it didn't involve a mistake on my part. I tossed the evidence of the misprinted check in the trash can just in case.

Elder Campos leaned through the doorway. "Presidente is sick. We need to give him a blessing."

"*We* do?" I asked, and he looked at me as though I was an idiot. "Yes, *we* do," he told me. "Come on, Elder."

Presidente was pacing in his office, hunched over, his face gray. "I think it is my appendix," he managed to say. Even though I'd never heard the word "appendix" in Portuguese before, it was similar enough to its English counterpart that I knew immediately what he'd said. "I must go to the hospital, but I want a blessing first." He looked up at me, his face twisted pain. "Elder Beckett, would you administer the blessing?"

I tried not to look surprised. For some reason, I had assumed Elder Campos would administer the blessing since he was the assistant to the president. "Of course," I said, trying to gather my scattered thoughts.

"What is your full name, Presidente?" Elder Campos asked before anointing him with the consecrated oil. After the anointing, we placed our hands on his head, gently. It was hard for him to sit completely still because of the pain. He seemed smaller than usual, vulnerable and hurt, hunched over in the chair like that.

I closed my eyes and took a deep breath. I tried to focus on what I needed to do. My initial nervousness about giving the Presidente a blessing had given way to concern about his condition. I blessed him with peace to know that the pain would soon be assuaged and with strength to bear it until then. It was a short blessing but the Spirit was strong, and I knew it was because of Presidente and Sister Marques and their faith. Presidente seemed to relax slightly as we finished the blessing.

We took our hands away from his head and moved around to stand in front of him. He managed a smile for us. "Thank you, Elder Beckett. Thank you, Elder Campos," he said. "Could you help me to the car?"

He put an arm around each of us and we helped him walk down

the stairs. He was lighter than I thought he would be, especially for being such a big man. It was probably because Elder Campos was helping me with his weight. Sister Marques hurried ahead to open the car door for us. We helped him stretch across the backseat. He lay down slowly, in increments, first sitting, then resting on his elbows, then finally laying his head down on a folded blanket Sister Marques slipped behind his head. I gently shut the door.

"Do you want us to follow you or anything?" I asked, wondering if she would need help.

Sister Marques was already climbing behind the wheel. "No, I'm sure the doctors will have a wheelchair there for him," she said. "I'll call when we know how he's doing."

We watched as Presidente and Sister Marques drove away to the hospital, which was only a few blocks away. It was a trip they had made before, with so many missionaries to take care of and look after, but this was the first time they had had to go for themselves.

Elder Campos and I walked slowly back inside and sat down at our places in the office. Before either of us started working again, Elder Campos said, "I think we should pray for Presidente." I agreed and we knelt by our desks. Elder Campos said the prayer, his soft voice carrying to every corner of the silent office. After we said, *"Amém,"* we both sat quietly for a moment before we went back to work.

I went back to the checks I was trying to print. There were still some strings of paper stuck in the printer, and suddenly I wanted to have everything done exactly right, so that when Presidente came back, the office would be in impeccable order. I would print these checks the way he wanted them done, or the printer would die trying.

I remembered the first time I had given my father a blessing. It had been a few months before I'd left on my mission and Chloe and I had gone over to his house for the weekend. He was really sick so I called his home teacher and together the two of us had given him a blessing. I remembered how odd it had felt to put my hands on his head instead of having it be the other way around. He is taller than I am, so I had never looked down on him before. I hadn't noticed how much his hair was thinning. He suddenly seemed so fragile to me, so mortal. It was one of those moments as a child when you realize that your parents are people who can be hurt and helpless, people like you.

It's kind of terrifying to realize that the status quo is going to change. Someday I wouldn't be just the little kid or the new missionary. I'd be a dad, a home teacher, maybe even a bishop or a mission president. Giving Presidente a blessing was a taste of that kind of grown-up responsibility. It was strange, and more than a little scary.

I remembered when I first came to work in the office, overwhelmed by the financial statements I was supposed to master. "I've bitten off more than I can chew," I'd muttered.

Presidente had corrected me. "No, Elder Beckett," he said. "You didn't. You were not in charge, except for a moment when you accepted the calling. The Lord called you. You should have more trust in Him."

At the time, I'd felt chastised. And later, when I kept making the same mistakes and Presidente Marques kept correcting me, sometimes with a hint of frustration in his voice, I felt that I'd started out wrong with that first comment and couldn't ever get right. When I wrote my dad and told him about how frustrated I was, he wrote back and said, "Your mission president is right. We receive callings because of what we can become through them, not because of what we already are. We have to grow, and unfortunately growth is often painful. Remember when I was called to be the Ward Choir Director, and I didn't even know how to lead music?" I smiled to myself. Of course I remembered that. He had been completely overwhelmed. Another thing I had never expected to see happen to my dad. He had made it, though. He had suffered through the embarrassing mistakes he had made in the beginning and done a good job.

I removed the last little strip of paper with the tweezers and dropped it into the trash can. The printer was clean—until it messed up again, which it would. And then I would fix it, and start over.

CHAPTER 10

JULY, ITHACA

Andrea Beckett

I sat on the porch steps, wearing shorts, an ancient Lakeview High cross-country T-shirt, no shoes, and eating a red Popsicle. I felt happier than I had in months. Julie and Mikey were coming to visit—the first visitors I'd had in Ithaca in the three years I'd lived there. They were flying to Buffalo (you can almost always get cheap fares into Buffalo), and they'd decided to stay there a day and visit Niagara Falls. And then . . . they were driving down to see me!

I couldn't wait to take the two of them to the Gorges, to Flatrock, to show them around campus, to feed the ducks at the Cornell Plantations . . . I felt like a tour guide, mapping out an itinerary. Nothing makes a place feel more like home than being able to show it to someone else. I'd looked forward to this visit all summer long.

My summer vacation, if you could call it that, had been a lonely one. Emma and Shannon had both gone home. A family from church had gone away for the summer, and they'd asked me to housesit for them until August. I'd jumped at the chance—it was a nice house in a quiet neighborhood, perfect for spending June and most of July studying for the GRE test and planning my application to graduate school. There's always some test with a lot of letters in the name looming over you during your school career—the SATs, the ACTs, now this. I couldn't wait to be done with it all.

After the breakup with Dave, I felt reckless. I decided that if I didn't want to go to medical school, I wouldn't. I had enough misery in my life from trying to forget about Dave. I decided to go for the master's degree in Marriage and Family Therapy that I hadn't been able to get off my mind. Taking the GRE was the first step toward my new goal. I'd taken the test the day before and was confident that I had done well. The next step was deciding where to apply. Syracuse was still high on the list. BYU also had a program that would work. After that, there would be other steps—figuring out how to pay for it, arranging my class schedule . . .

There was another step that I was postponing—telling my parents. I didn't know how to bring it up. I didn't think either one of them would be mad, but it was going to surprise them both and I still felt too fragile about the whole idea to tell anyone about it. It was my idea, my decision, my life, and I had to guard it and protect it until I was ready to tell everyone and ready to defend it.

I stood up and looked toward the street corner again, shielding my eyes from the summer glare. Nothing yet.

Living on my own over the past two months, I'd gotten into a routine, like a little old lady. I'd get up at 6:00 A.M. and go for a long morning run, then I'd go to work at the campus bookstore. I would bring my lunch in a brown paper bag and sit outside on the grass to eat, listening to the bells in the McGraw Tower and studying for the GRE. After work, I would go home and eat dinner, and then study until midnight. Then I'd wake up the next day and do it all again.

On Saturdays, I'd study all day, straight through except for meals. I'd take my books to the back porch if the weather was nice. If it wasn't, I'd sit inside and listen to the rain.

On Sundays, I'd take a break. I'd sleep in until right before

11:00 A.M. church, hang out with some of the other young single adults in the branch at potluck dinners afterward, and go to bed ridiculously early, trying to catch up on the sleep I'd missed the rest of the week. It had been a quiet summer, just me and my books and the few people I knew from the lab and from church.

In some ways, though, it *hadn't* been a quiet summer. I'd noticed noises I'd never heard before. Living alone for a month and a half, I'd starting noticing the humming the refrigerator made, recognizing the sounds of the neighbors' cars, identifying which floorboards creaked, and realizing how loud an airplane or a knock on the door can really be. And, alone at night, I'd sit on the porch, reading and looking up to see the fireflies come out, one by one, and then the stars. I'd close my book and simply watch, listening to the crickets. That became part of the routine, too. It let my mind stop working and let me go to sleep much more quickly when I went inside and got into my pajamas and brushed my teeth in the quiet house.

A car drove slowly past, then reversed, came back to the house, and eased up the driveway. It had to be them, but I stayed where I was for a minute, waiting to make sure. Then both of the front doors popped open and Mikey and Julie climbed out. They had the slightly confused look of people who have been driving in unfamiliar territory, and Mikey had a plastic wrapper stuck to her leg. She retrieved her flip-flops from the car and stepped into them. Julie shielded her eyes and said something to Mikey, checking to make sure that they were in the right place. They hadn't noticed me sitting on the steps yet.

I jumped up and called out to them. "Mikey! Julie!" When they saw me, they both broke into big smiles. I ran down the steps and across the long green lawn that I hadn't gotten around to mowing that week, stopping in my tracks as I approached the car. I'd meant to give them both a big hug, but I suddenly felt self-conscious.

"It's you!" I said instead, grinning at the two of them.

"It's us," said Mikey, giving me a hug. Julie followed suit. "It's so good to see you," Mikey said sincerely. I loved that about her. She honestly seems to mean everything she says. That kind of sincerity is unique in people our age—in people of any age, for that matter.

"It's great to see you guys," I said. "Do you want a Popsicle? Or some lunch?"

"Lunch sounds awesome," said Mikey. "Julie was determined to make good time from Buffalo to here, so we haven't had anything but snack food all day."

Julie picked the plastic wrapper off Mikey's leg and held it up. "As you can tell by this. They're all over the car."

"Come on in, then!" I said. "Welcome to Ithaca!" As the three of us girls went up the walkway together, laughing and talking, I thought: *My summer has finally started.*

• • •

Later, as we ate lunch at the kitchen table talking a mile a minute, I studied their faces, trying to see how they'd changed in the past few months and years. It is interesting to watch your friends' faces change and evolve and mature from their high school faces into their adult faces. They're different, but they're also the same. You can still see them, but the new experiences and years have changed them in tiny ways, ways that you only notice if you are a real friend and take the time to look, which I realized I hadn't really done the last time I'd seen them. Even though I'd seen both Mikey and Julie over the holidays, most of my focus had been on Dave. I'd been so busy figuring out how *he* had changed that I hadn't paid much attention to what was different about anyone else.

Mikey still had that air of assurance without being cocky that I admire about her. I think it's one of the things Ethan likes best about her too. Julie was still quiet, but then she'd always been the most calming person I'd ever been around. She still had the same habit of tipping her head back when she smiled at you or laughed at something you said, as though she wanted to drink it all in and not miss a thing. Her walk was more confident. Her voice was still gentle. It was good to see both of them. I wondered if they thought I had changed, or if there was anything different about me that they noticed, but I didn't ask.

"What do you want to do first?" I asked. "I know you've only got three days before you have to leave, so I've made a jam-packed schedule and also a more relaxed one."

"I vote for the relaxed one," Mikey said. "It's summer, after all." Julie seconded it, and now that I had some people to be lazy with, it was time to relax and let summer be summer, come what may. I felt a little reckless with the happiness of having people around again. If you'd told me a couple of years ago that I'd turn into kind of a people person and consider a degree in counseling, I would have laughed at you.

After we'd chatted a little longer, we went to Flatrock, a place in Fall Creek with slabs of slippery gray rocks and fast-moving water only a couple of inches deep. There were also waterfalls and deeper pools in other places along the creek. We splashed out into the water. Before we could get far, though, Julie went sliding across the slick, moss-covered rocks, and I tried to catch her, and then Mikey tried to catch the two of us, and we all fell down after a long, intensely uncoordinated skate across the mossy surface. I hadn't had a full-out attack of the giggles like that in a long time.

"This is beautiful," Mikey said, shading her eyes with her hand. The reflection of the sun on the water was so brilliant, it was blinding. "Have you spent every day this summer out here?"

"No," I admitted. "This is the first time I've been this year. You know me, lots of studying to do."

"That's sad," Mikey said. "It's a good thing we came along."

• • •

After dinner we went to an outdoor summer concert at Cornell on the Arts Quad. People scattered their brightly colored blankets across the grass like confetti, and, when they felt like it, got up and danced to the music. Tonight it was a local jazz band from Ithaca and they were *very* good, so a lot of people were dancing—kids, parents, teenagers, everyone. An elderly man next to us was dancing with his wife and shouted over at the three of us. "You girls should be ashamed! You're younger than I am, and you're not even dancing!" There was nothing for us to do after that but stand up and dance too.

It was late when we got back. I asked Julie and Mikey where they wanted to sleep. "There's plenty of room inside," I told them. "But we could sleep out in the back. It's supposed to be warm tonight, and this is a safe neighborhood."

"Let's do that," Julie decided. "I haven't had a chance to go camping yet this summer. This might be as close as I get."

I found some sleeping bags in the basement and we rolled them out in a row on the back lawn. Julie was in the middle, and Mikey and I were on either side of her. It was dark, but not quite pitch-black yet. There was an edge of deep dark blue on the horizon before it turned into black sky.

What is it about night that makes it feel like the right time to talk, to share confidences, to say things that you wouldn't say during the day?

"How are you doing?" Mikey asked, propping her head up on her elbow. "With the Dave thing, I mean." Even in the dimming light, I could tell she was looking right at me, not averting her eyes tactfully the way my mom did when she asked the same question. I thought about jokingly telling her it was none of her business, but I realized that I wanted to talk about it with someone who knew Dave.

Emma was a true friend, but she had never met Dave. She had never actually experienced his megawatt smile or the sheer joy of living that accompanied him wherever he went. She couldn't picture him the way these girls could, she hadn't seen us together as a couple the way Julie and Mikey had. In some ways, that had been invaluable. Emma had been able to help me look at things dispassionately. Ethan had known Dave and he'd written me the nicest letter, one I read over and over when I was feeling down, but I couldn't actually *talk* to him since he was so far away. Which reminded me . . .

"I'll tell you if you'll tell me about Ethan," I countered.

"You probably know as much as I do," Mikey said. "He's still writing, but they're still just friendly letters, nothing special." She paused. "That sounded bad. I'm glad that he's being a good missionary. But it's weird not knowing where I stand. And I won't know until he gets home."

"Are you dating anyone else?" I asked her.

"Not right now," she said. "I kind of started dating someone this spring, but it was never serious. It ended almost before it began. It's hard for anyone to compare to Ethan."

"What about you, Julie?" I asked, suddenly remembering. "What's up with you and Tyler? You brought him to Dave's party and everything. He seems like a good guy. Are you guys dating?"

Julie smiled. "No, but we keep in touch. He's never joined the Church, but he knows a lot about it since he goes to school in Utah and everything."

"You're running a good screen, Andrea," said Mikey, teasingly, "but we're still wondering how you're doing with the whole Dave thing." She grew a little more sober. "You heard that he and Avery got engaged in June, right?"

I *had* heard that. In fact, Dave had called to tell me himself, and seeing his number flash onto the phone had caused my heart to race, wondering why he was calling. We had e-mailed a few times since the breakup, but hadn't talked. Hearing his voice again was strange, and it was even stranger when I heard him say he had called to tell me he was marrying someone else. Even though that was the logical outcome—I knew he wasn't going to marry *me*—it was still difficult to hear. But I appreciated his making the call himself instead of letting me hear it through the grapevine, in spite of how painful it was for me at the time.

He told me that he and Avery probably wouldn't be getting married for a full year because her parents wanted her to have another year of school behind her. But still, the bottom line was that Dave was engaged only a few months after we'd broken up. When I'd gotten over the initial shock, I realized that the engagement hadn't had the same crushing effect that the actual breakup did. If the breakup had been an earthquake, the engagement was an aftershock. Not entirely unexpected, but still unsettling.

The grass against the backs of my calves felt good, and I rubbed my bare feet in it. There were grass stains on the bottoms of my feet now, which made me happy for some reason. I laid down, folding my hands behind my head. I felt pretty good, even though we'd been talking about Dave. I didn't dare entertain the thought that I might be getting over him because I didn't want to jinx it. "I think I'm okay," I said. "It was hard at first." I didn't know what else to say, so I repeated myself. "It was hard at first."

Mikey and Julie leaned back into the grass too. A firefly glittered past us and Mikey drew in her breath. "Was that a firefly?" she whispered.

"Yeah," I said. "They like to come out about now, after the rain in the summer. I don't think there are any in Seattle, are there? I've only seen them since I've moved here."

"I think you're right," said Mikey. Another one drifted by and she opened her hand, trying to catch it. She missed.

"I've never seen one before either," said Julie excitedly. "They're beautiful." There were more and more of them coming out from the bushes and shining around us. It was quiet for a few moments as we watched the shimmering lights.

"I'm probably going to go on a mission," said Julie suddenly, as if the announcement were something she couldn't contain any longer.

"I'm going to work this fall to save money and go sometime in November or December."

"That's great, Julie!" I exclaimed. "You'll be an amazing missionary."

"I hope so," Julie said. "My parents are a little baffled by it but at least they're supportive. My mom is hoping I get sent somewhere close to home. I don't know how well she'll do if I get sent somewhere like Russia or Africa, but we'll cross that bridge when we come to it."

"I'm impressed," I said and meant it. "I thought about going on a mission but never had the courage to do it."

"Did Mikey tell you she's going to Mexico?" Julie asked.

"Really?" I asked. "On a mission?"

Mikey shook her head. "BYU has a program where you can do your student teaching in Mexico. It works out perfect for me to go during winter semester, from January to May. I'll be able to see a new country, work on my Spanish, and get my student teaching done, all on the same trip."

"Doesn't that sound so fantastic?" Julie rolled onto her side. "Mexico in January *has* to be heavenly."

"Yeah," I said. "That does sound cool." I could picture Mikey teaching English, talking to people with that wide-open expression of hers, making mistakes in Spanish but then laughing at herself. Just like I could picture Julie on a mission, lighting up when she talked about the gospel, and listening to others with her eyes animated and alive with interest, the way she was listening to us now.

Hearing them talk, listening to their plans for the future, made me want to tell them what I'd been thinking about. I felt nervous, like I was about to bear my testimony or something. It was like I had a firefly buzzing around in my fist and I wanted to let it out to see what would happen.

"So this is going to seem a little crazy," I said, and they turned toward me. "But I'm not going to go to medical school anymore. There's something else I'm probably going to do."

"What's that?" asked Mikey. She sounded surprised, and with good reason. I'd been talking about going to medical school ever since I could remember.

"I think I'm going to get a master's degree and be a social worker," I said. I waited for them to laugh. Neither of them did. "Do you think that's dumb? I mean, my family hasn't exactly been perfect, and I know I'm not the easiest person to talk to. But I can't seem to get the idea off my mind. Isn't that a ridiculous idea?"

"Not at all," said Julie. "I've been to some family therapists before." She was quiet for a minute, and I realized yet again how much there was about Julie that I didn't know. "I think you would be really good at it," she said. When I started to protest, she cut me off, gently. "It's important to have lots of kinds of different people to talk to because someone different works for everyone else. You'll be direct, and responsible, and a lot of people will respond to that. Plus you'll work hard at it."

Mikey agreed. "If you want to apply for it, you should."

I wasn't done yet. I had opened the door and now I wanted to tell them everything. "One of the reasons I don't want to be a doctor anymore is that all the responsibility was stressing me out. I mean, being in charge of people's lives and health and all of that is scary. But this is even more personal. It's giving people advice on how to deal with the most important stuff going on in their lives. In a way, it's even more invasive than practicing medicine."

Julie thought for a moment. "I know how you feel. A mission feels like the scariest thing I could possibly do. But I also can't get it out of my mind, and even though I'm scared, I'm excited. And I feel like it's the right thing."

"That's mostly how I feel too," I said. "But I'm still more scared than excited right now."

Mikey broke in. "But you feel good about applying, right?" I agreed. "Then you should go for it. Sometimes answers come in steps." She paused. "At least, they do for me. So, for example, I don't know what's going to happen with Ethan, if we're going to get married or date again or what." She rushed through the words and kept going. "But I do know that it seems like writing to him right now is the right thing to do. We'll see what the next step is when we get to it."

I liked that answer. It made a lot of sense.

"So, a big year for all of us," I said. "I'm going to graduate and pursue a career that will possibly totally change my entire life, Mikey's going to Mexico, and Julie's going on a mission. There's a lot coming up."

They murmured in agreement. They were starting to wind down. I, on the other hand, could not have felt more awake or alive. My mind was firing a million miles a minute.

Something had ended when Dave and I broke up, that was true, but it hadn't been my life. Julie and Mikey had new beginnings in their lives, and I had them in mine. Sometimes all you need is one or two people whose opinions you value to tell you to go for something. Sometimes that's enough. Sometimes your prayers are answered through other people. I didn't know if I would get into the program or not, but I had enough courage to go for it, and I knew it was time to tell my parents. I'd call them tomorrow.

I relaxed into the grassy smell of the night and let myself be happy, effortlessly, close-to-perfectly happy, for the first time in months. There was still a little ache inside of me where I was healing, but it was getting smaller. The stars and the fireflies twinkled above me.

Neither of my friends answered me when I asked if they were awake a few moments later. I didn't mind. I rolled over onto my back and stared straight up into the night. A firefly flew past my face and I caught it without thinking about it. It blinked a couple of times in the cup of my hand, and I let it go into the night.

CHAPTER 11

AUGUST, ITHACA

Joel Hammond

Sitting in the foyer of the Ithaca chapel building, home to the Ithaca Ward and the Cornell Branch, it wasn't too hard to pretend that I was in an LDS church back home in Utah—or even in a building from my mission in Texas. The carpet was the same greenish-blue that seemed to be popular in the late 90s. An extravagant arrangement of fake flowers, heavy on magenta and a few other shades not usually seen in nature, sat on the end table in the foyer. The glass case behind me contained a map of the world and plaques for the different missionaries who were serving. There was a beautiful picture of the Savior hanging over the couch, which had a stray Cheerio or two stuck in the crevice between the cushions and the back. A bulletin board hung on the wall with pictures from youth conference and a handful of wedding announcements tacked to it.

I don't usually pay much attention to wedding announcements, but I wandered over to the board to look at all the happy, smiling faces, everyone paired off two by two. I was somewhere between the young guys in the mission pictures and the couples in the wedding announcements, somewhere in LDS limbo, neither a missionary nor a newly-married. I was just Joel.

Lauren and I had realized that for us to be together, one or both of us would have to make some significant sacrifices and changes. And apparently neither of us was willing to do that. I wasn't willing to give up grad school and wait for her to finish her undergraduate degree, and she wasn't willing to transfer out to a school in New York. The writing on the wall had been there for a while and as breakups go, it could have been worse. Still, it had hurt. One of the girls in the wedding announcements looked the slightest bit like Lauren, with curly blonde hair.

I left the happy couples behind and wandered over to look at the missionary plaques in the case. There were only two of them. There was one guy serving in India, of all places, and a girl serving in Japan. Each of them had a little red piece of yarn reaching across the map from New York to their mission country, stretched taut from pin to pin. They were both a long way from New York. I was a long way from home too.

My mission president always used to tell us, "The first three weeks of most things in life are the hardest. If you can gut it out for those first few weeks, usually things will get easier, or easier enough for you to keep on going." Since I'd been here about five days, I still had sixteen more to go before my three-week-relief would kick in. I looked around the foyer and down the long hall again. No one else was in the building, at least not that I could see. I could feel a little piece of yarn, you might say, tugging at my heart and making me feel the pull toward home.

I was waiting for someone I'd never met, which is always a strange feeling. After church on Sunday, our branch president had called me and said that someone named Brother Walker, a representative from the area's Church Educational System, wanted to meet with me at 5:00 on Tuesday evening. So here I was, waiting for Brother Walker. I looked at my watch. 5:02. I looked through the glass doors at the front of the building. I didn't see anyone who could be Brother Walker, but I did see someone else.

The funny, good-looking girl from the plane ride last spring was walking through the doors. She looked like she'd come straight from school, wearing jeans and a T-shirt and looking completely at ease. I remembered her walk from when we'd said good-bye at the airport, that perfect posture making her look even taller than she was. She hadn't seen me yet, and I racked my brain, trying to remember her last name. I'd kept an eye out for her last Sunday at the student branch, but she hadn't been there. Andrea something . . . Becker? Beckett? I smiled at her as she opened the second set of glass doors into the foyer. She did a double take. So she did recognize me, at least on some level. That was good. Man, she was good-looking.

"I know you," she said, and I remembered that directness about her as well.

"Yeah," I said, and watched her face to see if she would remember. It didn't take long, which I hoped was a sign that I had made a good impression.

"You were on the plane with me," she said. "At spring break. Joel, right?"

"Right," I said. "And you're Andrea, aren't you?" She nodded. Before I had a chance to say anything else, an older man hurried through the doors and she turned to greet him. "Hi, Brother Walker," she said. "This is Joel."

Brother Walker shook both of our hands. "Good, you two have already met," he said. "I wasn't sure if you would know each other, since Joel is new this year, aren't you?"

I nodded.

"We met briefly, a few months ago," Andrea explained.

"Good," Brother Walker said again. "I'm sorry for being late. I'd like to meet with both of you separately, if that's all right. Andrea, would you mind going first?"

"No problem," she said, and he opened the door of the nearest classroom to show her in.

"I'll be right back," he told me. He seemed like a nice man. He reminded me a lot of my grandfather. The white hair, the rumpled suit, the kind smile.

I didn't have to wait long. Andrea came out a few minutes later and sat down on one of the chairs in the foyer. "Your turn," she said. "Brother Walker said to send you on in."

"Thanks," I said, standing up and moving toward the little classroom.

Brother Walker shook my hand again and we both sat down. He asked me a couple of questions about my major and where I was from. Then he got down to business. "So, Joel," he said, smiling and leaning back in his chair, "I'd like to ask you to be the early-morning seminary teacher for the youth in the Ithaca area this school year. Actually, I'd like to ask you to be *one* of the early-morning seminary teachers. Andrea Beckett has accepted the assignment to be the other teacher."

I was surprised, and interested. "I'd be happy to do it," I told him. "I've lived in Utah my whole life, so I have to tell you that I don't know much about how early-morning seminary works. But isn't it usually taught by someone a lot—" I stopped myself from saying "older" just in time—"with more experience?"

The twinkle in Brother Walker's eye let me know that my pause hadn't gone unnoticed, but he tactfully chose not to comment on it. "Usually we do have a parent or someone from the ward," he said. "This year, though, our longtime seminary teacher moved away in the middle of the summer, and we in the area CES program thought it might be a good idea to have a teacher from the student branch this year. The Cornell Branch is full of young people that we feel would be good examples for the youth. We talked to your branch president and asked if he felt that would be too much to ask college students to take on during the school year. He thought it would be all right as long as we divided it up between two students, and then he gave us some names."

"Wow," I said. "I only got here last week. I'm flattered that he would think of me."

"We're grateful to you for accepting this assignment," Brother Walker said. "It's not a formal church calling, but it is a very important assignment. I think you'll find you'll receive a lot of blessings and insight from your work with the seminary students." He stood up, so I did too. "We'll need to discuss logistics with Sister Beckett. There are only a few weeks to prepare. The students start school after Labor Day, and seminary starts the week after that, so we have quite a bit to accomplish." I must have revealed how overwhelmed I was feeling with a nervous twitch or something, because he continued quickly, "We have lots of help for you. Manuals, lesson outlines, plenty of support. We won't throw you out there to sink or swim. We want you to be successful."

The two of us walked back out into the foyer. Andrea closed the book she had been reading and stood up, smiling at me. "Well?" she asked. "What do you think?"

"Should be interesting," I said. And boy, did I mean it.

Brother Walker didn't waste any time. He walked us down the hall to show us where the seminary room was, and then he sat us down at the tables and wrote a bunch of information on the whiteboard, instructing us to take notes. I was glad I had my backpack with me, but embarrassed when my pen didn't work and I had to borrow one from Brother Walker.

Brother Walker wrote down the class size (eight: a mixed bag of two freshmen, three sophomores, a junior, and two seniors), how long class was (fifty minutes), and the topic of study for the year (Doctrine and Covenants). I copied down every single thing he wrote, especially the list of students' names. I wanted to have them all committed to memory before the first day of class even if I didn't yet have the faces to go with the names. Since there were only eight students, it shouldn't be hard. It was finding out what was behind the names that was going to be the hard part—the part that counted—but the names were a place to start.

Then Brother Walker opened a closet and bombarded us with the tangibles of teaching seminary: keys, teaching manuals and binders, reading schedule, a box of scripture mastery cards, a stack of student manuals, and a carton of school supplies.

When he left an hour and a half later, Andrea and I stood in the seminary room staring at each other over a mound of seminary materials. Brother Walker's spidery writing covered most of the whiteboard. Even though he had promised to meet with us again soon, and even though he had given us plenty to work with as a starting point, I knew we were both wondering if we'd made a big mistake. It was overwhelming enough thinking about my own school workload; adding this was making me wonder if I had a death wish. Were there even enough hours in the day to get it all done? Still, there was an obvious bright side to the situation.

"It looks like we're going to be working together a lot," I said to her.

"It sure does. We'll have to coordinate lesson plans and schedules and talk about problem students with each other . . ." She shook her head. "I'm glad there are two of us. Can you imagine doing this alone?"

"No way," I said. "I already feel like I'll be drowning with my own school stuff."

"Do you want to meet tomorrow night to get our feet under us?" she asked. "We could both come here around six and put together a schedule. I know this will drive me crazy until I have a plan."

I agreed, of course. For me, it would be the event of the week. My roommates hadn't arrived yet, since there were still a few days before school started. I had met some nice people at church, but that was the extent of my social circle so far. It takes me a little while to make friends, but I usually can if I hang in there. Sixteen more days.

"Do you want me to bring some food?" I asked her.

"That would be really nice of you," she said. "I'll be coming straight from work, so I won't have had a chance to eat anything."

"Great," I said, standing up to leave the seminary room. "Are you leaving now? I'll walk you out."

She shook her head. "I'm going to stay a minute longer and look through some of this stuff."

"Okay," I said, wishing I hadn't gotten up to leave so quickly. "See you tomorrow."

• • •

Two of my roommates arrived the next morning. They seemed like nice guys and they went out of their way to talk to me and find out about me, but I was still the odd man out. They spoke in that shorthand that longtime friends have, where they can talk about going to Brandon's house without having to detail exactly who Brandon is or where he lives, or they say they're going to work and everyone knows what that means—where they work, how long the shift usually is, all that. I knew I would catch on eventually, but right now, it was like trying to watch a movie, but you keep having to get up to get popcorn or fix the volume or go to the bathroom, so you're getting the basic plot but missing some critical details.

I did have some working knowledge of Ithaca, though—I had found a grocery store. A few hours before I was due to meet Andrea, I drove there and spent some time wandering around the aisles before I decided to keep it simple and bring sack lunches. Even though I had plenty of time to make a real dinner, it would probably freak her out if I showed up with some sort of fancy, three-course meal. I filled my cart with bread, deli turkey, mayonnaise, mustard, cheese, apples, and cookies, plus some staples I'd already run out of—cereal, milk, spaghetti noodles. I even made my way back to my apartment without taking a single wrong turn.

It was fun to stand in the kitchen making dinner for both of us.

I cut the sandwiches into triangles like my mom used to do when I was a kid. In keeping with the elementary school theme, I should have put them into brown paper bags, but all I had were the plastic bags from the grocery store, so I put the lunches in them instead. One sandwich for me, one sandwich for her. I hesitated. I was going to have two sandwiches—should I make her two as well? It would be rude to give myself more food; on the other hand, I didn't want her to be offended and think I thought she was a big eater or something. I decided to err on the side of too much food, reasoning that it's harder to be in a good mood or have a good time when you're hungry. One cookie for me, one for her. An apple for each of us.

"What are you doing?" asked Jeff, one of my roommates.

"Making some food for the meeting tonight," I explained. "I have to meet with the other seminary teacher and I told her I'd bring some food."

"Who'd they ask to be the other teacher?"

"Andrea Beckett," I said.

He grinned at me. "Good luck, man."

"What do you mean?" I asked, but I kind of knew what he meant already.

"She's a cool girl, but she's tough. I went out with her a few times, had this massive crush on her last year, and she would not give an inch. We had fun, she was cool, but I could never get her to think of me as more than her buddy. She had some missionary she liked and wouldn't give any of us guys in the branch a chance because of him, and then he came home. I'm not sure what happened after that."

"She could be engaged, for all I know," I admitted. "I've only met her twice." But it had been enough to get me making sandwiches and taking some heat from my roommate.

• • •

I got to the seminary room before Andrea, so I turned on all the lights and set the bags of food on the table. I looked at the bare bulletin boards and tried to think of something we could do to make the room look more like a real classroom. I heard someone at the door and turned around. Andrea and another girl came in, both of them wearing backpacks and carrying water bottles.

"This is my roommate, Emma," Andrea said, introducing the girl with her. "She's the branch organist, so she's going to practice while you and I are meeting."

"Do you want some dinner?" I asked Emma. "I made extra."

"No, thanks," she said. "Don't want to get food stuck in the keys. Thanks, though." She gave me a friendly wave as she left.

We pulled two chairs up to either side of the table and I slid Andrea's bag of food toward her. "Thanks," she said, opening it up and looking inside. "This looks good." She pulled out her sandwich and unwrapped it. I followed suit. Organ music drifted down the hall from the chapel.

"What do you think would be the best way to divide up the teaching?" Andrea asked. "We could take turns doing Mondays, Wednesdays, and Fridays, and then switch, or we could alternate weeks. Or something else. What have you thought of doing?"

I smiled. "I've been too nervous to think of much. I'm planning on teaching college someday, but high schoolers are a different breed. And high schoolers at six-thirty in the morning are even more intimidating."

"At least we only have eight of them," she said. "And at least we're not teaching the Old Testament. Can you imagine? All those people to keep track of, and all those stories with violence and questionable morality?"

I laughed. She had a good point.

"And what better place to teach the Doctrine and Covenants?" I added. "There are so many sites around us, the kids probably have a better familiarity with some of the Church history than most high school kids. We'll have to know our stuff."

Andrea asked, "How did you feel when Brother Walker asked you to teach? Dazed, right?"

"Was it that obvious? Yeah, to be honest I was completely shocked. I don't even know how they thought of me. I haven't been here that long and I've never been in early-morning seminary. Where I lived in Utah, it was part of the regular school day. How did *you* feel?"

"I was shocked too." She looked like she was about to say more, but she didn't.

"So how *do* you want to break this up?" I asked her. "Should we alternate days? Weeks? Months?"

"It might be easier to alternate weeks," she said. "And maybe we should go to class even when the other person is teaching, at least at first, so we both know what's going on and everything."

"That sounds like a good idea," I agreed.

"Looks like we'll be spending a lot of time together," she observed dryly, and the way she said it made me laugh.

"I hope that's all right with you," I told her. "Personally, I'm thrilled about it because I spend most of my day with economics grad students, so you can imagine what a lively bunch that is."

She smiled. "About as lively as the group I hang around with all day. My major is biology, and there's a lot of us dorks in there." She balled up her plastic bag with the garbage and apple core inside and shot it toward the trash can. She hit it dead center, not even touching the sides. Somehow, I wasn't surprised. I did the same and hit it as well. Thank goodness.

"Nice shot," she said.

"You too," I told her.

"So, who goes first?" she asked. "Do you want to take the first week, or should I? I assume you're as excited as I am about the early hour."

I groaned. "It *is* early, isn't it? After my mission, I told myself that I would keep going to bed early and getting up early, but that didn't happen. I sure haven't been getting up anywhere near five-thirty or six for a long time."

"I'll take the first week," Andrea decided. "I might as well jump in with both feet. Plus, it's only two days long. Should I teach the next week, too?"

"No way," I said. "If you're willing to start it off, then you shouldn't have to teach extra days as well. I'm sure it will even out anyway at some point with all the holidays."

We looked over the reading schedule, which would kick in the Monday after school started, and adjusted it to fit the school district calendar we had. School started on a Thursday, and seminary started on the Thursday after that. The rest of the time, we followed the school district calendar to the end of the year, when seminary ended a week before school did.

With most of the business out of the way, I was ready to find out a little more about Andrea, but Emma returned and Andrea stood up.

"Thanks again for bringing the food," she said.

"No problem," I said. I walked with them to the door and pulled it shut, fishing my keys out of my pocket to lock the classroom. "Here we go," I told Andrea as the three of us walked down the hall. "Good luck with the first lesson."

"Thanks," she said. "I'll need it." For the first time, I heard a trace of undeniable nervousness in her voice. I wondered how much of what she'd said that evening had been bravado on her part.

• • •

I sat in the foyer for a little while after she left, trying to put my things together and organize my seminary stuff before I went back to my apartment, which was still pretty chaotic from three guys trying to move in at the same time.

I looked at the names on the roll, trying to commit them to

memory: Ben Allen. Camille Baron. Caterina Giovanni. Jason Hay. Melissa Hay. Steve Ward. Sarah Wren. Heather Wythe.

After I'd read the list a couple of times, I tried to write some lesson outlines for my first week, but I caught myself thinking about Andrea and what she might do the first week and how that might change my plans, and then I just admitted to myself that I was flat-out thinking about Andrea.

I'd thought about her in abstract a few times since the plane ride in March—cute girl, wonder if I'll see her again—especially after Lauren and I realized that we weren't going to work out. But it was abstract, just random wonderings about if there were more girls like her at Cornell and if one of them would give me a shot. Andrea had been fun to talk to on the plane and helpful with the Cornell stuff, but I had been preoccupied with how I was going to tell Lauren that I was, after all, moving to New York, so I might have seemed a little distracted. Plus, I had spilled orange juice all over my front and was wearing a Cornell shirt that I later found out still had the tag sticking out of it . . . Yeah, she probably hadn't been that impressed now that I thought about it. Hopefully, I could make a better impression now that we would be teaching together and hanging out.

I sat in the foyer for a few more minutes, trying to figure out what to do next. The problem wasn't that I didn't have enough to do—there were papers for my program already looming on the horizon, seminary lessons to prepare, plus all the minutiae of moving (changing the address on your magazines, opening a new bank account, etc.). There was plenty going on.

The problem was that I didn't want to do any of it. I wanted to talk to someone I already knew, someone who already knew me, preferably a family member. So while I was sitting in the empty foyer, I called my parents on my phone. No one was home. I called the brother I'm closest to, Eli, but he wasn't around either. After a moment's hesitation, I called my brother Seth, who lives in Boston.

"Hey," I said when he answered. "What's up? It's Joel."

"Hi, Joel," he said. Then before I could say anything else, he said, "Joel, I can't talk right now. We're trying to get the kids into bed. I'll catch you later." Click. Three strikes, I was out. There was no one else to call.

I guess I shouldn't have been surprised about Seth. He and I are very different people. Seth is four years older than I am, and he's always taken his big brother role seriously. Sometimes it ticks off Eli and me. Eli is two years younger than I am, and we've always been a little closer. But where Seth is concerned, we'll always be trapped in the roles of younger brother and baby brother. He was always giving us (unsolicited) advice. It didn't help our relationship that he's the only one married with kids. In fact, right after Seth got married, he and his wife moved back East for him to go to law school, and they've never been back home for more than a quick holiday visit. I hadn't really gotten to know Seth as an adult; maybe that was the problem.

I put away the phone and looked around the foyer one last time before I gave up and went home. I didn't know any of the names on the missionary plaques and I didn't know any of the people on the bulletin board. I didn't know anyone. And I could still feel a thread of something pulling on me, anchoring me to home.

CHAPTER 12

SEPTEMBER, ITHACA

Andrea Beckett

A lot of people think that spring is the best time of the year because it's time for a new beginning. I love spring, but I think fall can give spring a run for its money in the new beginning category. Maybe it comes from being in school for so long—this, my senior year of college, was my seventeenth year in school (if you count kindergarten, which I do)—but I've always felt that the year truly begins in the autumn. Everything starts over then.

And autumn in upstate New York is beautiful. Not just nice, isn't-that-pretty beautiful, but take-your-breath-away beautiful. I mean that literally. I have caught my breath plenty of times: at the sight of a vibrant sunset; as I've driven over the crest of a hill and seen a slope covered in thousands of trees, each a slightly different color of red or orange or yellow.

On that first day of seminary, two weeks into September, we were still about a month away from the peak of fall season. The leaves were barely turning on a couple of trees, and the weather was still hot and humid enough to remind you more of the way it had been in August than of the way it would be in October. But still, it was fall, and school was starting, and, instead of being excited and anticipatory, I was sick-to-my-stomach nervous in a way I don't ever remember being when I was going to high school myself.

I woke up at 2:00 A.M. and couldn't get back to sleep. I lay there in the dark, trying to convince myself that I hadn't really woken up—I was just having a very boring dream. I wasn't very convincing. Two hours later, I finally decided to get out of bed. There was no point lying there thinking about seminary and making myself crazy. If I wasn't going to be able to get any sleep, at least I could get up and do something productive with my time.

● ● ●

After I'd showered, I stood in front of my closet in my bathrobe, my hair swathed in a towel, completely stumped. It had been years since I'd worried about what to wear on the first day of school. In college, you realize quickly that if you wear jeans and a sweater, or jeans and a T-shirt, or jeans and almost anything, you're safe. You can wear almost anything and someone else will be wearing something better or worse.

But it seems like the options were more limited in high school. High schoolers have a definite idea of what will work on the first day of school and what won't, or at least it had been that way when I was there, four years ago. Had it been that long?

I pulled out a few different outfits. The first one was the trendiest one I had, but I was halfway through ironing the shirt when I decided that it wouldn't work. The second choice was a suit I had purchased in preparation for job interviews. That one actually made it all the way through the ironing and on before I decided that it was too businesslike, too dressy, not quite friendly enough.

My hair was almost dry and I was still in my bathrobe. Maybe it was good I had woken up so early, at the rate things were going. I threw the suit back on the bed, not caring that it would wrinkle again, and tried not to let my eyes fill up with tears. But they did. I sat down on the bed and put my hand to my head, closing my eyes.

What Joel didn't know, or Brother Walker either, was that I was in a world of trouble. I had never attended seminary in high school. I wasn't active in the Church then. Even when I started going back to Church at the end of my senior year, I never went to seminary. I'd thought it was too late. And my mom was the seminary teacher for our ward. Every morning, she and Ethan had gotten up early and driven to the Church for class. I'd used Chloe as an excuse saying I would stay home with her and help her get ready while they were at seminary, but we'd all known the real reasons I didn't go: I wasn't active; I wasn't interested. When I started being active and interested, my mom had offered to work something out so I could start coming to seminary with her and Ethan. "We'd love to have you. We can figure something else for Chloe if you want to come."

"No thanks, Mom," I had said. "It seems too late in the game to start now."

Apparently, Heavenly Father had a sense of humor. I'd missed out on that whole part of life and now I was going to teach seminary. I had no idea what to do. All I had in my mind to help me picture how a seminary class should be were the few details I remembered from conversations between my mom and Ethan. And I seemed to remember that my mom always wore a dress to teach. I looked at the clothes all over the room and knew the what-to-wear problem was the tip of the iceberg.

It was time to pull out all of the stops. I put my pajamas back on and opened up the scriptures to Isaiah 40:31, my special scripture since high school. Tucked in the pages was the letter my grandmother had written me right before she passed away. I read the scripture first and then her letter. I reminded myself to "wait upon the Lord" the way the scripture advised.

I thought about my mom, who had taught seminary for five years, a long time. What had her first day of teaching been like? Had she been nervous? What had *she* worn? I hadn't told her about my new assignment. Even though she and I were pretty close, there were some things we didn't talk about. We didn't talk too much about guys, and we also didn't talk too much about how I was in high school. I didn't want to bring up all those memories of her reaching out and me pushing her away.

Sometimes it's easy to forget that underneath the Mom-layer, there were so many other layers—child, teenager, adult, new mother, first-time seminary teacher. I remember watching her face as she talked about going to a dance when she was young, and it was almost like looking through a kaleidoscope—a little shift and I could see the animated, beautiful girl she had been in the animated, beautiful woman she was.

I finally settled on a blue oxford dress shirt with pinstripes and a long gray skirt. I decided it was the most teacherly outfit I owned. I could picture Mom nodding in approval, especially at the heels I chose. With heels on, I'm over six feet tall. My mom is tall too. "A tall woman should never be ashamed of her height," she used to admonish me when I was in my early teens and unsure what to do with all the extra length in my arms and legs.

I would have to come home and change before I went to school, though, or the heels were going to kill this unashamed tall woman as she walked all over campus. I usually wear a pair of my old running shoes to class, but the heels were a critical part of the ensemble. For a while I debated wearing my hair up in a bun, but in the end I wore it the way I usually did, in a ponytail. I put on a pair of silver earrings and my usual makeup—lip gloss and mascara—and I was ready to go.

When I got to the church building, I climbed out of the car and put on my backpack since I needed my hands free to hold the big "Welcome to Seminary" poster Joel and I had made to put up on the door. Neither of us had much artistic ability, so that's exactly what it was—a piece of white poster board with "Welcome to Seminary" written on it in black marker.

I felt a little silly wearing my backpack from school, but I didn't have the kind of bag I pictured a teacher wearing. When my mom had taught seminary, what had she carried? I didn't remember. A teacher would probably carry some kind of fancy leather bag with lots of straps and pockets, or a huge canvas tote bulging at the seams and a monogram on the side. I taped the sign to the door where the students could see it as they came to class and then I walked in.

I'd never walked into a classroom as the teacher before. The room was dark, the stage unset. It was all up to me to get things going. I turned on the lights and straightened the teacher's desk at the front of the room. The podium was sitting in a back corner; I picked it up and lugged it to the little table at the front of the room. I was going to need it. I had to have something to hide behind. I put my lesson plan and scriptures on top of the podium, squaring the edges neatly. I straightened the markers and erasers on the board. Then I read through my lesson plan over and over until it was almost time to start.

I propped the door open with a brown plastic doorstop, the exact kind I remember from my high school days. As it had then, it required some serious kicking to wedge under the door. I had just slammed it into place when the first student appeared in the doorway. She looked at me but didn't say a thing.

"Hi," I tried. "I'm Sister Beckett, one of the new teachers."

"Can we sit wherever we want?" she asked. "I'm Heather," she added, almost as an afterthought.

"Sure," I said, and she moved to the back table and sat down. Before I could try any more small talk with her, another girl came in. This one didn't make eye contact with me, but she did mutter, "Hi," in response to my "Hello" on her way to her seat.

I thought back to the only other teaching experience of my life, those days in high school when I'd done peer tutoring. Then it had been one-on-one. Now it was different. Now it was eight on one. Or it would be, if everyone showed up. It was time to start and only two people were there. Should I start anyway? Where was Joel?

I heard someone in the doorway again and I looked over to see who was coming in. It was Joel. He gave me a brief smile and sat quickly in a desk at the back. Despite the fact that it was my suggestion that we both come to class, I didn't know whether I was happy or sad to see him. On the one hand, I had some adult backup in the room. On the other hand, I realized that now he would see me teach and I had no idea how that was going to go. Well, there was only one way to find out. As four more students—two girls and two boys—came in and hurried to their seats, I decided it was time to take the plunge.

"Hello," I said. "I'm Sister Beckett, one of your seminary teachers this year. Your other teacher is Brother Hammond, who is sitting on the back row." They turned to look at him. Joel waved from his seat and I noticed a couple of girls looking at him with interest. "Brother Hammond and I are going to be taking turns teaching you the Doctrine and Covenants this year. Today it's my turn. So go ahead and get ready by getting out your scriptures and notebooks while I'm calling the roll . . ."

I stopped because a girl, one of the few who looked awake this hour, had raised her hand. "Um, aren't you going to tell us anything about yourself? Or let us play a getting-to-know you game or something?"

I don't like feeling unsure of myself, which is what I felt. But there was no way I was going to show any weakness or they'd figure out in a second that this was the first time I'd been in a seminary class. "We'll do that later," I said, as if I had been planning on playing getting-to-know-you games all along. "Right now I really want to get started on the first lesson. I'm going to call roll first so that I can know who's who. Let me know if there is a nickname that you'd like me to use instead of what's written here on my list." As I was making this announcement, a huge football player (he was even wearing his jersey) walked in and sat down. Seven out of eight students—not bad for the first day. I hoped my teaching wouldn't cause the numbers to dwindle.

The girl who had raised her hand turned out to be named Caterina Giovanni. She was tanned and freckled and stocky in an athletic way. Long strawberry-blonde hair, bleached by the sun, hung down her back in a single braid. "You can call me Caterina or Cate," she said. "I'll answer to either."

"I'd prefer to be called Sidney Rigdon," said the football player, whose real name was Steve Ward. He was perfectly deadpan.

"So we're really not going to do a getting-to-know-you game or anything?" said a panicked looking young guy sitting next to Cate.

"I thought you guys would all know each other from Church already," I said, losing my composure for a moment. Class was getting out of hand and all I'd done was call roll—or try to.

"We know each other, but there's still so much to learn," said Steve with feigned sincerity. Cate gave him a look that seemed harsher than necessary.

I had to get this back on track. "Actually, we have a lot to do and we need to get started. I have the reading schedule for the first week right here. Cate, would you pass that out, please?" She looked less than thrilled, but she stood up and took the papers from me.

"We'll start that on Monday. Today, we're going to write an essay about the Prophet Joseph Smith since we'll be studying his life and a lot about his history this year as we study the Doctrine and Covenants."

Cate stopped passing out the papers and turned to look at me. "You've *got* to be kidding," she said.

"I'm not," I said. Before they mutinied, I added, "It's not hard. All I want you to do is write what you know about him and how you feel about him."

They exchanged looks and a few whispers, but they started

writing and continued on through the next twenty minutes or so. Then we took turns reading from the Joseph Smith–History, going up and down the rows of students taking turns.

I watched their faces and listened to them read, trying to learn something about each of them. Steve kept falling asleep and had to be told each time that it was his turn and where he should start reading. The young freshman guy next to Cate—Ben, I think his name was—read so fast I could hardly understand him. Cate elbowed him and told him to slow down and that helped a little. Heather read so softly, I could barely hear her. The brother and sister, Jason and Melissa, read clearly and stayed on task throughout everything I assigned them, their faces impassive. Melissa sat at the end of the row next to Cate. Jason sat on the other end, next to Ben. Camille sat next to Heather and kept looking around, bored, but she read when I asked her to and didn't give me any grief. Everyone was too well-behaved.

They obviously all knew each other and had for a long time. They had that kind of closeness that being a small group for a long time brings. But there were probably rifts there, too, that I didn't know about. When I had called Sarah Wren's name during roll, they all looked at each other, but didn't say anything. What was the story behind the one student who wasn't there? There was so much I didn't know yet—about the material, about the students, about everything.

When it was time to go, I said, "I'll see you tomorrow," and collected their papers. I could see class hadn't been a raging success, but at least it hadn't been total mayhem. I would go home and talk to Emma or Shannon and try to figure out how this was going to get better, because it couldn't get much worse.

Joel hung around for a minute afterward, but I didn't want to talk to him. Stupid returned missionaries are always so good at teaching and they always know all of the doctrine and of course they've all been to four years of seminary throughout their perfect little lives. I tried to seem extra busy so that he would get the hint and leave. He must have figured it out, because he paused for a minute and then said, "See you, Andrea," and left.

Perversely, after he left, I was mad at him. How could he walk off and leave me like that? How was I supposed to get any feedback? How on earth was I going to figure this out? It was too bad Mom hadn't passed along some of her teaching genes to me along with her height.

•   •   •

Later that evening, I was working on the next day's lesson plan at the kitchen table in our apartment when I heard footsteps on the stairs outside the door. I also heard voices, lots of them. Then the doorbell rang, repeatedly.

"What on earth is going on here?" I growled as I went to answer it.

Emma called from the bathroom, "Don't you remember? Everyone's meeting here for the Young Single Adult activity tonight."

I froze for a second and considered running back to the kitchen, scooping up my books, and beelining for my bedroom to hide out. The activity was a hike to Taughannock Falls and then a trip to Purity Ice Cream for dessert. I was so not in the mood for this tonight. But it was too late. People could see me through the windows on the sides of the door and some of them were waving at me. I cursed Emma and her indefatigable hospitality under my breath as I opened the door.

I didn't know many people in the first group—there were a lot of freshmen—so I introduced myself and made a little small talk. When I heard Emma call out behind me, "Hey, everyone!" I made my escape, telling her I was going to get my shoes on. I knew that she would give me grief if I stayed behind. Plus they probably needed me to drive all these freshmen, who were usually carless.

I pulled out an old pair of running shoes from the back of my closet and shoved my feet into them, tying the laces. Then I sat on my bed for a minute. I didn't want to go out there yet. I heard a lot of laughter, more people arriving, talking. I heard Emma's voice rise above the rest for a second, and then quiet as someone else offered a prayer before the drive. Still I didn't leave my room. I might get lucky and no one would notice I wasn't there. I heard car doors slamming, people leaving, the apartment getting more and more quiet. Had I made it?

Emma threw open the door. "Come on!" she said. "We're about to leave. You don't even have to drive this time. There's a space in my car for you, and we're taking a couple of new freshmen with us. Hurry up!" She turned around, then turned back. "Oh, and grab those water bottles in the front room for me, will you? No one is getting dehydrated on my watch!" The two freshmen followed along behind us, wide-eyed and looking overwhelmed. The four of us climbed in Emma's car.

The good thing about the freshmen was that they were happy to talk. Emma got them started on where they were from and what they were studying and what they thought of Ithaca so far, so I didn't have to do much to keep up my end of the conversation. I looked back at them and couldn't help but realize how close in age they were to the seminary students. They were so young. I was twenty-one—almost twenty-two—and I felt ancient.

Whenever I talk to Mikey about her BYU student ward, it always strikes me how different our student branch is. We have such a big disparity in age, from the eighteen-year-old freshmen to the late twenty-something graduate students. It was weird to realize that this year I was closer in age to the new grad students than the freshmen. I guess I was becoming a bona fide adult.

Since Emma was in charge, she hopped out of the car and started organizing things, the two freshmen trailing after her like satellites. I ended up standing around alone while people spilled out of cars, chattered to each other, and milled around the trailhead. Groups of people can be so exasperating, especially when they're not moving in a direction but just standing or sitting or talking: one big blob of humanity. The blob sort of slurped toward Emma.

I was stuck at the back of the blob and it was driving me crazy. I moved around the side and headed for the front of the group. It wasn't hard to do: look purposeful, keep your eyes straight ahead, walk fast and don't stop. I disliked myself for being so easily annoyed with everything tonight. The buildup of fatigue, stress, and humiliation from the day had turned me into someone who should probably keep to herself until she became a little bit friendlier.

Once I had reached the front of the pack, I started walking fast, ahead of the group. "I'll make sure the trail isn't flooded from all the rain we had last week," I called over my shoulder to Emma as I started off. She rolled her eyes. She knew what I was up to, but she didn't protest.

I'd gone a little way up the trail and was putting some distance on the group when I heard something behind me. Someone was running to catch up. I sighed inwardly and turned around, putting on my game face. It was Joel, which surprised me. I didn't think he'd be the kind of guy to run after me. He seemed too reserved for that.

"Hey," he said. He was not out of breath, and he jogged like he knew how to run, not sticking his chest out like a football player and pumping his arms and legs way too high.

"Hey," I said. I didn't offer up my excuse about seeing if the trail had been flooded. I knew he wouldn't buy it. We walked in silence for a few seconds, which was awkward, but I didn't feel like it was my job to fill it. He was the one who had caught up with me after all. I looked over at him.

To my surprise, he was walking along easily, looking around the trail. He wasn't looking at me. He wasn't trying to talk to me. So why was he there? Why had he bothered to catch up with me if he wasn't going to say anything?

"I know I stunk it up at seminary today," I said, cutting to the chase. "I'll do better tomorrow. I've been thinking about it all day."

"You did fine," Joel said, sounding surprised.

"You're not a very good liar," I said to him. "I know it wasn't great."

"Andrea," he said, "it was fine. You did fine. While you were teaching, all I was doing was sitting there thinking about how terrified I was for my turn. I certainly wasn't passing judgment on how you were doing. Plus, I figure that we are only going to get better at this. It's not like either one of us are teaching majors or anything. I keep telling myself to let myself grow into it."

"You can't tell me it was a great lesson," I said stubbornly. "It was boring, and the kids didn't like it, and there wasn't enough participation . . . I could go on and on."

Joel smiled at me and shrugged. "I'm just going to be happy if I can make it through my first day teaching without soiling myself. Then, I'll work from there."

I laughed in spite of myself, but I wasn't done yet. "*You've* at least had mission experience. The only thing I've done that's even remotely like this is high school peer tutoring, and that was one on one."

"I bet you were a good peer tutor," he said.

"Not really. I was awful when I started, but I got better at it." I gave him a look. "Don't try to draw any parallels here," I warned him. "This is totally different." I didn't want to think about peer tutoring. Dave had been the one to help me with that, and I still didn't like thinking about Dave too much, especially when I was feeling vulnerable and unsure. My disastrous first day of teaching was even making me reconsider the idea of becoming a counselor. If I couldn't even teach a class coherently, how could I help people with their problems? I would be starting work at the student counseling center in the next week, and now I was tempted to quit before I'd even started. I was feeling pretty low.

"Let's make a deal," Joel said. "We'll agree to not take offense at each other's comments and to honestly tell each other some good things and some things that we could improve after each week. I know I've been joking with you, but I do take this seriously. I want to make a difference with those kids. I want to teach the gospel in a way that does it justice, as much as I can. I want to get good at this. You seem like you'd be willing to be honest with me."

"I can dish it out, but I can't always take it," I warned. "Sometimes I don't take criticism well."

"That's how everyone is. Sometimes I don't either. That's why I thought it would be nice for us to give each other feedback since we're both new at teaching high schoolers and we're flying without a net."

"All right," I said. "We can give it a try." Since we were talking about it anyway, I thought I'd go for broke and talk to him about my idea, the only one I'd come up with after an entire day of stewing about seminary. "Hey," I said, "Do you think it would be a good idea for us to have kind of a regular meeting at the end of each week? We could talk about where we are in the lessons and how the kids are doing, all that stuff? We could use that time to give each other our feedback too." And then, since I was on a roll and had nothing left to lose, I went right ahead and asked him, "Does Friday night work for you?"

The minute it was out of my mouth, I worried he would think I'd just asked him on a date. "At five o'clock or so," I clarified. "That way if we had other stuff to do, we'd still have time."

"I'd imagine that your Friday nights are pretty full," said Joel, in a kind of flirtatious, kidding-around voice. *Wonderful,* I thought. The last thing I wanted was for him to start flirting with me. He was a nice guy, a cute guy, even, but I didn't need someone to flirt with. I needed someone who would talk to me about seminary and help me be a better teacher.

When I didn't respond to his Friday night comment, he got serious. "Yeah, that would be a great idea," he said. "Kind of passing the baton from week to week, so to speak. Fridays are fine with me."

"So," I said, walking a little faster, "tell me what I did wrong today. Let's not wait until tomorrow."

Joel had enough sense to look wary, but to his credit, he went for it. "You didn't get to know the students. That was the only thing. They all wanted to connect with you and to get to know you a little, but you didn't give them much."

"What else?" I asked, feeling like I might have to heave Joel into Taughannock Falls once we arrived.

"That's it. Everything else was fine. You have good poise, you are articulate, you know your material, you adapted while you were on your feet. You have a good presence in a classroom."

"Huh." I wasn't sure what to say. I hadn't seen it that way. Was he sincere, or was he still trying to flirt with me? I walked faster.

"Look," Joel said, "if you want to run, let's run. But I can't keep speed walking like this without losing my dignity. Guys don't speed walk." I shot him a look, but slowed down a little.

"What are you thinking about doing in class tomorrow?" he asked.

"I was going to have each student pick a part of his or her essay to read out loud and share with the class. Then we were going to read an article about Joseph Smith," I said. "Then I was going to have everyone pair up with another student, do a little interview with them, and then introduce each other to the rest of the class. I know most of them know each other from Church, but you and I don't know them at all and it seemed like they wanted to do something like that." I waited. In my mind, I dared him to tell me that my lesson plan wasn't any good. I knew it wasn't exciting, but it was all I'd come up with after stewing about it all day. I was exhausted. I'd been up since four in the morning. I was ready to bite someone's head off, and if Joel didn't see that, he was blind.

"Sounds good," he said. "I'm still trying to figure out what to do about Monday."

"Do you really think reading part of their essays will be a good idea?" I asked. "Or will it be unbelievably boring?"

"I think it's a good idea," he said. "You can get an idea of what everyone is like from that."

"I remember my mom doing something like that when she taught seminary."

"Wait." Joel stopped in his tracks. "Your mom taught seminary? When was this going to come out? Why aren't we calling her every day? Why haven't we begged her for her lesson plans?"

"I haven't actually told her yet that I'm teaching."

"Why?"

I couldn't think of anything to tell him but the truth. "Well, she was *my* seminary teacher, and I never went. Not once."

"Oh." Joel looked at me, waiting for me to add to that. I didn't.

Instead, I changed the subject. "So what do you think of the kids in the class? I think that Steve guy is going to be a character, right? And what did you think of Cate?"

It worked. "Oh yeah, I was meaning to tell you. I found out a little more about Sarah Wren."

"How?" I asked, surprised.

"I called the bishop today. Apparently, she was baptized when she was eight, but her family isn't active and neither is she. She's a junior now, and she's never actually been to seminary, but they keep her on the roll in the hopes that she'll come someday. All the kids know her by name, but only Cate actually has any kind of friendship with her."

"That's all good to know," I said. "Thanks."

"No problem," he said. Then he asked, "How can we get her to come to class?"

"I think we should leave her alone for now," I said firmly. He looked surprised. "We need to find out more about her, first," I clarified. "Maybe she doesn't want us to bother her, maybe she would be okay with coming to an activity but not to seminary . . . you never know. We definitely need to find out more about her and what she wants before we do anything." I had strong opinions about this, having been in the inactive category myself in high school. Joel wisely agreed with me, and we started talking about who we should appoint to be the class president.

When we arrived at the waterfall, I was surprised to see that most of the group had caught up to us. One of Joel's roommates called to him and he went over to talk to him. Before Joel left he said, "Hey, Andrea. Consider calling your mom, okay? If not for your sake, for mine." He smiled as he walked away.

I looked around and saw Emma looking at me. She raised her eyebrows and widened her eyes at me, as if to say, "Hey, he's cute." Luckily, someone else came up to talk to her and she was diverted. I stared at the waterfall, thinking about seminary, my mom, the students, and Joel.

• • •

On the way back, Joel was talking to someone else and everyone moved ahead and paired off in clusters of twos and threes and fours. I ended up being behind everyone this time, partly by design and partly because I had been throwing rocks into the waterfall while I thought and hadn't been paying attention when the group had started down the path. They had almost left me behind.

Was this how I was going to be my whole life? Alone, because of a combination of accident and design? I was over Dave, pretty much, but that didn't mean I was ready to jump into a new relationship. In fact, I figured I'd wait until next year when I'd be someplace new and could start over and meet all new people. So was I going to hold everyone I met at arm's length for the rest of the year? It seemed like a very lonely way to be, walking along the path without any conversation or even anyone to keep pace with me.

• • •

When we got home, Emma wanted to talk and Shannon joined right in. "All right," Emma said, "you got to talk for the longest time to the nicest new guy I've seen in years, which wasn't entirely fair. I was stuck with a freshman girl who wanted me to take her grocery shopping, and then a freshman guy who wanted to find out more about the freshman girl. Were you two talking about seminary the whole time? Or something else?"

"Mostly seminary," I said.

"Is he cute?" Shannon asked us.

"Yeah," we both said at the same time, but Emma said it with more enthusiasm. Shannon laughed. Out of the three of us, she's still the only one with a steady boyfriend.

"Would you mind if I ask him out?" Emma asked. "He seems like a fun guy."

"Sure. Go for it." I was surprised. "Why would you think I'd care?"

"No reason," Emma said. "Just making sure. Or maybe I'll wait and hope he asks me out instead. But anyway, back to seminary. Are you ready for tomorrow?"

"Yeah," I said. "I spent half the afternoon writing my lesson plan and I think I have the whole thing scripted. I practically have stage directions. You know, 'Walk to the left. Pick up a marker.'"

Emma and Shannon both laughed. I went to my room to pick out my clothes for the next day. As I laid them out on the bed, I thought of my conversation with Joel, and I picked up the phone.

She answered on the third ring. "Hello?"

"Hi, Mom. It's me. I'm teaching seminary and I don't know what to do. Can I run this lesson plan by you and see what you think?"

END OF SEPTEMBER, BRAZIL

Ethan Beckett

When I was assigned to the office, sometimes I would daydream about how things would be going out in the field. I'd imagine myself walking along the dusty roads of the smaller towns or along the pockmarked sidewalks of the cities, surrounded by warm air and the sounds of Portuguese and the smells of the street. In the cities, the smells would be gasoline, meat cooking at the vendors' carts, and bread from the bakeries; in the country, the streets would smell like the nearby farms, beans cooking in the houses, and, after a rainstorm, like clean packed earth. I pictured myself standing outside in my white shirt with my nametag next to my companion, laughing and speaking in Portuguese with someone, holding out a Book of Mormon. I was realistic. Even in my daydreams, they didn't always take the book from me. But still, that was how I pictured it.

I definitely never pictured standing toe-to-toe with my companion in front of a dusty, rural bus station, both of our fists clenched, fighting with each other in English.

Elder Roy and I were waiting at the bus stop for him to catch a bus to his next area. He was already being transferred even though the two of us had only been companions for about a month. When we were assigned to our companionship, he was fresh out of the MTC and I was just leaving the office, feeling extra-motivated because I'd also been called as a zone leader.

We were both quiet while we waited for the bus, which wasn't unusual for our companionship. Elder Roy had had some trouble adjusting to being on a mission. He struggled with the language (something I could definitely understand), so I tried to help him like Elder Vickers had helped me. All through the month, I taped up words in Portuguese, kept us working hard, hauled him out of bed when it was time to get going. When he wanted to dwell on his girl-friend back home, I tried to change the subject so he wouldn't make himself homesick. I felt like I was dragging him through everything, but I reasoned that someone had to do it and he would start feeling better soon. I was surprised when he was transferred after only a month, but sometimes stuff like that happens on the mission. I hoped my new companion would be more enthusiastic about the work than Elder Roy had been.

As we stood waiting for the bus, I tried to make small talk. Elder Roy never said much. "I wonder why we never baptized anyone," I said. "We sure worked hard and had a lot of contacts. I can't figure out what the reason was behind it."

"You should look in the mirror," he told me. "You're the reason."

I almost smiled, sure that I had heard him wrong. He had to be joking. But one look at his face let me know that he was serious.

"What do you mean?" I asked him.

"Exactly what I said," he told me, and then the gates were down. His Portuguese still wasn't very good, so he spoke in English. There was no room for miscommunication. He knew what he was saying and he meant it.

"*I'm* the reason we haven't had any success?" I asked, trying to keep my voice level. "I'm the one who made sure we got up on time every morning. I'm the one who figured out where to go and came up with plans every day."

He rolled his eyes. "You're great at going through the motions. But all you are is a big fake. You're so proud of being a good missionary and a good zone leader that you don't even care about anything else." Then, to finish me off, he added, "That's why I asked for a transfer. I can't stand being here anymore."

I'm not usually a confrontational person, but I felt my blood boil and I stepped forward, my fists clenched. I wanted to go right ahead and let him have it. Everything in me was hurt, shocked, and livid at what he had said because I didn't think it was true, at least not the part about my being a fake. Elder Roy looked scared for a moment— I am taller than he is—but his look soon changed to one of contempt.

"What?" he taunted me. "You think you're gonna hit me? You think we're really going to fight? That would never happen." He was disgusted. "You don't have it in you."

It took everything I had to turn away. *Get a grip, Beckett,* I told myself. Two missionaries brawling in the street would definitely not be a good move.

I gritted my teeth in anger and walked a few steps down the road, away from Elder Roy. People were staring at us and for once I was grateful that Elder Roy's Portuguese was so bad. At least no one had understood what we were saying, since our fight had been in English, although I'm sure the tone of what we were saying was crystal clear.

The other two missionaries we'd been expecting to see at the bus stop hurried toward us. I was temporarily assigned to their companionship while I waited for my new comp to arrive.

"Sorry we're late!" called out one of the elders, waving.

I waved back, grateful for the distraction. From the other direction, I heard a bus coming down the road in the distance. Good. The sooner this was over, the better.

Elder Roy heard the bus, too. When the other missionaries reached me and we all walked back to join him, he already had his bag on his shoulder and his ticket in hand. He didn't make eye contact with any of us. He stared at the bus. The other two elders were too animated to notice, describing to me an encounter they'd just had with a man who wanted to tell them about his latest vision. I tried to act cool and pay attention to their story. I tried to ignore the person next to me, the person I was supposed to have taught about being a missionary, the person who had called me a fake and a coward.

The bus ground to a stop, metal gears grating on each other, and the little cluster of waiting people moved toward it. "Good-bye, Elder Roy," I said, as he climbed onto the bus. I tried to keep my voice even. The other two elders told him good-bye as well.

He didn't say anything for a minute, just kept climbing the stairs. When he reached the top, he turned back and looked at me. The people behind him in line made muttering sounds, wondering why he'd stopped. "You don't even know me," he said, anger and frustration thick in his voice. He hoisted his bag up higher on his shoulder and disappeared into the bus.

"What was *that* all about?" asked Elder Alencar.

I shook my head. "Nothing," I said, trying to downplay it. "Companion trouble." They both nodded, since we've all had that at some point or another, but this ran deeper. Luckily, we didn't have much time to talk since we were already late for our appointment to meet some members to go on splits. The bus passed us and we moved out of the way so we wouldn't get dirty. I didn't look up.

• • •

My mission has been a combination of two kinds of nights: the nights when I fall asleep almost before my head hits the pillow, and the nights when I lay awake, thinking for hours. This night was definitely going to be a laying-awake-thinking night, which wasn't helped any by the fact that I was sleeping in an unfamiliar place, on a cot in the living room of the other elders' apartment.

I wanted to ignore everything that Elder Roy had said. I wanted to write him off as a jerk and tell myself, "He's a mess. It's all in his head. Don't pay attention to anything he said." I knew I wasn't a terrible person, and I knew I was trying hard on my mission. I knew it wasn't all a show.

I also knew if I told the other elders about the conversation, they'd say all those same things to me. They'd point out that *he* was the one who had the problem, he was the one struggling with missing his girlfriend and being new on the mission, and he was taking it out on me.

I focused on being angry so I didn't have to think about how much his accusations had hurt.

• • •

Three days later, my new comp arrived. When he stepped out into the bus terminal, he stood out like a sore thumb with his bristly blond crew cut and his new suit and his lost expression. *Another American greenie from the MTC,* I thought. Exactly what Elder Roy had been. And that had gone *so* well. I told myself to remember not to be biased and to give the guy a chance.

"Hey. I'm Elder Beckett," I said, shaking his hand. The other two missionaries from my temporary companionship introduced themselves, too.

He shook everyone's hands. "Elder Park." Then, looking around the bus station with obvious distaste, he said in English, "Is the rest of the town nicer than this?"

What a question. "It's a nice town," I said in Portuguese. "You'll like it."

"You're seriously not going to speak to me in English?" he asked. "Why? You're American, right?"

"Our mission president says we should try to speak in Portuguese as much as possible," I said in English.

"Wonderful," he said sarcastically. But, to his credit, he did try to ask how we were getting home in Portuguese, only it came out sounding like *"A onda nós vamos"* which, technically, means "To the wave we go?" But it was close enough to *"Aonde nós vamos"* ("Where are we going?") that I figured it out. When I told him that we would have to walk, he grumbled a little and picked up his suitcases.

"Here," I said, reaching out my hand. "Let me carry one of your suitcases. It's a long walk." When he looked confused, I said it again in English.

"Não," he said in Portuguese. That I understood. The other two elders gave me a look that said, "Good luck," and they headed off to their next appointment.

So home we went, Elder Park and me, both of us lugging our baggage. Me with a chip still on my shoulder from Elder Roy, and Elder Park with his two suitcases. I could tell he was getting tired by the way his arms were hanging lower and the sweat beaded on his forehead. The suitcases kept bashing into his shins as he walked. I was tempted to let him suffer it out, since he'd already refused my help once.

I walked along, my bag over my shoulder and my arms swinging free at my sides. *All right,* I thought stubbornly, *we'll walk the rest of the way like this if that's what he wants.* We kept walking side by side in silence. After a block or so, I looked over at him again to see how it was going.

Elder Park looked absolutely miserable. His face was drawn with the exertion of carrying both his suitcases. He hadn't yet learned how to walk along the dusty road without kicking dirt all over himself, so a fine layer of reddish-brown dust covered his suit pants. His eyes were tired, and he looked ahead, not knowing what home looked like yet. We hadn't gone very many more steps before I stopped being a jerk and wanted to help him again, but I wasn't sure how to go about offering without looking like all the stuff Elder Roy said I was—a fake, a showoff, whatever.

Elder Park shuffled along, growing dirtier and grumpier and sweatier by the second. I shook my head, wondering what on earth was going on in his head, and I realized something. Among all the insults and the anger that he'd leveled at me when he'd left, Elder Roy was right about one thing, at least: I hadn't tried to get to know him. I had ignored signals that he was obviously struggling to reach out to me on some level. I hadn't asked him much about his life before the mission. I'd bulldozed through conversations and tried to be a leader, and even though everything I'd done had been stuff that had worked for me, I could have remembered more that people are different. I was proud that I had kept the rules and worked hard, but I was ashamed that I had done it at Elder Roy's expense. I racked my brain, trying to figure how to be a better leader, a good leader.

"Hey, Elder." He looked over at me. "Give me one of those bags, all right?" I smiled at him, trying to look as friendly as I could. I still expected him to turn me down, but I had to offer.

He looked like he was going to say no, but he surprised me.

"All right," he said in English, and then his face lit up, because he knew how to say the next thing in perfect Portuguese: *"Obrigado." Thanks.*

"De nada," I told him. *No problem.*

We walked a few steps more before I spoke again. "So, Elder Park, where are you from?"

CHAPTER 14

OCTOBER, ITHACA

Caterina Giovanni

Sitting in the backseat of my Laurel advisor's minivan, smashed between two other people (Melissa and Camille) and listening to three conversations at once, I was seriously questioning my commitment to be an example for the younger teenagers in the ward, which is what everyone always expects me to be. In fact, as a matter of principle, I was on the verge of deciding that I should quit going to Young Men/Young Women combined activities altogether. I'm getting way too old for these things. I end up hanging out with the leaders more than I do the other kids. Well, maybe not more than Melissa and Camille. They're both sophomores and I don't mind hanging out with them. And I like Heather and all the guys—but they're so *young*. At the very least, if I do keep going, I've got to start pulling rank and sitting in the front seat. And I don't care if Heather *does* get carsick and throw up if she has to sit in the back. It won't be anything I haven't seen before at Girls' Camp.

Even though we already spend plenty of time together every day in seminary and every week at church, our Young Men/Young Women leaders had planned a combined activity for Saturday afternoon. Technically, it's a combined activity because the Young Men and Young Women both go; but to me it's *really* the combination of one senior (me) and a bunch of underclassmen. Steve is always out of town with football or too cool to come, so I am *always* the only one there from my age group since in our ward I am the only active Laurel, and Steve is the only Priest.

Steve. I could feel my blood pressure rise just thinking about him, and not in a good way. I'm a happy-go-lucky person, but somehow Steve can always get me fired up. Last month, Brother Hammond and Sister Beckett had asked Steve and me to be co-presidents for our seminary class. It was going about as well as I had thought it would. So far Steve was not pulling his stupid, huge, football-player weight. I was the only one doing anything, the only one welcoming people to class, the only one asking people to do the devotional. It was probably a good thing Steve wasn't at the activity because I would have given him a piece of my mind. I'd held off long enough.

I looked out the window and my mood automatically brightened in spite of myself. I may have a bit of a temper, but I never stay too mad for too long. Especially when upstate New York looks the way it does in October. The sky was blue, the fall colors were in full swing, and we were going to be spending the day outside, which is where I always prefer to be. No clouds in sight, which is rare.

Ben looked back at me from the minivan's middle seat and I gave him a big smile. He lives down the street from me and my parents had told his parents that I would be happy to give him a ride to seminary each day. So every day, I went to his house to find him waiting for a ride, his eyes half open and his hair a mess from sleeping, clutching a brown paper sack. Today he was looking a little more alert since it was already mid-morning, but when he turned around I noticed that a sprig of brown hair still stuck up in back. *It must be a cowlick,* I thought, resisting the urge to pat it down for him. I was finding my little freshman sidekick more endearing than annoying today.

Part of my increasingly good mood could also be due to the fact that we were heading back to the place of my summer employment—Kayla and Matt's farm—for our activity. Every year around Halloween, they have a corn maze and a hayride and pumpkins to pick and fresh cider and donuts. People come from miles around to celebrate the season. I hadn't been to the farm in about a month, when I'd helped with the apple-picking. Matt had been gone, then, back at college in Cortland.

On Friday at school, I'd told Kayla we were coming, so she said she'd keep an eye out for me. She also told me that Matt had been coming home on the weekends in October to help out during the harvest season, so I'd probably get to see him too. I was glad. It had been a while since I'd seen him, since the last day before school started, in fact.

The wheels of the minivan hit the graveled road to the big red barn. The parking area was already almost full with people looking for pumpkins and hayrides. I waited until everyone had climbed out of the minivan and pulled the sliding door shut, standing next to the van and stretching for a second. Everyone else was hurrying for the entrance, anxious to get going right away, talking to each other a mile a minute. I lagged behind, looking around for a college guy with freckles and a Yankees baseball cap.

It didn't take long to find him. He was stacking pumpkins right inside the entrance when I walked in. He had looked up as our group started to walk past him, and he was about to look down again when he saw me. I waved.

"Hey, Cate," he said, grinning away. "Who're all your friends?"

"Hey, Matt. This is my Church youth group. We're hunting for pumpkins today." I gave him a look that said, "Bring it on, make fun of me." But Matt, being Matt, just smiled at me and didn't bite.

"Sure," he said. "We get a lot of that."

"Where's Kayla?" I asked, and Matt laughed. "She's stuck in the petting barn today with all the little kids," he told me. "It was my turn last Saturday. You'll have to go find her, talk to her a little. It gets old in there after a while."

"I will," I promised.

"Are you guys going on the hayride later? I'm driving the wagon," Matt said. He lifted the empty wheelbarrow and headed out for more pumpkins. "I'll save you a spot up front with me."

"I'm sure we will, and thanks for the offer," I said. "See you in a little while."

I caught up with everyone else as they walked through the barn and into the big open area where all the pumpkins were displayed. They were everywhere, in mounds and mountains, on wagons and shelves, in rows and piles. I almost ran into a little kid who stopped in his tracks and said, "Whoa." It was so cute. I've been coming here to pick out my pumpkins forever, so I sometimes forget how exciting it can be.

We all spread out among the piles of pumpkins. I watched the little kid grab the first pumpkin he saw and hold onto it for dear life, looking up at his mom with big round eyes. He'd found the one.

It took me a little bit longer. I always pick an ugly one. Forget looking around to find one that is perfectly round with a perfect little comma of a stem on the top. Give me a tipsy old one that's kind of lopsided any day. Or better yet, give me a gourd. Anyone can carve a pumpkin.

I found a super ugly and very large mottled green and yellow gourd. "This is the one," I said to no one in particular, and took it over to the cash register to buy it before anyone could talk me out of it. Matt and Kayla's mom was running the register and she wouldn't let me pay for it. I stayed there and chatted with her until the rest of my group arrived.

"You're still planning on coming back to work for us next summer, right?" she asked, and I told her that I was.

Finally, everyone had chosen their pumpkins. We carried them back to the minivan and piled them in the back cargo area. Ben had picked one huge pumpkin for himself and three little ones for his sisters. He carefully wrapped them in some of the blankets in the back.

"They look comfortable," I told him as I shut the back of the van. "Probably more comfortable than we'll be on the way back."

Now that we were finished with the only real business of the day, it was time to have some fun. "Okay!" said my Laurel leader, Sister Warnick. "Who wants to go on the hayride?"

It turned out that Ben was allergic to horses. And hay. Heather thought horses were stinky. Jason wanted to go through the haunted barn instead. Never mind that it was midday and that the haunted barn was never that scary, not even when it was after dark—everyone else seemed to think that was a great idea too. Sister Warnick thought she'd better go with them. So I was the only one from our group who wanted to go on the hayride.

I waited at the back of the line until Matt had helped most of the little kids and their parents into the wagon. "Hey," I said as he started to close the gate. "What about me?"

"Hey!" he said. "Where's the rest of your group?"

"It's just me," I said, shrugging. "They were all allergic or wanted to go to the haunted barn."

Matt laughed. "Come on, then. I saved you a seat up front." He helped me climb up next to him at the front of the wagon.

"Aren't I taking some little kid's spot?" I asked, feeling kind of guilty. When I was small, I'd always wanted to ride up high with the driver of the wagon instead of in the back with everyone else.

"Nah," Matt said. "My parents don't like us to let little kids ride up here for liability reasons. Plus, if anyone complains, we'll tell them you're a farm employee." He shook the reins and the Clydes started off.

The air smelled perfect, like burning leaves and sweet apples. I could smell some of the donuts baking back at the farm store. The fields I knew so well from the summer had already changed, lost some of their green, taken on new colors. I sighed. Matt looked over at me. "I miss working here," I told him.

"We miss having you around," he said. "I'm sure Kayla tells you that all the time. How come you didn't come back and work weekends? We need lots of help in the fall. October's about our busiest month."

"My parents thought I should focus on school more and try to raise my grades," I said. "They didn't want me to keep working once the summer was over."

Matt looked surprised. "I never thought you'd have trouble with school."

"I'm not horrible, but my grades could be a lot better," I told him. "My brothers and sister were all perfect students so I think my parents are a little freaked out that I might not get into college or something, since my grades are lower than theirs. It seems like it's late in the game to be worrying about that. Seems to me like I should be more worried about working and making money for college instead, but they don't see it that way."

"College costs a lot," he agreed. "My parents have had me saving for it forever. Kayla too. I wanted to spend it all on a car and they wouldn't let me. I guess I'm grateful about that now."

"Are you happy you stuck around?" I asked him. "You know, are you glad you went to school in Cortland instead of somewhere farther away?"

"Oh, yeah," Matt said. "I mean, how can I leave this?"

I looked around and, not for the first time, it struck me that all of this was his. Well, his, and Kayla's, and their parents', and their aunts' and uncles' and their families . . . but still. We were making a big loop around the fields in the wagon, and every field we passed was one they were responsible for, would take care of for years. Every little pumpkin and donut and fencepost and piece of gravel in the parking lot was theirs.

"How does it feel to be part of something so big?" I asked Matt. "You've always known that you'd come back and work here when you were done with school, right? Hasn't it been nice to know that this is all here for you?"

"Yeah," he said, but he looked serious. "But running the farm, it's a lot of work, Cate. You gotta know that going in. My freshman year of college, I thought, 'Maybe I won't go back to the farm. Maybe I'll do something else.'"

"But you're happy, aren't you? Even if it's not perfect, this is still what you want to do, right?"

"Absolutely," he said. "What about you? What's the plan, besides going to college?"

"That's all there is, right now," I said. "I've thought about going to nursing school, but I'm not sure where. I'm going to apply to a couple of places and hopefully one of them will take me."

"You don't want your life to just be what happens," he said. "You want to take control of it too."

"Oh, I know," I told him, and he laughed. "I haven't figured out what I want yet, but when I do, I'll go for it."

"I can believe that," he told me.

I looked at the colors painting the side of the hill. Red, green, orange, yellow, brown. Riding along in the wagon, you could pick out the individual patches of color and note them in your mind. Not like driving in a car where it goes so fast it's redgreenorangeyellow-brown and then becomes colorscolorscolors as you go even faster. If I stayed here, would I notice more of the nuances of things I'd taken for granted? Or would going away help me accomplish the same thing?

We were nearing the end of the hayride, making our way back to where we'd started. "You keep me posted on what's new with you, okay?" Matt said. "Kayla tells me some stuff, but you keep me up on it too. Kayla can give you my e-mail and all that, so you won't have an excuse, all right?"

"Sure thing," I said as the horses slowed down and we approached the gate. A bunch of kids and parents were waiting there for their turn on the wagon. Some of the kids were pointing at the horses and jumping up and down. I could hear the children sitting on the hay behind us talking and jabbering again.

Matt pulled on the reins and the horses stopped. Their hooves made satisfying "thunk, thunk" sounds in the tamped-down grass. Matt called out, "Here we are, everyone! Hope you enjoyed the ride!"

He helped me down from the front seat. I wanted to talk to him more, but the new crowd at the gate was already anxious for their hayride. "See you later," I told him, and he clapped me on the back and gave me one of those one-armed, big brother hugs.

"Good to see you, Cate. Keep me in the loop, all right?" I gave him a thumbs-up as I stepped back so he could open the gate to let the old riders out and the new riders in. I thought about climbing back up to the front seat of the wagon and riding around and around for the rest of the afternoon, but it was already time to find the rest of my cohorts.

I made my way through the thickening crowd toward the barn, keeping an eye out for anyone from my group.

Over the years, Matt has been like a big brother to me. He always has advice and is a good listener. It's nice to have someone of the opposite gender to talk to and help you through your high school years. Especially since my own brothers weren't around to do that for me. Maybe I would do the same thing for someone else someday.

I caught sight of the rest of my group standing in the donut line. Ben was near the front of the long line and he started gesturing to me and asking something I couldn't hear.

"What?" I yelled out in annoyance.

"Tell me what you want and I'll get it for you so you don't have to wait in line!" he yelled. Then he started calling out the kinds: "They have cinnamon, plain, sugar, powdered sugar . . ."

People turned to see who this litany was directed at and to fend him off, I yelled back, "Cinnamon's great, Ben! Thanks!" Camille raised her eyebrows at me, tilting her head in Matt's direction, telling me in universal girl sign language that Matt was sure cute.

I turned and waved good-bye to him one last time and he waved back, getting ready to take another load of kids off on another hayride through the fields and air and land that we all knew and loved. Matt had found the perfect balance between staying and leaving. I wanted that too.

CHAPTER 15

OCTOBER, ITHACA

Joel Hammond

It was Ben's turn to give the spiritual thought for the devotional. He hadn't been in charge of a spiritual thought before, which was unusual in a class so small. Somehow he had managed to give the prayer or read a scripture every time instead. When I found out that Cate had asked him to be in charge of the thought for the first time, I was interested to see what he would do.

After the song, he walked up to the front of the class, holding a bag, fumbling around with it, trying to get something out. It took him so long that the room fell perfectly quiet. I tried not to bury my head in my hands as I thought, *Oh no. He's going to try an object lesson. This is going to be excruciating.* I caught Andrea's eye and had to look away before I laughed or grimaced or did something that revealed how I was feeling. Cate pinched the bridge of her nose with her hand and looked worried. Steve was asleep at his desk. All the other kids looked at least mildly interested, except for the Hay twins, who were poker-faced as usual.

"I was thinking that the scriptures were a lot like this pumpkin," Ben said, finally succeeding in pulling a large orange pumpkin out of the bag. He set it carefully on the table in front of him. "So our thought today is about how the scriptures are like pumpkins." He stood there for a second, as if that was all that needed to be said. I wondered what Andrea thought about the scriptures-as-pumpkins analogy but didn't dare look her way. I peeked at Cate, who had taken Ben under her wing all year long. Her eyes were closed and she was still pinching the bridge of her nose.

Ben kept standing there. He honestly seemed to think he had covered it, but then I could tell from the slight blush on his face that he realized he might need a little help. "So, Ben, how are the scriptures like pumpkins?" I asked, looking straight at him. Out of the corner of my eye, I saw Andrea move her chair a little in the back, but I still refused to meet her gaze.

Ben turned to me, looking relieved. He didn't even address the class as he explained it. He talked just to me, so I maintained eye contact the best I could. "Pumpkins are like the scriptures because they are really messy inside. You open them up and you think that there is too much there and you will never get it all sorted out. But then, if you give it a try and if you work hard enough at it, you get it all cleaned out inside and it's a jack-o'-lantern." Having now spoken more words in the past few seconds than in the rest of the year put together, he seemed to think he was more than finished. He gave me a brief smile, picked up his pumpkin, and headed back to his desk.

Everyone turned to me, waiting for more. "That's a good point, Ben," I said. And it had been, except for the jack-o'-lantern part, which I hadn't quite followed. "And a really . . . visual analogy. Sometimes it is overwhelming to get started with scripture study, but with perseverance, you can make something out of it for yourself. It might be something different for everyone. Maybe you want to make a jack-o'-lantern, like Ben, so you have to scoop out all of the seeds and clean the pumpkin and carve it. Or, you might want to do something else, like roast the seeds, or make a pie."

Andrea raised her eyebrows at me from the back of the room,

but I didn't care. I was sailing with this analogy, and Ben was looking at me, fascinated and pleased that his spiritual thought had turned out so well.

I held up my scriptures. "It's like the scriptures because we each need a different answer, but the materials we use are the same. Someone might read the scriptures to find an answer to a problem with their parents, or to figure out what they should do about a particular situation or trial, or just because they know they need to. It can be messy and daunting to start, but if you take it a little bit at a time, seed by seed, it can be done and you can have the result you need. You can get the answers you're looking for, whether you're looking for the beginning of a testimony or for help with a specific problem."

Cate raised her hand. "You can also think of it this way: It took a long time for that pumpkin to grow, and you didn't grow it yourself. The farmer did. But you still get to reap the benefits. Kind of like Joseph Smith. He did a lot of the work of bringing back the gospel and translating the Book of Mormon, and we get to read it and have it just like that. We're lucky."

"Good point," I told her.

Melissa raised her hand too. "Also, when you read the scriptures, they can illuminate a question you've been having, but only after you've gone through all the mess. Just like a jack-o'-lantern can be a lantern when it's cleared out and sorted through—the scriptures can be lanterns for us."

Wow. I hadn't thought of that. I glanced at Ben and it was impossible to tell whether he had thought of it either. Was that what he had been getting at when he mentioned the jack-o'-lantern? Hard to tell. His facial expression remained exactly the same.

"What do you think, Steve?" I asked. He had his head down on the desk the way he usually did for the first half of class. We had a little pattern going with Steve. Every day, he stumbled into class, crashed into a chair, plopped his scriptures down on his desk, then folded his arms around them and used them as a pillow. He always woke up partway through class and participated, but he wasn't much to work with at the beginning. Andrea and I weren't exactly sure what to do. We knew he had a lot on his plate with football and school, and he wasn't a bad kid, but there was definitely room for improvement.

"I don't know," he said, lifting his head slowly, and Cate shifted in her seat in annoyance. "Sorry. I was kind of asleep. I was having a dream that you guys were talking about pumpkins."

"Actually, we were," I said. "Pumpkins and the scriptures."

"Whatever floats your boat," Steve said, already on his way back to sleep, and I looked over at Andrea. She shrugged at me. Cate looked from one of us to the other, and I could practically hear her saying, "*This* is how you're going to deal with him? *This* is the other class president I have to work with?"

I could understand her frustration. But I didn't want to alienate Steve and make it so he didn't want to come. At least he was showing up, and that was a start. It wasn't that I was afraid of him, although he could probably snap me like a twig if he felt so inclined. I wasn't sure what to do, and neither was Andrea. He had been the subject of several Friday night discussions. I let Steve be and finished teaching the class. As usual, he came alive about halfway through and started contributing. It was like clockwork. At least it was something, right?

• • •

But *something* wasn't good enough for Cate. Three days later, on Monday, we found out that things were going to change. At the beginning of class, we all sat there until it dawned on us that it was a minute or two past the time when class was supposed to start and nothing was happening. Usually, Cate stood up and welcomed the class and then turned the time over to whoever was doing the devotional. But nothing happened. Cate sat firmly in her seat.

Andrea, who was teaching, finally said, "Okay, let's get started."

Still, nothing happened. Cate folded her arms across her chest. "Um, Cate?" Andrea asked. "Are you going to get us started?"

"No," Cate said. "It's Steve's turn." We all turned to look at Steve, who was asleep, as usual.

"He doesn't look like he's quite . . . ready for this," Andrea said. Steve's hair, which was always covered with a baseball cap before and after class, stuck up like spikes on a hedgehog, and like a hedgehog, his face was tucked out of sight. Only the gentle up and down motion of his huge back showed that he was, in fact, alive.

"Too bad," Cate said. "I've been doing everything for the whole year. It's his turn." She stood up and poked Steve in the arm with her pen. Nothing happened. She prodded him again. Then she leaned over and whispered something in his ear. He sat bolt upright and looked around.

"What?" he said.

"It's your turn to welcome the class and do the devotional," Cate said. "It will be your turn for the rest of the month since I've had to do it since September and I'm sick of it. It's your turn now. So get started."

Steve looked at her, gauging how serious she was. Andrea and I gave each other glances that said, "What do we do? Do we step in?" She shook her head no, and I agreed. At least everyone was awake, surprised to see easygoing Cate getting after Steve. It was getting interesting.

Cate and Steve were still staring at each other. Cate broke the gaze first, but she didn't give in. She sat down in her seat and faced forward, looking like she was waiting politely for class to start. Steve sat there for a few more seconds, looking around. When nothing else happened and no one went to the front of the room, he heaved himself to his feet and went up to welcome the class. He's a good-natured guy, after all.

"Welcome to class," he said, then looked around again. "Who's in charge of the devotional today?" Camille raised her hand. "Okay, then, take it away, Camille." Then he went and sat in his seat. However, he didn't put his head down, probably because Cate had turned in her chair and was staring right at him until she was sure he was listening to Camille. Then she turned back and faced forward. She'd kept a poker face through the whole thing, but we all knew the victory was hers.

· · ·

That Friday night, I was running late to my meeting with Andrea. I hurried down the hall and through the open door. "Hey," I said, as soon as I walked into the room. "Sorry about being late. I had a paper due at five and I was working on it up until the last minute."

"Don't worry about it," Andrea said. Then she looked at my empty hands and raised an eyebrow.

I groaned. Way to go, Joel. "Was it my week to bring dinner?" She didn't answer, but I could tell she was trying not to smile. "I'm sorry, I'm sorry. I completely forgot."

"That's okay," she said. "We can hurry through our stuff. I actually don't have much to talk about this week. My mom sent me some more of her lesson plans and I thought we could review them and see if there were any ideas we wanted to use over the next few weeks."

"Awesome," I said. Her mom's lesson plans had been a lifesaver. We always changed them and adapted them to our kids and topics, but every now and then we couldn't come up with a single idea and Sister Beckett saved the day. "Listen, I feel really bad about forgetting dinner. Why don't you grab those plans and we'll go grab something to eat? I'll drive."

"Okay," said Andrea, after a brief pause. "I *am* really hungry. I missed lunch today."

· · ·

"Where do you want to go?" she asked me.

"You choose. You're the expert." I turned on the car and the CD player blared out "Like a Rolling Stone" by Bob Dylan. I grimaced. "Sorry," I said, turning it down. "I was kind of burning off some steam and singing along on the drive over."

She laughed. "I can't even picture that. You singing Dylan at the top of your lungs."

"Well, it's not something that the general public should ever have to hear," I admitted. Yet another reason to like her: the girl knew her classic rock. She'd recognized Dylan right off the bat. "So, where are we going?"

"You've got to give me something to work with. What kind of food do you like?"

"Mexican food sounds good," I said. "I don't think I've had any since I've moved here."

"There's only one place in town that's especially good," she said. "Hop on the 13 and I'll tell you where to go after that."

The restaurant she directed me to was my kind of place. The tables were covered in red-and-white-checked plastic tablecloths, no one was dressed up, the music in the background was lively but not too loud, the food was good, the prices were decent, and the service was fast. That last point was critical because my stomach had started growling with embarrassing frequency.

We dug into our food. I was pleased to see that Andrea could hold her own with a huge platter of enchiladas. "This is awesome," I said. "Thanks for recommending it. I'm sorry again about forgetting dinner. You must be starving, especially since you didn't have any lunch."

"Don't feel bad," she said. "If it had been my turn, I wouldn't have remembered either. It sounds like we both had a pretty crazy day."

"What happened to you?" I asked.

"It was a long day at work," she said with a sigh.

"Oh," I said, understanding. She worked at the student counseling center, partly as preparation for grad school, and the things that happened there were confidential, not something she could tell a fellow Cornell student. "I'm sorry."

"I've been working there since the beginning of the summer and I'm still not as good as I'd like to be at helping people, at talking to them. Today was another example of that." She sighed. "I used to think that if you tried hard enough at something, you'd be good at it. I keep learning that's not always the case. Especially right now. I'm not great at work, I'm struggling with the seminary teaching assignment—I feel like a fish out of water."

"I know how you feel," I commiserated. "I feel like I'm the only person in my economics program at school that is working so hard, but still not acing anything. And I can't find my way around Ithaca. It still doesn't feel like home yet. *I'm* more of a fish out of water than *you* are."

"Oh, yeah?" she challenged. "At least you don't get confused when you're teaching and make the kids hate you by getting their names wrong."

"But I forget what section I'm teaching sometimes. Remember last Friday?"

She started laughing. "I'd forgotten about that."

"I don't even know where the good restaurants are in town," I continued. "I can't find the post office. People start singing the Cornell fight song at the football games and I sit there grinning like an idiot because I don't know the words. Someone mentioned the Cornell Plantations the other day and I asked what crops they grew there. Turns out it's some sort of park or arboretum or something instead." I shook my head in mock sorrow. "I got lost going to the grocery store the other day, just when I thought that was the *one* place I could always find."

She threw up her hands. "Okay, okay, you win. You're the bigger loser."

"Thanks," I told her. "That means a lot to me."

"Tell you what," she said. "After dinner, we can drive around and I'll show you where everything is. But in exchange, you have to tell Cate and Steve that we'd like them to plan a class activity for the holidays." We'd decided on that a week ago but hadn't been sure how to go about telling them yet, since they would have to work together a lot and there was obviously still some animosity there.

"Deal," I said instantly. It was a small price to pay for a tour of Ithaca—especially if Andrea was the guide.

. . .

Our last stop on the tour, after the post office, grocery store, three restaurants, a bookstore, and several renditions of Cornell's fight song, was the Cornell Plantations.

"Oh good, we're in luck," said Andrea as we approached the entrance. "They're supposed to lock the gate at dusk, but sometimes they forget. We can still get in." We drove through the open gate and along the road.

Wide, grassy spaces opened up on either side of us. "Where should I go now?" I asked her.

"Follow this road for a little while." She sat back in her seat, watching the canopy of leaves above us as we drove through the almost-dark evening. "This is one of my favorite places in Ithaca."

As the road wound up and down some gently rolling hills, Andrea pointed out the duck pond, a grouping of geometrically shaped concrete statues, a few paths that she said were great to run on during the day. "Keep driving up to the top of this last hill," she instructed. "There are some parking spaces there. We'll get out and walk around."

We climbed out of the car and walked out to the viewpoint. I took a deep breath. "Wow," I said. Even in the dimming light, I could see the ponds and hills and trees below in the valley. A barn sat on the crest of one of the hills across the way. Clusters of trees rimmed the hills in other directions and the sky opened wide and dark and beautiful above us. There was just enough light to give depth to the black shapes below and a glimmer to the ponds. We stood there for a moment, looking. After a few moments, my eyes adjusted enough that I could see a few stars starting to emerge. I pointed them out to Andrea, who stood quiet and peaceful beside me, not full of the restless energy I could usually detect when I was with her.

"There's a bell here you can ring," she said. "Come on, I'll show you."

I followed her. The "bell" was a large metal cylinder suspended from a chain. "There used to be something you could ring it with, a kind of stick," she said, stooping down. She straightened up and held out a rock. "But now you have to use these." She rang the bell, gently hitting the rock a single time against the rusty metal, and a deep mellow sound rang out over the valley. We both stood there listening until there was nothing left to hear except the other sounds of the evening as it grew darker.

"You'll like it here," she said kindly.

I thought about saying, "I already do."

CHAPTER 16

END OF OCTOBER, ITHACA

Andrea Beckett

The air was cold enough that I decided to wear my favorite jacket, the one with the corduroy patches on the sleeves, the one that Joel calls my "Professor Beckett jacket." I had a bag of takeout Thai food to share with Joel at our Friday meeting, and the night smelled like burning leaves and curry as I opened the door. The trees in our front yard dripped gold into puddles on the ground, contrasting against the dark, charcoal-black trunks. It was such a perfect fall evening that I felt a little giddy.

"Here's the mail," Shannon said, coming up the pathway. "There's something for you. It's kind of fancy, and it's not from Ethan."

I hardly ever get real mail from anyone other than my brother, since my friends and family mostly call or e-mail, so I took it from her and looked at it, curious. It was a thick, cream-colored envelope. My name was written on the front in a dark black pen, the handwriting so fancy it looked like calligraphy. There was no return address in the corner, but when I flipped it over a fancy label on the flap of the envelope said, "Mr. and Mrs. Matthews" and listed their address. I knew then what it was, but I couldn't stop myself. I tore open the envelope.

It was Dave and Avery's wedding announcement. I'd thought they were waiting to get married until June, but it looked like they'd changed their minds. I read the words printed on the silver-edged page. The date: December 15. Too early for me to make it to the reception—I'd still be finishing up finals. I felt a little wave of gratitude for that. The temple: Seattle Washington Temple. Their names: David Gideon Sherman and Avery Camille Matthews.

And the picture, a black-and-white shot of the two of them. Dave, grinning at the camera with that same grin I'd known for years. Avery, looking beautiful and slender, holding his hand and smiling too. They were standing together on a dock, water in the background. It was a great picture. I was surprised how much it hurt me.

"What is it?" Shannon asked, sensing my anxiety.

"Dave's wedding announcement." I held it out to her.

"Oh, wow," she said, looking at the picture. "I thought they weren't getting married until June."

"Guess not," I said a little shortly. She started to hand it back but I gestured toward the table just inside the door. "You can just stick it there. I'd better get going or I'll be late."

• • •

I sat in the car for a minute to assess the damage. Once the initial shock of seeing Dave and Avery's engagement picture wore off, I realized that I was going to be okay. The old wound still ached a little, more than I'd expected in fact, but I was going to be all right. I was tough.

In a way, it was good that the announcement came when it did, I decided. I'd been starting to fall in *like,* I guess you could say, with Joel. We worked together all week and had a good time, and we had fun every Friday night. Especially last week, when we'd stood side-by-side in the dark at the Plantations, not touching, but close. I'd caught myself wondering if he felt the same little charge of electricity in the air that I did.

Well. I didn't want to go there again, not when I was going to graduate and move in a few months anyway. Even though the ache from the breakup with Dave wasn't an open wound anymore after so many months, I still wasn't ready to be hurt that badly again. I wasn't *completely* sure if Joel even thought of me as more than a friend and I certainly wasn't going to bring up the topic with him. But just in case, I was going to have to keep our relationship businesslike. We probably did spend too much time talking and joking around after we'd covered the basics, and I probably shouldn't have had him read my application essay for the master's degree at Syracuse. But he was so easy to talk to about almost everything. With him, I seemed to talk and talk. He drew me out by listening better than anyone I knew. And we *did* have fun together. But still. No more flirting. No more staying late and hanging out after all the seminary stuff was covered. The thought of losing all that hurt me, but I reminded myself how much worse it could be, how much it *would* hurt later if we did end up dating.

Because, let's face it, with me, relationships always ended in a breakup. And my family didn't have such a fabulous track record with commitment, either.

When I got to the classroom, Joel jumped up from his chair. "Hey!" He sniffed the air. "You smell good." He reached into the bag and started helping me set out the containers.

"I think it's the food," I said bluntly. I had to keep it formal right from the beginning. "I have somewhere I need to be later tonight, so we should probably keep this short."

"Oh. Okay," he said, sounding a little surprised. My tone had been sharp. I felt mean, but I wasn't quite sure what else to do. He was quiet as I divided up the food for us onto the little paper plates and handed him his plastic silverware. "Thanks," he said.

After I'd blessed the dinner, we started talking. We'd spent a lot of Fridays together, eating take-out dinners in that seminary room, laughing about the students or worrying about them or trying to figure out the best way to teach a particular section of Doctrine and Covenants. But I'd put a damper on the night's festivities. We went through the plans for the next week and talked about a couple of points we'd like to emphasize and agreed that things were going smoothly for now.

I stood to leave. "Okay," I said. "That sounds good. You've helped a lot. I'll see you at Church on Sunday, right?"

"Right," Joel said. He cleared his throat. "Andrea, I wanted to ask you something."

Oh, *no.*

"There's a dinner at this conference that my department's having and we're all supposed to bring a date. I wanted to ask you if you'd like to come with me." Joel smiled at me a little nervously. He didn't seem *too* worried about being turned down, but he wasn't being cocky. He was just being normal. He was a guy, I was a girl, we got along well and had a good give-and-take when we talked. His only mistake was that he didn't know whom he was dealing with.

"I'm sorry," I said to him, and I was. "I was in a long-distance relationship not that long ago and I don't really want to go anywhere near that again."

Joel blinked. He seemed to turn that over in his mind and didn't say anything for a minute. "Okay." He frowned a little. "But we live in the same town. It's not a long-distance relationship."

"Yeah, but I'm going to graduate in six months and leave. You still have a few more years after this one."

"I know," Joel said. "But I didn't think that would matter. We could cross that bridge when we came to it." He shook his head, confused. "I'm not asking you to be my girlfriend. I'm only asking you out on a date. You've gone out with other guys in the branch—"

"I'm sorry, Joel," I said. "I don't think it's a good idea."

"Okay," he said softly. I waited for him to argue with me or try to convince me otherwise. He didn't.

I tried to joke with him. "It's a conflict of interest, anyway. We have to remain absolutely professional at all times, remember? What would the seminary kids think if we were dating? They'd go crazy. Crazier than usual, that is."

"It's all right," he said. "I just thought I'd ask."

Neither of us knew what to say or do after that, so I grabbed the empty Thai boxes and threw them in the trash. Joel was still looking away and I wasn't sure what else to do. So I left, hesitantly.

I looked back at him when I got to the door of the seminary room, trying to think of something light-hearted to say, but he was still sitting there, and all I came up with was, "See you." He responded the same way. I walked out to the car alone. It was weird, after the past two months of walking out together and then standing next to our cars in the parking lot, talking for a while and laughing. Even though there were plenty of cars in the parking lot, it still felt strangely empty.

• • •

I didn't go home immediately. I went back to the library and studied for a while, and then, when I couldn't concentrate at all anymore, I decided to call Mikey as I walked back across campus toward my car. It only took two rings for her to pick up.

"Hello?" she answered cheerfully.

"Hey, Mikey," I said. "It's Andrea."

"Andrea! I was going to call you earlier, but I was worried it was already too late there and you'd be out on the town."

"No, I've just been studying. I got something interesting in the mail today."

"Dave's announcement, right?"

"Yeah. When did you get it? Did you know they were getting married in December?"

"I got it today, but no one checked the mail yesterday, so it probably came then. I had no idea they'd moved up the wedding!" She paused. "Are you okay?"

"I think so," I said. "It was kind of a surprise, though." I tried to laugh. "It sort of threw me for a loop."

I heard a guy's voice in the background. "Oh, I'm sorry! Are you busy right now?"

"I'm kind of on a date," she said hesitantly.

I felt like an idiot. "Oh, Mikey, I'm so sorry! It *is* Friday night." I felt sheepish. "I'll let you go."

"Are you sure?" she asked, concern in her voice. I guess I wasn't covering up my emotion as well as I thought I was.

"Of course," I said, and I even managed a convincing laugh. "I'm sorry again about bothering you."

"It's no problem. I'll call you tomorrow," she promised. "We have a lot to talk about. Did you know Julie got her mission call to Scotland? I'll fill you in."

"That's great," I said.

"Talk to you soon!"

I put the phone away. At least I wasn't the only one surprised by the wedding announcement. A cluster of people passed me, laughing and talking on their way to some event on campus. I walked faster toward my car.

• • •

When I got home, Emma and Shannon weren't back yet from their nights out. I sat on the couch and thought about what had happened tonight, about Dave and Avery, about Joel. I decided that I should tell Emma everything, that she should go ahead and go for Joel since nothing was going to happen between the two of us. Maybe something good could still come of this whole situation.

"Joel asked me out today, and I told him no," I said to Emma later that night, as she got ready for bed. I leaned in the doorway of the bathroom, trying to act unconcerned about the whole thing, like it wasn't that big of a deal. She looked over at me, as if to gauge if I were serious or not.

"Why did you say no?" she asked. "Andrea!"

"I said no because there's no way it would ever work out."

"That's such a lame reason!" she told me. "You don't know that it won't work out. Not until you try, and I *know* you like him. It's so stupid."

This wasn't the reaction I'd expected from Emma at all. My defenses came up. "No, it's not. It would be too awkward—dating plus teaching seminary. It would be like dating someone at work. There's probably a rule against it anyway."

Emma muttered something that sounded like, "You're so frustrating."

"Why am I so frustrating?" I asked her, standing up straight.

"Because I like him but now I know that he likes you. There's no way I can ask him out. Not now, when I know he's interested in you. I'd rather have a fair chance, thank you very much." She shut the medicine cabinet door hard. I was shocked at the force of her anger. Was this how our long friendship was going to end? Messed up by a fight over a guy? I hadn't pictured the conversation taking this turn at all.

"So you wanted me to go out with him?" I asked. "How would that have been good for you exactly?"

"Because then you would have given him a shot, and if it didn't work out, then maybe he'd ask me out, or vice versa. But by turning him down, I'm pretty much guaranteed to be nothing more than a rebound opportunity."

I shook my head, baffled. I couldn't believe that we were fighting, actually fighting, over a guy. A guy that neither one of us was actually dating in the first place.

"You still don't get it, do you?" Emma asked. I shook my head, not trusting myself to say anything. I was angry, and I don't do a good job of being angry.

"You act like you're too good for everything, like you're so far above everyone else that you don't even have to try." She was getting into it now. "You act like you are way too busy and way too perfect to give someone a shot. So what if your heart got broken over Dave? It's happened to all of us. You have to pick yourself up and try again." She stopped and glared at me, but before I could say anything, she started up again. "I take that back. Your heart probably wasn't broken at all. Your pride is probably the only thing that *really* got broken." And she marched off, slamming her bedroom door more loudly than necessary.

I stood there in shock. I'd never, ever seen Emma act like this. The door to Shannon's room cracked open and she peeked out at me.

"Are you okay?" she asked.

I shook my head, not trusting myself to speak.

Emma and I have been friends since freshman year, which, in college life, is a small lifetime. We'd been through it all together— the stress of starting college, being some of the few Mormons in an atmosphere full of underage drinking and promiscuity. We'd been through sad breakups and stressful finals and family problems and identity crises. She'd helped me through the rough semester after Dave.

I started to go back into my room, but Shannon didn't move. "What she said about you being too good for everyone and about your heart not being broken isn't true," Shannon told me sympathetically. "She's mad and hurt and she's had to play sidekick to you for a long time. She has a huge crush on Joel and that's what made her say those things. But you're a good person, Andrea. You know that, right?" I nodded because that was what she wanted me to do. She gave me a hug. "We'll talk tomorrow. We'll work it out." I hoped she was right.

I felt horrible and exhausted. "You stink at life, Andrea," I told myself as I climbed into bed.

A few of the things Emma had said rang true. I *had* felt all noble and self-sacrificing, telling her that she could go out with Joel after all. And my pride had been hurt a lot by Dave, more than I wanted to admit.

Wonderful. Now my mind was running at a million miles an hour again and wouldn't let my poor, exhausted body sleep. Who could I call? I cursed my stupidity again. I couldn't call Joel. I couldn't talk to Emma or Shannon. I didn't want to bother Mikey a second time in one night, especially when she was on a date. I thought about calling my mom for a second, but vetoed that idea, too. I wanted to write to Ethan, but that wouldn't be fair. I'd already unloaded enough on him with the Dave breakup, and he had a mission to focus on that was a lot more important than my pathetic dating life.

Thinking of Ethan made me wonder how Mikey's date with that other guy was going. I selfishly hoped it wasn't going well. I didn't want my brother to get hurt. The thought of that happening to him made me sad.

I was also sad that I had hurt two people that I cared about. I felt so frustrated that I wanted to cry. I thought I'd made a lot of progress over the past few years of being more friendly, more accessible, less prideful. I knew I wasn't Miss Congeniality, but I thought I'd finally shed the Ice Princess nickname, one that I hated so much it still caused me to grind my teeth when I thought about it. But still, after more than three years in Ithaca, I only had a few close friends—Joel, Shannon, Emma. And I'd alienated two of them in a single night. It seemed that I hadn't changed so much after all.

Although, I realized as I curled up on my bed, there was one thing that had changed since high school. Now I could, and did, cry myself to sleep.

NOVEMBER, ITHACA AND BOSTON

Joel Hammond

As I taught seminary the last, cold day before Thanksgiving break, I kept catching myself looking back to the last row, corner seat, the seat where Andrea usually was. She had left early to spend the holiday with her roommate Shannon and her family in Allentown, Pennsylvania, and her absence was strange. It was the first time she hadn't been in class all year. Even though it had been awkward the past few weeks, it still felt odd that she was gone.

Ever since she'd shut me down when I asked her out, I'd been trying not to glance back at her for those exchanges—smiles, raised eyebrows, a nod or a shake of the head—that we'd gotten used to during the lessons. Apparently if I was going to stop liking her as more than a friend, it was going to require a lot of effort. Maybe that was why I kept catching myself glancing back there now, because I subconsciously knew it was safe with her absent.

It was hard to get over someone you saw every day. Every time I saw her, I realized that she was still as cute as I thought she'd been. Maybe even prettier. And more than that, she was obviously crazy smart, and she always made me laugh. And even more than *that,* there was something about her that turned her from cute and smart and funny into cute and smart and funny—and can't get her off your mind.

I'd spent a lot of time thinking about what might impress Andrea Beckett. And I came to the conclusion that nothing would impress her. Nothing would change her mind. She's not going to wake up one day and decide that yes, she wants to date me after all. It's hard to let go, since we're still meeting Friday nights for our seminary planning and sometimes there will be these moments where it's like it used to be those first two months, where we're both laughing and on the verge of teasing or flirting, and then we both remember that things have changed, and it's serious again.

After class, Cate and Steve came up to talk to me. It had been a sparse class, a lot of the kids had left early for Thanksgiving break. Ben was gone, Heather was gone; there'd only been four in class that day.

"Hey, you two," I said. "What's up?"

"We've got an idea," Steve said.

"How worried should I be?" I joked.

"Not that worried," said Cate. "It's a really good idea, if I do say so myself."

"We've come up with an idea for the holiday class activity," Steve said. "It's going to rock your world."

"What do you have in mind?" I asked, grinning.

"A service project," said Cate, in that declarative voice of hers. "We've got an idea for it, but it's got to be a class project."

"Do you have a plan already?" I asked. Knowing Cate, it was a pointless question. Of course she had a plan.

"Yeah. It's simple. We'll have everyone donate what money they can, and then we'll take Christmas to a needy family as a surprise." She pulled out a piece of paper from her pocket. "I've already talked to Bishop Wilkes to see if he knew of a family, and he had one in mind. They're not members, but he knows them from his son's school. Their house just burned down. They're not very well-off and they don't have a ton of insurance, so they lost a lot of things. Bishop Wilkes and his family have done some stuff to help them, but he thinks an anonymous act of service would be the way to go, which is exactly how we want it to be anyway. I've got all the information."

"That sounds perfect, Cate," I said. "It sounds like you've already gotten the ball rolling."

"I'm getting there. I've been working on it for a while, and I thought Steve should be involved since he is class co-president." She shot him a look, which he chose to ignore. She added, grudgingly, "It was Steve's idea to do it a few weeks before Christmas instead of on Christmas Eve. That way they'll have presents under the tree to look forward to during the holidays."

"Pretty good idea, huh?" Steve grinned. He beamed proudly at Cate, and she tried to ignore him, although I could see that she was trying not to smile.

"I'm glad you're doing the project early," I said, "because Sister Beckett and I will both be out of school and gone by Christmas Eve. Do you need me to do anything? I can give you some extra time in class on Monday to announce it. And of course I'll donate and help with the shopping and everything."

"That's all we need," Steve said. "We're actually sort of organized, between Cate's tendency to obsess and my brilliant ideas."

Cate rolled her eyes but remained silent.

I congratulated myself silently on mine and Andrea's own brilliant idea of asking those two to be seminary co-presidents. It could have been a complete debacle, and at first had seemed to be going that way, but now, instead of antagonizing each other and bringing the class down, they antagonized each other and came up with service projects. Good for them.

"Sounds great," I said, moving toward the door along with them. I hit the lights and locked the door. We walked toward the parking lot together. It was snowing. As I turned toward my car and they headed toward theirs, I called out, "That's really a cool thing you guys are doing. I'm proud of both of you. Happy Thanksgiving!"

Cate waved at me as she walked toward her car. "You too, Brother Hammond."

Steve was still hanging around. His huge down winter coat made him even bigger. I thought, not for the first time, that it was a good thing Steve liked me because he could take me out without any trouble on his part.

"Hey, Brother Hammond," he said. "Do you have anywhere to go for Thanksgiving? You could come to my house. We're having the missionaries over and you could come too."

"That's nice of you, Steve," I said, touched by the thought, "but I'm going to my brother's house in Boston for the holiday. In fact, I better take off right now before this storm gets any worse."

Steve nodded and waved good-bye.

I scraped off the snow that had fallen on my car during class and double-checked the trunk to make sure I hadn't forgotten my bag. I climbed in my car, starting the heater and turning on the radio. Bob Dylan and I headed out into the snow.

It felt good to have someplace to go. By the time I passed through Whitney Point, the weather had started to ease up a little. The light snowfall turned into a stray flake here and there, so faint and delicate they could have been my imagination. I stuck a piece of gum in my mouth to help me stay awake as I drove and turned up the heater a little. It would take about five or six hours from start to finish to get to Boston, depending on weather and traffic. So far, it looked like I had the holiday traffic beat by a few hours. There weren't many other cars on the road.

This was my first Thanksgiving away from home, aside from the two I spent in Texas on my mission. I hadn't had enough money to fly home for both Christmas and Thanksgiving this year, and Christmas was the clear winner. Plus, Seth had invited me to spend Thanksgiving with him when he'd heard I'd be moving out to New

York. I was grateful for the invitation. I still felt more homesick than I'd expected. I wasn't exactly sure how things would go being a guest in my brother's home for the first time in several years. For the first time since he'd been married, actually. I'd only seen him when he'd come back to Utah for holidays and reunions and vacations. Now, I would be on his home turf and that was new.

After a couple of wrong turns and a few times re-reading the directions, I pulled into Seth's driveway. He lived in a suburb of Boston in a nice little house that probably cost plenty of money. There was already a Christmas wreath on the door and lots of snow in the yard.

I climbed out of the car and stretched. Then I picked my way carefully through the icy slush to the trunk. I was reaching into the back to grab my bag when the front door opened. I looked over to see Seth and his whole family standing there, beaming at me. Seth was yelling something, then started waving and crossing the yard. His wife, Maura, leaned against the door. His two kids, Henry and Celia, were hopping up and down with excitement. It was nice. It had been a while since anyone had made such an event of my arrival anywhere.

"Hey," Seth said, as he got closer. He slapped me on the back and took my bag from me. "Good to see you. Did you have any trouble with the directions?"

"No," I said, lying a little bit. "It was fine. Thanks for having me."

"No problem. You can tell we're all excited. It's the first time we've had anyone stay during the holidays. Usually we're on our own or back in Utah visiting the rest of the family. Kind of makes the holiday seem real, you know? We're glad to have you."

I was surprised. Aside from that first question, he was treating me like an adult, and he really seemed happy to see me. "I'm glad to be here," I answered. "How are all of you guys doing?" I asked as we approached the steps.

"We're doing really well," Seth said. "You haven't heard our big news yet, have you?"

I didn't think so. I shook my head. Had he gotten another promotion?

"We're having another baby in February," he told me. Maura grinned, and the kids latched onto me in an enthusiastic hug. "We wanted to tell you in person," he said. "So I warned Mom and Dad and Eli not to spill the beans."

"Wow, congratulations!" I said. "Maura, aren't you supposed to be showing by now? I couldn't even tell."

"Sweaters help with that," she laughed, and I noticed that she was wearing one of Seth's bulky cable-knit sweaters, one I remembered from when he lived at home. "And you're not going to be so thrilled because I'm *still* kind of queasy even though I'm almost six months along and *that* means you guys will have to do a lot more cooking."

"The turkey grosses Maura out when she's pregnant," Seth said, "so you and I are going to have to take care of it tomorrow morning."

• • •

True to his word, Seth enlisted me to help him with the turkey as soon as I'd finished my breakfast with the kids in the dining room. We walked into the kitchen together. The turkey lay there, bulky and enormous, luxuriating in the sink in a bath of cold water. "Maura says it'll be defrosted by now and should be good to go," Seth said, prodding it with a fork.

"All we have to do is stick it in the oven, right?" I said, heaving the turkey over onto its belly in order to read the directions on the label. It was like rotating a whale. Some of the water slurped onto the floor.

"Pretty much," Seth said, grabbing a plastic oven bag. "She says that if you bake it in one of these bags, it's foolproof." He started to open the bag.

"Hold on. We have to take out the giblets and rinse it and pat it dry first," I told him, reading from the back of the turkey.

"Okay," Seth said, putting the bag down. "I guess we *should* read the directions since neither of us knows anything about doing this. I mean, I've seen Maura do it before, but I've never been at the helm."

"So who gets to pull out the insides?" I asked Seth, beaching the turkey onto the shore of the counter.

"Ugh," he said. "You don't think I can claim morning sickness too, do you?" He snipped the plastic webbing that encased the turkey and it sort of relaxed into a huge mound of pimply, whitish, purplish bird flesh onto the counter. I briefly considered vegetarianism.

"I'll do it," Seth said. "Since you're a guest and all."

"Thanks," I told him. I'm not a wimp, but I hadn't been confronted with that much uncooked meat in a while and getting the giblets out of there had to be at least a little unpleasant.

"If I remember right, to get the giblets out, I have to reach into its . . ." Seth trailed off.

"Body cavity, yes," I said, referring to the instructions again.

Seth made a face and rolled up his sleeve. He reached into the turkey, made a face at the squishy sound it made, and pulled out the bag of giblets.

"Ewww!" we both said, sounding more like teenage girls than adult men.

"How's it going in there?" Maura asked, peeking her head around the corner to tease us. "Are you two okay? I heard you yelling and squealing. What a couple of sissies."

"I'm holding giblets in my hand," Seth warned. Maura beat a quick retreat to the living room.

Seth tossed the giblet bag into the trash and we went on to rinsing. We weren't sure how to rinse a bird that size—now that it was free from its constraints, the turkey was impossible to completely immerse in the sink—so we sort of gave it a shower, spraying it off with the sink attachment. Then we heaved it into the counter.

"Now it says to pat dry," I told Seth.

We looked at each other, drawing a blank. "Like this?" Seth said, patting the turkey briskly. He turned it over and smacked the under-belly as well. "Do you think I have to hit it a little harder to get the water to come off?" he asked me, and he started to pat with a little more force.

"What you're doing is more like *slapping* the turkey," I observed helpfully.

Maura stuck her head around the corner again. "Remember to heat the oven to . . ." she trailed off. "*What* on earth are you two doing?"

Seth looked up, mid-pat. "Just patting it dry, hon," he told her, and she snorted with laughter. "*What?*" Seth asked.

"Try using a paper towel," she said, still laughing. A few minutes later we could hear her on the phone with her mom. "You'll never guess what Seth and Joel were doing to the turkey . . ." she said. Maura has one of the most contagious laughs I've ever heard. It kind of reminded me of Andrea's laugh.

"At least we cracked her up," Seth said. "That means my stupid-ity canceled out the gross factor for a second. I haven't seen her laugh that much in a couple of weeks. Of course I *would* have to be the cause." He shook some flour into the cooking bag and held it open. I wrestled the turkey inside.

"Oof," said Seth, as he took it from me. "This thing is heavy." He slung the bagged turkey into the pan with a satisfying plunk.

I opened the oven and we put the bird inside. "See you later," I said. "Make us proud." Seth closed the oven door and brushed off his hands with finality.

"Now what?" I asked Seth.

"That's it," he said. "In a couple of hours we'll have to keep the kids out of Maura's hair so she can get the side dishes finished. She made pies last night. Later we'll need to set the table, too. And we have to keep checking on the turkey. That's the important thing."

"There's a lot that goes into this," I told him. "You seem to have it down to a science."

"We've done Thanksgiving on our own for a couple of years so we're getting better at it," Seth said. "But usually I'm in charge of the potatoes and other stuff. This is the first time Maura's let me be in charge of the marquee dish, so I don't want to mess it up." He stretched. "I'll go tell her that all systems are go."

As he left, Henry wandered in. "What're you guys making?" he demanded. He was four and still wearing his pajamas, which were the kind with feet on them. His bed-head was even more awesome than mine is in the morning, and his breath was rank. And he was totally self-assured about the whole thing. Little kids are the best.

I opened the oven door and Henry looked in. "Wow," he said, awed.

"Wow," I agreed. "It's a pretty big dinosaur of a bird."

Henry turned his gaze to me, his eyes perfectly round, like kids on cartoons. "It's a *dinosaur?*"

Oops, I thought. "Well, what I actually meant was—"

Before I could get any further, though, Henry ran back into the living room to announce the presence of a dinosaur in the kitchen. Maura started laughing and reached for the phone again. Seth raised his eyebrows at me as if to say, "What kind of nonsense are you feeding my kids?" I shrugged. It's my job as an uncle.

• • •

Later, after we'd eaten our fill of dinosaur (which tasted great, I should add), Seth and I started setting up a board game in the living room. We were waiting for Maura to finish talking to her sister on the phone so she could come play too. I don't know what it was, if I'd been lulled into a feeling of security by all the food and football and family, but I wanted to talk to Seth about something personal. "I'm beginning to think none of this stuff might happen for me," I said, fiddling with the game's dice.

"What stuff?" he asked.

"All this," I said, gesturing around the house, the kids' toys on the floor, the dining room where we'd had a genuine family Thanksgiving. "You know, married stuff. I've bombed out with two different girls this year."

"I heard about Lauren," he said. "Who's the other girl? Was it the one who teaches seminary with you?"

"Yeah," I admitted. "It's that obvious?"

"Pretty much," he said. "Well, if they're not interested, it's their loss. I'm sure there's a girl somewhere out there who'd be interested in you," he joked.

"Easy for you to say," I told him. "You've never had a girl decide she didn't like you, much less two girls in the space of a few months. The thing that really stinks is that I never even got a chance with Andrea. I mean, come on. She wouldn't even go out on a single date with me."

"Man, you gotta keep trying," Seth said. "You think I had it all easy, but that's just because you were a little runt when I was dating. Girls threw me over all the time. I was even engaged at one point, before I met Maura, and that didn't work out. Don't you remember that?"

I shook my head, surprised. "No. When did that happen?"

"Maybe you were still on your mission. We dated for most of the year and got engaged in the spring. The actual engagement only lasted about a week, though. I bet none of us even had time to write and tell you before she bailed. She told me that she liked me, but not enough to be with me forever. You want to talk about something hurting like crazy? I didn't think I was ever going to get over that one."

"But look at you now. You have Maura—everything's great."

"Yeah, but I didn't know that at the time. You'll meet someone too, you just don't know it now. The only guarantee that you'll be alone forever is if you give up."

I groaned. "I know, you're right. But I don't think I have it in me right now. I've been burned too many times too close together."

"Fine, take a couple of months off, let yourself go. Eat a bunch of chips and watch a bunch of sports on TV. Whatever. But don't let it become a permanent state of affairs."

"All right," I said, with no intention of being sincere. I wanted to end the conversation before Maura heard us. Her voice had stopped in the other room, so I knew she was on her way in. But later that night I turned over in my mind what Seth had said about being alone and about trying again. I hadn't known about the broken engagement. I guess we all think we're the only one in the world who's been torn up and thrown away by someone we cared about.

• • •

I felt good about moving on from the Andrea thing the entire weekend I was at Seth and Maura's house. Running around with the kids, helping Seth paint the dining room, coming up with new ways to eat the leftover turkey—it all kept me busy and cheerful. But then I had to go home.

The dark met me halfway into the drive, but luckily it didn't snow. I flipped on the headlights and turned on some Coldplay. It was a perfectly clear and black winter night. I couldn't help but contrast it with all the warmth and light I'd left behind.

I walked into my apartment and felt even more depressed at the dinginess and the empty cupboards. Our apartment sits right on the edge of one of Ithaca's famous rocky gorges and sometimes you feel like you are going to go falling, falling down with nothing to catch you. Once in a while, I imagine that if I jumped too hard on the floor the whole building would just sort of sigh and slide down into the ravine, without even a crash or anything. But there are steel bars somewhere holding this place onto the side of the hill. It's been here for a long time and it's still standing.

My cell phone rang right after I set my bag down and turned on the lights.

"Hey," said Seth. "I'm checking to make sure you got there all right."

"Who are you, Mom?" I teased, but it was nice that he called.

"Could be," he said. He made his voice about an octave higher. "Have you eaten supper yet? Are you making a vegetable? Have you seen the dentist lately?"

I laughed at him. "Thanks for a good weekend," I said. "And tell Maura thanks for everything, too. I'm going to write her a thank-you note too. She's a good sport."

"Yeah, she is," Seth said. He paused, listening to someone in the background. "Oh, yeah. Maura says to tell you she stuck a paper bag with a dinosaur sandwich in the trunk with your other stuff." He laughed.

"Tell her it sounds great," I said. "Whoever cooked that thing really did it right."

Seth chuckled. "You've got that right. You hang in there. We'll talk soon."

CHAPTER 18

NOVEMBER, BRAZIL

Ethan Beckett

The letters started arriving around the time they'd be celebrating Thanksgiving in the US, and they kept coming until Christmas Eve. They weren't all actual Christmas cards. In fact, only one of them was, one of the middle ones, from a boy named Ben. But they all had something holiday-ish about them. Stickers, or being written in red and green pen, or a Christmas tree inked into the margin with a leaky ballpoint pen, or just "Merry Christmas!" at the end of the letter. There were fourteen of them—seven for me and seven for Elder Park—which doesn't sound like all that many, but when you're on a mission, seven extra letters over the course of a month is a lot. Seven extra letters equaled seven gifts, seven unexpected envelopes in the mailbox, seven things to make our days a little better.

Our mission president doesn't allow us to e-mail anyone except our families, and that only happens if you're in an area where there's internet access. I wasn't in an area with access, so I was even more dependent on the mail than usual. When I had been in the office, my parents and Andrea and Chloe had been able to e-mail me, but now we were back to regular old slow mail. At least our mail kept coming, though. The mail famine a few months ago, when Elder Vickers and I got nothing for weeks, was still fresh enough on my mind to make me grateful for what contact I did have. And I was especially glad to be hearing from everyone during the holiday season.

In Brazil, people start putting up their Christmas lights around the beginning of November so it feels like the holiday season is even longer. In one of my letters to Andrea, I'd told her that it feels like the holiday season is two months long here, and she had pointed out that that happens in the US too. "The Halloween stuff is barely down before the stores start stocking the Christmas decorations," she'd written, and I had to concede her point. "But it's different when you're away from home," I'd written back. "It seems like it matters more, or you notice it more, because the holidays are the times you usually spend with your family." She hadn't mentioned it in her next letter, so I figured she'd gotten sick of my whining about Christmas. Little did I know she had something up her sleeve.

• • •

When the first letter came and I didn't know the person whose name was in the top left corner, I almost threw it away, wondering if it was some kind of joke. Then I saw the city and state: Ithaca, New York. That made me curious, so I opened it up. The paper was white with blue lines and three holes along the left side, the edge was ragged like it had been pulled out of a notebook. It was written in blue ballpoint pen, leaky blue ballpoint pen, because there were a few smears on the paper. In the margins, the author had doodled a snowman, a Christmas tree, and a stocking. It was a Christmas letter, even though it was still November. That much was definitely clear.

Dear Elder Beckett,
You don't know me, but your sister Andrea Beckett teaches my seminary class. She told us that the holidays are sometimes rough for

missionaries and said that any of us could write to you or your companion instead of writing in our scripture journals during class. I thought I'd give it a try today because I couldn't think of anything I wanted to write in my journal today, and because I have never written to a missionary, at least not that I can remember. So I hope I don't mess up.

How is your mission going? Are you having fun? Sister Beckett said that you are in Brazil. Do they speak Spanish there or something else? What do you do for Christmas when you are on a mission?

I think missionaries are great and I hope that you are having a lot of good luck and success in your work there. We'll all be praying for you here in seminary. We pray for all of the missionaries. Some of us are going to be missionaries someday. Keep up the good work!

Sincerely,
Heather Wythe

I folded up the letter and put it in my scriptures as a bookmark so that I would remember to answer it the next P-Day. I grinned to myself, thinking of Andrea teaching seminary and telling her kids to write to me. I wondered if anyone else would do it, or if they would all prefer to write in their journals instead.

I didn't have to wait long. The second letter arrived the very next day, the same day Elder Park got his first letter too. Both our letters were from a football player named Steve. His handwriting was big and blocky and he must have been left-handed, because some of the ink was smudged where his hand had dragged along the page. (Being left-handed myself, I notice that kind of thing.) The letter he'd written me was on the same kind of blue-lined, three-hole-punched paper:

Dear Elder Beckett,
What's up? My name is Steve Ward and I hope you are having a sweet time in Brazil. I'll be on my mission soon so let me know if you have any advice. Right now I have to make it through seminary though. Your sister is tough. She makes us write in journals and memorize

scriptures and plenty of other stuff. I'm sure it will come in handy on the mission someday.

Your sister is doing a good job with a tough crowd. There are only seven of us who come to class, and we've all been together in the same ward for years, so sometimes seminary can feel like it's an extension of Young Men's or Young Women's or something. Actually, some days it's probably more like an extension of Primary. Anyway, Sister Beckett and her partner in crime, Brother Hammond, do a good job of making us sit up and pay attention and not slack off. You can be proud of her. I'm sure you already know that. She talks about you a lot and I can tell she's proud of you. Keep up the good work!

If you get a chance I would like to hear what a mission is like. I'm planning on going on one but I'm sure I have no idea what I'm getting into. My dad served but that was about fifty years ago so I want to hear from someone who's gone recently. I've played football all through high school and I'll probably play in college, too, so I'm used to working hard physically. But what's it like to work so hard spiritually? How hard is it to learn a new language? I'm the oldest boy in my family so I'll be the first to go. Probably around this time next year I'll be sending in my papers. Crazy stuff.

I hope you have an awesome Christmas!

Steve Ward

While I waited for P-Day to roll around, I caught myself thinking all the time about how to answer their questions. When we went to meet an investigator and he was drunk and embarrassing his family, I wondered how to tell Steve about something like that. Should I tell him how hard things were, like the time Eduardo didn't show up for his baptism? Or what about the family who was so interested the first few times we visited, but then talked to other people and decided that the Church was evil? "I'm sorry, we can't be associated with you any more," the father had said, politely but firmly, and shut the door as we stood there on the doorstep. Thinking about that still called up a hollow, sick ache in my chest.

No one had told me these kinds of things, specifically. They had told me general things, like "It will be hard," or "Your mission will be the best and the worst two years of your life," but no one had gotten down to specifics. Even Dave, the few times he'd written, had simply said, "It was a rough week." Or maybe they had told me. Dave might have said, "It was a rough week because an investigator we had didn't get baptized," and I hadn't known the agony that would be behind those words. I hadn't known what those words meant, until I'd experienced them myself. Isn't that the way it always is?

Of course, you can get to feeling good again pretty fast—all it takes is a great discussion, a promising street contact, a baptism, or a comfortable meal talking and laughing at a member's house.

Elder Park and I started hurrying to the mailbox to see if either of us had "seminary mail." For a while, I was ahead in the count, but then he got four letters in one day.

"Are you going to answer each of these individually?" he asked me.

"That's what I was planning on," I told him. "What about you?"

"Yeah, me too," he agreed. "I mean, how can you not when they took the time to write?"

My next letter, the one from a kid named Ben, was a piece of plain white paper folded lengthwise to make a long, skinny Christmas card that fit in a regular-sized envelope. He'd written "Merry Christmas" in red and green marker on the front and drawn a picture of some holly underneath it. Inside was almost nothing but questions:

Dear Elder Beckett,

Merry Christmas. I am one of your sister's seminary students. My name is Ben Allen. I have some questions for you. How long have you been on your mission? Do you like it? Does it ever get too hot there? Do you like the food there? Do you like the people there? Do dogs chase you? Have you gotten fatter or thinner on your mission? Do missionaries really get Dear John letters? Do you want to go on another mission when you are older and have a wife?

Merry Christmas and good luck.

Ben Allen

After Ben's letter, I got one from a girl named Melissa, in handwriting that appeared to be a computer font, it was so tiny and precise. Hers was the first letter written on actual stationery, the kind with envelopes that match the paper, and her writing was more formal than the rest of them had been.

Her brother's letter came a few days later. His handwriting was less precise and his letter was a little less formal. The sister–brother relationship reminded me of Andrea and me. She was always going first and leading the way, too.

Six days before Christmas, my second-to-last letter arrived, from a girl named Camille. This one was on pale purple paper folded in some sort of complicated way. It took me a while to figure out how to even open it. At the top of the paper, she had drawn a picture of a palm tree with Christmas ornaments hanging on it and presents stacked underneath.

My last letter arrived in the mailbox on Christmas Eve, which was great because it was the most Christmassy letter yet. The envelope was bright red and there was a sticker of Rudolph the Red-Nosed Reindeer with a very glittery red nose stuck to the back:

Dear Elder Beckett,

If you had to choose one thing to take out of a burning building, what would it be? (All of the people and animals are already safe.)

I always ask this question to break the ice. I'm convinced it can tell you a lot about a person. Who knows if you'll have time to write me back, but if you do, let me know your answer.

I'm Cate, and I'm a senior in your sister's seminary class. We're studying the Doctrine and Covenants right now and it's nice because so many of the Church History sites are only a couple of hours away, it makes it easier to picture the events and everything. Have you ever been to the Sacred Grove? You should, if you haven't. It's a really amazing place. I wish there were a better way to express that, but I'll have to leave it at that. I feel lucky to have been able to go there so often growing up. It's one of the best things about living here, and there are a lot of awesome things about New York!

What are some of the awesome things about Brazil? Do you get to stay in any one area long enough to get attached to it?

I hope your mission is going well. My two older brothers both served missions and I know it's a lot of work. We pray for the missionaries in seminary almost every day. And remember, people in all the temples across the world are praying for you, too. That's what my mom always told my brothers and they said it helped. Merry Christmas, and good luck in the New Year.

> *Sincerely,*
> *Cate Giovanni*

P.S. I would bring my journal. (If I could grab just one thing out of the burning building.)

I liked writing back to the students. It was a good chance to reflect on some things as I thought about how to answer their questions. Even after I'd put the letters in the mail, my answers stayed in my mind, and I turned them over and over again:

My mission is going well. I am having fun, but it's a different kind of fun than I've had before. We speak Portuguese in Brazil. Learning a new language was one of the hardest parts of the mission for me, but it's true that the Lord will bless you if you work hard.

For Christmas, we open our presents, call our families, eat Christmas dinner with some of the members. We also try to do something helpful, some kind of service activity, for the people here, talk to some people about the gospel. When I write it out that way, it probably doesn't sound very different from what you do, too.

Working this hard spiritually is more draining and more exhilarating than anything else I've ever experienced.

I've been here for a year and a half, and I love it, even though it does sometimes get too hot. I love the food—most of it—especially the fruit. Yeah, dogs chase us sometimes. We do get Dear John letters.

I would love to go on another mission when I'm older and have a wife, but I have to finish this mission first before I think about another mission. Or a wife.

There are tons of stories or experiences I could share. Some of them are among the best experiences of my life—like seeing an entire family step into the waters of baptism one after the other, or playing baseball with some kids in the branch, or running through the streets of Brazil while it was raining, or giving the mission president a blessing. But some of the experiences are more painful—a man deciding not to be baptized, finding out that a companion didn't like me. But, bad or good, each experience is part of my mission experience as a whole and has made me grow.

We do read the Doctrine and Covenants on our mission, but we really focus on the Book of Mormon.

I have never been to the Sacred Grove. I hope to go there when I come back to the United States. It is one of the places I most want to visit in my life.

The most awesome part of Brazil is the people I've met here—both the people who live here and the missionaries I've served with. I've gotten attached to every area I've been in while on my mission.

P.S. If I could only bring one thing from a burning building, I would bring my journal too, my missionary journal. There's no way I want to forget anything that has happened to me here, even the hard stuff. I want to hang onto these memories for the rest of my life. At the beginning of my mission, it felt like it would never end and I would never get to come home. Now it is going by much too fast, and I wish time would slow down.

CHAPTER 19

DECEMBER, ITHACA

Caterina Giovanni

I was so excited about our service project that I got to our meeting spot in the mall before anyone else did, and for once, I didn't have Ben in tow. I stood by myself, waiting for everyone else. I couldn't wait to get going because we had a lot to do in one night. We had to pick out all the gifts, take them back to my house, wrap them, and deliver them. Sister Beckett and Brother Hammond were going to meet us there for that part, and I didn't want to keep them waiting.

Since there were only a couple of weeks left before Christmas, and since it was a Friday night, the mall was packed. The bell ringers for charity were especially enthusiastic with their bell ringing. The contrast between cheerful people and grumpy, stressed-out people was more and more evident as I studied the faces walking by me. I sighed impatiently and turned to look back at the entrance again. I was surprised to see everyone except Steve headed my way.

"Hey!" I called out to them, waving. "Did you all come together?"

"Me and Jason and Heather did," said Melissa. "We ran into Ben and Camille in the parking lot on our way."

"It figures Steve would be the last one here," I muttered and regretted it almost immediately. *That's no way to start a service project, Cate,* I told myself.

"There he is," said Ben, pointing. "And he brought someone else with him."

"Who?" I asked, turning to look. And my jaw dropped. "Oh," I said. And I *really* regretted bad-mouthing Steve earlier. Because walking next to him was Sarah Wren. I'd mentioned the service project to her earlier, but it looked like Steve had actually convinced her to come or picked her up or something.

"Who is it?" Ben asked me.

"It's Sarah Wren. Don't you recognize her?"

"Oh, yeah," he said, comprehension dawning. "Wow! Does this mean she's coming back to Church? Is she's going to start coming to seminary?"

"It means she was willing to give the service project a shot," I clarified, speaking as quickly as I could before they reached us. "What it means is that we are all really nice to her but don't make a big deal out of it and scare her off, okay?" Luckily, everyone nodded in agreement. It even seemed to get through to Ben.

"Hey, guys," I greeted them. "Are you ready to get started?"

Steve, standing behind Sarah, grinned at me and raised his eyebrows, wanting me to acknowledge how awesome he was for getting Sarah to come along. I ignored him, of course.

Sarah stood with her hands in her coat pockets, looking casual like she usually did, but also a little uncomfortable. "I have somewhere I need to be in a few hours," she said. "Plus a paper to write." She and I have English together and we talk now and then about homework so I knew which paper she meant. It wasn't actually due for another week, but I could tell she wanted to have an out if she needed one. We needed to move fast to keep on schedule and I didn't want to give her a chance to get bored and leave.

"Okay," I said, reaching into my purse and pulling out envelopes. "We're going to work in pairs. I'm giving each pair an envelope with the age and gender of the person you're shopping for written on the back. There are four people in the family, so it works out perfectly. For example, my partner and I will be shopping for"— I looked down at my slip of paper—"a ten-year-old boy. You also have a few items listed that you'll need to get for the family. We're getting them a little tree, for example. Your budget is written on the top of the paper and the money is inside the envelope. We'll meet back at my house in an hour."

"Who's with who?" Sarah asked. I was wondering the same thing. I had planned on grouping Melissa, Jason, and Heather together and giving them two envelopes, but having Sarah show up changed things. I had to think fast and shuffle it around.

"You're with Steve," I said. That seemed like the safest bet since he'd been the one to get her to come. "Melissa will be with Camille, and Jason will be with Heather." Oops. I'd left myself with Ben. Oh, well. I handed each pair an envelope.

Steve grinned as he read the back of his envelope. "This is awesome," he said. "We get to pick out stuff for the littlest kid in the family. She's six. This is going to be great. We can get her all kinds of stuff, a bike or something . . ."

Sarah caught my eye. "I'll try to keep him under control," she said.

"*Thank* you," I said. "That's why I put you two together." Then I added to everyone, "And remember to get the practical stuff too. I mean, of course toys are good, but each of your lists has a practical suggestion that I got from Bishop Wilkes, so make sure you include that in your budget. Like our kid, for example, needs some clothes for school, so we'll need to look for that."

Ben and I grabbed a shopping cart and started through the aisles of Target, the mall's biggest store. We didn't say much at first, sort of like our rides to seminary in the morning. It takes Ben a few minutes to warm up to a conversation. Having him follow me around all of the time and knowing all his idiosyncrasies was kind of like having a little brother. It was actually probably a *lot* like having a little brother. He was kind of sweet and helpless, but half the time he made me so annoyed I didn't know what to do with him. Like now. He insisted on holding the list and walking right by me. I was getting a little claustrophobic, plus we weren't moving fast enough for my taste. I tried to send him off to look at clothes while I checked out the toys, but I should have known better. He wasn't about to do something that required that much autonomy.

Ben followed me into the toy aisle.

"Okay," I said, suddenly glad he was there as I stared at the display of hostile looking superheroes and miniature, chromed-up cars and trucks. "What on earth can we get him?" I asked Ben. "I thought toys would be the easy part, but none of this stuff looks right."

"I don't know," he said. "It's been a long time since I was that age."

I looked at him, wondering if he was serious. He's barely fourteen, barely taller than any of the girls his age, endearing and awkward and only able to talk to me because our families have known each other forever. He was studying our list without any hint of irony, so I decided he *was* serious.

"Come on, Ben," I said. "Help me out. At least you *were* a ten-year-old boy at one point. I don't even have that to help me here."

"Ummmm . . ." he said, looking at all of the stuff. "None of this looks good. Maybe we should get him a gift card."

I groaned. Forget what I said earlier about Ben being endearing. There's a fine line between endearing and maddening and Ben seems to cross it, frequently. "Ben, that's the whole point of this. We want to get them *actual gifts*. All I know from the info Bishop Wilkes gave me is that he likes sports, he needs some school clothes, and he's ten years old. You have to help."

"Well," Ben said, scrunching his forehead in thought, "I guess when I was his age I was really into Pokemon."

"You would be," I said under my breath.

"What?"

"Nothing," I sighed. "Any other ideas, before I grab something off the shelf?"

He shrugged. "What about the sporting goods aisle?"

"It's worth a try," I told him. When we got there, I saw one of those basketball hoops that you can hang over the back of a door. It came with a couple of little basketballs. "What do you think about this?" I asked Ben.

"That works," he agreed.

"Great," I said and tossed it in our cart. We headed over to the clothes. This was easier because the bishop had written down the boy's size and some specific things he needed (a hoodie, some T-shirts, socks). I held up the options and Ben vetoed them if he thought they were dumb. The ones that were "not dumb" were the ones that made it into the cart. We were finished with the hard part, to my relief. The rest, the gifts for the whole family, would be easy.

"That wasn't too bad," I said, looking at my watch. "We're doing good on time, too. Let's pick up some Christmas candy and the tree and we'll be out of here." We were in charge of buying a small fake tree for the family. That didn't take long because there was only one that fit into our budget.

I pushed the cart toward the cash registers and Ben wandered along next to me. While we stood in line and I piled the items onto the moving belt, Ben seemed to be deep in thought. He wasn't helping me at all. I made an unnecessary but dramatic "oof" sound when I lifted the tree box onto the counter. Still nothing from Ben.

"What's up, Ben?" I asked. "How about a little help here?"

He picked up a bag of Christmas candy and slowly set it on the belt. He still seemed to be thinking about something. "You know that question you're always asking people? The one about which thing they'd save?" He set a single spool of shiny ribbon precisely on the belt while I loaded the rest of the items onto the counter.

"Yeah?" I said, shoving the empty shopping cart forward.

"You should ask these people because they actually had to do it. What did they save?"

"Good point," I said. I thought for a minute, looking at him. The cashier asked me how I'd like to pay for the items in a tone that said this might not be the first time he'd asked that question today. I hurried and paid for everything and Ben and I pushed the cart back to the car together and loaded it up, Ben actually managing to pull his weight this time.

Different cars were converging at my house by the time we arrived. I could see other cars already in the driveway and all the lights on the ground floor were lit up. The Christmas lights that my dad had strung up in our yard twinkled in the snow. I gave a little sigh of happiness. Ben looked over at me.

"It's so Christmassy," I explained to him, and his face lit up in a grin, too.

"It sure is," he said. We sat there for a second, watching people carrying in armloads of shopping bags and wrapping supplies and food and candy and decorations. Then we climbed out of the car and went in, too. We weren't the only ones in a good mood.

"Hey, guys!" Steve called out from the kitchen where he had already started eating the Christmas cookies provided by my mom. We were the last to arrive, except for Sister Beckett. The doorbell rang, and I went to answer it.

It was Sister Beckett. "I'm sorry I'm late," she said. "I was trying to get a package mailed to my friend Julie before the post office closed at seven. It's a Christmas package, and it had to go all the way to Scotland, so I wanted to get it in the mail today. Anyway, it took longer than I thought. I'm sorry."

"Don't worry about it," I told her. "We're just getting started. Come on in." She followed me into the kitchen. It was kind of weird having the seminary teachers at my house. Sister Beckett stood there for a minute looking awkward, while my dad hung up her coat. Brother Hammond waved at her from the living room, where he had started sorting out the gifts.

She smiled hesitantly at him. Then she turned to me for direction. "You guys did a nice job," she said, looking at the mound of presents. "Should I start wrapping?"

"Yes, please," I said. I *hate* wrapping presents. Buying them is a lot more fun. In fact, more than once, I'd taken a gift right to the person and given it to them immediately, sometimes even forgetting to take off the price tag. I'm not that patient when it comes to gifts. Especially when I know I've gotten someone something they're going to love. I've been known to give people their birthday presents weeks before their birthday because I couldn't stand waiting any longer to see them open it.

Sister Beckett took some wrapping paper and ribbon to the dining room table and people starting bringing her gifts to wrap. The guys—Steve, Jason, and Ben—were doing their usual Sister Beckett drift, where they all kind of wander over to see what she's up to. It looked like she would have some help with her project. She started showing them how to make perfect corners, but she wasn't as uptight as she is in class, and when Steve joked with her, she actually laughed. A Christmas miracle.

Brother Hammond looked for a second like he wouldn't mind joining them, but instead he came and sat down with me and Heather and Sarah to put together the food basket. I introduced him to Sarah and he was perfect. "Nice to meet you," he said, and he kept making friendly jokes, but didn't freak out or make too big a deal that Sarah was there.

Sarah, for her part, had finally relaxed and looked comfortable setting all the food in the basket and arranging it to look right. "I'm going to tie a bow around some of the bigger boxes," she said. "That'll make it look more like a gift and less like a bunch of groceries plopped down on their doorstep." She gave me a questioning glance. "That is what we're doing, right? Leaving it on their doorstep and then ringing the doorbell and running away?"

"That's the plan," I told her.

"Great," she said. "I think I'll stick around for that part, too. That should be fun."

As I went back to the pantry to get some more treats for everyone, Brother Hammond caught my arm. "This was a wonderful idea, Cate," he said quietly, for about the thousandth time, and I beamed, for about the thousandth time. Brother Hammond is so sincere. "It's nice to have everyone here." He nodded slightly at Sarah.

"It is," I agreed.

• • •

Finally, we were ready to take everything over to the house and we loaded all of the gifts into Steve's car and all the people into a couple of other cars. I must have checked the address from the bishop about fifty times, and I'd even done a drive-by earlier in the day to case the joint. The family was living now in a duplex on a quiet street in town with lots of trees and shrubbery to hide behind . . . perfect for our purposes.

Once we were there, we started Operation Drop-Off, as Steve insisted on calling this part of the project. He had begged to be in charge of taking the presents to the door and was even wearing camouflage cargo pants with his huge puffy jacket. He had enlisted Ben's help. Even when I'd pointed out that Ben could be clumsy, Steve had held firm.

Steve and Ben parked next door to the family's house and flipped off the car's headlights. When the trunk popped open, I whispered, "It's time," and we all ran quietly to our hiding spots, crouching behind garbage cans and mailboxes and trees. Steve gave us a little wave and he and Ben each lifted some of the gifts. They needed to make a couple of trips to haul everything to the door before they could ring the bell. This was the part none of us wanted to miss, the part when we watched from our hiding places and saw the family open the door and find Christmas all wrapped up on their porch.

I held my breath as the two of them carried the presents up the stairs and put them in front of the door. I was crouching behind a row of prickly bushes, poking my head up enough to see what was happening. Sister Beckett crouched next to me, grinning like a kid. It was dark and cold, but I could almost feel the smile on everyone's faces. I looked over and saw Sarah and Melissa crouched behind a garbage can. They were both beaming, too.

After a couple of trips, Ben and Steve made the final trip up to the door. It was time for them to knock and run. The rest of us squished even closer together in our hiding spaces behind the bushes. I was glad it hadn't snowed since yesterday and the sidewalks were clear. We needed to make a quick getaway.

"No, no, no," Sister Beckett said under her breath. "They're not even trying to walk quietly. I can hear them from here. What a couple of elephants." She muffled her laughter behind her hand. She was right. Steve and Ben were marching up the few steps to the door—pound, stamp, shuffle, pound—without trying at all to be stealthy. But when they set the last of the gifts and the food basket down, they did it very quietly, so at least they got that right. Steve raised his hand to knock on the door.

Suddenly the porch light flipped on. Everyone froze. "Oh, no," I said, and Sister Beckett caught her breath. Steve and Ben looked at each other and I saw Steve's lips move. Then they started running down the steps, making a colossally loud sound, which meant that they really *had* been trying to be quiet earlier because this was deafening.

The door opened behind them and a man yelled, "Hey!" By then they were down the stairs and heading down the driveway.

Steve and Ben kept going, running right past us, down the road. One by one, we all popped up from behind the bushes and started running too. Sister Beckett and I lasted the longest, then we looked at each other and jumped up too. We didn't say anything. I can only imagine what we looked like to the man on the porch. First there were two kids, then four, then more and more and more, emerging from the bushes and taking off into the night. None of us looked back to see what he was doing. No one even talked. Everyone just ran as fast as they could.

Sister Beckett was beyond fast. She was almost to the end of the street before she looked back and noticed that no one was keeping up with her. Without missing a beat, she checked her speed, turned around, and ran back. She wasn't even breathing hard. She had almost caught up with Steve, and he's known for his sprints down the football field *and* he'd had a head start on her. Brother Hammond was bringing up the rear, jogging next to Heather, who wasn't moving as fast as the rest of us. We made it around the corner and to our cars, and there were met with an interesting sight.

Steve was standing at the end of the street, throwing up as only a guy can do, lots of output without a lot of extra noise. It was impressive. Gross, but impressive.

"Oh, no!" said Sister Beckett. "Are you all right?"

Steve nodded, standing up. "Too much eggnog and too much excitement," he said. "Let's go back to Cate's!" Everyone hopped into the nearest cars, not paying attention to who was riding with whom, terrified that the family would catch us. Steve actually peeled out as he drove away and I shook my head. The sound of squealing tires was *so* not inconspicuous.

But no one chased us. We were still undercover. Operation Drop-Off was a success. I guess you don't try so hard to follow someone when you trip over the presents they brought and realize it's not a prank or an intruder. Still, I was relieved. The whole point was to be anonymous and it would have been awful if we'd been caught!

Ben and I ended up in Sister Beckett's car, along with Brother Hammond. I hopped in the front with Sister Beckett. We laughed and talked about our near miss for a while. Ben drew Christmas trees and snowmen with his finger on the condensation on the inside of the window.

I am determined to crack the Sister Beckett façade and see what she's really like under there, even though she refuses to give any of us an ounce of personal information. The guys think it makes her mysterious that we don't know that much about her. I think it makes her just plain frustrating. I don't need to hear her life story every day she teaches, but I keep feeling like she's not putting any of herself in her teaching. If she never shares her personal experiences or insights, how can she expect us to share *our* experiences or insights? She doesn't know it, but that's the reason we all respond so much better to Brother Hammond, even though she probably has more natural ability as a teacher. Although Brother Hammond does have that nice deep teaching voice . . .

"Sister Beckett, can I ask you a personal question?" I asked, when we'd finished talking about what had happened at the house and there was a lull in the conversation.

Sister Beckett turned to look at me, a little surprised at my question. Then, in typical Sister Beckett fashion, she said, "You can ask. I might not answer." I can never tell if she's serious or joking, so I plowed ahead.

"If there were a burning building, like with this family and their house, and everyone else was safe but you were the last one, what would you grab before you ran out? What would you save, if all the people and animals were already safe?"

Sister Beckett didn't even seem to consider the question at all before she answered. "Nothing. I'd just run."

I was surprised. No one had ever given that answer before. It made sense, though, considering I'd seen how fast she could run. "What about you, Brother Hammond?" I asked. Brother Hammond gave it a little more thought, as Sister Beckett steered us toward my house and into the driveway.

"Well," he said as Sister Beckett turned the car off, "I think I'd grab my emergency backpack."

"Your emergency backpack?" I said.

"Yeah. It has a 72-hour kit and a folder with copies of important documents and a first-aid kit inside. And some water. A while ago, President Hinckley gave a talk during the priesthood session of conference about being prepared. I ran across it again right before I moved out here and I thought I should probably do something about it. So I put together that backpack."

Sister Beckett looked at him. "Are you serious? You have an actual emergency backpack ready to go?"

I could see she had hurt his feelings somehow.

"Yeah," he said. "I can't help it. That's the way I am. Predictable and boring."

Ben looked up from his window drawings and looked at me quizzically. Even he had picked up on the fact that something was going on. I wasn't sure what, though. Sister Beckett tried to fix it.

"I think that's great," she said to Brother Hammond. "Really, I do."

He kind of smiled in response. "Sure," he said. Then he changed the subject. "What's the plan now, Cate?"

We went inside the house to watch *It's a Wonderful Life*. Steve, none the worse for wear, replenished his eggnog supply. Sarah agreed to stay for the movie. I would have suspected her of having a crush on Steve, except he is very much not her type. She's more interested in the cute class president/newspaper editor kind of guys.

Sister Beckett and Brother Hammond excused themselves and went home in their separate cars. I guess they felt like it would be weird if they stayed, but it would have been fine. As is usually the case with movie parties, we all ended up talking through most of the movie instead of watching it, except for Heather and Steve, who'd never seen it before. They ended up sitting with their noses almost against the TV to watch and tune the rest of us out.

Some friends of Sarah's arrived to pick her up right as the movie ended. "Thanks for everything," she said to me. "This turned out to be really fun. I'm glad you guys told me about it."

"Thanks for coming," I told her. "See you in English Monday."

"See you," she said. "Bye Steve! See you, Melissa! Bye everyone!" she called out as she left, and everyone responded.

Steve was the last one to leave. He hung around helping me pick up the popcorn and cups from the floor and put the leftover treats back in the fridge. "How did you get her to come?" I asked him. "I invited her, but she was pretty noncommittal about it when I talked to her."

"Sarah?" He started to grin. "I went over to her house and asked if she wanted a ride to the seminary service project tonight. She looked kind of surprised but then she said sure. She called her friends and told them she'd be late." He shook his head. "And then she used some of her money to help buy the stuff. That's how we were able to get so much food. She really wanted to help."

"Way to go the extra mile," I told him. "I didn't even think about going by her house. I guess I thought she wouldn't come, especially on a Friday night."

"It was a long shot," he said, "but I'm glad it worked. She had fun, don't you think?"

"Yeah," I said. "I think she did."

• • •

After Steve left, I started thinking a bunch about Brother Hammond and Sister Beckett. I had moved into the dining room to clean and noticed that Sister Beckett had taken care of all of the wrapping mess in the dining room before she left. I appreciated that. I wondered if she and Brother Hammond had had a good time. It must be kind of hard to be their age. I'd never thought about that before. They don't fit in with the teenagers anymore, and all their own friends from high school are far away, back in whatever towns they came from. Hopefully they had plenty of new college friends, but they also seemed like they might both be loners, though for different reasons.

I wondered what I would be like after high school. For the first time in my life, I wondered if I was a loner. I don't think so—I have a lot of friends, even though I'm not what you'd call popular, in the sense that I don't hang out with the typical popular crowd. But my friends are people I've been around for a few years, at least, and so I've never had to start all over making friends, the way you have to do if you go away to school. I can never tell if the idea of starting over again like that appeals to me or makes me nervous.

Would it be so wrong to stay at home and go to school? Would that be taking the easy way out? It's split about 50–50 with my high school friends. About half are staying at home, working at jobs or going to one of the colleges around here—the community college, Ithaca College, Cornell, or Binghamton. About half are going farther away, either away in-state or to colleges out of state.

I can't decide what to do. The rest of my family all ended up at BYU, so part of me wants to do that, too. But part of me wants to stay here, where I know everything and everyone, where I don't have to try to figure out who Cate Giovanni is, because everyone already knows.

Still, do you ever *really* know who someone is? Sarah and Steve had both surprised me tonight.

CHAPTER 20

DECEMBER, ITHACA AND SEATTLE

Andrea Beckett

The morning after the Christmas service project with the seminary kids, I woke up with a blah, yucky, something-is-off feeling. That's not usually the feeling I get after a service project, so I knew it had something to do with something else, something other than the service project itself—namely, the situation with Joel. I tried to fall back asleep since it was only eight o'clock on a Saturday morning, the perfect time to catch up on all the sleep I'd missed over the past week.

But it wasn't meant to be. My mind wouldn't give me a break. I climbed out of bed and took a look out the window. When I saw that it wasn't snowing and that the roads were clear, I decided to go for a run. Neither of my roommates were up yet, and I knew very few college students would be conscious this early after a Friday night spent partying, studying, or working late. I would have the roads, the sidewalks, the trails, all to myself.

The air was frigid. I put on my warmest pair of running pants and layered a long-sleeved top and a jacket over my short-sleeved T-shirt. I hate running in a hat, but it was cold enough that I needed one or my ears would hurt the whole time. I found my gloves and pulled them on, then stretched in the living room so I could hit the ground running outside before the cold could get through me.

I started off running toward campus, and then veered off onto the trail around Beebe Lake. It was cold enough that the mud around the lake had frozen solid so my feet didn't sink into it, they pounded into it instead. I ate up that loop and ran it again, then headed off toward the Cornell Plantations where there were a few good hills to get my pulse racing. A car horn honked at me. I passed a couple of older ladies out for a jog, a man walking a sweater-wearing dog, some kids rolling up snowballs to make a snowman in a field.

I ran harder. Ever since I stopped running competitively and started running for fun, I have enjoyed it more. But once in a while, like today, I feel that urge to go beyond running fast to running wild, running a little too hard. That was what I did. I pulled off my hat and stuck it into the pocket of my jacket. I was fully warmed up now. I cut through the Plantations and across Route 366, then down a road that had a trail with a mile marked out on it. I clicked the timer on my watch and burned the mile, spending every ounce of energy I had. I checked my watch as I crossed the mile marker: 5:51. Not bad for being a good five miles into a run and being out of top competitive shape.

I leaned down and spent a few moments catching my breath. Then I started to jog slowly back toward my apartment to finish the long loop. It would be a long run back; I had burnt up most of my energy.

There was a couple walking and holding hands along the path. They were smiling at each other, and as I ran past, they both said, "Good morning."

"Good morning," I said back, darting out to the side and around them.

I wanted to be like that, didn't I? Then why wouldn't I let anyone in? Because of what happened with Dave, that's why. It had been great, but had fizzled and died over time. It didn't end in tragedy, it didn't end with a big scene and one of us getting mad at the other (which, like I've said, was how all my high school breakups had seemed to go, so at least I'd made some progress). But fizzling out still hurt. It had been mature, and a clean break, and very grown-up and cerebral and all of that. And it had still stunk.

Was that what had happened with my parents? I'd always assumed that there was some final scene that we kids hadn't witnessed, but maybe it had simply fizzled out. Something had gone wrong and had never been fixed. I was amazed that my parents were even willing to date other people again after going through something a million times worse than my breakup with Dave.

Maybe I needed a big scene. Maybe there was something cathartic about that for me and that's why I had created one all of those other times before Dave. I thought I was getting better, but then why wasn't I willing to go on a single, simple date with Joel Hammond? Why was I still thinking about this, weeks after he'd asked me out? It should be old news by now. But it still felt raw, like the wind that whipped my face. My ears were starting to burn. I wasn't running fast enough to keep the cold at bay anymore, so I pulled my hat back on and picked up the pace a little. I could tell I was going to be tired when I finished, which was good.

I was home. I stretched for a second on the curb, but without staying in motion it was too cold to stay outside. The wind cut through my jacket and I gave an involuntary shudder. I opened the door to my apartment and walked into my room, and then, with complete disregard for my poor muscles, I kicked off my running shoes and climbed back into bed without stretching, pulling my comforter over my head and staring at the way the light seeped through the fabric. I was trying to get warm.

I was tired enough from the run, from finals, from seminary, from not sleeping, that my guard was down and the answer to my question—Why hadn't I gone on a date with Joel?—finally made it through: I said no to Joel because Joel could hurt me, because I *could* like him. Going out with Joel would be opening myself up to liking Joel, maybe even liking him a lot. Going out with other guys was safer, other relationships were safer—I knew they wouldn't develop into anything else.

But Joel had potential. He was attractive, funny, and smart; we had chemistry. I watched his eyes when he taught. I knew the way he moved. I looked at him during class to see what he was thinking. Even after I'd turned him down, I hadn't been able to break myself of that habit. And when he wasn't looking at me, I wanted to get his attention. Joel! Look over here! I want you to notice what I'm doing, and help me figure out how to get better at this.

When he walked into seminary, I felt that little catch, the one I wasn't sure I'd feel again after Dave. When he said something to me at church, or asked me about something after seminary, I replayed things he said and the way he looked in my mind afterwards.

We still met to talk about seminary, but our meetings were brief these days. I missed the long talks about the students and about our teaching processes and about the lessons we were teaching. I missed the dinners on Friday nights in the seminary room. I missed standing by our cars in the parking lot and talking. I missed it all.

Every guy I've ever dated, I've let do most of the work. I've let them do the pursuing, even Dave. I mean, they can tell that I'm interested, I do know how to hint, but I never say or do anything big. I never put myself out on a limb. Was it time to do that with Joel? How stupid was I going to look? He hadn't said anything to me about going on a date since the night I turned him down. I knew that he had gone out with some of the other girls in the branch, including Emma once or twice, which had only made things even more awkward around our apartment. The night I knew he was taking Emma out, I made sure I was gone so I didn't have to watch the two of them together.

I'd been easy for Dave to get over—he'd gotten engaged only a few months later, for heaven's sake. I was sure Joel wasn't pining away after me.

I'd thought I'd been almost completely healed from the breakup with Dave, but healing from a heartbreak and feeling whole enough to risk another are two entirely different things.

I was starting to get warmer, so I poked my head out of the comforter and stared at the window, overhung in dripping icicles now that the sun was out. I'd been doing something suspiciously like pining for Joel.

Well then. I might as well do something about it. But what? It was almost Christmas, so I could give him something and write something on the card that let him know how I felt. The gift would have to be something meaningful, though. That was hard. The only time I could remember giving a particularly meaningful present was a homemade album I'd given Ethan for his birthday a few years ago. Ethan had loved it and I toyed with the idea of doing something like that for Joel, but couldn't think of what to photograph for him. I definitely wasn't going to stalk him and take *his* picture.

Finally, I remembered something Joel had said about the Sacred Grove in winter, how he thought it was even more beautiful then than in the summer. We'd had a beautiful snowstorm a few days ago, and the roads were clear. Today would be perfect.

I jumped out of bed, suddenly in a hurry to get showered and out the door before Emma or Shannon saw me. I wanted to get started as soon as possible and I didn't want either of them to ask me any questions. I showered, dressed, and threw my camera, some granola bars, and a water bottle into a bag and hurried out to my car, tossing the bag inside and turning the heater on. I'd made it. It would be a clean getaway.

Once the car was warmed up, I started the drive. The Sacred Grove is only about an hour and a half from Ithaca, but it feels like a longer drive, as you wrap around the lake and up through the string of small towns dotted along its shore. Not for the first time, I thought about Ethan and how I wished he could come to the Sacred Grove with me. I was sure he would, someday. But all I had right then was myself, so I went alone.

• • •

I pulled into the parking lot near the Sacred Grove, one of only two cars there. Although the warm lights of the visitors' center tempted me to go inside, I knew what I was looking for was out in the cold. I zipped up my coat, pulled on my gloves, and tromped through the snow with my camera to find the perfect shot. Sometimes looking through the camera gives you a different perspective. Sometimes not. Sometimes it looks exactly the same, only smaller and less exciting than the real thing.

There were a few images I thought might work: Snow lining each branch. The row of trees on the lane leading from the Sacred Grove to the farmhouse. The cooper's shop, with the door open and the wood looking warm and inviting against the starkness of the snow. A shot from the Joseph Smith farm, looking toward the spire of the Palmyra Temple. The white spire with its golden angel Moroni stood out even more against the dark, spiky, bare winter branches. My hands were freezing even inside my gloves, and the clouds over me started to block the sun. I didn't have much time before the best morning light was gone (or before frostbite set in). Still, I didn't rush.

I didn't see a single person while I was there. No one else was out. Even the missionaries who worked at the site were snug inside the visitors' center and the Joseph Smith home, and I didn't go in. It was the first time I had ever been to the Sacred Grove or the other sites without friends or family or even other people there. It was peaceful.

I turned from the farm and walked back down the lane from the farmhouse to the Grove. This time, I wasn't looking for pictures. I just looked. The snow was still fresh enough that it hadn't yet gotten crunchy, so it gave way easily beneath my feet. It might have been my imagination, but it felt warmer in the grove. I looked around to make sure I was alone and knelt in the snow.

Later, when I climbed in the car and turned on the heater, blowing on my hands to warm them up, I looked back at the Grove for a long time before I pulled out of the parking lot to go home. It was hard to leave the peace.

• • •

I toyed with the idea of turning the pictures into black-and-white prints for effect, but I decided I liked them better in color. I popped out the memory card from the camera and drove straight to the photo store to print them out. Finals could wait. Studying could wait. Papers could wait. Figuring things out with Emma could wait. I knew I wasn't going to be able to relax or think about anything else until I had finished Joel's gift, so I thought I'd better get on with it. The sooner it was done, the sooner I could stop acting pathetic and get back to being a focused, driven, mature college senior.

While I was waiting for the prints to be finished, I wandered around the mall looking for an album to put them in. I couldn't find an album I liked, so I decided to make one myself out of supplies from the craft store, like I had for Ethan.

It had been a long time since I'd been in a craft store and I got lost. I wandered around, stuck in a forest of fake flowers and wreaths and enormous painted wooden snowmen and Santas before a kind worker took pity on me and guided me to the cardstock and paper and string and photo corners. I gathered all my supplies and picked up the prints and went home to work. My roommates were both gone, studying at the library or out with friends, so I had the place to myself. I ate a bowl of cereal standing up to fend off hunger, but I hurried. I wanted to get started.

Like I said, it had been a while since I'd made Ethan's album, so I had to throw away my first attempt and go back to the craft store for more supplies. But I got it right, or close enough, the second time. I made the album small since there were only a few pictures. I didn't want it to seem too girly so I used a dark red color for the cover and framed each print with a simple black backing on white pages. I punched holes along the side and tied the whole thing together with some heavy string. It took some doing to get all the edges straight and to center each picture perfectly. I spent almost all afternoon and most of the night sitting at the kitchen table, measuring and cutting and gluing. Shannon and Emma both came home partway through the second round of album-making, but neither of them said much besides "Hello." They were in the throes of finals too.

"What are you making?" Shannon finally asked as I started to adhere the pictures to the pages.

"A book for someone," I said. I didn't want Emma to know it was for Joel. Their one or two casual dates hadn't turned into anything more and I wasn't sure how she felt about it. Emma didn't look up from the couch, where she was surrounded by textbooks and index cards and Kleenex. She had a rotten cold and it was only a matter of time before we all had it, the way it was going through the campus.

"You're sure spending a lot of time on it," said Shannon, coming over to check it out. "It looks amazing. Where are all these pictures from? I know this one is your temple, right?" she asked, pointing to the shot of the Palmyra Temple spire.

"Yeah," I said.

Emma came over to look too. "These are really good. This one is my favorite." She touched the page that had the picture of the lane on it. "Who are you making it for?"

I'm not a liar, even though sometimes it would be easier. "Joel," I said. Then, since I was being honest, I added, "I'm hoping it lets him know I regret saying no when he asked me out earlier this year."

Emma looked surprised. "You mean you do want to go out with him after all?"

"Yeah," I said, taking a deep breath. "In fact, I think I might like him."

I could feel, rather than see, Emma stop at the table, across from me. "So you're finally admitting it to yourself?"

I didn't expect to cry. I wiped my eyes angrily with my sweater sleeve so I wouldn't drip on the photos. I couldn't look up at Emma. "Yeah."

"Good for you," Emma said softly. I looked up at her. "I'm glad you're giving it a chance. If it works, great, and if it doesn't, then both of you can move on." She walked back over to her spot on the couch. I looked back down at the album.

It was the only bit of hope I had to cling to that Joel might still be interested—that "you can both move on" phrase. Maybe Emma thought he was still interested in me. Since it was all I had, I took it. I picked up the album and walked back to my room. I glanced at Emma as I went, but she was deep in studying. My first priority was this gift for Joel. My second was to think of something for Emma, even if it was something small. The little interaction we'd had that afternoon had given me hope that maybe things between us weren't beyond repair. Maybe enough time had passed. Maybe she and I could be friends again.

Finals were moving further and further down on the priority list.

· · ·

Later that night, after Shannon had left with Rich and Emma had crashed in her room with a killer migraine, I returned to the kitchen table to work on the hardest part of the gift. The card. I went through so many different versions of it that I finally ran out of time and energy. It wasn't perfect, but it was the best I'd done in about seven different drafts so I figured it was as good as it was going to get. It was definitely direct and to-the-point, almost embarrassingly so, but I didn't know what else to do.

I read it one last time:

Merry Christmas, Joel. I hope you like this gift. It's easier for me to write things than to say them, but this is still hard to do. I regret turning you down when you asked me out earlier this year. I would love to go on a date with you if you're still interested, even though I know that's a long shot. We have spent a lot of time together this year, and I've realized that I care about you as a friend, and as something more, too. If you're not interested, you can rip this up and we'll pretend it never happened.
Andrea

To make sure I wouldn't be tempted to change it, I sealed it in the last envelope I had, taped it to the gift, and wrote "Open on Christmas Day," across the front. That way he wouldn't open the present and card while I was there. I didn't think I could handle that. If I was right there, he might feel obligated to ask me out again, and even though I hoped he would, I didn't want it to happen out of pity. I wanted him to ask me out because he really, truly wanted to ask me out.

I tucked the card and gift in my backpack and went to work making Emma's favorite white chocolate cranberry oatmeal cookies. It was almost midnight, and I was exhausted, but there was no way I was going to sleep while there was still work to be done.

• • •

A couple of days later, Joel and I met at my apartment to discuss seminary stuff for the last time before Christmas break. We went over the outline for the first few weeks of January. My late nights were taking their toll on me and the cold I had caught from Emma had turned into an all-out winter special. I kept punctuating our conversation with sniffs and snuffles.

"So, when we get back"—sniff—"we'll pick right up here in D&C. What do"—snuffle, attempt at a discreet noseblowing into a Kleenex—"you think we should ask the kids to"—sneeze—"sorry about that" cough—"read over the break?" It was so bad it was almost comical.

I caught Joel looking at me with an amused expression once or twice as I hacked and sneezed through the meeting, trying to pretend that nothing was wrong. I had dressed with more care than usual—my most flattering sweater, my best jeans—but I might as well have worn my pajamas because my cold was doing its best to render me as unattractive as possible.

Do you like chapped red noses, Joel? I thought about asking. *What about bloodshot eyes? Do you like girls who have wads of used Kleenex in their coat pockets? Does seeing me like this make you glad I said no when you asked me out?*

It was a short meeting, even including all the time we wasted due to my constant trips to the bathroom to blow my nose. (I couldn't stand to do it in front of him, not when I was trying so hard to win points.) We were both worn out from finishing up finals and papers, and we both still had to pack up before we left for the holidays.

As he stood to go, he handed me a box. "I have this Christmas present for you." That was as good a cue as any.

"I have something for you too," I said, reaching into my bag and pulling out his gift. My hands were shaking a little, so I handed it to him as quickly as I could, sort of dropping it into his hands as if it were a hot potato. I hoped he wouldn't notice how nervous I was.

"Thanks," he said. He read the instructions on the envelope and looked a little surprised.

I wasn't sure what to do next, or where to lead the conversation—Did he want me to open his gift now? Should I try to explain his gift without giving away what it was?—but he gave me a quick hug, a guy hug, the kind where they sort of side-hug you with one arm around your shoulder.

"Are you okay? I mean, do you need me to get you some chicken soup or something?" he asked.

"No, thanks," I said. "You're nice to offer, but I'm going home tomorrow and my mom will take care of me, I'm sure."

"Okay," he said, looking a little unsure but deciding not to press the issue. "Thanks again for the gift," he added as he walked to the door. "Have a Merry Christmas."

"You too," I told him, and I stood there for a second as he walked down the pathway. It had snowed the night before and the sidewalks were slick, so he walked very carefully, setting his feet precisely in the footprints he'd made before when he came to the door.

When he got to his car, he looked back at and saw me standing there. "Merry Christmas! Get better!"

My throat was too sore to yell anything back, so I waved in return. I closed the door and watched him leave through the front window. The two little jets of light from the headlights on his car swooped and turned in our driveway and then he was gone.

Emma came out of her room, ready to leave for the holidays. "Did it go okay?" she asked. Our relationship was starting to thaw, just a little.

I nodded. "I think so," I told her. "I won't know for sure until he opens it at Christmas."

A horn honked outside the house. It was Emma's ride to the airport. She picked up her suitcase and started for the door. But before she left, she turned to me and said, "Merry Christmas, and good luck." I could tell she meant it.

I carried Joel's gift back to my room. At first, I planned to wait until Christmas to open it. It was only fair, since I had asked him to wait. That resolve lasted all of three hours. While I was packing to go home, I kept looking over at the package on the top of my shelf, wondering what was inside. Finally I sat down and tore it open, my heart beating fast, trying to breathe through two tissues stuffed in my nose.

It was a copy of the Joseph Smith biography that I had wanted to read as background for class. There was a card too: "Merry Christmas. I hope this comes in handy with teaching next semester. Joel." It was a nice gift, a thoughtful gift, but it definitely wasn't anything along the lines of what I had given him. I was glad he had given me something, because it made me feel less awkward, but now I was seriously worried for when he opened his gift. I wondered if he would really wait until Christmas. I wondered what he would do once he opened it.

Well, he would have a surprise coming for him. I hoped it was a welcome one. I didn't know if I felt better for having done something or scared. Or if I felt just plain sick. I blew my nose again, packed the book in my bag to read when I got home to Seattle, and went in search of some cough drops. I stuck a cherry-flavored one in the right side of my mouth and lodged a eucalyptus one in the left side. I dug through my desk until I found my plane ticket. I put it on the night-stand and set my alarm. I blew my nose one final time. It was time to go home.

• • •

By the time Christmas morning rolled around, my cold was almost completely gone, thanks to extremely sluggish behavior on my part and good caretaking on my mom's part. When I had arrived home, I'd felt like the living dead. I took up residence on the couch in the family room where Chloe and I played endless rounds of Uno and Monopoly together, while my mom did work for school and brought me orange juice and soup.

Mikey came over to visit a few times and we talked and talked. She'd been to Dave and Avery's wedding reception and told me all about it. I was surprised to realize that it was actually kind of fun to hear all the details. We also talked a little about the guy she was dating, but she told me it wasn't very serious. We had a good time hanging out and watching movies and writing letters to send to Julie. I ended up telling Mikey about Joel and the gift. She made me promise to keep her posted on how things went. It was easy to get better with so many nice people around me letting me be lazy. I contemplated getting a cold every holiday season but realized that wouldn't be fair.

So when Chloe bounced into my room and hopped on my bed at the unearthly hour of 6:00 on Christmas morning, I assessed the situation and decided that I felt 99% back to normal—except when I thought about a certain Christmas present that would be opened somewhere in Utah that day. Then I felt a little sick. But since there was nothing I could do about that, I didn't make Chloe go back to bed. We went into my mom's room and woke her up together.

"Let me call Paul before we start opening presents," she said to us groggily. "I promised him I would."

I expected Chloe to raise a gargantuan fuss since she's only nine and she really, really wanted to get Christmas started, but she didn't complain. I took that as a sign of how much she liked Paul, my mom's boyfriend of the past few months. (It seems so strange to call a forty-something doctor with three kids of his own a "boyfriend," but that's what he was.)

My mom hung up the phone. "He'll be right over. Let's get dressed and I'll stick the breakfast casserole in the oven, and then we'll be all set." Paul's kids were with their mom that Christmas, so we were the only game in town as far as he was concerned. I didn't mind having Paul over, but we were definitely not ready for combined Christmases with all the kids yet.

Paul knocked on the door about fifteen minutes later, which was a smart move since any extra time delay could have resulted in a downgrade in Chloe's affection. Chloe and I answered the door; apparently Paul still rated a little makeup as far as my mom was concerned and she was still getting ready.

"Hey!" he said to both of us. "Merry Christmas!" He was dressed in his hospital scrubs. "I'm on call," he explained to me.

Chloe, without preamble, told him, "Then let's go into the living room and get started."

I had thought all along that Chloe was excited about digging into the presents, which was what I'd been most focused on when I was nine, but I was wrong. When my mom came down the stairs and we were all together in the living room, Chloe indeed went right for the presents, but not for the ones that were for her. She had a box for each of us that she handed out.

"Open them," she said, her eyes merry and bright.

My box held a certificate saying that a $10 donation had been made in my name to the cancer research center where I'd interned after my senior year of high school. It was a place that was very important to me, even more so now that I wasn't going into medicine. It was a place where I had done a lot of growing and learning, where I had started to be able to look past my own pain and empathize with the pain of others (something I was still working on).

"Chloe," I said, "this is a wonderful gift."

My mom and Paul were looking at their certificates as well. Mom had tears in her eyes. "Thank you, Chloe," she said. I looked at her quizzically. "Chloe gave a donation in my name to the women and children's center," she told me.

"Mine was to the cancer center," I told her.

"Mine was to Doctors without Borders," Paul added.

We all looked at Chloe, who was blushing and grinning. "My Primary teacher said that we should try to think more about giving than about getting this year because that's what Jesus wants us to do. So I tried to think of good gifts for all of you. Then I heard one of my friends at school say that her family was giving money away to people or groups that needed it instead of buying a lot of presents. That seemed like a good idea because you'd still get a present from me but it's also giving to someone else."

"How did you manage to do all of this?" my mom wondered aloud.

"Dad helped me," she told us. "I had to let someone in on the secret. It was really fun driving around with him. He kept calling me an elf. 'Do you need to run any elf errands today?' he'd ask me." She grinned. "But he doesn't know that I got him one of these too. I donated some money in his name to that place that makes all those toys for kids who don't have any—the Happy Factory. I found their address online and sent them some money in an envelope."

"But where did you get the money for all these gifts?" Mom asked her.

"I've been saving my allowance for a while," Chloe said. "Plus my birthday money, you know."

"You used your *birthday* money for this?" I couldn't help exclaiming. It was one thing for her to ferret away her little allowance each week. That was unselfish enough. But to use her birthday money, too—that went right off the charts from sweet and cute into something you'd read about in the *New Era.*

For the first time, Chloe looked worried. The smile left her face for a moment. "Yeah . . . is that bad?"

I hopped up from the floor and gave her a big hug. "Of course it's not bad. It's wonderful."

She beamed. Then, turning back into a normal nine year old, she asked, "So . . . did you guys get *me* anything?"

Mom and Paul and I looked at each other and laughed. "Well, Chloe, you're going to be a hard act to follow," Mom said, "but I think there is something under this tree for you, somewhere."

I ducked my head under the evergreen branches and found one for her.

Christmas had officially started.

• • •

Chloe was unwrapping the last gift of the morning when we heard a electronic version of "Jingle Bells" ring out loudly.

"What's that?" I asked. "Chloe, is that something of yours?"

"I don't think so," she said. "Is it yours?" she asked my mom. My mom shook her head.

"Did someone sit on their keychain and set off the car alarm?" Paul asked helpfully. "You've done that before."

We Becketts may be book smart, but we're always a little baffled by any new technology.

"Is it your beeper, Paul?" Then I recognized it. "It's my cell phone!"

"Would you answer it, please?" my mom asked. Right as she said that, it stopped ringing.

"Who set my ringtone to 'Jingle Bells?'" I asked, digging through some of the wrapping paper in hopes of finding it.

Chloe got a guilty look on her face. "I did, but I forgot. It was last week when you first got here. Haven't you heard it ring since then?"

"I guess not," I told her, realizing that I hadn't gotten any calls in a long time. Since it wasn't ringing anymore, I was heading back to my spot near the tree when it started all over again.

"Andrea . . ." My mom had a touch of frustration in her voice.

I finally remembered that I'd left the phone on the end table to charge after I first got home. I waded through the wrapping paper to answer it, wondering who would call, twice, on Christmas Day. When I saw the number, my heart skipped a beat. It was Joel. For the past hour or so in the excitement of Chloe's gift and of Christmas, I'd actually forgotten about the gift I'd given him.

"Hello?" I said.

"Andrea," he said. "It's Joel."

"I am so glad to hear your voice." *That* came out of nowhere. Heads turned to look at me. My mom raised her eyebrows. Chloe asked, "Is it Ethan?!?" I shook my head at her silently. It suddenly became apparent to me that this conversation wasn't one I wanted overheard, so I moved toward my room. I could feel three very interested pairs of eyes boring into my back, following me up the stairs.

"Hey," he said, and I could hear the smile in his voice. "Merry Christmas."

"Merry Christmas to you, too." I was climbing the stairs as fast as I could. When I got to my room, it still didn't seem private enough. I cast my eyes around to find a better place.

"I loved your gift," he said. "I had to hide in my room to call you because I wanted to tell you that it was my favorite gift and it would break my mom's heart if she heard that. She put a lot of work into making me a cookbook for school because she thinks I'm starving. Anyway, it was beautiful."

"I'm so glad you liked it," I said. "And thank you for the biography." I sat down inside my closet, behind the clothes rack full of plastic-bagged prom dresses and my letterman jacket and the clothes I'd left behind when I went to college. I closed my eyes, as though not being able to see would somehow lessen the embarrassment that might be coming my way as a result of this conversation.

"I hoped you would like it," he said. "But I feel kind of dumb. Giving you something like that when you did something so thoughtful for me."

"Did you . . ." I wasn't sure how to ask this, except directly. "Did you read the card too?"

"I did." He paused. "I was about to bring that up. It was the part I liked best about the gift, actually. It gave me the courage to ask you a question."

"What's the question?" I asked, squishing myself even farther back into the closet, eyes still closed.

"Can I come visit you? This break is five weeks long and I should be working, but all I can think about is how much more I would enjoy the holidays if I could spend them with you."

My eyes flew open. Was he serious? He would come all that way to see me? It was too good to be true. All I'd dared to hope for, at most, was the chance to go out with him on a date when we got back to Ithaca. And now I might get to see him before then . . .

"Andrea?" he asked.

"Of *course* you can come visit me," I said. A heavy coat slid off the hanger and landed on my head. I batted it away.

"How long is the drive?" Joel asked.

"About twelve hours, give or take," I said. "It can get rough in the Oregon mountains, though. Have you checked the forecast? Do you know how to get here?"

He had, and he did. "It should be clear sailing. I'm borrowing my mom's car. I'll leave tomorrow morning and be there sometime in the evening. I've got your address and a map from online. I'll call you if I get lost."

"That sounds perfect," I said. I didn't know what else to say. I wanted to ask him lots of things all at once, but I also wanted to talk to him in person. It couldn't be a bad sign if he was willing to drive all that way to see me.

"I'll see you tomorrow then?" he asked. "I can't wait."

"I'll see you tomorrow," I said. We both said good-bye, and I sat looking at my phone until the light on the display screen faded and I realized I was sitting inside a very dark closet by myself, grinning like a madwoman.

I crawled out of the closet and marched down the stairs and into the room where Mom, Chloe, and Paul were starting to play a new game, Settlers, that we'd opened for Christmas.

"Okay," Chloe said, reading from the instruction sheet, "this is going to get complicated, so pay attention."

Before anyone could ask who had been on the phone or what was going on, I made a preemptive strike. "Joel is coming to visit tomorrow," I announced, and for once in my life I didn't try to play it cool. "I hope it's because he likes me."

For a minute, they didn't seem to know what I was talking about. Then my mom's brow cleared and she asked, "Joel is the other seminary teacher, right?"

"Right," I agreed.

My mom looked shocked, and then she laughed. "I think there's a good chance of him liking you, then, if he's coming to visit for Christmas."

"I hope so," I said. I felt so good I didn't know how to contain it, so I ran back up to my room, taking the steps two at a time. I picked up Joel's gift and looked at the cover again, flipping through the pages. It didn't seem awkward to look at anymore. It seemed immeasurably thoughtful, and hopeful. I started reading it right away so that I could tell him how much I loved it the next day when I saw him. *When I saw him.* He was driving all the way to see me.

• • •

Later that day, my dad arrived for Ethan's call, and we all talked to Ethan one after the other. Ethan sounded more reserved, more grown-up than the year before. It was wonderful to hear his voice. I couldn't believe it had been a whole year already. So much had changed since our last conversation for both of us.

I didn't want to pass the phone off to Chloe, to break the connection, but I did. Her face lit up the moment I handed her the receiver and she heard his voice. We all missed him.

After Ethan's call, Chloe and I went with my dad to his house for Christmas dinner. We opened presents and watched old holiday movies with him. He dropped us back off late and we were both good and tired. Still, if it hadn't been for my cold medicine, I probably wouldn't have slept at all that night. The anticipation was too great.

• • •

About 4:00 the next afternoon, my mom, Chloe, and I were chopping up vegetables and herbs for spaghetti sauce when the doorbell rang. We looked at each other. I didn't think it could possibly be him, not that early. He would have had to leave at 4:00 A.M. Still, who else were we expecting?

"I'll get it," I said, strangely calm as I wiped off my hands on a dish towel. I walked toward the front door, and as I got closer I could see someone with dark hair through the small frosted glass pane. I walked faster and opened the door.

There he was.

"It's me," he said.

"I see that," I said, smiling idiotically and holding the door open, not sure what to do next. (Inviting him in would have been a good place to start, I later realized.) What would he do? Play hard to get? Act cool until he knew exactly how things stood? Make me suffer a little since I'd given him the runaround?

But no. This was Joel, so he wasn't going to play games. He reached out and gave me a hug. Since I was standing a step up from him, inside the door, I was a little taller than him. Partway through the hug he stepped up so our eyes were right at the same level.

"You made it here earlier than I thought," I said. "We haven't even had dinner yet."

"I drove straight through after I woke up this morning. Well, maybe one little bathroom break in Boise."

My mom appeared in the doorway. I was surprised she'd held back that long. "Hi, Joel," she said, and I stepped back to introduce the two of them. I showed Joel where he could stash his bag in Ethan's old room, and then he came into the kitchen to meet Chloe. She was still sitting at the table, chopping away at the vegetables, pretending to be very busy. She looked up when we entered, her eyes bright. "Hi!" she said.

"This is my sister, Chloe," I said. "Chloe, this is Joel."

"Hi," he said. "It's nice to meet you. Thank you all for letting me come crash your holiday break."

"Have you ever been to Seattle before?" Chloe asked him. "Have you seen the Space Needle yet?"

"This is my first visit. All I've seen so far is the drive to your house."

"You should take him someplace before it gets dark," my mom suggested. "The Space Needle might be a little ambitious, but there's plenty of other things to see."

"Aren't you tired?" I asked Joel. "You've driven a long way today."

"I think I'm still running on adrenaline," he said.

"You could take him to Snoqualmie Falls," my mom said. "That's a pretty place, and you can walk a little on the path to get your blood moving again. Burn some calories so that you have room for dinner."

I borrowed the car keys from her. When I went out to the garage, I felt a little sad looking at the ancient Ford Taurus. It was yet another way my mom had sacrificed for me. She'd insisted I take the nicer car to school so I would have something reliable to drive in the Ithaca winters. I'd argued with her a little but had ultimately been happy to take her up on it.

"You'd think they were trying to get rid of us," Joel said as I started driving.

"I know," I agreed. "Maybe they thought we had things to talk about."

• • •

It's not much of a hike, walking to the Snoqualmie Falls overlook, but it's still a beautiful view, even in the almost-dark before night falls, which is early up here in the Northwest. No one else was at the overlook. I guess going to see a waterfall in the cold isn't everyone's idea of something fun to do the night after Christmas. All the rain we'd had lately meant that the falls were huge. They roared and bellowed and foamed over the edge, sending a cold spray right into our faces.

We had talked a lot in the car, chattered, almost, telling each other about Christmas Eve and family traditions and what we'd been doing since we'd last seen each other. But as we walked to the falls together, we didn't say a word.

It's always interesting to try on silence with someone. You know you've taken a step. Can you be silent together? Is it awkward? Will the person be offended by your silence, or you by his? Or does it feel okay, like you don't have to say something if you don't have anything to say?

I don't know what Joel was thinking about. But I know what I was thinking. It was as though I were standing right at the edge of that waterfall and knowing with absolute certainty that I was about to go over and it was both exciting and terrifying. I had chosen to be there, I had chosen to stand on the edge like this.

I had chosen to let myself fall in love again. I was going to open myself up to all the heartache and joy and hurt and pain and rawness and possibility again. I was going to do it because I wanted to do it. I had tried to shut myself away from it but it was too late. I would miss too much if I didn't give love another chance, I knew that now.

Joel turned to me. He had to lean very close to speak so I could hear him over the water. "Beautiful," was what he said.

"It really is," I agreed.

"I meant you," he said, and he brushed my hair away from my face.

I hoped that meant he was going to kiss me.

It did.

CHAPTER 21

JANUARY, BRAZIL

Ethan Beckett

Elder Almeida and I had given up. Not on the mission, not on each other, not on our investigators or the members. Just on sleep. It was almost midnight on New Year's Eve, and neither of us could get any rest with all the commotion going on outside. Elder Almeida was reading his scriptures, and I was writing down my New Year's resolutions. I had zero so far.

Even though it was New Year's Eve, we'd gone to bed at 10:30 P.M., the same as every night. But it was impossible to sleep. Motorcycles roared up and down the street, engines revving, people were singing, laughing. Everyone was trying to yell above the cacophony of the celebrations going on all around us. It was way too hot to close the windows to shut out the noise.

"This is impossible," Elder Almeida had said, at about 11:00. He got out of bed and flipped on the light. "I can't sleep, and I'm listening to everyone and all their bad language instead. It would be better for me to study the scriptures or something."

"Good idea," I agreed. I was tired of lying awake, listening to other people's yelling, other people's celebrations, when we were stuck inside. I reached for my scriptures, but changed my mind and got out my missionary journal instead. I wanted to write down all my resolutions for the New Year. There were only a few months left until I went home in early May (or June, if I was lucky enough to get an extension). I was determined to make every day count.

Elder Almeida went out to the kitchen and returned with two bottles of Guarana. "Happy New Year," he said, handing me one of them on his way back to the sofa where he was reading.

"Thanks, Elder," I told him. Our fridge wasn't working, so the soft drink tasted warm and slightly flat. I didn't mind. It still felt celebratory.

Before I started writing, I reread my last entry, the one from Christmas Day. Elder Vickers had been right. Christmas this year had been easier than last year. So easy, in fact, that I almost hadn't wanted to call my family. I didn't want to lose the groove I'd found after all this time. But, of course, I called them, and I was glad I did. If I hadn't, I would have missed out on hearing Chloe talk about how excited she'd been to give her Christmas gifts to everyone. I also would have missed out on hearing actual giddiness in Andrea's voice when she told me that Joel was driving all the way from Utah to visit her.

One of the reasons I didn't like thinking about going home was that I knew there would be a lot of change there. Chloe would have grown up. My mom was dating someone, a doctor named Paul. Andrea was about to graduate and start a real, adult life, and there was a new guy in her life, a guy I'd never even met. My pre-mission friends were all changing, doing new things. My latest letter from Mikey proved that.

Dear Ethan,

This is one of the last letters I'll be able to write before I leave for Mexico. It should get to you just a few days before I arrive in Colonia Juarez. The return address on this letter is my new one there, so make sure you write to me at the right place—I don't want to miss any letters!

Did you get my last letter, by the way? The one where I told you about coming home over Thanksgiving and hearing Julie speak at Church for her farewell? I've gotten a couple of letters from her now and it sounds like she's doing really well. She's about to leave the MTC in Preston, England, and go to Scotland. Have you heard from her yet? She said she was going to write to you and get some advice about being a good missionary.

I'm back home in Seattle now. I was lucky and didn't have any finals for my classes, just final projects that were due on the last day of class, so I got to come home early this semester. I made it just in time to go to Dave and Avery's wedding reception. They were so happy. Avery looked really beautiful. She had a really simple, pretty wedding dress and she wore little white flowers in her hair. (I'm sure you care about these little details.)

The reception was really elegant, but there were definitely some Dave moments, too. The wedding cake, for example—Avery must have let Dave pick it out because it was this huge, massive, chocolate cake covered with chocolate frosting and M&Ms. It was a really elegant cake and they had arranged the candy in a fancy pattern but it still had Dave written all over it.

At the end of the reception, Dave read Avery a poem he'd written for her and it was hilarious, but also really sweet. I saw Mr. Thomas there— can you believe he finally retired from teaching English?—and our high school principal, Principal Downing. She looks great—I heard her cancer is in remission. I stayed until the very end because I ran into a bunch of people from high school and it ended up being really fun.

After that, it was only a couple of days until Andrea got home from New York. She's pretty sick—she's got a cold—but she seems to be doing really well. She had a lot to say about Joel! He sounds like a really nice guy. I'm glad she's home over the break so we can hang out a lot. I've been getting advice from her about teaching. I'm starting to get so nervous about teaching my classes when I get to Mexico! Andrea had a lot of good advice (and some funny stories, too).

She and I talked about how crazy it is that it's already been three-and-a-half years since Julie's baptism. Can you believe that? Everyone is scattering and spreading out across the globe. It makes me wonder if we will all be in the same place at the same time again. Wow, I feel really lonely now after writing that. It's a good thing I'm setting off on my own adventure soon!

This has been a really long and rambling letter. I promise to be more cheerful in the next one! ☺

I've said it before and I'll say it again: I admire your courage in taking off for two years to do something worthwhile. I hope to do the same, in some small way. Thank you for everything, as always.

Love, Mikey

Dave was married. Julie was on a mission. Andrea had met someone new. Mikey would be in Mexico in a matter of days. I hadn't talked to her on the phone in almost two years; we'd just written letters. What would it be like to see her again? What would it be like to see any of them?

I loved my family and my friends, but I didn't know their day-to-day lives anymore. Seattle seemed almost unreal even though I could picture it in my mind. BYU seemed far away, too. The lives that seemed real to me now were the ones I spent the most time around: Elder Almeida, our investigators, the other missionaries in our area, the people on our street.

Another firework popped outside, reminding me of the ones the little kids had set off on Christmas Day. "Remember Christmas Day?" I asked Elder Almeida, and he gave me a look that said, "Of course I do."

"Remember those kids, with those fireworks?" I asked, and he started laughing. We had walked around a corner and right into some fireworks that a group of little kids were setting off. To their delight, we had both jumped a mile and yelled. They had followed us almost all the way home, laughing, saying, "Merry Christmas!" Now when we ran into any of them on the street, they'd ask me,

"Remember the fireworks, *Alemão?*" (They always call me *Alemão*, Portuguese for *German*, probably because I'm so pale.) Then they pretend to have more fireworks and pretend to throw them; Elder Almeida and I act all scared and pretend to run. The kids think it's hilarious. Elder Almeida and I wonder what's happened to our pride.

Before we'd run into the kids with the fireworks, we'd been walking home from taking a Christmas package to a family and heard a brass band playing "The First Noel." We stopped in the street to listen with a cluster of other people. The fat, round bass notes plopping out of the tuba hung in the air after they finished. They played a few more songs, then started packing up to leave and go to another street to continue. I couldn't stop myself. I wanted to hear it again. "Please," I said, pushing my way through the crowd. "Please, could you play 'The First Noel' one more time before you go?"

The trumpet player looked at the others, then shrugged. "Okay, one last time. But everyone has to sing along." And everyone did, or most of us, anyway. After the last note drifted off into the night, it was quiet for a second, and then everyone began to cheer and call out "Merry Christmas! Merry Christmas!" as the crowd dispersed into the night.

My journal page was still blank when the clocks struck midnight and the year changed. I wasn't watching the time myself, but we could hear people outside counting down. Then the whole street erupted in cheers, slightly apart from each other. The music became louder, and a new burst of fireworks went up, popping into the sky.

Elder Almeida raised his head and we both looked out our window. There wasn't much to see, but there was still plenty to hear.

"Happy New Year," he said to me, raising his soda in a toast.

"You too." There was one swallow of Guarana left, so I held it up in his direction.

After our makeshift toast, Elder Almeida teased me, "Maybe next New Year's Eve, you will be kissing a pretty girl at midnight."

I laughed, shaking my head. After that, we were both silent for a minute, listening to the people celebrating outside and wondering where we'd be the next year. At least that's what I was doing. Would I be home in Seattle for a visit? In Provo, working over the school break? Somewhere else, in some situation I couldn't yet picture?

The past year had definitely had some situations I hadn't anticipated, like being made financial secretary for the mission and working in the office, finding out what Elder Roy really thought about me, learning how to be a zone leader, and getting sicker than I'd ever been and spending three days in the bathroom. Still, over the past year, I'd also learned a lot about the gospel and about myself.

Elder Almeida sighed and stood up. "I think the worst of it is over now that midnight is past." He closed his scriptures and stretched. "I'm going back to sleep."

"I'm going to stay up just a minute more," I told him. "I'm almost done." I'd never actually started, but I knew what I wanted to write before I let the last year go into the past.

Under the heading of the date and place, I wrote one resolution, the only one that really mattered: "I resolve not to forget what I've learned here."

CHAPTER 22

JANUARY, SEATTLE

Joel Hammond

My last night in Seattle proved to be one of those nights. You know the kind—where you set your alarm for, let's say, 6:00 A.M. So, consequently, you wake up at 3:00 A.M., at 4:00 A.M., and then at an accelerated pace—5:13. 5:33. 5:41.—because you are absolutely sure that you are going to miss your alarm. When I woke up at 5:41 A.M., certain that it was 7:00 and I'd completely overslept, I gave up. I grabbed my towel and slipped into the guest bathroom to shower before the rest of Andrea's family was awake.

After I showered and dressed, I folded the blankets, cleaned up my room, and packed my bags. Then, I didn't know what to do. I sat there on my bed, looking at my suitcases, and checked my watch. 7:00 A.M. I couldn't figure out why I was waking up so early. I didn't want to leave. I really didn't want to leave. Then why was I waking up and acting like a kid on Christmas morning? I realized it was because I wanted to spend every last minute with Andrea that I could. I hefted the bags to my shoulders and walked downstairs. I'd sit in the living room and wait for her to wake up, and then I could see her right away, when she first came down the stairs.

At the bottom of the stairs, though, I almost knocked over Andrea's mom with my bags. "Oof," I said, lurching to a stop. "Sorry, Sister Beckett."

"Good morning, Joel," she said, smiling. "I think Andrea is out for a run." That surprised me—I'd assumed I'd be the first one up by a long shot, but the Beckett women had me beat. "Do you want to come help me make breakfast?" she asked.

Of course I said yes. I followed her into the kitchen. "What would you like me to do?" I asked her.

She looked at me thoughtfully. "Let's have you make the orange juice." At first, I thought she meant make it from concentrate, which even *I* know how to do, but she had something else in mind. She pulled out a juice squeezer and plugged it in. "There's a crate of oranges in the garage," she said. "Would you bring those in and cut them in half and juice them?"

The loud shrillness of the juicer made conversation difficult, so we didn't talk much. I sliced and juiced and tried to look friendly. Before too long, the noise woke Chloe up and brought her staggering into the kitchen, wearing sweats and a T-shirt and fuzzy bunny slippers, which I had never seen before in real life. I was glad to see Chloe. I hadn't wanted to miss out on saying good-bye to her, and unlike her mother and sister, she had a tendency to sleep in.

"Hey, Chloe!" I said. "Do you want to help me make orange juice?"

She gave me that direct, serious, squinty, slightly irritable stare of someone who has just woken up and can't quite make out what it is you're saying or what, exactly, you're demanding of them. After a minute, she said, "Yeah," and climbed up on the barstool next to mine at the counter. I handed her an orange half and slid the juicer toward her. She mashed the orange slice right on top and ground it into pulp in no time flat.

"Wow," I said, impressed. Even still half-asleep, she was about twice as fast as I was.

Sister Beckett smiled at us. "Chloe has it down to an art form," she told me, bringing a plate of pancakes to the table and covering them with a clean dish towel to keep them warm while we waited.

"I can see that," I said. "I'll stick to slicing them and keep out of her way." Chloe was still squinty and tired, but she cracked a smile at me and mashed the next orange down on the juicer.

We had finished the juice and were debating whether or not we should wait for Andrea when we heard the front door slam.

Andrea hollered, "I'll be right there. I'm just going to shower."

"Breakfast is ready, though," Andrea's mom called back.

"You guys eat without me," Andrea said. She popped her head around the corner and grinned at us. "I'll ruin your appetite if I don't rinse off first." She pounded up the stairs, taking them two at a time, from the sounds of it.

"Dainty, isn't she?" said her mom, rolling her eyes. "Let's eat, then." She offered a very nice blessing, making mention of their being glad to have had me there and praying that I would have a safe trip home.

• • •

After we'd eaten our pancakes and juice, Chloe and her mom left to run some errands. I think it might have been an excuse to let Andrea and me have some privacy to say good-bye. I thanked Sister Beckett and Chloe for being so nice, and they both hugged me good-bye. I checked my watch after they'd gone: 8:00 A.M. My 8:30 target departure time was not going to happen. There was no way I could only see Andrea for a pitiful, measly half hour before I left. I revised the departure time to 9:00. And Andrea teases me for not being flexible!

Before she left, Andrea's mom handed me a thick book bound in green leather. "Lakeview High School" was written across the front in gold. "This should keep you interested while you're waiting for

Andrea to get ready," she said, smiling a sneaky mom smile. "It's Andrea's high school yearbook."

I was going to start clearing the breakfast dishes, but I couldn't resist peeking at the yearbook. I had barely cracked the cover open when I heard the sound of feet on the hardwood floor in the hall.

Andrea came into the kitchen with her hair still wet, wearing jeans and a pale green sweater that made her eyes even more alive than usual. She smiled at me for a second, until she saw what I was reading. Then she moved fast, reaching over my shoulder and grabbing it away from me with a shriek.

"Who gave this to you? My mother?" she asked. She didn't seem too mad, and she bumped me playfully as she took the book away, so I figured we were all right.

I grinned. "She also told me a little bit about your high school résumé. You never said you were homecoming queen. Or valedictorian. Or the state cross-country champion."

"Does that matter to you?" she asked a little grumpily, plopping down next to me at the table, so close I could smell the shampoo she'd used. "Do you think the stuff you do in high school is that important?"

"Yes and no," I said.

"What do you mean, yes and no?" she asked, rising to the bait in spite of herself. "That's so enigmatic."

"Well, high school obviously doesn't define who you are for the rest of your life, or at least it shouldn't. You should make a lot of progress beyond high school—grow up, try new things, all that stuff. But you do take with you some of what you learned and who you were in high school, so in that sense it does matter. I know you at twenty-one, but part of you at twenty-one is who you were at seventeen."

"Okay, Joel," she said. "Fine. So what would your yearbook say? What would I find out about you in high school? Did they even have yearbooks way back then?"

I rolled my eyes. She always likes to joke about how I'm three years older than she is. I keep trying to remind her that a three-year age difference only really matters, say, in elementary school, when the gap is so huge. The gap seems to get smaller and smaller as you grow older and older. At my age, which Andrea assures me is elderly, you can even get to the point where you almost start thinking of your parents as your friends.

"No, seriously. I want to know. Did you do *anything* in high school? Or have you always been the shy guy?"

"I've always been the shy guy." I smiled.

"Driving up to visit someone in Seattle over the break doesn't seem shy to me," Andrea teased. "That seems really forward."

"That's me," I agreed. "I'm that kind of guy. I'm shy. I'm forward. I'm unpredictable and mysterious." I grinned.

She shook her head at me and opened up the yearbook. I slid a little closer to her. She held her long wet hair back with one hand and tried to hold open the book and turn the pages with the other.

"Allow me," I said, taking her hair. It was impossible to be that close to her and not want to kiss her. So I did.

"I haven't looked at this in a long time," she said. "High school's kind of a time I'd rather forget, except for my senior year."

"We don't have to look at this," I said, reaching forward to close it.

"No, it's all right," she said. "I wouldn't mind seeing it again."

There was a large picture of her a few pages in, a professional quality shot of her as Homecoming Queen. "Wow," I said. She looked beautiful, of course, and younger. She wasn't smiling, just looking directly at the camera, or something right past it, her face serious.

"There's a story behind that picture," I said, not asking.

She nodded. "It was taken right before I walked off the stage." She brushed her fingers over the glossy picture of herself. "I didn't have a date to the dance that night and I was under all this pressure from taking state cross-country and applying for scholarships and trying to be perfect. I was humiliated that I didn't have any real friends and sick of putting on an act for everyone. I was embarrassed about standing up there on the stage at halftime in front of everyone with no date. I had to get out of there, so once I got off the stage, I started running and didn't stop. I ran to the parking lot and ran into Dave and he gave me a ride home."

Dave. Were we finally going to talk about the elephant in the room? I knew about Dave from little things Andrea had said throughout the year, and Emma had filled me in a little more on the background when I couldn't figure out why Andrea wouldn't even give me a chance. I knew Andrea had liked him a lot, that they'd broken up, and that he'd married someone else from their high school a few weeks ago.

"Is that when you guys started dating?" I asked.

"No. It was the start of our being friends, though." She flipped a few pages to the senior picture section. "This is Dave," she pointed. I looked closely. So this was the guy. He was grinning away, and he looked like a good guy, I had to admit. Still, something had to be seriously wrong with him. Who in their right mind would not go after Andrea? And even worse, let her go and break her heart?

"He looks like a good guy," I told her.

"He is," she said. Then she started flipping the pages, looking for something else. "Here's Mikey," she said. We'd hung out with Mikey a couple of times and I really liked her. Especially because I'd overheard her telling Andrea that she thought I was "awesome" and "perfect" for Andrea.

"And here's Ethan," she said, showing me her brother's picture. It looked a lot like his mission picture that hung in the living room.

"I hope I get to meet Ethan someday," I said.

Andrea gave me an appraising look. "I think he'd like you," she told me.

"I hope so," I said. "I want your whole family to like me so they can tell you what a great guy I am in case you ever need convincing."

"You've already gotten my mom and Chloe wrapped around your little finger," she said.

"What about your dad?" I asked her. I'd only had a chance to meet him briefly one night after he brought Andrea and Chloe home from the ballet. (One of their holiday traditions was to go to the Nutcracker Ballet, and it had been impossible to get an extra ticket for me with such late notice.) I'd spent the evening with her mom and Paul, playing Scrabble (which I am terrible at) and feeling desperately like a third wheel, even though they were nice about it.

"I don't know what he thinks yet," she said honestly. "I'll ask him and let you know."

The next pictures she showed me were in the sports section. We flipped through the black-and-white pages of football stars and cheerleaders and then to the cross-country section. There were two pictures of her there—one of her running and one of her holding the state trophy, staring down the camera. We looked at the pictures in silence.

"Wow," Andrea said. "It seems so long ago. Is it because the pictures are in black and white?" She kept looking at her eighteen-year-old self. "It's so weird to look back because the Andrea in these pictures is already gone. Even though it's only been three years or so, these pictures seem to belong to another person, another lifetime." She looked up at me.

"I feel that way when I look at my mission pictures," I said. "I know it was me, and I remember it well, but it's one of those eras that was so huge for me that it seems crazy it could ever fade into the background, but it does. And then when you look back you're surprised at what you've forgotten."

"Were you happy on your mission, when you were in Texas?" she asked me.

"Yes," I said. "Very happy, in a way that's kind of hard to explain. It was no piece of cake in a lot of ways. But I was happy."

"I wonder if these pictures are so hard to look at because I wasn't happy. I wish I could go back and tell myself to lighten up and let go, let everything be okay." She shook her head. "That's a lesson I'm still learning. I hope I'm getting better at it."

"Are you happy right now?" I asked her.

She wrinkled her forehead and pretended to consider the question, and I groaned. "Of course I am," she said. "Very happy. Of course, if you kissed me, it might be even better."

If there's one thing I love about Andrea, it's her honesty.

• • •

"I'd better get going," I told her. "I don't want to go. But my parents are going to be mad enough as it is that I skipped out on them for so much of the break."

Andrea looked worried. "Really?"

"No, they'll be fine. But my brother Seth is coming into town with his family for a few days and my mom is so excited to have us all together again." I smiled at her. "Otherwise I might be tempted to overstay my welcome. I've had a really good time."

"Me too," she said. We were both quiet for a minute, looking at each other. I *really* didn't want to go.

"I'd better put my bags in the car," I finally said.

"I'll get my coat and meet you out there," she said.

I popped the trunk and shoved my bag in the back. It was my old black suitcase from my mission, a little frayed around the edges. I slammed the trunk shut and there was Andrea, standing next to the car with her hands stuck deep into her coat pockets.

"I'm going to miss you," she said. "It's a good thing I'll be seeing you in a couple of weeks. I'm warning you now that I'm terrible at the long-distance thing, so don't write me off until I get back there."

"There's no danger of that," I told her. "Thank you for this week." I reached out to give her a hug. She took her hands out of her coat pockets to hug me back.

"Thank *you*," she told me. We looked at each other, so close I could see that some of the strands of her long red hair were actually gold as they caught the early morning light. I kept looking at her, and she at me, until she broke into a smile.

"Well?" she said, teasingly. "This is the last chance you'll have to kiss me for a few weeks."

"Then I'd better make it count."

I thought about that kiss all the way home.

CHAPTER 23

FEBRUARY, ITHACA

Caterina Giovanni

I heard back from BYU–Idaho. Accepted. I also heard back from SUNY Cortland. Accepted.

Why doesn't Heavenly Father make things easier for us? It would have been perfect if I'd been accepted to only *one* school. Then the decision would be made for me and I wouldn't have to worry about it for one more second. That had been my plan. Well, now it was time for another plan. And I totally wasn't up to the task.

When the acceptance letter from SUNY Cortland came, I fell dramatically back on my bed and covered my eyes with my hands and muttered, "No, no, no." But, as always, I got bored with being dramatic on my own and decided to find an audience. "Mom!" I yelled, opening the door.

"What, sweetie?" she called back.

"I got accepted to *both* schools!" I held out the letters as evidence. "*Now* what am I going to do?"

My parents are no help in situations like these. Having raised five other kids has taught them to leave themselves out of the decision-making process as much as possible so us kids can't come back and get mad at them later for their advice.

"I honestly think either place would be great for you," Mom said. "You could grow a lot from leaving, but it would also be wonderful to have you here. They have decent nursing programs in both places. I want you to make the decision that is right for you."

After a practical reaction like that, and after my dad gave me a hug and patted my back and said, "I know you'll do the right thing, hon," I still needed an audience for my drama. I'm afraid that was when Steve called and asked me to go to dinner and a movie with him that night. I said yes, even though the way he extended the invitation was less than glamorous:

"I finally decided where to go to school," he told me over the phone. I almost hung up on him then and there since that was so not what I needed to hear, but he kept going. "And I want to celebrate and for some weird reason I kept thinking, 'Hey, I should call up Cate and take her to dinner. That would be a cool way to celebrate.'"

He could have used a little more finesse, but it was still flattering, even though it was Steve. And if he'd decided where he should go, maybe he could give me some pointers.

Steve and I have come a long way. We can actually stand to be around each other now. I never would have thought it would be possible after all those years of antagonism in Primary and Young Men's/Young Women's that we'd be able to hang out . . . much less go on a date, even as friends. We'd bonded over the seminary president stuff and over the struggle we'd both been having about where to go to school. Steve had been agonizing over choosing between BYU and the University of Binghamton, which was only about an hour from where we lived. And now he'd made a decision. Lucky guy.

One of the nice things about going out with Steve was that I didn't have to obsess about what to wear. I found an outfit that I thought looked good on me (black dressy pants and a light gray blouse), combed my hair, put on some new lip gloss, and I was good to go.

Steve didn't ring the doorbell. He knocked on the door, loudly. "See you guys later," I called to my parents as I picked up my coat and opened the door.

"Hey, Steve," I said. "You look nice." He had dressed up a little, too, and was wearing khakis and a light blue, button-down shirt.

"You too," he told me.

My mom emerged from the other room. "Have a good time, you two," she said, and I felt a twinge of embarrassment, even though this was Steve and he'd known my mom for years. At least she didn't pull out the camera or call out after us, "Be home by midnight!" Even though I complain that my parents are low-key because they've been through it all before, sometimes it does have its advantages.

Steve and I got to the car and split around it, me heading toward my side and Steve going toward the drivers' seat. "Ahem," I said, standing next to the door with my arms folded.

"Oh, yeah, right," Steve said, coming around to open my door. He was getting better. Before, he would have stared at me blankly. I had been trying to help Steve with some of his social skills even though he kept insisting they were perfect—better than perfect, in fact—and I should stop bugging him so much about them. Steve's gotten too used to girls who are so excited to go out with him they let him slide on that stuff, but someone has to train the guy. I want a thank-you note from his wife. Forget that. I want them to name their first child after me.

"So do I have to come around and open the door to let you out, too?" Steve asked. I decided to let him off the hook a little bit.

"Tell you what," I said. "You just work on remembering to get the restaurant door for me when we're going inside, and I'll let myself out of the car."

He rolled his eyes at me, and, of course, to prove that he could remember it all, when we arrived at the restaurant he raced around and opened my door with a flourish in spite of what I'd said.

I was almost too distracted to notice because he'd taken me to one of the fancier restaurants in town. "Wow," I said. "Are you serious? This is really swanky, and kind of expensive. I've never actually eaten here." The restaurant had low lights, fresh flowers on the table, tasteful piano music in the background, and very, very fancy food. I was suddenly glad I had dressed up a little.

"Nothing but the best for you," he said, grinning. "Also, I might have a gift certificate."

I pretended to be offended. "Oh, okay. I see how it is."

"Come on," Steve said. "I thought you'd like it. I've had it all year and thought this would be a great time to use it."

"It's fine," I told him. "Now I feel like I can order something really expensive."

Steve laughed. "Go for it. The sky's the limit, and I'm saying that seriously. I owe you a nice dinner after all these years of tormenting you."

The candles glittered and fluttered as we walked by. The lighting was low enough that it made everyone look more beautiful and mysterious. Couples held hands across the table. A narrow rectangle of glass at each table held a single tall flower, and each table was lit by candlelight. It was very romantic. A little *too* romantic, perhaps. I glanced over at Steve suspiciously. Was he trying to put the moves on me? But Steve looked totally unconcerned, and the next words out of his mouth reassured me.

"I'm starving," he said, looking around. "They better not serve teeny tiny little helpings of everything."

"So," I said as we sat down, "when are you going to tell me what you decided?"

A lot of people would build the suspense, but not Steve. The waiter came up to us but Steve didn't wait at all. "Binghamton," he blurted out, and then "Raspberry lemonade." That was for the waiter.

"Me too," I told the waiter. I thought about teasing Steve about the raspberry lemonade, then decided against it. The waiter walked away, leaving us with our menus.

"Binghamton? Really? I thought you were leaning toward BYU."

"Yeah, me too," he said. "In fact, I actually mailed the acceptance letter to BYU. I was out running errands for my mom, and I had the envelope with the letter in it, and I stuck it into one of those blue mailboxes, the one by the grocery store. Right after I did that I totally freaked out. I couldn't stop thinking about all the reasons I should go to Binghamton instead—it's closer, it's a good school, I could always apply again to BYU later, after my mission, and, of course, it's cheaper." He was so excited he accidentally blew out one of the candles at our table. A little squiggle of smoke drifted up toward the ceiling.

"Oops," said Steve. After checking to make sure our waiter wasn't in sight, I lifted the burnt-out candle and tipped the wick into the flame of the other candle. "Good idea," he said approvingly, but I dripped a tiny little spot of wax onto the tablecloth. Without batting an eye, Steve covered it with the pepper shaker and went on with what he'd been saying.

"I couldn't stop thinking about all the money I could save for my mission if I stayed here and lived at home and commuted to Binghamton. I'd thought about that before, but after I mailed the letter, I couldn't get it out of my mind. So I sat there and waited until the mailman came and could ask for it back. He was totally cool, though. He said that happens more often than you think, that someone puts something in the mailbox and then changes their mind. Anyway, then I knew for sure it was Binghamton." He laughed. "Pretty stupid, huh? I mean, I had good feelings about it all along. I don't know why it took me so long to recognize that."

"That's a great story," I told him, and I meant it. We had to break the conversation to order our food. I ordered filet mignon because I had never actually eaten it and it was what fancy people in movies always seemed to order. Steve ordered duck, which kind of grossed me out, but I didn't say anything.

We talked a little more about his decision, about the classes he wanted to take, and about the campus at Binghamton. Even though I still didn't know where I was going, talking about his school adventures-to-be made me excited that I would be experiencing those same things, but at a different place. Talking to Steve made me lean towards staying. Talking to Kayla, who was leaving, made me lean towards leaving. I didn't seem to have a mind of my own these days.

My thoughts kept going back to Steve's story about the mailman having to give people their letters back. I brought it up again with Steve when we were eating our dessert (I had cheesecake; Steve had crème brulee). "I wonder what other letters that mailman has had to give back."

"Maybe breakup letters, stuff like that," Steve suggested.

"Or maybe letters that tell someone what you really think of them."

"You know what's going to be the scariest letter to open?" Steve asked. "The mission call letter. That'll happen about this time next year."

"That would be something," I agreed. "Your whole life for the next two years all wrapped up in one single letter."

"Are *you* planning on going on a mission?" Steve asked me.

"I'm not ruling it out. We'll see when I get there." I shook my head. "I can't think that far ahead! I can't even make the decision that's right in front of me." Then I remembered why we were there. "But tonight isn't about me. This is about Steve Ward, Binghamton student." I raised my glass of water. "To you, Steve."

Steve returned the toast noisily. Luckily, the crystal didn't shatter. He was grinning and I could tell he was feeling good, his decision made and done. Well, if nothing else, dinner had been inspirational.

I was going to go home and take a page out of the book of Enos and pray for days if I had to. It was time to get an answer!

As we stood up to leave the table, Steve grabbed me by the arm and leaned in close to my ear. What the . . . ?!? Was Steve making a pass at me? And just when I thought we really understood each other.

"What are you doing, Steve?" I tried to put the appropriate amount of grumpiness into my words without going overboard.

"Stop squirming, look very slowly over to your right, and you'll see something *very* interesting," he said.

For once, I didn't argue with him. I turned and looked over, very slowly, and he was right. Brother Hammond and Sister Beckett were walking toward a table together, both of them looking their best. And it was obvious they weren't thinking of themselves as Brother Hammond and Sister Beckett, but as Joel and Andrea, college students on a date. Her hair was long and loose, her eyes were sparkling, and she was wearing gray slacks and a cream-colored top. He had on a dark sweater that I'd never seen before. Neither one of them could take their eyes off each other. He was saying something and she was laughing. They were holding hands and walking right next to each other. *They were on a date!*

I had been right all along! There *was* something going on between the two of them. I wanted so badly to tell Steve "I told you so!" but it wasn't the right time.

Brother Hammond pulled out Sister Beckett's chair for her and she smiled at him. He didn't stop looking at her for a second as he sat down in his own seat.

"We should go over there and say hello," Steve said with a grin. "It's the only polite thing to do."

"I agree," I said, grinning back. I led the way. We wove through the chairs and arrived at their table. They were so involved with each other that they didn't even notice the two of us making a grand progression as we approached their table. They hadn't sat across from each other but had taken the two chairs right next to each other.

They were still holding hands, not even bothering to look at the menu yet.

Steve and I both said, "Hi," simultaneously, and they both looked up, startled. Steve was following me so closely that he almost ran into me when I stopped, which would have sent me sailing into their table.

"Hi, Cate," said Sister Beckett, at the same time Brother Hammond said, "Hi, Steve."

"Hi," I said meaningfully, hoping to draw something out of them, but Steve went for the direct approach.

"So, Brother Hammond," he said, before either of them could say anything else, "is there anything you should be telling us?"

They didn't drop hands or look guilty or anything.

"You caught us," said Brother Hammond, grinning. "We're dating." He looked at Sister Beckett as if he couldn't believe it were true. It was so cute it made my heart ache. "Actually, it's not a secret or anything, but I didn't think we should make a big announcement."

Sister Beckett looked too happy to be uncomfortable. "So . . . should we be expecting to hear a similar confession from the two of you?" She looked from me to Steve and back again, taking in our dressier-than-usual clothes and the fact that we were at a restaurant, not a fast food place. She was teasing, I think. I didn't even bother to respond, other than my shocked look, but Steve started grinning and nodding. I hope she knew better than to believe him.

"Do you want to sit with us?" Sister Beckett suggested.

Wow. That would be all kinds of awkward. I was relieved we'd already eaten. "No, thanks," I said. "We just finished." Then, to make sure they knew that Steve had been joking about our being a couple, I added, "We're celebrating Steve's college decision."

"Binghamton, baby!" Steve stuck his hand in the air and they both high-fived him, laughing at his enthusiasm, drawing some looks from some of the other guests in the restaurant.

"That's great, Steve!" Brother Hammond said. We made small

talk for a few minutes more and then made our escape. I'm sure they weren't too sad to see us go. They spend plenty of time together with us. It's probably a relief to be alone for a little while.

Still, I couldn't help talking about it the moment we were out of earshot. "Can you believe that?!?" I exclaimed, slugging Steve in the arm. "I was right all along! They do have something going on."

I could tell Brother Hammond had it bad for Sister Beckett from Day One. It was only to be expected. She's the kind of girl that the rest of us want to look like: Tall, that thick, straight model-like hair, eyes that kind of change colors to match her outfit, like the ultimate accessory. And she had that confident walk that always turned into a strut when I tried it on for size. How do you walk like that without looking like you're showing off? At least she was a pretty crummy teacher when she started. It was nice to find something wrong with her so you knew she wasn't perfect.

"That's crazy," said Steve, shaking his head. "Go Brother Hammond! I wonder how long they've been together?"

"I don't know," I said, frantically trying to figure it out. "They definitely weren't together when we did the Christmas activity. They seemed not to like each other all that much then."

"This is awesome," said Steve. "We've got to tell everyone. They'll never believe this!"

I agreed. "Everyone's going to go crazy. Our teachers are dating! That's so funny. Wouldn't you think that would be against the rules?"

Steve kept laughing. "We should have figured it out a long time ago. They're always hanging out together. I know they take their teaching seriously, but come on. No one hangs out that much without there being some other reason, too. We should have known!" He opened the car door for me and I hopped inside.

• • •

I picked up Ben for seminary Monday morning as usual, and he sat there eating part of his lunch, as usual.

"Can you believe this about Brother Hammond and Sister Beckett?" I asked him. "And did you hear about Steve deciding to go to Binghamton?" I hadn't had a chance to talk to him the day before because his family had been at the Trumansburg Branch for a mission farewell.

"The dating thing is kind of weird," Ben said, stabbing a straw through the little foil hole in his juice box and taking a huge bite out of his apple. He's the only person I know who brings a juice box to high school. "But everyone's acting like it's such a big deal when it's not. They're only dating. They're not getting married or anything."

"Not a big deal!" I said to him, startling him enough that he dropped his apple on the floor and had to bend over and fish around for it. "It's totally a big deal!"

"If you say so," said Ben, locating his apple and rubbing it on his coat sleeve before he started eating it again.

I keep having to reassess how I feel about Ben and adjusting the percentages. Usually, I feel Ben is about fifty percent infuriating and fifty percent endearing. If this is how I acted when I was younger, it's no wonder my brothers and sisters never hung out with the baby of the family.

"Ben, seriously," I said, "you have no interest in life. Come on. Admit that this is at least a little bit entertaining."

Ben smiled at me and kept eating his apple. He'd taken off his hat, and his hair, as usual, was a mess. As always, his cowlick was standing up, and, as always, I had to resist the urge to smooth it down. He was so endearing. Then he started crunching into his apple too loudly and it bothered me. He was so annoying. How do parents *stand* it?

"Then what about Steve?" I asked. "*That's* interesting, right? That he's going to be around next year?"

Ben agreed with that, at least. "He's going to save up lots of money for his mission," he told me, sounding knowledgeable. He talked about Steve's plans for the rest of the ride to seminary; I didn't let on that I already knew all the details.

Even if Ben didn't think that Sister Beckett and Brother Hammond's relationship was interesting, other people seemed to disagree with him. Melissa, Jason, and Heather were waiting for us in the church parking lot, already buzzing with excitement. Brother Hammond was teaching that week, and I was thinking of lots of good ways to tease him about the weekend and bring up the big news in case anyone had missed it.

But when I walked into the classroom, my jaw dropped. On the whiteboard in big red letters he had written, "YES, SISTER BECKETT AND I ARE DATING. I HAVE NO COMMENT." He had stolen my thunder. I glared at him as I got out my scriptures. Someone tried to ask a question about him and Sister Beckett, but all he did was point to the whiteboard and smile. Sister Beckett wasn't there yet.

When she came through the door, about ten minutes after class had started, all of us turned to look at her, including Brother Hammond. She pretended not to notice and sat down. When she saw what was written on the board, she sent Brother Hammond a pointed look, but when he winked at her, she couldn't contain her smile. We all watched their exchange with great interest.

Brother Hammond tried to get the class back on track. "So, in the early days of the Church, lots of the Saints had to make painful choices. Sometimes joining the Church meant losing almost everything—their family, their friends, even their country of birth since many of them came to join the Saints in America. I can't imagine how hard it would be to make those kinds of decisions."

I raised my hand. "Brother Hammond, why do you think that we have to make so many decisions? I know it's because of our agency, and that making choices is important to grow, but couldn't we accomplish the same thing with a few less decisions?"

"Amen," said Steve, who appeared to have the agony of the college situation still fresh on his mind.

The more I talked, the more fired up I felt. "I mean, it's great and all to say 'seek and ye shall find,' but sometimes you don't even get an answer after you fast and pray and do everything."

Brother Hammond smiled at me. "You sound like you might have some personal experience with this, Cate."

"I do," I said. "And I can't be the only one. It's so frustrating!"

Sister Beckett raised her hand from the back and Brother Hammond gestured for her to go ahead and speak. "Sometimes you have to wait longer than you want for the answer," she said. "It's not that you're doing anything wrong. It might not be time yet. Look at Joseph Smith and his life. Even though he was living righteously at the time he prayed for things, he still had to wait for answers, or for the time to be right. Even for him, it wasn't instantaneous."

"And," Brother Hammond added, "there are some things that we won't know the answer to in this life."

I gave a colossal groan and Steve laughed from the back row.

• • •

After seminary was over, we all drifted toward the parking lot together. Steve gave me a pat on the back as we reached our cars, which were parked next to each other. His idea of a friendly pat was so strong that I could feel it reverberate through my body even though I wore my fattest down jacket.

"You'll figure it out, Cate," he said. "And when you do, *you* can take *me* to dinner to celebrate."

"Thanks, Steve," I told him, laughing. The weather was way too frigid for us to linger outside, so we waved good-bye and I climbed into my car, turning on the heater before I even shut the door. Ben slid into the passenger seat and pulled his hat down over his ears. The two of us waited in silence for a few minutes while the car got warm enough to drive.

"What do you think I should do, Ben?" I asked as we pulled away from the Church building and started our drive toward school. "Should I go to BYU–Idaho or stick around here?" I figured Ben might as well earn his keep, since I'd been chauffeuring him around every single morning all year long and he didn't provide a lot of entertainment. Well, intentional entertainment, that is.

"I don't know," Ben said. "You'll have e-mail either place, right?"

It was such an irrelevant comment, I wasn't quite sure how to respond. "Yeah," I said, finally. "But what does that have to do with anything?"

"Nothing," Ben mumbled, looking out the window. "I was thinking that you could still e-mail me no matter where you went and that would be good. At first I wanted you to stay here so I could still see you around but that would be kind of selfish. You should do what you want to do." We drove in silence until we'd reached the point where I dropped him off, near the annex where he had his first class. He hopped out of the car and stuck his head back in. "See ya."

Good old Ben. I shook my head as I drove around looking for a parking spot. At least there was someone who would miss me if I decided to go. I was surprised by how much his comment had meant to me. Although I couldn't imagine what on earth we'd e-mail about, it was still a nice idea. My parents would miss me, but then their lives would close over the gap I'd left, just the way they had when all of my brothers and sisters had gone away. I knew my parents loved me and that they'd cry and miss me, but life would go on, for all of us.

I'd like to think that I'm such a force of nature that the minute I leave, everything is different. "Where's Cate?" everyone in Ithaca would say the moment I boarded the plane or bus or train, taking off for something new. But really, it wouldn't change much. If at all. People would still go to the Farmer's Market on Saturdays and come away with flowers and vegetables and smiles. A whole new group of high schoolers would trudge through the halls without ever knowing I had been there, walking those same halls and thinking some of the same thoughts.

My leaving would be like throwing a rock into Cayuga Lake. For a minute, there would be a splash and some ripples, but then the water would smooth over and it would be like nothing had ever happened. It was a humbling thought. You grow up in one place and feel so tied to it that you think it couldn't possibly go on or continue to exist without you when, really, everything and everyone would do just fine.

CHAPTER 24

FEBRUARY, ITHACA

Andrea Beckett

I descended into the depths of the Willard Straight Hall and headed for the Ivy Room. Even though I've eaten in the Ivy Room cafeteria plenty of times, I'm always surprised by the incongruity of the shining, stainless-steel salad bars and the neon lights in that gloomy, grand old dining hall. The wood carvings, stone floors, and wavy, old-glass windows seem to tolerate those things the way they tolerate the students wearing their flashy clothes and talking away on their cell phones. "Do what you need to do while you're here," the building, and much of Cornell, says. "This was here before you came and will be here after you're gone." You feel as though they are patient, the benches and stones and walls, patient in a way that only inanimate objects can be. That's the good thing about being rock or wood or concrete, I guess.

I was going to meet Joel and his mom, who was in town visiting him. Since it was only 11:00 A.M., there weren't many people in the Ivy Room. We were eating early on purpose because during the lunch hour there are students everywhere, calling and yelling and swearing to each other, and because Joel had a class at noon. "You can come

253

meet us for lunch," Joel had said, "and then could you show her around campus for an hour while I'm in class? Then we can take her to the Syracuse airport together. Would that work?" Joel's mom had arrived only the day before. It was a quick visit, a stopover on her way home from Boston, where she'd been helping Joel's brother Seth and his wife with their new baby.

"Sure," I said. "Will you give me a list of things to talk about with her?"

Joel laughed.

"No, seriously," I told him. "That would be helpful. I don't want to mess up and have her not like me."

"She's going to like you," Joel told me. But he relented and told me more about her, giving me some information I could work with to make polite conversation. I found out that she liked to cook desserts but hated cooking dinners, that she had been a runner herself when she was younger but now preferred swimming, and that she played the cello in the community orchestra.

I tried not to let Joel know how scared I was. I wanted him to think I was looking forward to meeting his mom, which I was, in a way. It was kind of how you look forward to meeting your teacher on the first day of school when you're a little kid. You want to find out what he or she is like—and you want to find out really bad—but if they seem mean or if they don't like you, you know right then you're sunk.

I didn't see Joel or his mom in any of the lunch lines—the pasta bar line, the burger line, the salad line—so I assumed they must have already gotten their food and were sitting down somewhere. I went into the dining part of the cafeteria, carrying my brown-bagged lunch over to the spot near the back where I usually sat with Joel. Sure enough, there he was with his mom. I hadn't met any of Joel's family members before. She was the first. I tried to look friendly and not nervous as I approached their table.

Joel was facing me and saw me first. He stopped mid-sentence and his face lit up. His mom turned to look at me while Joel jumped up from his chair and came forward to meet me. "Andrea!" he said. "This is my mom, Claire Hammond."

I stuck out my hand to shake hers. She shook mine back. Joel pulled out the chair next to him and I sat down. "You brought your lunch *today?*" he asked me, and I nodded sheepishly. I know he doesn't have much money so I always pack a lunch when we're meeting on campus. He's always trying to get me to knock it off so he can buy me something. Sometimes when I pack a lunch I bring him something, too, but I hadn't today. I hadn't wanted to seem weird or possessive or excessively smitten to his mom.

But now it seemed like I'd been rude. I didn't know what to do. I freeze up when I feel out of place and this was no exception. I sat there smiling at both of them and put my hands under the table so they couldn't see that I was clenching my fists in embarrassment. Joel reached over and held my hand. That helped.

"It's so nice to meet you," Claire was saying. "Joel has talked about you all year long, from the moment he found out you two would be teaching seminary together." She got a mischievous look in her eye. "And when he told me he was going to drive to Seattle to visit you over the break . . . I knew something was up."

Joel looked from me to her and shrugged his shoulders. "What can I say?" he asked us. "But before you embarrass me even more, Mom, let's go get some food. It'll be crazy here in a minute." They both stood up. I didn't. I was staying right here and thinking of five good things to say before they got back.

"I'll stay here to save our spot," I offered. Then the three of us were what Ethan calls pointlessly polite. Joel and his mom offered to stay and save the spot instead and I insisted they go and they insisted they stay and we ended up right back where we'd started, but at least everyone had *tried* to be polite so the bases were covered. When you have divorced parents, you see a lot of pointless politeness (if you're lucky). I remained firm about staying, and Joel caught the look in my eye, so he and Claire headed over to the food lines together and I sat stolidly in my chair.

I didn't know if I'd committed a faux pas. I knew Joel would think it had been fine, but I hoped his mother didn't think I was being rude or too forceful. I never know what to do in social situations and Ethan has warned me that I can come across as snobby, even after working on it all of these years. I wonder how many people, like me, have a reputation for being snobby when all we're doing is freezing up in an uncomfortable situation. Why is it such a crime to be quiet? Why do people seem to think that silence is grounds for being hurt, or offended, and think that you should say something, anything, even when you have nothing to say?

My college adviser, the one whose class got me thinking about the master's degree, thinks this is one of my strengths, which surprises me because I have always thought it was one of my weaknesses. "You're not afraid of silence. You can wait and draw people out," she said. I guess that was one way to look at it.

As more and more people came in, the Ivy Room grew louder and louder. Girls arrived and screamed and threw their arms around each other. Guys yelled. Cell phones rang and chairs scuffed and screeched along the old flagstone floor. But above all, everyone was talking, talking, talking, while I sat there quietly, as usual.

I watched Joel and Claire slide their trays along the metal bars and make their selections. Joel talked to his mom a mile a minute. He kept looking over and waving at me. I waved back.

Claire Hammond wasn't what I had expected. My eyes followed the two of them as they paid for their food and started walking back toward me. I guess I had pictured her looking more like my friends' moms. Cozy, wearing jeans and a brightly patterned sweater, a head full of tousled grey curls, and eyes with crow's-feet around them that you *know* came from lots and lots of laughter. Instead, she was almost Joel's height, at least five nine or so, very trim, and wearing a black corduroy blazer, a cream-colored blouse, and charcoal slacks.

Her gray hair was perfectly coiffed. She was intimidating without meaning to be.

When they returned to the table, she sat down right across from me, and Joel sat next to me. I'd been nervous before about showing her around for an hour. Now I was petrified. But there was no way to get out of it. Joel gave my hand another squeeze and I knew that it couldn't be all bad.

• • •

"Would you like to walk around a little?" I asked her after we'd dropped Joel off at his building. Even though it was cold, we both had coats and scarves, and I knew she hadn't had a chance to see much of the campus.

"That would be nice," she said. "I'd like to see more of Cornell than I have so far."

We started walking up Tower Road and she asked me the usual questions: how I liked Cornell, whether or not I missed my family moving so far away, a little about my major, and if I was excited to graduate in the spring.

As luck would have it, we had only been walking five minutes before it started snowing, soft and thick and heavy. What was I going to do with Joel's mom for the remaining time until we met him back at Uris Hall? Claire was wearing black dress shoes, not at all right for walking in this kind of snow. We stopped, almost simultaneously.

"This storm looks like it's here to stay," she said. "Is there somewhere inside we could go?"

I racked my brain for ideas. "I guess we could go to the bookstore and look around," I suggested lamely. "Or we could go to the Cornell Dairy Bar. They have hot chocolate there, and it's not too far away."

"Let's do that." By the time we made it up there, the lunchtime crowd was starting to thin and we were able to find an empty table next to the window. I grabbed a napkin and wiped up the evidence of other lunches, other spills, before we sat down with our Styrofoam cups.

Something about the snow outside the window and the cup of hot chocolate in my hand made me feel cozier, more comfortable. "How is the new baby?" I asked Claire.

"She's doing wonderfully," she said. "She's such a sweetheart, and she's going to have to hold her own, with her brother and sister." She smiled. "She's our third grandchild and the thrill never wears off. They're all beautiful and unique and so much fun to meet."

I took a sip of my chocolate, nodding, thinking of my deep bond with my own grandmother.

"Do you have any nieces or nephews in your family?" she asked, right as I filled my mouth. I shook my head "no" as I swallowed it down. My tongue and throat felt scalded, but I smiled anyway.

"That's right, Joel told me you were the oldest," she said. "And there are three children in your family, right?"

"That's right," I said.

"Just like us. Although we have three boys, no girls. They were a handful." She smiled at the memory. "Especially during the Little League and high school years. It seemed we were always watching baseball games. Of course, things got even busier when they got to high school. Joel, especially, with everything he was involved in."

"What did he do?" I asked her, curious. "He hasn't told me much about high school."

She laughed. "That sounds like him. He was a mixed bag in high school. He was on the soccer team, and also president of the chess team. He was one of those quiet, under-the-radar guys that everyone knew and liked and who did a lot, but never drew a lot of attention to himself."

Joel's mom was a fountain of little-known information. "Chess club president?" I asked in disbelief. "Soccer team?"

Claire laughed. "Joel doesn't like to talk about himself. I didn't know that he was the assistant to the mission president until he got home. Sometimes, I don't know whether to be proud of him or driven crazy by him."

I knew the feeling. She smiled at me across the table, and I felt much more comfortable. Even though we didn't know each other well yet, we knew Joel and that was the best starting point I could imagine.

"So," I said, leaning closer to her, "tell me more about Joel."

"What would you like first?" she asked. "Embarrassing childhood moments or stories about his teenage years?"

"I want to hear it all," I said.

• • •

The snow had eased up by the time we left campus for the airport, but Joel still drove carefully all the way to Syracuse. Claire sat in the front with him, because I insisted, and I sat in the back, watching the occasional snowflake drift by, listening to their conversation and feeling warm and safe, the way you do when you're in a car driven by someone you can trust. Toward the end of the drive, they started talking about his brothers, whom I hadn't met, and they apologized. "Sorry we keep talking about our family," Joel said. "You'll meet Eli and Seth soon, I hope."

"It's fine," I assured him, and it was. "I'm learning a lot. It's been a very . . . educational day." Claire turned around and gave me a conspiratorial smile. Joel caught the end of it.

"Should I be worried?" he asked.

When we reached the airport, we went inside with his mom to say good-bye. After Joel had hugged her, she hugged me, too, and we both said it had been nice to meet each other. Then she walked briskly toward the line to check in, but she hadn't fooled anyone. You could see she'd been tearing up, and at the last second, she turned back to Joel and called out, "I love you!" He called it back.

We got back into the car and turned on the heater. It was getting dark, and it was freezing. Joel pulled on his gloves and started driving, still carefully because of the snow from earlier that day. Neither of us said anything for a few moments as we drove through the lights of Syracuse. It was one of what I'd come to think of as our trademark silences, when we are both deep in our own thoughts and completely comfortable.

It was a good time of day for thinking, one of the best, when the daylight is fading and the other lights are blinking on—lamps in houses, streetlights, each little car snapping on its two little beacons of headlights. Joel flicked the car's headlights on and their beams of light shone out onto the dark road.

We started to thaw, and soon we were a warm little cocoon of a car, racing through the sharp cold air.

Joel turned to look at me. "So . . . what did you think? Did you like her?"

"I did," I said. "I liked her a lot. And the whole experience was very intriguing."

"How's that?"

"Your mom gave me your résumé today when we were talking."

"My résumé?" he asked, confused.

"You know, all the highlights of your long and distinguished career here on the planet. Assistant to the mission president. Soccer team star. President of the chess team. Pulitzer Prize winner."

Joel rolled his eyes.

"Okay, I made the last one up," I acknowledged. "Still, I'm very glad we had the chance to talk. It was very . . . enlightening."

"*Mom,*" sighed Joel in mock disgust. "What was she thinking? Sorry about that. She's like most moms, always trying to talk me up."

"I'm glad she did. It was nice to hear a little bragging. Why do you always have to be so modest?"

Joel looked truly uncomfortable. "It's not that. I didn't want you to think I was bragging or showing off for you or being self-centered. Plus, if you didn't like me, finding out that stuff wouldn't make a difference at all."

"It's weird, though," I said. "Here I thought I was dating the antithesis of the guys I dated in high school—the popular jock—and now it turns out that I'm dating . . . the popular jock."

"Well, if jocks can play chess, then yes," Joel said. He got a glint in his eye. "So, we're dating?"

I rolled my eyes at him. "Of course we are. We've been dating for months."

"It's nice to hear you say that." He glared at me playfully. "You keep introducing me as, 'This is my'—then you pause—'friend, Joel.'"

"Well, how do you want me to introduce you?" I teased him. "This is the man who changed my life? This is the man who makes my heart go pitter-patter?"

Joel burst out laughing. "I never thought I'd hear you say the words 'pitter-patter,'" he told me. Then he grew serious. "I think 'boyfriend' would be nice."

"Point taken," I told him. "From now on I'll say that."

"Mom really liked you."

"Are you sure?" I quizzed him. "What exactly did she say?"

"Let's see if I can quote it verbatim," Joel teased me. "As far as I can remember, she said something like, 'I really like her, Joel. And I can see why you do, too. She's beautiful and sweet and intelligent and quick-witted.'"

I groaned. "You are *so* making that up, Joel Hammond."

He shook his head. "I'm not. She had fun with you. She said chatting with you was one of the highlights of her visit."

"That's nice of her," I said. "I had a good time too. She's great. When I first met her I was scared of her, though. She's really put together and—well, kind of intimidating."

Joel laughed. "I wonder who else is like that?" He reached over and gave my hand a squeeze.

I shook my head at him in mock disgust. "Eyes on the road," I reminded him, teasingly. "I don't want us getting in a car accident."

He smiled and looked back at the road. It was unfair because *I* got to look at his profile the whole time. Even in the dimming light, you could see how handsome he was and how kind his eyes were. The shadows on his face gave it depth, and when a passing car's headlights shone on us, he looked over at me and for a second we were both covered in light, looking right into each other's eyes. Then the light was gone and he was looking back at the road, a little smile on his face. This time, I reached for his hand.

"I love you, Joel," I said, trying the words on for size. They fit perfectly.

"I love you too," he said.

MARCH, BRAZIL

Ethan Beckett

P-Day again. I was trying not to count how many I had left. I stuck with my irrational theory that if I didn't keep track of how much of my mission was left, maybe it wouldn't have to end. I wondered if all missionaries felt like this: you finally knew what you were doing, and then it was time to go home, where you didn't know what you were doing anymore. Probably not. Probably plenty of them couldn't wait to go home. I had to admit that my mood swung that way, too, now and then.

"The mail came," called Elder Almeida to me as he walked through the kitchen. "I'll go get it."

"Thanks," I said, my head still stuck under the sink. I was trying to figure out why it wouldn't drain. I had a bad feeling about the answer. I should probably call the plumber, but I wanted to give it a shot first. Anything was better than doing laundry, which I was going to have to do at some point. *That* was one thing I wouldn't miss, the hours spent soaking and scrubbing and hanging the clothes out to dry.

Elder Almeida came back in, holding a few letters and a small package. "It's for me," he said, catching my eye and giving me a half-apologetic grin. Packages are the gold standard of good mail. A package day is a red-letter day. "Sorry," he said. "It's from my mother. If she sent food, I'll share it."

"Thanks," I said. I didn't duck back under the sink yet. "Anything for me?" It had been over a month since I'd heard from Mikey, the longest I'd gone without a letter from her (not counting those months where we didn't get any mail at all). I was blaming the mail system in Mexico where she was doing the study abroad program.

Elder Almeida set his package on the kitchen table and flipped through the envelopes. "Another letter from your dad," he said. "Your dad is awesome. Does he write every week or what?"

"He writes a lot," I said.

"Every week," Elder Almeida said again. "At least every week since I've been your companion."

He was right. My dad did write every week without fail. I had come to rely on the consistency of his letters. He'd kept it up through my whole mission. I caught the letter Elder Almeida tossed me and set it next to the sink to read when I was finished. Before I got started again, though, I heard Elder Almeida say something. "What?" I asked.

"Another letter for you," he said, flipping another envelope toward me like a Frisbee. I caught it in midair, hoping it was from Mikey.

It wasn't. The return address in the corner was from Elder Caxias, Brazilian MTC, and the envelope was the thin kind they have here in Brazil. It made me curious. Who had sent this? I didn't think I knew an Elder Caxias.

"Do you know an Elder Caxias?" I asked Elder Almeida as I opened the envelope. He was already deep in a letter from his mother (who wrote even more than my dad) and shook his head without looking up.

I unfolded the paper. It was a short letter, only about a page, and it was written in small, very precise handwriting. The paper was waxy, thin, almost transparent. I looked at the signature at the end: "Elder Marcelo Caxias."

"No way!" I yelled as recognition shot through me. *Marcelo.* He had been an investigator Elder Vickers and I had found shortly after Eduardo's failed baptism. Marcelo was a young guy, a great kid, and I could picture him instantly in my mind, even though it had been months since I'd seen him. I'd always called him Marcelo. I'd forgotten his last name, especially when it was paired with the title "Elder."

"Hey, Elder Almeida, listen to this," I said, and started reading the letter.

Dear Elder Beckett,

This is my first letter as a missionary, except for one I have written to my mother. Now that I am a missionary, I wanted to write to you, since you are the one who found me. I want you to know that I will be serving in the Brazil Recife Mission. I am still in the MTC right now.

Elder Almeida interrupted my reading. "So I take it this isn't from your girlfriend? Are you going to tell me who it *is* from?"

"A kid—a man—that I baptized about a year ago is serving a mission now and wrote to tell me." I felt a grin spread across my face.

"Very cool," Elder Almeida said enthusiastically. "What else does he say?"

I started again at the beginning, continuing through the letter.

I have only been on my mission about one week and it is already very hard and very exciting. I am sure that you know this. I miss my family very much but they are doing well. My mother and sister are both still working at the restaurant and we have had some blessings to help me go on this mission. They are working very hard to help me be here and I will not let them down. I will also not let you down. Thank you

*for teaching me the gospel. My prayers are with you and I know yours
are with me. Please write if you have time.*

I quit pretending to fix the sink and sat down to write to
Marcelo. When I finished and reread the letter, I had to laugh at
myself. I'd written so many exclamation points, my letter looked like
one of Chloe's. Still, it reflected how happy I was about what
Marcelo was doing.

I looked at my watch. I had time for one more letter before our
shirts would be done soaking. I pulled a piece of paper out and
wrote, "Dear Mikey," at the top. Then I muttered to myself and
balled it up, standing up to throw it in the trash can. My eye caught
my companion's.

"What are you doing?" Elder Almeida asked, amused.

"I'm trying to decide whether or not I should write to Mikey," I
admitted. "It's been a month since I've heard from her."

"Just write to her," he said. "What's so bad about her knowing
that you care about her? The mail might be bad in Mexico. She
might be sick. You should never give up on a person if you don't
know for sure."

That sounded right. So I wrote to Mikey, careful to sound businesslike but friendly, careful not to be too obvious about how I felt.
When Elder Almeida was finished writing to his mother, we ran the
letters to the post office at the corner, waving at the kids who cried,
"*Oi, Alemão!*" *Hello, German!* along the way.

Later, after hanging up our laundry, fixing dinner, and companion study, we were on our way home from a meeting with the branch
president when it started to rain. Elder Almeida and I looked at each
other. "Our shirts!" he yelled. We ran home, sprinting hard, splash-
ing through the puddles, even though we knew we would be too late.
Our shirts, hung across the back of the yard, were drenched. We
brought them inside and strung the clothesline across the kitchen so
they could dry. This had happened before and we both knew that

tomorrow we would be wearing damp white shirts, but we were both in a good enough mood to laugh about it.

Before I went to sleep, I finally read the letter from my dad. As always, it was full of encouragement and faith. In some ways, I thought, being a parent is like the ultimate missionary experience. You plant these seeds and you work hard to nourish them and sometimes they bear fruit right away. And sometimes they don't. Sometimes you have to wait for years. But my dad had faith—in the Church, in missionary work, in the gospel, in *me*.

There wasn't time to write him a letter that night. It was late. But I would write him as soon as I could and tell him all about Marcelo. I could hear the rain outside and the shirts dripping on the tile of our kitchen as they dried, and I closed my eyes.

MARCH, ITHACA

Andrea Beckett

I sat in the library on campus, alone. I'd carved out my own little space by finding a spot where most people didn't go, a place that wasn't on the main thoroughfare where everyone sits to see and be seen. I was tucked away in a corner, far away from the computer area and windows and anywhere else people like to study. I had made a barrier by choosing a quiet place, by setting up lots of books and pencils around me, by putting my backpack on a chair, and by not even looking up when other people passed me. You'd think I was studying for my prelims, to look at all the notebooks and textbooks and index cards. But it was all a decoy. I wasn't actually studying.

I was making a list. The list was titled: Pros and Cons. It was about Joel.

There were quite a few items in the Pros column. It was a long list, in no particular order. I kept rereading a few of the listed items.

I like the way he puts his hand on my back when we are in a crowd.
He has a great laugh. A laugh that is quiet but full.
He listens to everyone with a thoughtful look on his face.

He worries about people—me, the seminary kids, his family, everyone.

He is strong—in the gospel, in his convictions, and in his ideals.

In class last month, I told Cate that sometimes when you prayed, you had to wait a while for an answer. I'd been waiting, but time was running out. I knew exactly how she felt. I had to decide if the program in Syracuse was what I truly wanted to do. I knew that Joel was hoping for Syracuse, but didn't want to sway my decision. He'd gone away for a few days to a conference, and I wanted to make a decision before he got back.

I sighed, loudly enough that I looked around to make sure that no one else had noticed. They hadn't. My relationship with Joel was getting serious. That was what I had wanted. I had consciously decided to let myself fall for Joel. I knew I was letting myself in for this eventuality, but you never quite know how it's going to feel to be in love. I had even been the one to tell him I loved him first, which was not something I had planned on doing, but I had wanted to say it. I meant it. I loved him. And I knew that if I stayed in New York, things would get even more serious.

In a way, going to school in Syracuse bought us some time, because I'd be around for two more years. But it also meant seeing our relationship out to the finish, whether that meant heartbreak or happiness. There would be no using geography as an excuse. If it didn't work out, it would be because of some other reason, something deeper, something personal. That was scary.

There weren't many items in the "Cons" column. Only three, in fact:

1. I don't want to end up getting a divorce like Mom and Dad did.

2. I'll have to compromise and change because that's what marriage is all about.

3. What if someday he decides he doesn't love me anymore?

One and three were fairly close, but they were still different enough that I separated them out when I wrote them down. I wondered what Joel would say if he could see me listing things out like this. It would have to be kind of insulting. But I didn't know what else to do. My mind was not clear. My vision was not steady.

When I was with Joel, I was sure being with him was what I wanted. I was sure most of the time we were apart, too. But I didn't know if wanting to be with him and loving him meant that I was supposed to marry him, and I was afraid to ask. Dave and I had never even gotten close to this point. Even though I had loved him and cared about him, this was different, deeper. If I thought losing Dave had hurt, it would be nothing compared to how it would feel to lose Joel now or, worse, at some point even later down the road.

I remembered Steve telling our seminary class a story about putting the envelope into the mailbox and then realizing that he'd made the wrong decision and what the right decision really was. Maybe that was what I had to do—take some drastic action to find out how I truly felt about the whole thing.

I made a reconnaissance mission after leaving the library to check the pickup times on the blue mailbox on the corner. Pickup was scheduled for 11:00 A.M. If I dropped my acceptance letter to Syracuse through the slot at 10:45, then I'd only have to hang around for fifteen minutes if it was the wrong decision.

• • •

The next morning, the manila envelope slid easily through the blue metal slot. I stood there for a minute, watching, waiting, and . . . I felt fine. No panic, nothing. And why would there be? It was an amazing program, in a good location. It meant I could stay closer to the man I loved. I started walking slowly back toward my apartment. As I turned around, I almost hit someone on a bike, who cursed at me and rode away. Even that didn't make me feel uneasy.

I made it all the way home and felt fine. Joel was still in New York City at a conference, and though I wanted to call and tell him the good news on the phone, some news is better delivered in person. It was hard to wait, but I did.

"How was your day?" he asked me when he called that night.

"Fine," I said, trying not to let on that anything was up. But I'm horrible at subterfuge. He could tell right away.

"What's up?" he said. "You sound happy."

"It's because I'm talking to you," I told him.

• • •

When I arrived to teach seminary the next morning, I was surprised to see the lights already on, the door already propped open, and Cate already sitting at her desk. I must not have locked up the day before. I grimaced, picturing the irate message the building custodian would leave me if he found out.

"Hey, Cate," I said, then stated the obvious as I hung my coat over the back of my chair: "You're here early."

She looked up at me. Her face, usually cheerful, usually full of life, looked tired. And not the I-woke-up-at-5:30-A.M.-so-I-could-be-here kind of tired. It was the kind of tired I'd felt before. Worn down, worn out.

"Cate?" I sat down in a desk near her. "Is everything okay?"

"No," she said. "I was kind of hoping that Brother Hammond would be here to talk to."

"I'm afraid you're stuck with me. Joel—Brother Hammond—is still at his conference in the City."

"You'll do," she said, and before I could laugh, added, "That was a joke."

"I hoped it was," I told her, smiling. "What's going on?"

"I've realized that I'm not very important," Cate said.

"What do you mean?"

"I'm all stressed out about where to go to school, and it doesn't matter, does it?" she asked.

"Of course it matters," I said. "It will change your life in a lot of ways."

"That's just it," she said. "It will change *my* life, but it won't really matter to anyone else."

I frowned. "What do you mean?"

"I'm realizing that everyone will get along without me fine, and it's hurting my pride. If I go away, my parents will miss me, but they'll be okay. My friends will miss me, but they'll be fine too. It seems kind of pointless to go away if no one's going to care." She laughed a little. "I know how weird that must sound."

It didn't sound weird to me—I'd left home to go to school far away after all—and I told her so. "We all want people to care about us and miss us. That's not something that's only important to you. And we're *all* going to miss you, a lot."

"There's something *you're* trying to decide about, too, isn't there?" She was direct. I didn't expect anything less from Cate.

"Yeah," I said, "but I can't tell you what it is. No offense."

"None taken."

"You remind me a lot of myself," I told her.

She laughed. "*Really?* We're nothing alike."

"Yeah, we are," I said. "Or maybe I'm flattering myself. You're actually a lot more centered than I was at your age, and probably more put together than I am even though I'm almost done with college. But we both like to call it like we see it and sometimes that gets us into trouble."

Cate grinned. "That's true."

"But we're different too. You're more easygoing. You're much better with people than I am. You have always been completely and unapologetically a Mormon and Cate and comfortable with that." I paused. "I wasn't even active in the Church when I was your age. You have a lot of inner strength that I didn't have then. And you're a natural leader. Everyone likes you, everyone looks up to you. You make friends wherever you go.

"So, you're probably right," I said, trying to laugh. "Maybe we're not that much alike after all." I couldn't picture Cate being afraid to ask a question of anyone—not of herself, not of anyone else, not of Heavenly Father. And it was becoming more and more apparent that I was.

· · ·

Joel called when he was a few minutes outside of town. I told him to come right over to the apartment.

"I put something in the mailbox recently," I told him.

"Really?" he asked. "And what was that something?" He sounded very alert, and I had to laugh.

"I'll tell you when you get here."

He pulled into the driveway a few minutes later. I was waiting at the window. I couldn't wait to see him and I didn't want to sit around inside any longer. Before he had a chance to get out of his car, I pulled on my parka and grabbed my hat and gloves and ran out to meet him. He rolled down the window.

"Let's go for a walk at the Plantations," I said.

He looked at me as if I were crazy. "It's freezing outside!"

"It's at least forty degrees," I told him. I tried to look imploring. "Please?" When he nodded, I ran around to the other side of the car. He reached across and opened the door for me.

"Before I drive this car an inch, I need to know what, exactly, you put into the mailbox," Joel said after I'd kissed him.

I didn't hesitate. "My acceptance letter to Syracuse."

Joel whooped and gave me a bone-crushing hug, reaching across the seat to do so. "That's the best news I've heard all day. All week. All month. All year!" he told me. "You're going to stick around!"

"For a couple of years, anyway," I told him, still smiling.

Relief at having made *one* of my big decisions made me giddy. I kept hugging Joel as we walked through the Cornell Plantations. To keep from freezing, we parked at the bottom of the hill near the duck pond and ran to the top of the hill and rang the bell. We sat together on a wooden bench, looking out at the tops of the trees, which were starting to come alive with green. I hooked my ankle around Joel's and leaned on his shoulder. We both sighed at the same time and then looked at each other and laughed. Our eyes locked and Joel held my gaze. I held my breath, waiting for him to kiss me. Instead, he did something else.

"Will you marry me?" he asked.

He took me by surprise. I wasn't ready. I had answered one big question, but I wasn't ready for the next one, not yet. Even though I loved him, I needed more time. I looked into his eyes, pleading with him to understand.

"No," I said.

CHAPTER 27

MARCH, ITHACA

Joel Hammond

There ought to be dress rehearsals for proposals. I'd pictured how I might propose to Andrea several different times. Blurting it out in the middle of a happy moment and getting completely shot down was not the way I had pictured it in any of my imaginary scenarios. I should have known that my forte was not spontaneity.

Try teaching seminary with someone you've proposed to who asked for a deferment. Kind of interesting. Try dating someone after you've taken that plunge. It felt like that, like I had taken a colossal jump into the water, expecting her to be right there with me, then belly flopping instead and looking up to see her standing on the side, waving politely. It hurt. And it was embarrassing.

But it could have been worse. After that first, initial, gut-wrenching, heart-stopping, "No," I had sat there like a big slab of Joel-shaped stone. I could feel my face falling, losing all of the happiness and confidence I'd felt just moments before. I'm not an idiot. I wouldn't ask a girl to marry me if I didn't think she was going to say yes. I thought that her deciding to go to school in Syracuse was a huge step. It was, and that's where I made a mistake. I was so happy that I took things one step further, and she wasn't ready for that.

After she said no, I opened my mouth, like the stunned fish I was, then realized that I had nothing to say. I didn't even know where to begin. I closed it quickly.

"Joel," Andrea said, sounding worried, "are you mad at me?"

I shook my head. I wasn't sure what I was feeling, but I knew it wasn't anger.

"I'm not breaking up with you," she told me, and I began to thaw. Of all the possible scenarios that were going through my frozen, sluggish mind, I knew that one was the worst.

"Good," I managed.

"I need some more time," she told me, and she reached out and grabbed my hand. "Can you just give me some more time?"

"I can give you all the time you want," I told her. "I can wait as long as you need me to wait."

"But," Andrea said, hesitantly, "what if you wait and give me all the time, and I end up telling you 'No' again? I don't think that's what is going to happen, but I don't know for sure what I'm going to want to do. I need to think about it and pray about it and everything."

"You haven't done that yet?" I asked. She shook her head. I felt like a giant fool all over again, because I had. And I felt like I'd had an answer. But if she hadn't asked that question, it was no wonder my proposal caught her flat-footed. "So you're telling me to give you some time but not hold you to one particular outcome?"

She nodded.

"I can do that," I told her. "I love you, and the last thing I'd want is for you to rush into something when you're not ready. I'm sorry I proposed before you were ready. I promise I wasn't trying to rush you into anything."

"I know," she said. Then she started to ask me something, and stopped.

"What is it?"

"Are you sure about *me?*" she asked. "Are you sure I'm the one for you?"

I opened my mouth to answer, but she shook her head. "You keep thinking about that while I'm thinking too. We both have to be *sure.*"

• • •

A few days later, Andrea went to Syracuse early in the morning to meet with some people at the university, and I taught seminary alone. It was strange to look out at the classroom and know that she wasn't going to be sitting at the back today, signaling me or laughing at the students or taking notes on something that had caught her attention or drumming her fingernails when I got boring, which was something she didn't realize she did. I realized with a pang that this was how it was going to be next year if they kept me as the seminary teacher by myself. Andrea wouldn't be commuting from Syracuse to teach the class. No matter what happened between us, the end of the school year would be the end of the Sister Beckett–Brother Hammond era.

My cell phone rang a few moments before class was due to start. Cate and Ben, the only students there so far, turned to look at me. I shrugged. Who would be calling me at this hour? Was everything okay with Andrea? I looked at the display and saw Seth's name.

"Hello?"

Seth sounded terrible. "The baby's sick, Joel," he said, and even though I know next to nothing about babies and sickness, I could tell this was not a run-of-the mill cold. "Lucy's got a respiratory virus—RSV—and she's in the hospital. They think it's turned into pneumonia, and she's so little. She's not doing so well." He paused, and I could tell he'd been crying. "I need to go back to the hospital, but I was calling to ask if you would call Mom and Dad and see if Mom can come out here to help us out with the other kids. I can't get hold of anyone and I want to stay with Lucy and Maura as much as I can."

"Of course," I told him. "I'm so sorry, Seth." I had a million questions in my mind: What does this mean? Is she going to be okay? How bad is it? I could tell from his voice, though, that it was bad and so I asked the only question that mattered, "What can I do?"

Seth took another ragged breath. "Just pray, and get hold of Mom and Dad if you can. I've gotta go."

"Okay, Seth," I said, and sat there looking at the phone for a minute. Then I looked at the class that had somehow filled up while I had been on the phone. "Cate, do you think you could get class started?" I asked her. "I'll be right back. My niece is sick and I need to get in touch with my parents as soon as I can."

Cate nodded and quickly came to the front of the room.

It took about ten minutes of calling my parents' home and getting no answer before I thought to call Eli. He was groggy and confused, since it was so early in Utah, but he did know that my parents were out of town and he knew where they were staying. I called my mom and passed along the information, relieved at being able to do the one thing Seth had asked of me. Well, one of the things. I also knelt and said a prayer for Lucy. I walked back into class in time to start the lesson. Camille was finishing up her part of the devotional and sitting down right as I entered.

I had a hard time getting started. Everyone was feeling emotionally drained. The day before, our lesson had been about the martyrdom of the Prophet Joseph Smith and his brother Hyrum. On that sober note, it was hard to pick back up. Plus, I knew a lot of the kids were going through some rough times, not to mention the things they were going through that I knew nothing about.

And it was March. You forget that, in addition to the promise of spring and the warm days that pop up here and there, you also have three more months of school to get through and freezing rain and mud. There's always that mud.

I felt like I was slogging through mud as I taught. I started writing a timeline of the events between the Prophet's death on June 27, 1844, and the meeting on August 8 of the same year. Halfway through, I dropped my marker, and as I turned around to pick it up, I caught a glimpse of my class.

Cate was resting her head on her hand. As I glanced at her, she closed her eyes for a moment and didn't reopen them very quickly. Ben unraveled a thread from his sweatshirt sleeve, broke it off, then twisted it around his finger, turning the tip bright purple. Cate murmured something to him without seeming to open her eyes and he unraveled the thread and dropped it on the floor. Steve dropped his pencil and didn't bother to pick it up. Heather doodled on her scripture reading chart with such flourish that I could see the design from where I stood.

I turned back to the board with my timeline in hand and copied down the rest of the words and dates without saying anything. I tried to gather my thoughts. I was sorely tempted to just slog through the lesson and then go our separate ways. But if I was feeling down and Marchy, I knew the kids must be too. The school year and the bad weather and our own personal trials had sucked the life right out of us, as individuals and as a group. Everyone, at least for today, seemed to be going through the motions, plodding through the mud.

It's happened before. Sometimes Andrea takes care of it. Sometimes you can count on Steve with his bluntness or Cate with her energy or Ben with his awkwardness to pull you out of it. And sometimes you have to do it yourself.

"Can you guys imagine how these people must have felt?" I asked, and something in my voice made them all look up. It could be due to the fact that I had regressed momentarily to puberty and my voice had cracked a little with emotion.

I erased my timeline and wrote down some words that came to mind. "Scared. Confused. Worried. Brokenhearted."

A couple of the students called out other things. "Tired. Lonely.

Doubtful." I wrote them down too. We had about half of the class alive now. Heather was still doodling but her head wasn't practically touching the paper anymore. It had come up a few inches.

"They felt all these things," I agreed. "Does that mean they were bad people? Or they didn't have enough faith?"

"Having faith doesn't mean you're never scared," said Ben. "But it does mean you don't give up." He met my gaze briefly, then found a new string on his sweatshirt sleeve to interest him.

Cate opened her eyes and looked over at him.

"That's a good way of putting it, Ben," I said. "In this case, the Saints had to wait more than a month before they knew what was going to happen with the Church. Can you imagine how long that month must have felt to them? Even though Brigham Young knew that the Twelve held all the keys and that the presidency and the Church would move forward, he wasn't there yet. There was a lot of confusion and uncertainty for these members."

"Plus they were probably feeling really down about what had happened to Joseph and Hyrum," said Steve.

I walked back to the board. "You're right. They didn't know what was going to happen. What if they had sacrificed everything for nothing? They loved and knew Joseph and Hyrum, and they had both been killed. It must have been a frightening and sorrowful time. So why do you think most of them were able to stay faithful until Brigham Young came back and the question of succession was settled?"

No one answered. I wasn't quite sure what I was looking for, but I knew it wasn't silence. I kept waiting.

Cate spoke up. I think it was the longest she had ever gone in a class without talking. "I think they stayed faithful because in their hearts they knew the Savior loved them, even if things weren't working out so great at the time."

"Good answer," I said. I erased the board again. "So, what can we do to stay faithful in difficult times?"

"Remember how it felt when things were going right," said Steve from the back.

"Keep praying even if you don't feel like it," Cate offered.

Heather had stopped doodling. "Talk to your friends about it or to someone else you love a lot."

Jason, for the first time ever, offered his second comment in a single class period. "Remember other stuff you've gotten through because if you got through that, you can probably get through this too."

"That's true too," I said, adding it to the list. No more hands were forthcoming. "Everyone get out your journals," I told them, and they did so with less groaning than usual. "I want you all to think of something that you're going through right now. It can be something little, like you're having a horrible day because you have a bad cold, or something big. Write down what it is you're going through and one idea of how you could try to make it better. Even if it's not going to fix it, try to think of something that might help."

"Like eating chocolate?" Cate asked. Everyone laughed. "I was serious," she said.

"Sure," I told her. "Eating chocolate is fine. Whatever you think might help in some way."

They wrote for a few moments. I did too.

"Now, think of someone else you could help. Someone who might be going through something tough, whether it's little or big. Write down their name and what they might need, something you might do for them. Maybe you could give them some of your chocolate," I told Cate, and she smiled wanly at me.

"Your homework assignment for the weekend," I told them, "is to do the things on your list, both something to help yourself and something to help another person. We're not going to have a big brag session on Monday about how nice we were or anything, but I do want us to generally share how we felt, if serving someone else really did help us feel better or not."

Everyone picked up their things and left. Everyone, that is, except for a certain co-class president and her freshman sidekick. Cate and Ben stayed put, Cate staring off into space and Ben finishing his lunch and packing up next to her without leaving his seat.

"What's up, Cate?" I asked, sitting next to her and Ben at their table. "Everything okay?"

"Yeah," she said, sounding tired. "I'm still waiting for my answer. Still reading my scriptures and praying. I know it will come eventually."

"I know," I said, more sympathetically than ever. "I'm in the same boat." I could tell she wanted to ask what I was waiting for, but she refrained.

"Your lesson gave me an idea, though," she said. "I think I'm going to start praying for help in hanging in there until I get the answer. Also for help in recognizing it when it comes. I think I'm expecting it to hit me like a ton of bricks and that might not happen." She stood up. "Okay, Ben," she told him. "I think I'm ready." Ben picked up his lunch bag and his scriptures from his desk and started to walk after her.

"Hey, Cate," I heard him say on his way out. "I brought an extra juice box for you . . ."

There are a lot of us waiting. Cate is waiting for an answer. Andrea is waiting for an answer. I'm waiting for Andrea. Our whole family was waiting to find out what was happening with Lucy. It's what you do while you wait that matters, I guess. I looked at the name I had written down and tried to think of what would work. What did Seth and his family need right now?

I called my mom again. "The soonest I could get a ticket was for Sunday," she said, sounding worried, "but that's two days away. What are they going to do until then? Someone has to watch those little ones. I'm sure they have nice people in their ward, but I wish I could be there. I think I'll try standby, but things seem very crowded."

"I'll go," I said, surprising us both.

"Don't you have class today?"

"Not on Fridays," I said. "Cornell doesn't usually schedule classes on Friday, just sections with the TAs. I can miss it."

The relief in her voice was obvious. "That is wonderful, Joel. I'll call Seth and leave him a message to let him know that you're coming."

"I'll go straight to the house," I said. "He can have whoever's taking care of the kids meet me there in about seven hours or so."

• • •

I had barely driven out of the Ithaca city limits, such as they are, when my cell phone rang. It was Andrea, returning the message I'd left her earlier about what was going on. I pulled over to the side of the road to answer it.

"Where are you?" she asked.

"I'm just leaving Ithaca now on the 79."

"Hold on a second. I'm getting out my map." There was some light rustling in the background. "Okay, I've got it. You keep going, and I'll get on the 81, and I'll meet you in the town of Greene. We can leave my car at the LDS chapel there. In fact, we can meet at the chapel. Do you know where it is? It's right on the main road through town."

"Yeah, I know where you mean. But what about your meetings today?" I didn't want to ruin anything for her, but the idea that she might be able to come along was a very tempting one.

"I asked if we could reschedule for next week and they were fine with that."

"You don't have any of your stuff for the trip."

"I'm sure I can figure something out." There was a pause. "Joel, would you rather I didn't come? Maybe they'd rather I wasn't there. I mean, they've never met me and—"

"No," I said quickly. "It would be great if you came. I'd like you to come. I'll see you in an hour or so."

"Okay," she said. "Call me if anything happens and we need to change plans."

"Thanks, Andrea," I said, feeling better. Then, "I love you."

We said it at the same time.

• • •

My phone rang again right as we were leaving Greene. Andrea answered it for me. "Hi, Sister Hammond," she said. "This is Andrea." Pause. "Yes, he's right here driving. I'm coming with him." Another pause. "I'll tell him. Thanks, Sister Hammond." She shut the phone and turned to me. "Seth will meet us at the house with the other kids."

"All right," I said. "Any other news?"

"Not yet," she said, resting her hand on mine on the steering wheel.

It was one of those times, of which there are many in life, when it's good not to be alone, when it's good to have someone sitting next to you, someone giving your hand a squeeze, someone reading the map for you while you navigate, someone covering the miles with you, even when they're not saying anything, even when all you're doing is worrying together.

To my surprise, Seth opened the door and started crying when he saw me. Andrea was waiting in the car to give us some privacy. It's awkward for guys when one of us starts crying, especially if it's the tough brother who never cries. It made me uncomfortable, so I started rambling to him. "I can't really help with the baby," I told him. "But I can watch the other kids and make dinner. I can vacuum, I can clean toilets, I can plant flowers and take out the trash, I—"

He laughed through his tears. "I don't need a résumé. Come in."

CHAPTER 28

APRIL, ITHACA

Caterina Giovanni

Brother Hammond helped me lift the cooler out of the trunk of my car. "This thing is *full*," he commented, as we lugged it to the picnic table.

"I know," I said, staggering. "Steve basically wanted a five-course meal for this picnic. We have sandwiches, two kinds of salads, a fruit plate, drinks, and three kinds of dessert. We're lucky it didn't rain. It would have broken his heart if something went wrong to mess this up."

Steve and I had planned a seminary class trip to visit the sites in Palmyra and have a picnic, and April in upstate New York is a very fickle month. We were lucky the sun was shining and we could get by wearing jackets instead of parkas. You can't ask for anything better this time of year.

"And all that food is in *here?*" Brother Hammond asked.

"Steve has a cooler in his car too."

"Good grief," he said, but he was smiling. "I guess I should be grateful. He and Ben alone could probably eat half of this stuff."

"That's true," I agreed. We'd made it to the wooden picnic table and heaved the cooler up on top.

"It seriously could not be a nicer day," I told Brother Hammond as we both gazed off at the Sacred Grove. The trees were that color of bright green in between new green and summer green. I caught myself humming "Oh, how lovely was the morning," and he started humming along with me. He was in a great mood, for a very good reason. He'd told us that morning that his little niece who lived in Boston was finally healthy again and out of ICU. He'd been so worried about her. Sister Beckett had been too.

"I always think of that song when I come here," he said. "Well, maybe not the first time I came. That was last March and the bees weren't exactly humming. It was still amazing, though. This is where I got my answer about which school to attend," Brother Hammond said. "The same might happen for you." He laughed. "Not to put any expectations on this trip for you or anything."

"I would love it if I came away with an answer today," I told him. "I feel like I'm getting closer to knowing, but I'm not quite there yet."

We opened the cooler up. "Oh, man," he said. "Are these mint brownies?"

"Yes," I said, "Steve's secret recipe. And he won't give it to you, so don't ask."

Sister Beckett returned from her car with the paper plates and napkins and joined us. "I think they're almost done," she said, nodding to the rest of our group who were walking around the Joseph Smith farm with the missionaries. We had excused ourselves a little early to set up the picnic. Steve had stayed with the rest of the group to keep them in line. Or vice versa.

As had been the case with all of our activities since the Christmas service project, Sarah Wren had come along too. She still never came to class, but it was nice to have her along for the activities and she genuinely seemed to have a good time. I hoped the tour was going well and that Sarah was liking it. She said she hadn't been to the Church sites in years.

"I'll go help herd them over here," Brother Hammond said, heading off in the direction of the farm. He palmed a brownie as he left.

"I saw that, Brother Hammond!" I yelled after him, and he turned and grinned at me.

"What did he do?" Sister Beckett asked.

"He stole a brownie," I said. We looked at each other. "I think that means we get to eat one too," I told her, and we did as we started unpacking the food together.

"These are so good," she said. "Do you think Steve will notice if we sneak another?"

At the beginning of the year, I would never have thought that I would spend a Saturday with Sister Beckett, and a long period of time alone with her, without it being awkward. It wasn't awkward at all. In fact, I decided to ask her something I'd been turning over and over in my mind.

"What does it feel like to be the one who leaves?" I asked her.

She looked surprised. I tried to clarify.

"I mean, I'm the youngest in my family, so I've never actually been the one to go anywhere. You'd think it would be easier to do something like that, after I've watched everyone else go, but for some reason it's not. What is it like to be the one who goes away, to college or somewhere else?"

"That's a good question," she said thoughtfully. She was silent for a few moments. "I think I like leaving," she told me. "I like being on the move, not having to stay too long in one place or one situation. Part of it might be because my parents are divorced and my dad moved away. That hurt so much I never, ever wanted to be the one left behind again." She looked away. "That's part of why I went so far away to school. That's also probably why I broke up with all of my boyfriends before they could break up with me, except for one of them." She laughed, a little self-consciously. "That's a lot more than you wanted to know, I'm sure."

"No, it makes sense," I said. Even though it didn't exactly apply to my situation, I could still understand what she was saying. How could I find out if I liked moving, trying something new, if I never did it? College or work would be a change no matter what because it would be different from high school, but I knew myself. If I could stay in a safe, comfortable groove, I would. If I wanted a change, a big change, a go-for-broke kind of change, I would have to throw myself out of my comfort zone entirely.

"Thanks," I told her. I sat down hard at the picnic table and sighed. Sister Beckett smiled at me across the table.

"This kind of decision is one of the hardest kinds to make," I mused. "For me anyway. It's a lot easier to choose between a good choice and a horrible one than it is to choose between good and good."

"What about choosing between an exciting but scary choice and a safe but boring one?" Sister Beckett asked me. Or maybe she was asking herself. She wasn't actually making eye contact with me when she said it, but gazing off toward the Joseph Smith house and the path where our group was coming into view.

I wanted to ask her what she was talking about, but then everyone else started streaming over toward where we were sitting. Heather said a blessing, and we dug into the food.

"Awesome sandwiches, Cate," said Brother Hammond as he piled his plate high.

I waved my hand at Steve who was standing behind me in the sandwich line. "He's the one who made them."

"Here's my secret recipe," Steve leaned around me to talk to Brother Hammond. "I mix together orange juice, white vinegar, a little sugar, and some oil. Then I sprinkle that over the lettuce before I put it on the sandwiches."

Brother Hammond looked more and more amused but he listened intently.

Sister Beckett, Brother Hammond, and I sat down at the picnic table. Everyone else was at the other table because there wasn't much room at ours, what with all the food spread out on it.

"Cate, there's something that Brother Hammond and I have been meaning to ask you," Sister Beckett said.

"Yeah?"

"We were wondering if you would be willing to give a short talk at seminary graduation. Steve's already said yes, but I haven't had a chance yet to ask you. We would love it if you agreed. In addition to being a senior and co-president of the class, you're someone everyone in the class looks up to. I think they would all love to hear from you."

"Sure," I said. It couldn't be any worse than giving a talk in Church, and I'd done that lots. In fact, this would probably be a lot like giving a talk in Church, since everyone going to the seminary graduation would either be a member of the ward or a friend or family member.

"Thank you," she said. She pushed the potato salad toward me and I took some more. Paprika was Steve's special ingredient in this one, and he had almost had a heart attack when he thought I might have sprinkled too much on top.

"The potato salad tastes divine," I called out to Steve as I carried the bowl over to their table. "The amount of paprika is perfect. You must really have had a good assistant for this one."

"Was it you?" Ben asked seriously.

"There's an extra secret ingredient in that salad," Steve grinned at me as he took the bowl from me.

I took the bait. "Oh, yeah? What is it?"

"Love," he said. Everyone stared at the two of us and I shook my head at him. Why did he always have to tease me about this kind of stuff, especially lately?

"Okay, okay," he said. "The secret ingredient is friendship." He gestured widely at everyone. "So it should taste good to all of you."

I gave him the thumbs-up sign and swiped his spoon of potato salad. "To friendship," I said, lifting the plastic spoon in a toast that everyone echoed.

• • •

On the drive home, almost everyone else fell asleep. I think it was all the food—everyone was so full they couldn't keep their eyes open with the motion of the car and the warm sun slanting in through the windows. I was the driver, so I didn't have that option. I looked back at my passengers—Ben (of course), Sarah, and Heather. Ben slept with his mouth open. Heather was about to slump over onto his shoulder. That would be interesting if it happened. Sarah, who was sitting next to me in the front seat, had balled her jacket up into a pillow and was leaning against the window. I tried to drive carefully so I wouldn't wake up anyone. Steve passed me with his car full of sleepy people and honked and waved. I waved back.

Even though the car was quiet and warm and I was full too, I wasn't sleepy at all. I drove in silence through the small towns and fields. I reached the point where you can see Ithaca, sitting on the other side of Cayuga Lake.

As I looked out over the water toward the towers and spires of Cornell, I thought about all the good-bye scenes I'd been through before with my family. First the college good-byes, then the mission good-byes, then the marriage good-byes. Even the little good-byes we went through every single time they came home.

At first, when I was little, I'd cried and cried at every good-bye. Eventually, after so many farewells, I got a little jaded. "I don't think you even care that we're leaving," my older sister, misty-eyed, said as they were leaving after Christmas. I didn't know how to explain to her that, as the youngest child, I had to have a thick skin.

With all the comings and goings and, most of all, the good-byes, you have to get pretty tough or you'll never make it, getting left all of the time. Sister Beckett seemed to understand that. I'm almost sure it's easier to be the one leaving than it is to be the one who is left. But I wouldn't know. I've never had a chance to try, until now.

CHAPTER 29

FIRST WEEK OF MAY, ITHACA

Joel Hammond

Bleary-eyed, I walked out of my class, my last class of the semester and my last class of my first year of grad school, with no thought of anything but getting outside of a classroom and breathing some fresh air. Standing there waiting for me in the concrete and metal building, in the hall with industrial tile and scuff marks along the paint and the ugly, life-draining fluorescent lighting and the smell of graduate students, chalk, and disinfectant, was . . . Andrea.

She'd been in Seattle for the last few days to see Ethan, who'd just gotten home from his mission. It had been a long few days without her, and I didn't care I was holding up the hallway traffic when I gave her a hug right there and then. She gave me a quick kiss and someone walking by whistled at us. Neither of us cared.

"You're back early," I said. "I didn't think I'd get to see you until this afternoon. Aren't you exhausted?" Her return flight had been a red-eye.

"No, actually I slept a lot on the plane. I've come to take you on a walk," she said, pulling me along with the crowd. "How does that sound?"

"That sounds perfect," I said, falling in step with her. She was walking fast.

"Hurry, though, or I'm going to get a parking ticket. My ten minutes are almost up." She looked at her watch. "In fact, they *are* up."

Holding hands, the two of us hurried through the hall and burst through the doors to the outside world. Even though it was May and sunny, it was still a little chilly. Not cold enough to feel unpleasant, just cold enough to make you feel alive.

When we were sitting in her car, she looked over at me with a mischievous glint in her eye. "Buckle your seat belt, Joel. I have a destination in mind."

She drove to the Cornell Plantations. I started to say something. We hadn't been there since the scene of the botched proposal. "What?" she asked, turning to look at me.

"Nothing." If it didn't bother her, I wouldn't let it bother me. Finals were over, she had come back early, and we were escaping campus for a while.

Andrea parked in our usual spot near the duck pond, and without saying much, we walked to the bench at the top of the hill and sat down together. Even though we'd returned to the scene of the crime, so to speak, I felt comfortable. The trees, which had barely been frosted with green before, were enveloped in leaves now. There were flowers in bloom at the top of the hill near the bench, the first truly blue flowers I had ever seen. It smelled like grass and rain and sun all at the same time.

Absolute contentment washed over me. I put my arm around Andrea and she rested her head on my shoulder. Neither of us said anything for a few minutes.

"Yes," she said. "I would love to marry you."

I pulled back to see if she was kidding. She was smiling, but it didn't appear to be a joke. I started smiling and couldn't stop.

"But I didn't even ask!" I protested.

Andrea smiled, and just raised her eyebrows at me, waiting. I sat there for a second, trying to play it cool, but we both knew what was going to happen. Or at least, I was hoping I knew what was going to happen.

I got down on one knee, laughing at first. When I looked up at her, I saw tears in her eyes, something I had only seen once or twice before. Still, she was smiling, and I smiled back, reaching for her hand. "Will you marry me?"

"Yes," she said. "Of course."

I waited to see if there was anything else she wanted to say, but she was quiet. We looked at each other for a long moment. There would be more to say later. Still holding her hand, I leaned up to kiss her.

• • •

After a little while, some other people reached the top of the hill and started to wander around, looking at the scenery, chatting idly and pointing out the sights. Even though I felt like I loved all of humanity at that moment, I also didn't want to be with anyone but Andrea. So we started winding back down the hill toward the duck pond. We took our time.

A few minutes later, when I had come down from cloud nine to cloud eight and a half, I asked her, "What made you certain?"

"I was hoping you'd ask me that," she said, stopping in her tracks. She pulled a folded piece of lined paper out of her pocket. "This is a list," she told me. "A list of the pros and cons about you."

Only Andrea would do something like that. "Let me see that list!" I said, reaching for it. She pulled it away, and before I could do anything, she tore it in half, then in half again, and put the fragments in her pocket.

"That list doesn't matter," she said. "This is the one that does. This is a list of things I love about you."

"I don't see anything," I said, looking for another piece of paper.

"I didn't write it down. I don't have to. I know it by heart." She started counting on her fingers. "You have a great laugh. You are a good listener. You care about everyone. You have a strong testimony. You're a good kisser—"

I couldn't let that one go by without giving her a kiss to prove it, just in case.

"Okay," I said a moment later. "You can go on with the list now. Or was that it?"

"There's more, but I'm not going to tell you everything at once," she said, the teasing back in her voice. "I'll tell you a few things now, a few things later. I'll probably be adding to that list our whole lives."

"What about the list you tore up?" I asked her, half-seriously. "You're always so thorough. I'd love to see what the cons were about marrying me."

"The cons on the list had nothing to do with you," she said. "They were all about me. You're perfect, for me anyway."

There was nothing to be done after that but to give her another kiss. We stood there on the path, holding each other, for a long, long time.

"So where's my ring?" she teased as we finally pulled apart.

"We'll have to take care of that. I didn't know I was going to be proposing to you today, you know," I said. "I guess we'll have to take care of a lot of things—when and where and all of that—but we don't have to do that right now."

"You're right," she said.

About fifteen minutes later she said, "I think June would be a perfect time," she said so seriously that I couldn't help but laugh. "What? What's so funny about that?"

"Andrea," I said, "it's May. June is only a month away. I don't know if we can even get the temple scheduled by then, much less our families, much less get the reception organized."

"Oh," she said. Then, "We can try though, right? It's *early* May.

We could at least try for the end of June, and if it doesn't work, we could do July instead. We should look for an apartment in Cortland since that's halfway between Syracuse and Ithaca."

"This is all happening so fast," I teased.

"Not really," she said. "We've known each other since September, and I've been thinking over your proposal for almost two months. I'd say we're actually on a slow track. Almost two months between the question and the answer is a long time."

"It was a long wait," I agreed.

"Was I worth it?"

I laughed, thinking she knew the answer for sure, but then I could see the seriousness in her eyes.

"Yes," I said. "Of course you are. Am I?"

"Absolutely."

CHAPTER 30

JUNE, ITHACA

Caterina Giovanni

"There's one last party to organize before we ride off into the sunset," I told Steve, pulling my chair right up next to his at the table so it would be hard to overhear our conversation unless you were right next to us. Steve and I were sitting in the seminary classroom, waiting for Sister Beckett and Brother Hammond so we could go over the program for seminary graduation together.

"What's that?" Steve leaned forward in his chair. "Some kind of graduation thing?" He looked around. "Should I be whispering? Is this a secret?"

"Kind of. Brother Hammond and Sister Beckett shouldn't be able to get away without a wedding party, or some kind of party, in their honor," I told him, and he started to smile.

"I'll do the food," he offered. "I bet some of my mom's friends will be willing to help. I'll ask Ben too."

"I'll do the decorations and the invitations."

"So you think it should be a surprise?" he asked, a glint coming into his eye.

"Yes, I do," I said, and I didn't even have to ask him if he agreed. He was practically rubbing his hands together.

"When can we have the party, though?" Steve wondered. "They're not getting married until the end of June, and I'm leaving right after that for my sister's wedding in Utah. We'll be gone for three weeks."

"Then we'll have to have it before you go," I said firmly. "We're not doing it without you. We'll just have it before the wedding."

"We could have it after seminary graduation," Steve suggested. "I know! We could ask the bishop if we could have it here in the classroom right after graduation. Then we could set everything up and everyone would be sure to be there."

"Perfect," I told him. "We—" I closed my mouth fast as Sister Beckett and Brother Hammond came in the door. I'm sure we looked guilty, but they didn't seem to notice.

"Hey, guys," said Brother Hammond, grabbing two chairs and pulling them up to our table.

"Hey," we said back. Steve looked perfectly nonchalant. I tried to look innocent too.

"I have a question for you, Cate," Sister Beckett said, reaching into her bag to pull out a rough draft of the graduation program.

"What is it?" I asked. Then a thought hit me. "Do you want me to be a flower girl or something at your wedding? I'd be willing."

She laughed. "I appreciate the offer, but we're going to have my little sister do that."

"I could be the ring bearer," Steve offered, which cracked Brother Hammond up.

I couldn't resist the urge to find out more about the wedding, now that the door had been opened. "What else can you tell me about the wedding? What are the colors? Where are you guys going on your honeymoon? What temple are you getting married in?"

In the old days, you couldn't get Sister Beckett off topic for love or money. Now, love worked. "We're getting married in the Palmyra

Temple," she said, smiling at Joel. "There's not going to be a wedding reception, just a family dinner afterwards. We both wanted to keep it low-key."

"But you have a flower girl?" I asked, confused.

"Well, you know how it is when you get married in the temple. That's the important part. But my sister, Chloe, is the only one who can't come to the ceremony out of all of our brothers and sisters, and we wanted her to feel like she had something special. She'll be a flower girl and have a special dress to wear and a bouquet to carry for the pictures."

"What color is her dress?" I asked Andrea.

"Pink, of course," Andrea said, smiling. "I let her choose and she wouldn't have chosen anything else."

I made a mental grimace at the thought of pink, which seemed very un-Sister-Beckett-like to me. I must have made an actual grimace as well because Sister Beckett started laughing.

"I know," she said. "I'm not a pink kind of girl either, but it's what she wanted."

"So is pink one of your wedding colors?"

"Yeah, but the only pink thing will be Chloe's dress. The rest of the flowers and decorations will be yellow and purple, kind of a summer mix."

"Oooh, what's your bouquet going to look like?" Not only was it fun to find out the details, but it was good information to have for planning the party. Then we could kind of match the décor with their wedding colors. Ever unappreciative of my genius, Steve pretended to fall asleep next to me and I elbowed him. If I was going to have to do all the legwork for this surprise party, the least he could do was be supportive. I was getting lots of good information. I didn't hear him gathering anything useful.

"It's going to be a mix of white and yellow lilies," she said, laughing at Steve as his head lolled back against his chair. "I know, I know,

Steve, I'm sorry. This girl talk is probably killing you. We should get back on topic." We returned to the graduation program.

But I had found out enough for my purposes.

• • •

When you have only two graduates, seminary graduation is pretty short. Ours lasted less than an hour. There was the class musical number, then Steve spoke, then I did, and then there were short addresses from Brother Hammond and Sister Beckett and a longer one from the bishop. It all went according to the program.

After Ben had given the closing prayer, Steve stood back up at the microphone. "We have a special surprise for Sister Beckett and Brother Hammond, if they'll agree to be blindfolded for a minute." The other seminary students and their parents vanished, heading to the seminary room to take their places.

I tied the yellow blindfold around Sister Beckett's eyes while Steve took care of Brother Hammond.

"What is this all about?" she asked me.

"You'll see in a minute," I told her. "Would you rather Steve or I led you?"

"You, please," she said, laughing. Steve took hold of Brother Hammond and we steered them down the hall.

"I feel like we're going to the seminary room," said Brother Hammond. Steve had tied his blindfold on so tight that I worried Brother Hammond was losing circulation in his head.

"You may be right," Steve said, guiding him around a corner. "Then again, you might not."

We took off their blindfolds and the waiting crowd yelled, "Surprise!"

Sister Beckett and Brother Hammond looked dazed.

"Oh my," said Sister Beckett. "This is unbelievable."

I had to give the whole seminary class credit. Everyone had really pitched in to help with the party. Sarah especially deserved some recognition. She had arranged all the yellow and white flowers I'd picked up at Matt and Kayla's farm and they looked awesome. Little white lights were strung all over the room along with yellow and purple streamers. A huge banner stretched across the back of the room: "Welcome to Joel and Andrea's Wedding Reception." I'd made that. It had been weird to write their first names instead of "Brother" and "Sister," but since graduation officially marked the end of their time as seminary teachers, I figured it was all right.

Brother Hammond shook his head. "This is amazing, you guys. I can't believe it."

Sister Beckett, to my surprise, seemed to be a little choked up when she turned to me and Steve. "You two are the best class presidents ever," she told us, giving us both a huge hug. Then she started hugging all the other students too. For a minute, things were turning mushy, but I didn't have to worry that they'd stay that way for long.

"Let's get the party started!" said Steve, and everyone clapped and cheered.

• • •

It wasn't a typical wedding reception at all. For one thing, the person in charge of the music appeared to be about fourteen years old because it was Ben and he *was* fourteen years old. For another thing, the guests were mostly high school kids and their parents. For another, the groom was wearing a white shirt, khakis, and a tie, and the bride was wearing an eyelet summer skirt with her hair pulled back. But still, even without the wedding dress and the tuxedo, you knew they were the bride and groom. You could tell by the way they looked at each other.

Andrea went out to her car to get her "wedding folder" so she could show us some pictures. Of course, we girls were the most interested. "This is Chloe, my little sister, the one who's going to be the flower girl," she said, and everyone exclaimed over how cute the serious nine-year-old was. "This is my younger brother, who just got back from Brazil," she said. "I took these pictures when I went back to Seattle in May for his homecoming." She showed us a few pictures of a very handsome guy, wearing a suit and tie. The girls gathered in a little closer.

"This is Joel's brother Seth with his family," she said, showing us a picture of a young couple and their three kids. "The baby is doing great."

She even had a picture she'd cut out from a magazine to show us what her wedding cake was going to look like.

Steve pretended to be underwhelmed. "Wait until you see the cake *I* made for you guys. In fact, let me go get the food right now."

Steve and his mom had outdone themselves. He brought so much food that the card table literally groaned and sagged a little under the weight. They had to get another table to help hold all the food. Joel helped him and so did Ben, and I was surprised to see that Ben was almost as tall as Steve. He had grown so much in the past year.

But the pièce de résistance was definitely the wedding cake. Steve had made a five-layer chocolate cake with white fondant frosting and raspberry filling. A bride and groom figurine perched on the top. Only upon closer inspection the bride and groom appeared to be sinking. "I think I set them right on top of the part with the filling," Steve said. "We should probably eat it fast before they disappear into the center of the cake."

Andrea and Joel cut the cake together and even fed it to each other at our request, laughing. They refused to smear it all over each others' faces the way they sometimes do at wedding receptions, saying that it would be a waste of Steve's hard work.

After we'd mingled for a while, and most of the parents had gone, Steve looked over at me and raised his eyebrows. I nodded. It was time for the group gift. We'd had a heated discussion about what to get them, but we'd finally settled on a beautiful picture of the

Palmyra Temple which we'd had professionally framed. Heather, who'd been in charge of picking it up and wrapping it, stood in front of Brother and Sister Hammond and a hush fell over the room. Everyone was excited about the gift.

"We got this for you," Heather said. "Congratulations, and thank you for everything you've done for us this year."

They tore open the wrapping paper and from the looks on their faces, they loved it. "This way, you'll think of all of us every time you guys see this picture," called out Steve from the back. "So you'd better hang it right in your living room."

"It's perfect," Sister Beckett said softly. She looked down at it for a moment, and then up at all of us and smiled. "You are all invited to come see us at the temple, you know. I know it's a bit of a drive, but we'll be taking group pictures afterward and we'd love to have one with all of you. After all, if it weren't for all of you, who knows if we would have spent so much time together and fallen in love."

Sister Beckett and Brother Hammond beamed at us and then at each other. I couldn't wait for the day that someone would look at me like that. Instead, I saw Steve trying to catch my eye for something. What was he mouthing? Oh, the price tag from the framing store was still on the bottom corner of the picture frame! I darted up and peeled it off the back before Sister Beckett—soon to be Sister Hammond—could tell what I was doing.

I lingered by Sister Beckett to ask her something. "Do you think that's true, Sister Beckett? Do you think you guys might not have fallen in love if it weren't for us? Do you think that's the way that love works? If you and Brother Hammond had missed out on teaching seminary, like if one of you hadn't accepted the assignment, would that have been it? You'd have missed your one chance?"

Sister Beckett looked thoughtful. "I don't know if that's true," she said. "I like to think you have more than one chance, or even more than one person you could be happy with. But when you find someone great and make the decision you're going to go to the temple together, then they become *the one.*" She smiled. "And that feeling, hopefully, gets stronger and stronger as you go through life together."

That made sense to me.

I looked around at the group in the room. It would be one of the last times everyone would be together, because things were going to change as they did every year. People were going to move on. This time, I was going to be one of the ones leaving. I wouldn't be coming back next year to sit in the seminary room and think about how much had changed and how different the new teacher was and wonder about how the seniors were doing, off at college or on their missions or gone.

This time, it was my turn to stand up and wave good-bye and walk out the door toward something different and new. I would sit in a totally unfamiliar classroom in Idaho and walk across a campus I didn't know and live in an apartment I hadn't even seen yet. Wow.

About half of me could hardly wait to start something new, to meet new people. But you do care about the ones you leave, too. My parents, for example. And there was someone else I would miss, too, someone who would grow up and change without me there to drive him around. Ben was the closest thing to a little brother I was going to get. And Steve. I would miss Steve. A lot. And Matt and Kayla and Sarah . . .

When Brother Hammond and Sister Beckett had gone, the rest of the seminary class pitched in to help us clean up. They trickled away one by one as we got closer and closer to being finished and soon it was just two of us, me and Steve. Steve found the vacuum in the hall closet and ran it across the floor, picking up the last of the debris. I folded up the tablecloths and threw away the crumpled paper napkins.

"Well, this is it," I said, as I put the last of the decorations in a box. "It's really over. Our reign as co-presidents has come to an end."

"Too bad," Steve said. "We would have rocked a second term."

"Yeah, we would have," I agreed. There was a pause, and then we both said, "Well—" at the same time and stopped.

"Do you want to go on a date when I get back from Utah?" he asked me.

"Sure."

"A *real* date," he added.

"Steve, we've *been* on real dates," I reminded him. Had he forgotten?

"I mean one where I tell you that I like you or that you look good and you take me seriously," he said. "And you don't laugh. And when I try to hold your hand, you don't act like it's a big joke. *That* kind of a real date."

"Oh." I was at a loss. I couldn't crack a joke, not after what he'd just said. Then I started to smile a little. "I'd like that." Steve grinned.

"Ready?" he asked.

"Ready," I said, picking up the box of decorations.

As we left the room, I looked back one more time. For some people, it was time to stay. For me, it was time to go, but that didn't mean that I still didn't belong here in some way.

Good-byes are messy. You hardly ever get to make a clean break. There are always loose ends and threads trailing behind and memories reaching back even as you reach forward for your new life.

And that's fine with me.

JUNE, ITHACA AND PALMYRA

Andrea Beckett

Joel laughed at me because I couldn't stand still. I bounced on my toes, checked the flight information six or seven times, craned my neck to see as far past the security checkpoint as possible. I couldn't wait to see my family. I'd been the one getting picked up at the airport for so long, and now everyone was coming all this way for me, for Joel, and for our wedding.

"I don't see anyone yet," I said to Joel. They were all arriving together—my dad was coming on the same flight with my mom, Ethan, and Chloe. Even though it was going to be strange in some ways, I was glad both my parents were coming and could be in the temple. "The screen says their flight has landed. Do you think it's wrong?"

"Don't worry. I'm sure they'll be here any minute. You know it takes a while to get off a plane, especially if you're stuck in the back." He smiled at me. "What they need is a giant stuffed whale. Do you remember the first time we met?"

"Of course. How could I forget that?"

"A lot has changed since then."

"Oh, yeah?" I teased. "Like what?"

"Oh, you know, we were both dating other people then, and now we're going to get married."

"We didn't even know each other's names at the beginning of that plane ride," I said. "We had no idea we were going to teach seminary together, much less marry each other."

"And now I'm waiting to meet your family for the second time, and your brother for the first time. Maybe he's going to hate me and you'll tell me to get lost."

"Neither of those things are going to happen." I was certain about that. "He's going to like you, and I am *never* going to tell you to get lost."

"Good thing," he said.

I thought of another family member who hadn't met Joel, and who wouldn't, not in this life. Grandma would have loved Joel; I knew that. I imagined her smiling at me and approving of my choice.

I squeezed his hand and he pulled me into a bear hug in return. We stood that way for a while until someone near us said, "Here come the passengers," and we broke apart to look for them again.

Several people walked through the doorway. I kept looking, trying to see someone from my family. It didn't take too long. The first person through the door was my dad, holding Chloe by the hand. Then came my mom, who was turning back to say something to someone who was walking behind. Ethan.

"That's him!" I told Joel. "That's my brother." I started waving frantically at Ethan, who didn't see me for a second. Then, he did, and he waved back. I still couldn't get over the fact that he was really here instead of in Brazil.

I gave Ethan a big hug before he could protest or act embarrassed. Then I gave Chloe one, too. She was beaming from ear to ear and holding a dress bag. "What's in there?" I asked her.

"My flower girl dress," she said.

"You carried that the whole way?" I asked, incredulous.

"She held it on her lap the whole way," Ethan said. Then, teasing her, he added, "She really gave that dress the royal treatment. She practically gave it its own seat, shared her pretzels with it, took it to the bathroom . . ."

Chloe gave a semi-annoyed huff. "I did not. I just held it on my lap. I wasn't going to *check* it, or stuff it in the overhead compartment. It's my flower girl dress!"

"I know, Sis," Ethan said. "I'm supposed to give you a hard time. It's my job." We were all standing around, grinning at each other, and I remembered the important introduction I had to make. It almost seemed superfluous; it felt like everyone should know each other already, since I loved them all so much.

"Ethan, this is Joel," I said, and Joel reached out to shake Ethan's hand.

"Great to meet you," Joel said. I laughed out loud. I couldn't help it—everything was falling into place. Now Joel had met everyone. Now the people I loved with all of my heart knew each other.

• • •

"The rain's letting up," Ethan told me. "Hopefully you'll have a clear day tomorrow."

"That's good news." I peeked out the window of the hotel's foyer. He was right. The clouds were starting to move away. It was getting late and we had to be up early, but I was in no mood to go to bed.

"How's your jet lag?" I asked Ethan. "Do you want to keep me company for a little while? I don't think I'm going to be able to sleep."

"Sure," he said. I went upstairs to leave a note for my mom and Chloe, who had gone in search of a toothbrush for Chloe. I went back to the foyer, which was empty except for the desk clerk, and around the corner to an alcove with some couches and a TV. A loud game was blaring, and Ethan turned off the TV when he saw me. "NBA Finals."

"You can keep watching if you want," I said. "I'll hang out here with you."

"Where's Joel?" he asked. "Is he still at the airport picking up his parents and his younger brother?"

"Yeah. I hope he gets back soon." Everyone in the wedding party was staying at the same hotel, but on different floors. Seth and his family had arrived a couple of hours earlier and had already put their little kids in bed for the night.

"How come you didn't go with him?" Ethan asked.

"I wanted to stick around and hang out with you guys since it will be my last chance to do that for a while. We're both spending most of our time with our families tonight."

"It's bad luck for him to see you anyway, isn't it?" Ethan asked.

"I don't think that kicks in until tomorrow, the actual wedding day," I told him. "And anyway, I'm not superstitious. Plus I've been with him all day today, remember?" After we'd picked up my family at the airport, we'd all had dinner together. It had been busy, fun, chaotic in the best possible way. But now things were quieter and Ethan and I could have a face-to-face talk. I already knew the topic I wanted to bring up.

"So . . ." I said. "What do you think?"

"He's a great guy," Ethan said simply. "I mean, of course I don't know him that well yet, but I like what I know." He paused. "And you're happy, aren't you." It wasn't a question. "It's good to see you this way." He grinned. "It seems like Chloe's the only one in this family I can count on to not get married. This Paul guy seems like he's sticking around. Even Dad is dating someone."

"Speaking of dating . . . what's going on with you and Mikey these days?"

"Not much yet," he said, fiddling with his cell phone and not looking at me. "I got off the phone with her right before you came, actually. She just barely got back to Provo from traveling around Mexico. It's the first time we've talked since before my mission."

"How did it go? How did she sound?"

"She sounds good. I *think* it went okay, but I probably need time to de-weird. Chloe keeps telling me I'm different. But she still seems to like me." He paused. "Chloe, that is. I'm so out of practice at reading Mikey that I have no idea if she still likes me or not."

"You've got that little accent now," I said teasingly. "I bet she liked that."

He looked surprised. "I do? Do I sound weird?"

"No, girls love accents. I'm sure she thought it was cute." I changed my tone. "It'll be fine, Ethan. You'll figure stuff out."

"I hope so. So tell me more about this program you're starting in the fall. You realize you're going to have to talk to families about their problems," he teased. Apparently, we'd talked enough about Mikey and dating. I understood. It was hard to define a situation you yourself were uncertain about.

"I know," I said. "It might be terrifying. But it's less scary now that Joel's around. It's nice to be part of a team instead of flying solo."

"You guys *are* a great team," Ethan told me. "It's cool to see. Do you think it's because you worked together teaching seminary for so long?"

"That's probably part of it," I said. I laughed. "We did go through a lot together with seminary, but also just with dating."

"When we have more time, I want to hear all the stories you're willing to tell," Ethan said.

"And I can't wait to hear all your mission stories. We didn't have nearly enough time to cover it all when I was home."

"No, no," Ethan protested. "This trip is for your wedding. I'm not going to steal your thunder by talking about my mission the whole time. But when you guys come home for Christmas, be prepared. I'll save up all my pictures. I'll put together a huge slideshow on Mom's laptop, with background music, and make you watch the whole thing. And there will be a quiz afterward. It's too bad I didn't do all that before the wedding and make Joel pass the quiz, initiate him into the Beckett family."

"It would be a trial by fire," I agreed, laughing.

"There you two are," said my mom. Chloe was right behind her, holding a toothbrush in a plastic bag. I was glad to see them, but I wished Ethan and I had had more time to talk one-on-one. "Don't you think you should be heading to bed, Andrea? It's a big day tomorrow and it's almost ten o'clock."

"I wouldn't be able to sleep," I told her. "I'd make myself crazy. Besides this will be the last time I get to see all of you for a while."

She smiled at me. "All right, honey. I'm going to take Chloe upstairs, though, so she can get some sleep."

"Oh, Mom," Chloe pleaded, "please let me stay up too."

Before my mom could respond, Ethan and I joined in. "Yeah, Mom, come on. It's a special occasion. Please . . ."

My mom threw up her hands in mock despair. "How can I say no when you all gang up on me like that?" Chloe bounced happily onto the couch between Ethan and me.

I stood up. "I'm going to go get Dad. He should be here too. What's the number of the room you guys are staying in, Ethan?"

• • •

An hour later, we were still in the foyer, talking. People came to the front desk and checked in and carted their suitcases up the elevators. People came and went. But the Beckett family stayed.

Joel and his family finally arrived from the airport and there was another flurry of introductions all around. In the middle of all the chaos, Joel found me and we stood there holding hands, smiling while the people we loved best in the world met each other.

"Aren't you coming, Joel?" teased Eli, as the Hammonds started to move upstairs.

Joel grinned. "I'll be up in a minute," he said, and wrapped his arms around me. "I want to stay and talk with the Becketts for a little while." He glanced at my family. "If that's all right with you, of course. I don't want to interrupt your time as a family."

"Of course it's okay if you stay," said my dad. "You're *part* of our family."

Our family. We weren't perfect. My parents were being very careful not to say the wrong thing to each other. Ethan kept lapsing into Portuguese. Chloe was asleep, her mouth wide open, snoring a little. As I looked at them, my imperfect family, I felt a wash of love for all of them and was grateful that they were willing to be with me and support me in my wedding.

And Joel. When I looked at him, it all overflowed and I couldn't sit still any longer. I stood up, pulling him with me, and everyone looked up at me from their places in the chairs and couches and on the floor.

"You guys, come check this out," I told them, gesturing toward the door. My family followed me, raising their eyebrows and grumbling, but going along with my whim since I was, after all, getting married the next day and the bride *always* gets her way.

I wasn't sure if they would be there, but I had a hunch. It had been raining and there were thick green bushes around the front of the hotel. It was the right time of the year. We might be lucky.

I walked barefoot into the wet parking lot. They *were* there. The fireflies were just starting to come out into the night and there were so many of them, I didn't even have to point them out or tell my family what they were.

"Wow," breathed Chloe.

I held tight to one of Chloe's hands and tight to one of Joel's, to my family and my family-to-be, as the fireflies sparkled around us all in the dark, warm night.

CHAPTER 3 2

JUNE, PALMYRA AND SALT LAKE

Ethan Beckett

I glanced at the two suitcases on the bed and everything piled around them: shirts, socks, shoes, towels, jackets, books. There was no way it was all going to fit. Since I was flying straight to Provo after the wedding, I'd had to pack everything I might need for the next six months, until I went back home for Christmas. Had my stuff multiplied since the last time I'd packed, back in Seattle? My dad came in and looked at the cluttered bed.

"Wow," he said, raising his eyebrows. "And I thought Chloe had a lot of stuff when I was loading it into the car this morning. You're giving her a run for her money."

"Yeah, right," I told him. "Remember, I'm packing for months, not days. When Chloe goes to college, there's no way she'll be able to fit everything she needs for an entire semester into two suitcases. Plus, I'm a pro at cramming everything I need into two bags. That's how I've been living for the past couple of years, remember?"

"I know, I know," he said, sitting on the bed next to the suitcases. "I guess you'll just buy dishes and stuff for your apartment when you get there, right?" he asked. "I feel bad we didn't get to load up a car full of stuff and drive you to school in style."

"That's okay. I'll pick some up when I get there, as soon as I get a job and get some money."

My mom and Chloe had left that morning for Seattle. My dad and I were flying together as far as Chicago. He had a business meeting there and I was catching a flight to Salt Lake City, and from there, a shuttle to Provo.

I already had a spot in the same apartment complex as some friends of mine from before the mission. My goal was to find a good job in Provo and save up some money before school started in August and all the students descended on BYU en masse. My mom kept asking me if I wanted to stay and relax in Seattle for the rest of the summer instead of jumping from one place to the next. Even though I'd had a great time reconnecting with my family during the month and a half I'd been home, I had been a little restless. I had a lot of reasons for wanting to get started on my new life in Provo. One of them was a girl named Mikey.

"It's hard to watch you pack up to leave," Dad told me, refolding a dress shirt of mine and making less of a mess of it than I usually did. "I've seen both you and Andrea leave a few times now, but it still tears me up a little, even though I'm happy for you. And it's *really* hard to say good-bye to both of you in one weekend."

"It *was* kind of weird to see Andrea drive away like that," I agreed. Watching my sister leave with Joel had been a strange feeling. It reminded me of everyone I had left behind in Brazil. There had been a lot of good-byes in my life lately.

"Joel is a great young man," my dad said reflectively. "I'm glad they found each other."

"I liked him, too," I agreed. "It's good they're coming to Seattle for Christmas so we can get to know him better."

I was trying to smash my bag of hygiene stuff—toiletries? cosmetics? It all sounded so girly—into the first suitcase, half of which was taken up by my huge winter coat. The little bag wouldn't fit. Fine. I'd save it for the second one. I started to close the lid and couldn't. It was close, but didn't quite make it.

"Want me to hold the lid down?" Dad asked, and I nodded. Between the two of us we got it zippered shut. We started on the second suitcase, both of us folding shirts and rolling ties.

"It looks like a game of Tetris in here," I said, as we configured and strategized our way through the second suitcase. I paused. "It seems kind of obscene for me to have so much stuff, when so many of the people in Brazil didn't have anything."

"I remember," my dad said. "Is that why you wouldn't let us buy you any new clothes when you got back?"

"Yeah," I said. I gestured at the suitcases. "I gave away a bunch of stuff before I came home, but my closets at home were still full."

I finally settled the problem by unpacking the bag of toiletries and sprinkling them throughout the rest of the clothes. I slotted a little tube of toothpaste in between my ties. I stuck my deodorant into a shoe. We closed the last suitcase.

• • •

"Dad?" I asked him later, as he walked me to my gate in the Chicago airport. "How do you remember it all? How do you keep yourself from forgetting about the people from your mission—the converts, the companions, everyone?" There was a time when his mission stories bored me to tears. Now I wanted to hear them all, and not just because we'd gone to the same country.

He sighed, looking thoughtful. "Keeping in touch, as much as you can, helps you remember. So does finding other ways to do missionary work."

"It makes me sad to think about how much I will miss them," I told him. "Our lives intersected for the briefest, shortest time, but it mattered a lot to all of us." I paused. "Or, at least, I'd like to think it mattered to them. I know it mattered to me."

He nodded. "You'll think about them your whole life." He glanced out the window of the airport, and I wondered who he was thinking of then. "It's bittersweet because you miss them, Ethan, but it also motivates you. You don't want to fail them. You want to see them again, standing in the celestial kingdom someday." He laughed a little. "Sometimes I think they'll all be there without me, but I have to keep trying."

We'd reached the gate. "Well, I guess this is it," Dad said, and I was surprised to see tears in his eyes.

"I'll see you in a couple of months, Dad," I reminded him. He was coming to Utah for General Conference—it coincided with a business trip—and we were going to the Priesthood session together.

"I know," he said, trying to laugh at himself. He gave me a hug. "I'm proud of the man you've become, Eth," he told me.

I watched him walk down the hall, getting smaller and smaller as he left, and was proud of the man my father was, too.

• • •

When they told me at the Salt Lake City airport that they had lost my luggage and they weren't sure where it was but they would do the best they could to find it, I couldn't help but laugh at the irony. In a way, it made things easier. I shouldered my backpack and found the shuttle bus to Provo. Only one other person was riding it that night, so it was a perfect time for thinking.

The night before the wedding as we stood watching the fireflies, I had asked Andrea, "Are you nervous?"

She'd smiled at me. "Not at all. Which is weird because I keep thinking I'm going to be. Ask me the same question tomorrow."

But I didn't. I didn't have to. She was excited, I could tell, because she kept forgetting things as we got ready to drive to the temple. She was sitting in the car, seat belt buckled and everything, when she realized she'd left her wedding shoes in the hotel room. It happened again when she realized she'd forgotten Grandma's red garnet earrings, which she wanted to wear for the pictures outside the temple. Both times, she didn't get upset—she just laughed, ran in to get them, and said that all she really needed was her recommend and her temple clothes, which she had right there, and Joel, and the people she loved.

When they came out of the temple, we all cheered, including the seminary class she and Joel had taught together, the same kids who'd written me all those letters. After all the pictures, there had been the family dinner, and then they were gone, off on their honeymoon.

I looked in my backpack to see what supplies I had for the next few days now that my suitcases had gone missing. I had my temple recommend, my scriptures, my wallet, and a couple of books and notebooks. It was enough to work with for a little while, at least.

I thought about the question that Cate from Andrea's seminary class had asked me in her letter: "What would you take from a burning building (all the people and pets are safe)?" I set my nearly empty backpack on the empty seat next to me and thought about how I would answer her question now. I think I'd tell her that it doesn't matter what you take with you, not as much as you'd think. You find a way to get by with what you have.

But maybe she would point out that you can choose what memories and feelings to keep with you, and that could be considered a kind of packing as well. Put some memories right on top, take them out and look at them often. Bury some a little deeper, but don't forget about them, because they still matter.

I looked out into the summer night. I could see the stars if I craned my neck back far enough. It reminded me of another night on another bus, when Elder de Oliveira and I were riding home from zone conference. He had sung hymns to himself the whole way while I had looked out the window and thought about people back home, worrying about Andrea and wondering if she'd find the happiness she wanted. Now here I was, back in the United States, back home, and Andrea was fine.

I thought about Elder de Oliveira and wondered how and where he was right at this moment and how the members were. So much had changed, and yet so much hadn't. I guess people's hearts were meant to be reaching out around the world. I guess it's more common than not to feel torn between two places, or to miss people who aren't there with you.

When I graduated from high school, there was a lot said about how it was both an end and a beginning. I hadn't realized until now that almost everything in life was like that. Something ended every day. Something started every day too. Every day was another first day.

Andrea's single days were over; so were Joel's. It was the commencement of their new lives together. Some of their students were ending their high school years and starting something new. My mission was ending, and a new part of my life was beginning.

I wonder why we're so surprised by change. It's happening all the time, all around us. Things are always ending and beginning in life. The surprising thing, I guess, would be if things weren't changing. We're always moving on, or someone near and dear to us is taking a new step. The best you can do is make sure that what you carry within you are the things that are important, the things that matter, the things that will last forever.

The shuttle to Provo arrived at my stop. I stepped out into the night, my backpack on my back and my heart full of hope. It seemed that what I had was, after all, enough.

ABOUT THE AUTHOR

Allyson Braithwaite Condie received a degree in English teaching from Brigham Young University. She went on to teach high school English in Utah and in upstate New York for several years. She loved her job because it combined two of her favorite things—working with students and reading great books.

Currently, however, she is employed by her two little boys, who keep her busy playing trucks and building blocks. They also like to help her type and are very good at drawing on manuscripts with red crayon. She enjoys running with her husband, Scott, reading, traveling, and eating. She lives with her family in Ithaca, New York.

You can visit her website at www.allysoncondie.com